Praise for The Lenticular

"A potent SF depiction of humanity victimising peaceful aliens."
Kirkus Reviews

"… wild and expansive, and just so totally out there." *Aurealis Magazine*

"There is much to like about this novel, including the representations of good and evil in both humans and aliens, and also the strong female characters …" **Carol Ryles**, author of *The Eternal Machine*

"… space opera done as space opera should be done" **Richard Harland**, award-winning author of *Ferren and The Angel*

"… weaves a complex and enticing web of future humanity, alien races, and murky motives …" **Mitchell Hogan**, award-winning author of *A Crucible of Souls*

THE LENTICULAR

BOOK TWO

TRAITOR'S BARGAIN

KEITH STEVENSON

First published in paperback in Australia in 2024

by coeur de lion publishing

www.coeurdelion.com.au

© Keith Stevenson 2024

www.keithstevenson.com

cover artwork and design by Jeff Brown Graphics

Print ISBN 978-0-6457466-0-0

Ebook ISBN 978-0-6457466-1-7

NATIONAL
LIBRARY
OF AUSTRALIA

A catalogue record for this book is available from the National Library of Australia

1

The transport ship was hunting me and I had no way of knowing where it was. I was going to die.

I nudged the thruster, bringing the pod I'd stolen closer to the asteroid's rough striated surface. A flash of brilliance to my left, and a smaller rock burst apart at the far edge of the asteroid field. Debris smashed into neighbouring rocks, setting up a rippling cascade of collisions. The direction of the burst gave me a momentary fix on the transport's position.

I eased the pod around the asteroid, so close now the hull scraped across it. A wave of dizziness took me and my vision faded.

∞

I lay on the table where they'd excised me. But my mantle was already gone. What more could they take?

Bright lights. Alien voices. But no pain this time. No sensation at all.

∞

I jerked awake as the light from another blast blossomed silently near the centre of the asteroid field. I was still sheltered against the large rock, but if I blacked out again …

The next explosion was closer, but behind me. The pod's hull rang with an ominous sound then another long scrape. A second asteroid had been pushed against the pod. I was trapped on both sides. If I moved again I'd disturb the rocks I was nestled between and the transport would find me.

The best thing to do was sleep. Conserve air.

I got as comfortable as possible, then concentrated, slowing the rush of air through spiracles. I felt my pulse points slow in response and let exhaustion take me.

∞

"Udun?"

The voice that spoke my name sounded odd. Attenuated, like sound through a door. Like I was the door, vibrating in sympathy.

White walls glowed with their own inner light. Someone spoke again. But they were too far away to hear me answer.

∞

I woke. A light flashed on the control array. The air supply was almost gone but I hadn't been asleep that long. Whoever owned the escape pod hadn't kept the tanks filled. If I drifted back into comfortable unconsciousness I'd suffocate. But each second I survived made me hungry for another and another. If I was going to die, I'd die doing something.

I eased the thrusters back and forth, gently pushing against one asteroid then the other. There was a disconcerting scraping noise, but it was working. The gap between the rock faces opened until I could see stars above me. I sent the pod moving up. As I cleared the rocks, I looked through the ports front and back, to the side and above, trying to spot the transport. I wanted to see the ship if it was going to fire on me.

No killing shot came. But the transport might be on the other side of the field, manoeuvring towards me.

"Come on," I said, my voice hoarse and desperate. Where were they?

A chime sounded. My air was exhausted.

I floated above the asteroid field, close to the centre. The thin air wheezed through my spiracles. I blinked as a darkness deeper than the starfield closed around my vision. I was losing consciousness.

The pod turned. There was movement out near the edge of the field. A ship. Or maybe my imagination.

∞

"Udun." The same voice spoke my name.

I opened my eyes, but they refused to focus even with the desert eyelid. A shape moved closer. I tried to speak but something was clamped to my feeders. I made to lift my claws to brush it away. My arms were bound at my sides. My hoofs couldn't find purchase.

"Udun, it's Emba. Calm down. You'll hurt yourself."

I pulled harder but I couldn't move. I was submerged in liquid, but a liquid I could breathe.

The shape moved again. Hard to see. Emba? We'd met on Telsus IV when I was setting up the secret trade deal for Hierarch Czerag. Emba had introduced me to Atalna, who'd warned me about … the Hegemony. The invasion. I had to warn him but the thing around my feeders made it impossible. I kicked and my hoof hit something. There was a dull ringing. I kicked again.

"Stop! You'll smash the tank. Wait."

My body was pulled down and I touched bottom. The liquid was draining into the floor.

"Just wait," Emba said again. "You've been sick. Injured. We had to put you in a coma while you healed. The tank's cleansed the radioactives from you."

The liquid continued to drain and the level dropped past my eyes. I blinked, the inner eyelid flicking over, and saw Emba through the crystal wall of the tank.

"You're healed now," he said.

But I'd never be completely healed. I still felt the laser searing away my mantle flesh. When I closed my eyes I could see my sister Isza blown apart on Treaty Mount steps.

My arms were released, but as the liquid sucked away gravity fully asserted itself and I slumped against the tank wall, barely able to stay upright. The crystal slid aside and the cold air stung the hide beneath my plates.

Emba tried to help me stand but I was too heavy for him. I fell forward, taking him with me, and we landed together on the floor.

He wriggled out from under me.

"Emba," I rasped, "I have to warn y–"

"You have to help me get you into bed. Then you can warn me." He scuttled behind me and helped me to sit up. Then he grabbed at my torso plates and dragged me backwards. "Come on. We need to do this together." He grunted as he gave another pull. "I told the house staff to take a holiday when I knew you were coming."

I pushed with my hoofs against the carpet and in this way we slid across to the bed. With his help I was able to haul myself up on to the broad platform. Finally, I lay across the mattress, out of breath, but I couldn't wait any longer.

"The Hegemony – they've invaded Homeworld. You have to warn the Lenticular."

Emba was puffing as he sat on the edge of the bed. "Save your words, Udun. We know what's happened on Homeworld."

I lay back ready to hear more, but Emba was silent. "And?" I asked finally.

"And nothing. Hierarch Kergis contacted the Lenticular Assembly and explained that there's been a regime change on Homeworld. Trade is unimpeded and life goes on. It's not for us to interfere in internal politics."

Kergis. I remembered the battle at the Point. The Hegemony ships streaming through, being met by our own forces. And then the Kergis ships pulled back and fired on the other Kresz Defender ships. Betraying us.

I tried to push myself up, but my arms were too weak and I collapsed back onto the pillow. "There's been an alien invasion by highly aggressive forces from outside the Lenticular," I said. "Doesn't that worry you?"

"It's highly unusual."

He wasn't making any sense.

I tried again. "My people are dying. You need to help them. The Lenticular needs to help them."

"Kergis has assured the Assembly that the Hegemony is no threat to the wider Lenticular," Emba said.

"And you believe him?"

His snout wrinkled, showing sharp teeth. "Of course not. We're on high alert. But there's nothing to be gained from attacking them on Homeworld. If they move against us, we'll be ready. Right now it's a stalemate." He stood. "You need to rest, Udun. We can talk about all of this when you're stronger."

I tried to push myself up again, but it was no good. "Does anyone know I'm here?"

"No. You were delirious when they picked you up, but you had enough wit to say my name. The freighter captain is a friend of mine. He contacted me and we felt it more prudent to bring you here with a minimum of fuss."

Prudent. This wasn't the time to be prudent. I closed my eyes and saw the Hegemony ships boiling out of tenspace and our Defender craft exploding in gouts of flame. And then on Homeworld, the Hegemony troops firing at us on the runway of the spaceport, killing indiscriminately. Even forewarned I'd been unable to prevent the invasion. I should have done more to convince Czerag to alert the other houses.

"It was harder getting the tank installed when the doctors told me you needed one," Emba continued. "But you can —"

"I want to see Atalna."

Emba stared at me. "That's not a good idea."

"Pl—" My voice failed me. I tried again. "Please. Bring him here."

At least the Betlaan would understand what we were dealing with. He'd already suffered through a Hegemony invasion on his world.

"All right. But only if you promise to sleep."

I felt I could never sleep again.

∞

When I woke, the light filtering through my eyelids felt wrong. The wall beside me glowed blue-white. Of course. I was in Emba's house.

Without thinking, I rolled onto my back and realised there was no pain. I reached around to feel the ridge of flesh where the Hegemony had cut off my mantle. I'd become so used to the constant nagging ache or sharp shock if I jarred it, but now the skin was puckered but firm.

The room was empty except for the bed and the tank I'd woken in. The tank looked out of place here, its crystal door still open, pipes and cables snaking from its sides across the carpet and into the wall.

I pushed the bedcovers back and stood slowly. No dizziness. My muscles were tired but I felt I could walk a little.

The door opened into a short corridor that ended in a blank wall with a sparkling piece of sculpture composed of shifting light and not much else. To my right the corridor led into a wide, low room with a long table and a sitting area with padded chairs. A crystal wall ran the length of the house and through it I could see a garden, illuminated by overhead lights set into a transparent dome. A gravel driveway separated the house from a central flower bed dominated by strange, many-stalked plants with fat pods on the end of thick, curling branches.

The house seemed empty. I remembered Emba saying he'd sent the servants away. Right before he told me his government knew about the invasion of Homeworld. Why weren't they and the other Lenticular governments planning a counterstrike? Were they all too scared to act? Or – worse – had they struck their own bargains with the Hegemony, just like Kergis? I needed information. Even a lie would tell me something.

I heard the whine of a turbine, then a vehicle ground along the drive and came to rest in front of the window-wall. The vehicle's door axed up and Emba climbed out.

I stepped forward and the crystal wall split and moved aside. The air was warmer outside and smelled of growing things.

"Udun. You're up," Emba said as he went to the far side of the transport and helped his passenger stand.

"Atalna!" I called, and walked out onto the rough gravel to meet him.

The Betlaan turned stiffly, his leg obviously paining him, but I was by his side and supporting him while Emba closed the vehicle door.

"You're well?" I asked.

"I bear my scars. As I see you now do, Udun. It is good to see you."

Emba bared his teeth at the two of us. "It seems I have a weakness for looking after lost souls."

"I was on Telsus when Emba sent word," Atalna said as we walked together into the house. "He organised a fast transport here."

"This isn't Telsus Prime?" I asked. But then a gout of smoke and flame flared up through the bushes, and I saw past the lights in the dome that the sky was a dark blanket of brown and yellow cloud reflecting a red glow from below. This was Telsus IV.

"We're at my estate," Emba said.

"Udun, you look like you've been through a terrible ordeal," Atalna said as I helped him to a chair at the long table. "I'm sorry that my fears of a Hegemony attack have been fulfilled more swiftly than even I imagined." He glanced towards Emba. "If only I could have done more."

I pulled up a stool and sat opposite him without replying. I could plot my own "if onlys" all the way back to when Sakat sucked the poisons from our world and set the first proto-Kresz to live there. There was no use in "if onlys".

Emba noted my silence and changed the subject. "Udun, you haven't eaten since you got here. And you've slept around the clock since we talked last. It's time for breakfast."

He crossed to a wall of cupboards and pulled out plates of fruit, bread and some kind of cured meat that he placed on the table before us. I was hungry and piled berries and slices of dark bread onto my platter.

Emba poured us all a drink from a crystal ewer filled with a green liquid. "It's goja juice. Try it."

He took a long gulp, exhaling loudly as he finished his own glass, and refilled it. "So, Atalna," he said, "you're well? How is the dwelling?"

"I am well, thank you. And the house you found me meets all my needs." Atalna turned to me. "Emba provides me with a stipend. Far more generous than I deserve. I have money enough to live. And it's peaceful there."

"I could do the same for you, Udun," Emba said. "I have more than enough resources. You know I'd be happy to help."

The piece of bread I was chewing felt suddenly thick and too salty on my feeders. Some juice helped and I swallowed the mouthful. "Have the Hegemony surrendered or withdrawn?" I asked.

Emba's snout dipped. "No. Everything is the same. But you escaped. You were lucky to get away alive."

"Others were not so lucky," I said.

Emba glanced at Atalna again, then sighed. "It was clear from the first moment I met you that your hierarch was playing a dangerous game and the political situation on your world was far from stable. Your side has been out-manoeuvred and you've been caught up in the consequences of that."

"This is more than some internal power struggle," I said.

"But is it? Kergis chose to get help from outside. Unconventional for a Kresz, but not difficult to understand in the scheme of things. Now he's formed a new government which is making all the right noises to my political masters and the rest of the Lenticular. The Point is being rebuilt. Though the Hub has been damaged by terrorists acting against the legitimate government –"

"It sounds like Betlaan all over again," Atalna said.

"The point is, things are calming down," Emba finished.

"You're talking as if all the killing that *will* be done on Homeworld *has* been done," I said. "As if all the suffering has passed. Kergis is destroying our way of life and anyone who stands in his way is put to death. How long till he decides to execute anyone who's not House Kergis just to be rid of an inconvenience? I can't stand by and watch that happen."

"What can you do?" Emba said. "You're one Kresz and not even ... well ... an injured one at that. It's over for you. You survived. Come to terms with that, because if you don't it will only end in your death. Either you'll throw your life away on some foolishness, or you'll make such a nuisance of yourself Kergis will reach out from Homeworld and crush you." Emba leaned over and touched my claws. "I can help you. You want a place to live, somewhere you can feel safe. Somewhere you can stop running. Somewhere the Kresz and the Hegemony will never find you. I can do that for you if you'll let me. The fight is over. Be kind to yourself."

I pulled my claws away. "Have you forgotten what Atalna told us? The fight is never over with the Hegemony. You can sit here and fool yourself you're safe, but eventually they'll come here and take everything you have too."

"I brought Atalna here to show you there are alternatives to fighting and dying." It was clear Emba was struggling to keep his voice calm. "He escaped the Hegemony. They're still out there, but Atalna has found peace."

There was a grunt from the other side of the table. "Friend Emba, you have made my life very comfortable, but I cannot say I have found peace. Not the peace that comes from knowing that justice has finally been done. The people of Betlaan are enslaved. The fact they are light years away does not alter that fact, and there is not one second of every day that I do not think of them and wish I could make their suffering stop. I ran, and that is my shame. But I could see nothing else for me. I stopped running because, again, I was weak. I do not want you to think I am ungrateful for your help.

But I would throw myself into the fight against the Hegemony again in an instant if I could only see some way I could hurt them. Even if it cost my life."

Atalna hesitated. Emba's face was unreadable. "Again I'm sorry, Emba. I do not mean to toss your kindness back in your face. But I think I understand Udun more than you can." He grasped my claws across the table. "Don't become like me, Udun. The daily bread of life is poor feeding when you can't share it with those you love."

I grasped his hand back. "Believe me. I will not give up until the Hegemony is gone from my world."

Emba slammed his glass onto the table. "You are both as insane as each other."

"I pray you don't get to share in our insanity when the Hegemony comes to your world," Atalna said.

"Emba," I said quickly, "you want to help – I know that. You are genuinely a friend. One of the few I have left. Please. I'm asking you for the sake of our friendship, for the dead and suffering Kresz on my world, for the sake of your own loved ones. Please help me."

"I thought I *was* helping you," he rasped. "I don't know how else I can. What do you want, Udun? No one cares about your world enough to intervene."

His words hurt but they were true. The Kresz had never bothered to make alliances beyond expedient trade links with the Lenticular.

"Just do one thing for me," I said. "Arrange it so I can speak to the Lenticular Assembly. It's not a small thing, I know, but I hope, I pray, you can do it. Let me help them see what I have seen. Give me a chance to change things."

Emba stood. He looked like he'd lost his appetite. "Finish your breakfast," he said. "I'll make some calls." And he went out of the room.

"He'll be all right," Atalna said. "He has a habit of doing the right thing. It's unavoidable for him. And this is the right thing."

I blinked. "I don't know. Emba's right that I'll be putting myself in harm's way again –"

"You are doing the right thing," Atalna said. "Believe someone who relives the consequences of his actions every day I draw breath. The faces of my dead family never leave me. Let me help you. You won't have to fight the Hegemony alone."

"I …" I stopped; I didn't know what to say. "Thank you," I managed, and squeezed his hand again, embarrassed by how much his words affected me.

2

The combined Brell, Totek and Sissilak force was strung out in a column across the dark Voss Space chamber: massive, illegally armed support carriers interspersed with destroyer escorts and equally outlawed battlecruisers, accompanied by a swarm of Sissilak Talon fighters and delta-wing Brell singlecraft. Rhees froze the recording, then spun the holo to orient her view at ninety degress to where she knew her Hegemony Diplomatic Corps scoutcraft had been, hanging back on the lip of the chamber as she, Denev and Volmar followed the rebel force.

She hadn't seen the attack ships transit first time around, but she was looking for it now. Maagba fighters, shaped like horseshoes standing on end, phased into the chamber at its apex. They speared down on the convoy, which was already breaking apart as limited sensors registered the intruders. A series of explosions rippled through the disintegrating column, and ships veered madly to escape destruction.

Another wave of Maagba ships and more missiles, and then the Sissilak, Totek and Brell began firing back. Lasers and particle weapons lanced out and dark bulbs of energy formed as the Voss Space field reached criticality then exploded in searing plasma blasts, burning ships out of existence. In the mayhem, the pace of attack stepped up and the Voss Space chamber began to break down, walls shifting and tunnels extruding to crush unlucky ships, singlecraft stuttering in and out of existence. That was when Volmar had insisted they transit.

The image shifted to space. Rhees could see her scoutship, mostly disabled and too close to the planet. While she was crash-landing – heavy on the crash, not so good on the landing – the other half of the Maagba force that was waiting safely in space mopped up what was left of the rebels sent to attack it. Sent by Volmar – although the poor rebels hadn't known he was the source of the intel Denev had fed them through his network on Herakli.

The Brell, Sissilak and Totek had only been defending themselves from a series of attacks from the Maagba that had already killed billions. But somehow they'd hidden their own considerable attack force from the Hegemony auditors. It was far more than they were allowed for a local militia. They still didn't deserve to be sacrificed by Volmar so he could make an alliance with the raiders.

Rhees fast-forwarded the images. She knew what happened next. The Maagba had captured them on the planet – but only after she'd punched Volmar in the face. That at least had felt good. Then Volmar made whatever slimy deal he'd been planning all along with the Maagba and offered Rhees up to them as a blood sacrifice to seal the bargain. That shouldn't have surprised her. Volmar had been looking for an excuse to get rid of her ever since she'd been thrown out of Fleet for killing her boyfriend – Denev's brother – in a training exercise and ended up in HDC. Except the Maagba hadn't killed her. She'd won her fight with them and they'd gifted her a ship. Something Volmar and Denev didn't know.

She watched to the end of the recording, saw the HDC scoutcraft she'd piloted leaving without her, heading back to Hegemony space. The sensor channel running along the bottom of the image showed the ship contained two humans. So Denev had survived. She hoped he was still safe.

She'd been picked up by the Jantri ship and Nok a few hours later. The alien had offered the recording when Rhees had asked if he knew what had happened to her companions, though she didn't give a shit about Volmar. She hadn't expected to see such a comprehensive record of Volmar's treachery. Now she wondered just how long the Jantri'va had been observing Cygnus Sector, and did their surveillance extend deeper into the Hegemony?

We don't just want information on the Hegemony. We want you to help us defeat them. She hadn't been able to sleep since Nok had dropped that bombshell.

Part of her felt it was the perfect solution. What she'd seen of the Hegemony Diplomatic Corps, Volmar and the ruthless acts of the Central Administration disgusted her. The species bigotry she'd witnessed on Herakli, and Volmar's deal with the Maagba – a plan her father, Fleet Admiral Gart Lowrans, had signed off on – were shining examples of how low Earth had sunk. So if the Jantri wanted her help to defeat the Hegemony and free humanity and every other species in its grip … Why not?

But could she really support a bunch of powerful aliens who wanted to attack Earth? Twenty years ago the K-Chaan had come close to wiping out the human race and the Hegemony had been created to make sure that never happened again. Since then though, the Central Administration had lost its way, seeming to believe any action was justified in order to maintain control. The majority of humanity thought itself safe and secure, but that safety came at a terrible price. Privacy was just a word. No secret was left undisturbed under the gaze of the HDC. Freedom was another illusion. It was freedom with hard barriers. Freedom to do whatever you wanted as long as it accorded with what the Central Administration judged was right and good. Meanwhile, HDC and Fleet moved out into space and subdued, threatened and corrupted any alien species they encountered all in the name of keeping the peace. But that wasn't how lasting peace was won, was it? Even a Fleet brat like Rhees could see that.

And now HDC had stirred up a bunch of aliens from a star system she'd never heard of. From what she'd seen of this ship and Nok's armour, the Jantri'va looked at least equal to the Hegemony in technology – and may be more advanced in some respects. There would be other species in the Lenticular who were equally unhappy with the Hegemony's incursion. HDC was already picking a fight with the Hanloi out towards galactic centre. Just how many battles on how many fronts did they want to start?

She shifted on the mat, still far from sleep. Her gaze took in the table where she and Nok had sat. There was no way she could afford to trust him – it – whatever. But they were already aligned in one respect. The Jantri'va wanted to stop the Hegemony encroaching on their space; she wanted to change the paradigm under which the whole Hegemony operated.

She barked a short laugh. When had she developed such lofty ambitions?

But she knew she was right. It was important to protect Earth, yes. But do it through cooperation, alliances, friendships, not fear, suppression and – what did Nok say? – by destroying the souls of entire species.

If she worked with Nok, she would be branded a traitor. There were those who would never forgive her. Her father, who she'd had little contact with growing up, already saw her as an unreliable hothead. This would put her beyond the pale.

There were also no guarantees she'd be able to influence how the Jantri'va ultimately acted. It was easy enough to aim a weapon and fire the kill shot. It was far more difficult to pull your aim to simply wound your adversary, and then hold back from firing again. Especially when a wounded foe was the most dangerous of all.

But what was the alternative? Run away? Fuck that.

She stood, feeling like her brain was wrapped in cobwebs. The door opened at her touch – Nok had insisted she wasn't a prisoner – and as she stepped over the threshold, a light track set into the deck strobed sequential lights leading away to her left and around the corner. She was being shepherded again. She almost turned right in defiance, but she was too tired for games.

She followed the lights, taking everything in: the walls, ceiling, control panels, ducts, doorways, other passages, trying to get a feel for the internal topography. Finally she came to a broad entrance.

The lights disappeared as the door scissored open. Nok stood there, or at least the suit did.

"I'd like to hear more," Rhees said.

"Come inside," Nok said.

There were two other suits in there, operating wall stations. Maybe they were robots. Maybe Nok was too. As she entered, she was surrounded by a web of light: wildly looping beams all connected into a network floating around and above her. She raised a hand tentatively, brushed at a light trace with the back of one finger. She heard a low hum and the light felt cool against her skin.

She joined Nok in the centre, ghost fingers of light brushing against her face and arms.

"This is the – Voss Space, you call it – network for the galactic arm," Nok said.

"All of it?"

"As much as we've mapped, which now reaches into Hegemony space and back past the Lenticular. Speaking of which." He caught a loop of light in one gauntlet and pulled it towards them. The network shifted, expanding along the line Nok was following. "This is near-Lenticular space. And this intersection is where your Hegemony emerged to attack the Kresz Homeworld. As you see, the local branchings open into a much larger passage that leads through the rest of the Lenticular. We detected another, much larger Hegemony force advancing on the same corridor a few days ago. We feared a further invasion force, to consolidate their hold on Homeworld before launching an attack on the rest of the Lenticular. It was certainly a large enough group. But instead …" He expanded the view of the main Voss Space corridor crossing that part of space. "They passed right through the heart of the Lenticular and kept going. They're currently passing a gravitational anomaly at the far end with no sign of slowing. There's another similar Hegemony force heading to the Lenticular now. It's not clear whether they'll follow the others or stop once they reach that part of space."

Rhees plucked at the main passageway. It felt slippery

against her fingers, like soap. She rotated the view, turning it end to end, studying the branchings. The anomaly Nok mentioned was impossible to miss. Voss Space bent round it in a distinctly ungraceful way, and beyond it was a local network of crosspaths that opened into another, much wider chamber extending further into the arm towards galactic centre. That second Hegemony force had to be the Hanloi attack group. Volmar had said the Hegemony was going to war. Which meant the destruction of the Kresz was collateral damage. The poor bastards were just in the way.

She could tell Nok about the Hanloi, but she wasn't ready to share just yet.

"So what's the plan?" she asked.

The suit was silent. Was it reading her? Did it know she was holding back information?

"We are not ready for a plan yet," Nok said eventually.

"They're already killing your Kresz friends. Don't you want to do something about that?"

"Any unilateral plan to attack and subdue the Hegemony in the Lenticular has already been considered and discounted. The K-Chaan learned that lesson and the Jantri will not repeat it."

So the Jantri knew about the K-Chaan. Just how long have they been studying us, she wondered.

"Any solution must be owned by those it most directly affects," Nok continued. "We are not saviours, we are facilitators."

Rhees shook her head, then wondered if the gesture would be understood. "That's just an oblique way of justifying not doing anything. What happens if 'those it most directly affects' are too beaten to see a way out or fight back?"

Eddies of gas sparkled behind the Jantri's faceplate. "Then they will be trapped in the situation."

Fuck. She'd been about to say that was inhuman. But look at what she was talking to.

People were being crushed but who was worse – the group doing the crushing or the group that stood by while it happened?

The Hegemony had stripped itself of its humanity. The Jantri had none to begin with. But they'd chosen her to help. Why?

"But we don't believe that's the current situation," Nok said, bringing her back to the present.

"So you wait? For what?"

"For the necessary elements to align."

"And how long will that take?"

This was insane. Should she cut and run? Could she? They wouldn't just let her leave. And there was no way she could outrun this ship. But she needed space around her.

"I need to get outside for a while," she said. "I think better out there."

The faceplate looked down at her, unreadable.

"You said I'm not a prisoner. Where's my ship?"

Nok crossed to a door at the far side of the room. As it opened, his head – disconcertingly – turned one-eighty degrees on his shoulders to face her. "The hangar is below, but we have something better than the Maagba craft you brought."

She followed him into a large elevator, and the car dropped a long way. The doors opened onto a blindingly white hangar. Rhees blinked, not able to get a sense of how big it was. The vessels studded along the deck – including her "gifted" ship – looked like toys.

"You can take your own ship out if you like, or you could try one of these." Nok pointed a gauntlet towards a singleship unlike any she'd ever seen.

The hull was featureless grey, shaped like an ellipse, pointed at the front and flowing up and back into a sleek hump. It didn't look like anything Rhees had ever seen but somehow reminded her of a dolphin, or an artistic abstraction of one.

"Gravity drive, of course," Nok said, "but it also generates an inertial field I think you'll find interesting. Far more manoeuvrable than Hegemony ramcraft and no need for you to be entombed in a gel coffin."

"For someone who's only recently encountered the Hegemony, you know a lot about them," Rhees said.

Them, she thought. Not *us*. She'd crossed a line. In her head, at least.

Taking one of their ships guaranteed she couldn't just run. But the pilot in her was intrigued. "How do I ..."

The hump of the ship split open, flowing back like putty. The interior seemed made of the same material as the hull, some of it bulging into the approximation of a crash-seat. She glanced at Nok but he said nothing. The floor of the cockpit was spongy, giving beneath her weight as she climbed in. The chair moved around her as she sat, and the hump flowed back over her head, plunging her into darkness.

Control faces lit up around her – lightboards floating in space – and she forced herself to relax. The seat supported her, easing back a little, and a view of the hangar opened up just above the controls. Then ... it was as if she'd blinked very slowly and opened her eyes on a new way of seeing. She couldn't still be looking through her eyes, but it didn't feel like the synaptic shunt of immersion either. She could see the hangar all around her, the controls superimposed on her view as if the ship hull wasn't there. But that wasn't all of it. Somehow she had a complete three-sixty-degree view. She saw everything without turning her head or focusing on a particular area. It was like suddenly being given a third arm – weird but obviously useful. Especially for a combat pilot. She'd used broad-range sensors before but this was more immediate, like it was a part of her. And instinctively she knew her sight extended far beyond the visible spectrum now. She also realised she knew exactly how to fly this ship.

Nok was standing patiently by the hangar entry. Rhees activated the launch sequence – a moment's concentration on the blinking icon – and headed for a new opening in the larger vessel's hull.

The stars waiting beyond were tinged slightly green by what her augmented senses knew was a force curtain holding in the hangar's atmosphere. She punched for full thrust as soon as she was clear. She knew exactly how fast she was accelerating, and Nok's ship dwindled to a pinpoint in less than a second, but she may as well have been sitting on the bed in her apartment. Inertialess. Intellectually it was impressive, but her body missed the rush of the ramcraft. Still, that would mean …

She plotted a series of manoeuvres that would pancake a ramcraft pilot even in the most advanced gel coffin, and activated commit. Three seconds later she was back where she'd started, and the craft had traversed the six planes of a cube five hundred kilometres on an edge and executed twenty-four ninety-degree turns at the vertices. She hadn't felt a thing.

There wasn't one ship in the Hegemony she couldn't fly rings around. But flying was only half of it. Her view expanded, magnifying local space and shifting into ladar. There. A tight cometary swarm, way out on the long orbital axis of whatever sun it visited in an epochal cycle. Weapon interfaces shouldered into her awareness. Pretty impressive armaments.

She imagined her ship from outside: a dolphin pausing for a moment, sonar penetrating the depths in search of prey, then diving in a flash of fin and tail for a glittering shoal. Again, she couldn't feel the acceleration, but she saw the comet swarm leaping towards her and sensed the tightening in her chest and belly.

There were six cometary masses. Dirty accretions of rock and water-ice, packed so close the tenuous gas halo enveloped them as one. She was headed straight for the centre, counting down seconds to impact.

This is the last thing Petar saw, she thought. She'd never be able to forget the sight of his gel coffin burst apart. But she pushed the ship faster, the wall of ice rushing to meet her. She screamed. Almost broke off at the last moment.

Then weapons engaged – laser clusters breaking out along the length of the ship's body, an expanding shell of missiles, the harsh grunt of a rail gun mounted in the nose. The rushing ice vapourised ahead, and around her each rock and pebble freed from the conglomerate was tracked and slagged by lasers or burst into dust by pinhead rockets, the gas halo lighting up like an aurora. And then she was through, with nothing bigger than a grain of sand left in her wake.

She brought the ship to a full halt and let out a long breath. Going by the holo records she'd seen, it was clear the Jantri had been observing the Hegemony for a long time. Nok might be content to wait for the 'necessary elements to align', but she needed to know everything the Jantri knew. There *was* no going back, no matter how many caveats she put on it.

∞

When she stepped out of the dolphincraft, Nok was waiting by the door as if he hadn't moved the entire time.

"I'll work with you," she said. "But only as far as our goals align. I'm not handing over everything just because you want it."

"That is acceptable."

"The Hegemony forces you've been tracking. They're not interested in the Lenticular. They're heading further out to engage the Hanloi at galactic centre."

Nok's faceplate glowed the same as always. "I see."

"I need to know everything they're doing," she said.

"Follow me."

They re-entered the elevator and got off at the same level as before. Rhees followed Nok down a series of corridors. She was expecting him to take her to some kind of surveillance hub crammed with listening tech. Instead he led her back to her room.

"Everything you need is here," he said.

The room filled with light – coherent interfaces floating in midair, control surfaces that Nok pulled into place, arranging them around his visor. Rhees moved to stand beside him, already recognising some of the functionality.

"These can be reconfigured any way you want," he said. "And

you may as well be comfortable while you work." He pointed at the mat she'd failed to sleep on and it twisted and folded to form an angled chaise longue.

Rhees settled herself on it. "Got anything worth eating onboard?"

"I'll see what we can find," he said, and left her to it.

3

Atalna and I were looking at the garden when Emba came out of the house.

"There's some people I need to see," he said. "I'll be back, but I'm not sure how long this will take."

"Will the Assembly let me address them?" I asked, feeling guilty at the trouble I was putting him to.

"I hope so." He looked at Atalna. "Try not to hatch any more crazy plans while I'm gone." He climbed into his ground car and followed the curve of the driveway behind the house.

"He's not really angry," Atalna said.

"You've come to know him well," I said.

"He's done more than house me. He's been visiting. More regularly lately, sometimes to talk, sometimes just to sit with me." The smooth mosaic skin of his face crinkled. "I have the impression his work isn't going as well as in the past. That he's fallen out of favour. Not that he's said anything to me directly."

"I'm sure this isn't going to help," I said. "No one likes the bearer of bad news."

"It may be worse than that. If the Hegemony is on your planet, they may be here also. It's not a good time to look like an opponent."

"Do you think they are here?" Hearing Atalna express my own fears made them more of a possibility, more real.

"I have seen nothing to suggest it, but that means precisely nothing. The bigger question is why they're in the Lenticular at all."

"You warned us they were coming."

"I warned they may come some day. But I never thought it would be this soon."

I took his arm and we walked along a winding path through the garden. The plants clearly thrived in the rich, dark soil, and I could hear insects rustling between the stalks and leaves. As we passed through a stand of tall, thin trees, we could see where the thick dome wall melded with the ground. Outside was bare, glassy black rock running for several spans then abruptly ending in fire and smoke. Molten lava, red and hungry-looking, spat and smoked in a line that followed the curve of the rock plate. There were other islands like this one in the distance, floating through drifts of thick smoke that occasionally covered them from sight. Further away, plumes of fire or liquid rock shot up into the yellowed sky. It was hard to conceive a less hospitable place to live. Inside the dome, however, I felt none of the deadly heat. The still and cool of the garden shrouded us and the chaos outside could have been a holo for all the effect it had. I saw now why the Telsans had been so keen to access a cheaper source of tekla. Its energy-absorbing and insulating properties were vital to this type of construction. I thought they'd wanted it for ship hulls like most of the rest of the Lenticular.

We sat on a bench on a patch of grass near the dome wall and looked out into the toxic clouds and living fire.

"The Hegemony took your mantle," Atalna said. "What happened on your world?"

"They took everything," I said.

Without my mantle I'd lost my empathic link to my people and become an outcast through no fault of my own. But I would have gladly ripped it from my shoulders myself if those I loved could still be alive. Up to now I'd been able to build a barrier between me and much of what had happened, just as Emba's dome kept out the inferno beyond. But here I was safe, if only for now, and that seemed so wrong when everyone I had loved, everyone who'd ever helped me or been kind, was dead. Isza, my breach-sister. Gurud, the huge Defender who was her lover. Elrak, the shopkeeper who had preferred the company of excisees like me, was most likely dead too. So many had died in the massacre at the Point, on the streets of Aktiuk and on Treaty Mount.

"You told me you wished you'd been killed when the Hegemony came to your world," I said.

"I still do. But I have to believe I survived for a reason." He paused. "I can't understand why the Hegemony came so far so fast, skipping who knows how many civilisations in the process."

I thought about how the Hegemony had arranged the rendezvous with Kergis in deep space, and the secret meetings with Kergis that must have taken place afterwards. And their fleet suddenly appearing at the Point. Such things didn't happen quickly or easily.

"Does your world have something they might want?" Atalna asked.

What would an alien species want with Homeworld? "We have tekla ore," I said. "It's used for spaceship hulls. And for Emba's house and this dome too, I think."

A momentary crease ran across Atalna's otherwise smooth forehead. "No. They have mineral wealth aplenty and their ships are advanced. More advanced than your own, I suspect."

"What did they want with your world?" I asked.

"With us it was far more straightforward. The Hegemony acts with an almost paranoid fervour which would be insane if it weren't so effective. With the expansion of their territory, it wouldn't have been long before our part of space was on the border of their own. That alone brought us to their attention. I'm sure it was nothing related to Betlaan or its people except in the broadest terms, because, you see, even though we were peaceful there was always the chance, however vanishingly small, that we might one day attack the Hegemony. This is the way they think. In order to rid themselves of the risk of potential attack, they prefer to strike first. It didn't matter to them that we were an insular race, wanting nothing they had. It didn't matter that we had no ships, no weapons that could threaten them. It didn't matter that in the tens of millenia before their ships came we had never known war, had no military and barely even need for a police force. We were close to their territory and we weren't under their control. Those two factors sealed our fate. But one day they will regret ever setting foot on Betlaan. They will regret their aggression against us. They have made me their enemy. I, who would never have considered the violence I wish now to bring down upon them."

His attention seemed focused inward, as if he were seeing those ships landing on his planet once again. I knew exactly how he felt. But then his cheek slits vibrated and he settled back on the bench, his anger subsiding as quickly as it had come.

"My pardon for the rantings of an old man. But I will help you in any way I can. Our causes are aligned now. You oppose the Hegemony as much as I."

We sat in silence for a while, looking out on magma lakes and basalt islands. The violence beyond the dome mirrored my own inner landscape.

"I feel the same anger you do," I said. "I'd never hurt anyone before this happened, but now I'll suddenly be filled with an urge to lash out for no reason. I want the comfort that only violence can bring; the comfort of inflicting pain rather than being the target for it. It scares me that I'm no better than those who attacked us, who did this." I indicated the mantle stump.

"No, Udun. You're nothing like them. These feelings, they're a reaction to stimulus. An emotional response. The Hegemony acts without emotion. Their people apply violence and torture coolly, as the logical end point of a set of arguments which, to them, make perfect sense. But your rational side is shocked by the anger you feel. That's another point of difference: you feel horror; they … I'm not sure what they feel."

"Can an entire species be evil?" I said.

"You mean can the morality of a species contain values that are diametrically opposed to anything we know? I'm not sure. Look at the member species of the Lenticular. You are all so diverse and yet you live harmoniously enough. There is a common ground for understanding. Life seems to have a set of rules hardwired into it, no matter the environment that begets it. I don't dispute there are individuals who have been twisted by their upbringing perhaps or some genetic weakness to become evil as you say, but they are the exception. It seems to me that no civilisation could exist without at least some utilitarian morality: that to do good for others is to increase the good directed to oneself and to the benefit of the whole as a secondary effect."

"And yet the Hegemony does inflict evil on others," I said. "You said they attacked Betlaan to prevent a future potential threat. That's a twisted application of the utilitarian principle. And yet they seem able to justify it to themselves."

"True," Atalna said. "It's counter-intuitive but they don't seem to see it. Eventually some enemy they create through their actions is going to make them pay for what they've done."

"But even if they were friendly to other species, in a vast and diverse universe they'd eventually come across a powerful aggressor," I said. "At least this way they act from a position of power when that time comes."

"You think they don't care that their policy multiplies the chance they will eventually be attacked?"

"Apparently not. But is the Hegemony such a unanimous force? Do they all subscribe to the motto of 'attack first and dominate'? If we agree a species cannot be philosophically and fundamentally evil, then surely there must be those inside the Hegemony who question its actions."

Atalna's black eyes regarded me. "I said before you are unique. You question where others would simply decide and move on. Myself included. But even I was forced to look beyond the surface detail when I fled Betlaan. I searched for a weakness in the Hegemony's war machine. I found none, but I did learn a little of their politics. The Hegemony's rulers are strong but there are dissenting voices. I couldn't find out much more than the name of the opposition group: the Inclusionists. But its existence at least suggests the Hegemony is not some all-conquering force of nature. There is a chance it can change."

That seemed a far-off possibility. I needed to change things here and now.

"If the Hegemony does have some other goal in the Lenticular beyond Homeworld, it might be useful leverage," I said. "If I can talk to the Assembly, get them to think of themselves as potential targets …"

"Nothing focuses the mind more fully than the thought of imminent death," Atalna said. "Believe me, I know."

∞

Telsus IV's single sun had passed its zenith when we heard the ground car return. By the time Atalna and I reached the house, Emba was already out of the vehicle. Another Telsan was with him, larger than Emba, although still short by Kresz standards.

"Well, Udun, you've got your wish," Emba said. "Not the entire Lenticular Assembly, but the Inner Council. They're waiting for you."

"Now?" I said, startled.

"Apparently."

"I didn't realise you had this much power."

Emba nodded to his companion to climb back into the car's cockpit. "Well, there are a lot of things you don't know about me. Atalna, we'll have to leave you, I'm afraid – we're going straight to the broadcast spire. You'll have to make your own way to Fa'ar Rojen's."

"I'll be fine," Atalna said. He patted my forearm. "Good luck, Udun. I hope they listen."

"Come on, Udun," Emba said, already standing by the car's open rear door. "These people don't like to be kept waiting."

"I'll see you later," I said to Atalna and squeezed into the car.

Emba sat beside me and rapped the screen between us and the cockpit.

The car started moving immediately, taking us slowly round the house and under an arch in the clear dome. There was a short tunnel where we stopped while the dome sealed behind us. An airlock. The yellow-brown mist from outside flowed in through a widening gap in front of the car.

When the outer doors were fully open, both Emba and I were pushed hard back into our seats as the car sped along a short span of road, whipping the smoke into shreds, and then became airborne. I couldn't see anything through the cloud around us, except the occasional plume of lava from below or a flameball of exploding gas. And then we were above the cloud deck. The sky was violet, thinning to black, and the planet below was shrouded in a patchwork of browns, yellows, pinks and reds.

Emba was quiet. I wondered if he was still annoyed with me for not 'being sensible'. But there wasn't really anything I could say. He wasn't going to change his mind, and I couldn't.

The car dipped back into the clouds again and Emba eventually broke the uneasy silence. "It won't be long now. I hope you're ready."

The nerves I'd been feeling since getting into the car intensified. Was I ready? It was all happening so quickly. But if I could make the Inner Council see that the Hegemony was a direct threat to their own sovereignty, that it couldn't be trusted to stop at Homeworld alone, I might convince them to act. I had to trust they'd believe me.

4

Elysem, Telsus IV / Telsan Sector / Lenticular

We were low enough now to see the rivers of lava beneath us give way to a large plate of rock that extended into the fog left and right. The car landed smoothly, running along a broad roadway. I still couldn't see the city – the smoke was too thick – but a roof passed over us and then we were joining rows of cars filing into a series of locks like the one at Emba's residence except much larger. The outer door closed behind us and a strong jet of steam from above played over the vehicles and was sucked down into the floor. Then the inner door opened and we were driving into Elysem, this time up a ribbon of road that rose quickly past tall buildings towards the crystal dome that covered the entire city. At this height, our destination was easy to see. The broadcast spire was the tallest structure in a forest of giant structures, its thin needle terminating just below the apex of the dome.

Our driver moved the car easily from ribbon to ribbon until we were on a wide avenue that led to the spire building: a broad pavilion enclosed by a basketwork of thin cables that held the spire in place. The size of the structure was more than just for show. The antenna boosted the frequencies needed to punch a signal into tenspace and then modulate it into an even more tightly packed dimension to cut broadcast lag between planets down to almost nothing. Homeworld had one but it was hardly ever used: instantaneous communication with outworlders wasn't often necessary. Even so, I suspected Kergis would have moved to capture it as soon as the Hegemony attacked.

The car ground to a halt at a low run of steps up to the main entrance. Emba pulled at the door and leaped out. I followed, taking the steps quicker than he could so we were abreast as we came to the entrance doors. Emba paused and looked back. His driver was right behind us.

"Can't you wait?" Emba snapped at him.

The driver said nothing.

The doors opened to reveal two Telsan guards with guns strapped to their chests. They looked at me intently, beady black eyes in impeccably combed furry faces.

Emba raised a paw and they stood aside. One of them pointed to the first in a series of doors that ran in an arc around the base of the spire.

Emba's driver followed us into the room and I saw the guards take up position on either side of the closing door. The driver sealed the door and stood with his back to it. It was obvious he was more than just a driver. Why all the security?

I didn't have time to ask because Emba was thrusting a pair of goggles and a set of hearing buds at me. He looked angry. With me, I supposed. Had this meeting cost him more than I realised to set up?

The hearing buds fitted into my ear gaps well enough, but as I put on the goggles the room seemed to lurch. Emba still stood beside me, although the goggles and buds he wore had disappeared and so had the room. We were at the edge of a circular platform that curved gently away from us to the centre. I looked behind. The platform was suspended over a deep black chasm that I stepped quickly away from. Then I realised it was as if the spire above us had flipped around to beneath us and we were standing on an impossibly large siphon. Had our broadcast images appeared out of that hole? It seemed likely. This was a virtual space, I understood that.

The sky above us was dark green and purple lightning shot across it, illuminating a group of three or four figures further along the platform's rim. Beyond the rim the landscape quickly faded into a dark neutrality.

"Watch Lintal," Emba said. "He's our representative on the Inner Council."

His tone made me instantly alert. Something was wrong.

As we approached the group I saw more clearly there were four others here; although if I hadn't eagerly read everything the escarpment's records hall held on the Lenticular's inhabitants, I might have mistaken one for a pile of mud. The Aphsans were rough cone shaped mounds. Their only distinguishing feature – at least for me – was the thick brow ridge that ran just above the centre of their lumpen bodies and protected a band of sensory tissue.

The other beings were more easily recognisable. The giant to the Aphsan's right was a Svestan. It was similar to a Kresz Defender in height and build but its exoskeleton was covered in thick spines that rattled as it turned to watch Emba and me. To the left was a Jantri – clad in the usual golden pressure suit, although there was no need for it in this virtual space – and then another Telsan. This must be Lintal.

The group split, whatever they were talking about cut short by our arrival.

"Emba, can you introduce your companion," Lintal said.

"This is Udun, emissary of House Czerag from the Kresz Homeworld."

"I am Lintal, Minister of the Exterior for the Telsan Congress. With me are representatives of the Inner Council: Tol Imnan of Svesta, Nok of Jantri'va and Goraan of Aphsus Prime."

These four represented the core governments of the Lenticular. There were other species in the Assembly, but these were the strongest, the most technologically advanced. I only had this one chance to convince them to help Homeworld, and I felt sick hope and fear of failure all wrapped up together.

"Thank you, council members, for agreeing to see me at short notice," I said.

Thunder rolled across the vault of the sky, then I realised the sound had come from Tol Imnan.

"What do you want, little shell thing?" it said.

Svestans were notoriously aggressive, but they were also pragmatic. I had to appeal to that side of its nature.

"I've come to warn you of danger and to ask for your help."

"Speak then." This from Goraan, I guessed, only because the mound shifted slightly.

"The Kresz people have been invaded by a ruthless enemy from beyond the Lenticular and betrayed by a hierarch who has seized control –"

"We know what has happened." Goraan again.

"What happened is what happens to all who are weak," Tol Imnan said. "You only have yourselves to blame."

I looked at Emba, trying to understand if I was missing something, but he gave away nothing.

"The younglings and elders I saw lying dead and broken in Aktiuk did not deserve their fate," I said. "This isn't some bloodless coup. The killings have been brutal. The excisions," I turned to show the scar of my mutilation, "even worse."

"And yet there has been no call for help," Lintal said. "Hierarch Kergis assures us no assistance is required. How can we of the Inner Council take it upon ourselves to encroach on the sovereign territory of the Kresz uninvited?"

I couldn't believe this. "Those that aren't dead or suiciding because of excision are being worked to death right now as forced labour. Some still fight or are hiding in the deep desert waiting for rescue. You have a moral duty to act."

Tol Imnan shrugged his massive shoulders and the spines rattled together. "Your people have always shunned contact apart from what trade suits them. They must look to their own for help."

The Jantri had been silent during the exchange. But now it spoke up. "That demonstrates as short-sighted a view as the Kresz you're criticising."

"The Hegemony has come hundreds of light years to reach the Lenticular," I said. "They're not going to stop at the Kresz

Homeworld. They're a threat to all of you. They must have recruited Kergis to their side before the invasion. Right now they could be infiltrating your own worlds."

"And if they take your air-breather worlds," Tol Imnan continued, "why should we care?"

I couldn't keep the anger from my voice. "The Hegemony is more than one species. It's possible they have methane-breathers. And if your planet has something they want, your atmosphere won't stop them."

Tol Imnan stepped closer. It was a threatening move and I was glad this was only telepresence. "Svesta is not so easy to take as you think."

"This has gone on long enough," Lintal said. "We know about you, Udun. Your own government has branded you a criminal. That is why you bear the mark of excision. You escaped custody on Homeworld and now you're out here spreading alarm to destabilise the sector."

I looked to Emba for help, but he'd vanished.

"That's a lie," I said.

"A warrant has been issued for your arrest," Lintal continued. "To be honest, we wouldn't have allowed this audience if some among us hadn't insisted."

The Jantri spoke again. "I still believe it was useful."

"A Kresz ship is on its way to pick you up," Lintal said. "You'll be confined until then."

"This is all lies," I said and ripped the goggles from my eyes. The world lurched around me and I almost fell over. I was back in the broadcast booth.

Emba was there, leaning over the prone body of his driver.

"We have to get out of here," he said. "The door's guarded, but that wall …" He indicated the curved wall opposite the door. "I don't think it's very thick."

"Why didn't you tell me?" I said.

"No time." Emba nodded at the driver. "And he was listening

all the way. Udun, we have to go!"

I tapped the wall Emba had indicated. It sounded hollow. There was nothing else in the room I could use, so I took a step back and ran my shoulder into it. The panel broke easily. Behind it was a narrow corridor arcing round the base of the broadcast spire.

Emba followed me into the space. "Go left," he said. "Quickly."

Lintal would alert security. It wouldn't be long before they broke into the booth and found us gone. I ran, hunkered over in the cramped space, until we'd worked our way to the other side of the spire.

"Out here," Emba said.

It was another blank wall panel, hopefully leading into an unoccupied booth. I leaned against it and kicked hard with my hoof. The panel split, and another kick broke it open wide enough to push through. The room was empty, the outer door closed.

Emba put a paw on my arm. "The car's waiting outside where we left it. I don't think the guards will shoot us."

"That's reassuring. But where can we go?"

"That depends on Atalna." There was a voice in the corridor behind us. "Move!" Emba said.

I keyed the outer door open and we ran back along the curve of the spire towards the bright entranceway. There was one guard looking into the booth we'd vacated. He heard us coming and turned, clutching at his gun, but my momentum carried me into him before he could fire. He bounced off me and slid along the polished floor.

I was already at the exit before he'd stopped. I leaped down the steps and into the rear of the car. I didn't know how to drive it.

"Come on!" I yelled out the open door.

Emba was panting loudly as he half-fell, half-jumped into the driver's seat. The car slewed round and I was thrown back, just managing to get a claw to the door to pull it shut.

We accelerated along the broad strip leading away from the spire, then the car swerved. "Hold on," Emba said needlessly. I was already gripping the armrests tightly.

There was a loud whine as the car came to the edge of the roadway and was slowed by some invisible force. Then our momentum carried us through whatever it was and we were off the road and dropping down. Turbines roared, the car bucked around, and I thought we were going to hit a supporting pillar beneath the roadway, but the car angled down until we were on a steeply descending ramp.

"We have to get to a smaller service lock," Emba said. "Lintal will have the obvious exits guarded, but I got the feeling he's not that keen to catch you."

"I thought you'd betrayed me back there," I said. I wasn't proud of it, but he deserved to know the truth. "It seems you've saved me. Again."

"Not yet, I haven't."

"The others didn't believe me," I said. "Or didn't care. I don't understand it."

I'd thought I could rally the Lenticular. A call to arms, with me – the outsider, the excisee who couldn't even keep his breach-sister safe – at the front of an avenging fleet swooping in to rescue Homeworld. It sounded pathetic now.

"Bad news is hard to swallow. And people don't generally thank the bearer of it," Emba said.

The ramp levelled and soon we were tearing along a narrow way between the foundations of buildings wreathed in darkness, their tops lost somewhere in the brightness above. Emba's furry paws were gripping the control stick, his whole body leaned forward in concentration. We were going much too fast for such a narrow street and the car's lamps did little to penetrate the shadows. There could be all kinds of unseen obstacles ahead.

"You know where you're going?" I asked.

"I managed to get word to Fa'ar Rojen before I acquired my 'bodyguard'."

"Who's Rojen?"

"The captain who found you in the asteroid field and brought you here at my request. The rendezvous isn't far. With luck Atalna should be with him. It's best you both leave."

The car slowed and we turned into an equally dark alley, then emerged from between the buildings to see the dome wall in front of us. Set into the wall was a dimly lit airlock. There was no one around.

"Wouldn't Lintal have had all the exit ports in the dome locked down electronically?" I asked.

"As I said, he's not that keen to catch you. He doesn't like diplomatic incidents. Too much apologising and Lintal never apologises. He alerted your government. I couldn't talk him out of that."

"Why allow me to address the Council then?"

"That's the strangest thing. When I was in Lintal's office he got a call from Nok. Somehow he knew you were here and wanted to see you."

"I don't understand."

"That makes two of us. Look, don't worry. I'll work on Lintal. The Hegemony is too much of a threat for him to ignore for long. But for now he's done the minimum to keep our government, and his own hairy hide, out of trouble. If you happen to slip past our security and get off-planet … Well, then you're someone else's problem. Besides, this service exit is so old and out of the way, it's easy to forget in a general shutdown. I don't even think the automatics work any more. That's the reason I like it." His snout wrinkled, the lips pulling away from sharp teeth.

"You're enjoying this," I said.

"Best fun I've had in ages."

"And you won't be in trouble for helping me escape?"

"I probably won't be welcome in Kresz space anytime soon, but that's no great loss. Lintal will publicly reprimand me, just to appease your government if they complain too much. An enforced period of leave. Not much more."

I was glad Emba wouldn't be in too much trouble, assuming I

escaped, but I couldn't quite see it his way. I'd failed to get the help Homeworld needed.

Emba scurried out of the car and ran to a panel at the side of the lock. Moments later he was back and the door was grinding upwards.

"Mind you, there's something to be said for a peaceful life free from violent incident," he said. "After this little adventure a holiday might be rather nice."

The outer door opened and thick brown mist swirled in around the car. There was no sign of any pursuit behind us and, as we moved out onto the brittle rock of the planet, no one here to stop us either. After a short run, the car took to the air. I felt safer flying through the impenetrable smoke, though I was sure our vehicle could have been tracked if Lintal wanted it.

"What will you do now, Udun? Where will you go?"

I had no idea, but I didn't want Emba to know that. It would make his recent rescue efforts seem redundant.

"It's best if I don't tell you," I said. "But you make sure to keep yourself safe, Emba. Don't trust anyone."

"I've never trusted anyone in my life. I'm not about to start now." There was a ping on the cabin processor. "We're here."

The car descended through the smoke and a sinuous band of amber appeared: a river of lava, just a thin strip. We flew over it, dropping all the time, and then the wheels hit solid rock again and the car slowed quickly to a crawl. Emba was navigating by screen, staring intently at a point on the display.

There was a thump on the outside of the car. I jumped and looked out the window. Something had latched onto the door on the right.

"It's not really standard to enter a ship this way. But then there's nothing standard about today," Emba said.

The smoke cleared and I saw a thick ring attached to the metal outside with a ribbed tube stretching up from it into darkness. I couldn't see anything outside the curve of the ring, so I didn't know where it led.

"Just give it a moment," Emba said. "They're replacing the atmosphere." He turned in his seat to look at me. "This is where we part, Udun. I really wish you the best of luck. Rojen will take you wherever you want to go. I'll do what I can here."

"Be careful, Emba." I reached over and held his arm. "It was good to have a friend for a while in the middle of all this."

"If you need anything more from me, all you have to do is get in touch."

The door opened to my side with a slight hiss. There wasn't anything else to say, so I let go of his arm and pushed out into the tube. It swayed a little under my hoofs, but I managed to stay upright. I found that if I leaned forward and took some of my weight on my arms as well as my lower knees, it didn't bend as much when I began to climb. Through the thin plastic of the tubing was searing heat and deadly gas. I felt instantly vulnerable, but the plastic was cool to the touch.

Finally I got to the ship's hatch. It slid aside and a stocky Telsan dressed in a baggy flight onepiece stood in the entrance. His face had the typical pointed snout, the floppy ear flaps and the dark eyes, but his fur was shot through with patches of white.

"In more trouble, Kresz?" he said. "It seems to follow you. Come on."

He reached for my arm and helped me into the inner lock. The door shut behind us; there wasn't much room in there.

He flicked at a wall panel. "I've got him, Emba. Make yourself scarce."

I didn't hear Emba's reply, but there was a churning sound outside – the tube retracting, I supposed.

The inner door opened and I followed Fa'ar Rojen down a corridor that split at a junction. The roof was low and draped with cabling; I had to stoop, my shin plates scraping along the metal decking.

"We need to get you strapped in and get out of here," Rojen said. "Security already know where we are."

"Where are we going?"

"Where I can get rid of you with no questions asked."

That made me stop. Was Rojen going to give me up?

The Telsan turned around. "Come on, Kresz – assuming we get off this ball and out to tenspace, it'll be safer for you and for me if we part company with no knowledge of the other. Whoever's after you will be looking for me too now. I'm taking you to Maelstrom – a tenspace junction at the in-arm point of the Lenticular. It's busy enough for even you to get lost in the crowds. After that I'll have no idea where you're going."

He turned and kept walking. I followed, feeling a little better. He *had* picked me up from the escape pod and brought me to Emba. That must count for something.

"Here's your old cabin," Rojen said. "Though I doubt you remember it. You'll have to share this time."

He keyed the door open and I looked inside. Atalna was strapped into one of two couches in the cramped space.

"So Emba was right – it *was* a trap," he said.

The ship shuddered and I held the doorframe to stop from falling.

"That's the lift sequence starting up," Rojen said. "You can say your hellos strapped into the couches." He left.

I sat in the second couch and pulled the straps tight around my legs and waist. The couch fitted the Betlaan a lot better than it fitted me but I felt secure enough.

"Lintal told the Kresz I was here," I said. "We're not sure when they're going to turn up so it's safer we leave now. But why are you here?"

"I told you: I want to help you. I can't do that staying behind."

The cabin lurched again as we took off. Rojen wasn't wasting any more time. We climbed, then levelled a little, still in atmosphere.

"I'm glad you came," I said. "Thank you."

Atalna was silent for a moment. "Purpose in life is hard to discern, if it exists at all," he said eventually. "But it comforts me to think this may be why I met you on your first visit. And why I'm here now. We all have to make sense of the world somehow."

I couldn't see much sense to the world right now. I was grateful for Atalna's company, but how much help could he be? He was old and crippled. Any long trip would be hard for him.

I looked at him quickly, concerned that he might have picked up my emotions. But it was a redundant reaction: my feelings were locked solely within me. Here was the privacy and solitude I'd craved when I left Homeworld for the first time on Czerag's mission. It was the bitter fulfilment of a wish by an Udun I felt little connection to any more. Too much had happened to change who I was.

5

Rhees got comfortable on the chaise. A simple gesture brought the panels down to eye level and she organised the array more logically – at least to her. The functions were pretty standard: vessel location and tracking; a range of sensor types – some fairly exotic; and comms interception. She reviewed the data Nok already had. The Jantri had been tracking Hegemony ship movement for quite some time and analysing and cataloguing ship types and deployment.

No attack force in human history had travelled so far to engage an enemy, Rhees thought. From her time in the HDC Datahive, she knew analysis of Hanloi strength and force deployment was short on detail and long on conjecture. It looked like Central Administration's strategy was to throw an overwhelming force at the problem. But what if that wasn't enough?

What the Jantri data lacked was a comms analysis. Did this show a gap in their technical prowess? Shortly after Voss had made his breakthrough into what the theorists up to then had called hyperspace, another theoretical physicist – Randolph – worked out how to use Voss Space to focus communications into an even higher dimensional fold, supporting fast or near-instantaneous communications depending on how close the sender and receiver were to a booster relay. Hegemony-occupied space – and the Voss Space channels it contained – was saturated with relays. Outside the Hegemony, relays were carried by any suitably sized ship from a battlecruiser up, providing a local hub for their ship group to link to the network.

In the Hegemony, every citizen had standard comms access through their band. But Fleet comms used quantumly entangled encryption, and HDC encryption went one step further. Still, her band should let her visualise the comms traffic even if she couldn't read it. She centred the comms portion of the lightboard, linked her band into the Jantri ship and sent a connect query propagating into Voss Space. There was no knowing how long she'd have to wait for an answer.

She looked down to see a tray on the floor beside her with a tumbler of water and some kind of steamed bun. She had no idea how it got there. The bun tasted like a wet donut but it filled her up and she'd had worse. Then she slept on the chaise and when she woke, the answer was waiting for her: <unregistered request – access denied>.

Fuck. Volmar – the consummate bureaucrat – had cancelled her band. Of course he would. He thought he'd killed her and he wasn't the kind to leave loose ends. Still, it meant he couldn't ping her if he came to suspect she wasn't dead – silver linings and all that.

If the Jantri couldn't brute-force their way into Hegemony comms, they were stuck with raw movement data. She needed a different intel source.

She opened an intra-ship channel. "We need to talk."

"We can meet in the observation lounge," Nok said. "The light strips will guide you."

Rhees had been staring at readouts for too long and the corridors seemed dark to her. The light track led her along winding passages and for a short trip up in an elevator. She couldn't get the ship's topography straight in her head.

The elevator doors opened onto a large room dominated by a curved floor-to-ceiling window. The ship was hurtling down a Voss Space corridor and the rush of plasma walls past the window made her wish she was strapped securely in a gel coffin.

She walked right up to the window. Below she could see the shape of the main hull, projecting forward and flanked by the sweeping curve of weapon or engine pods, or both. Despite their speed, the plasma walls only emitted a dull glow, but with an unusual yellowish cast to them. She wasn't sure if the window was tinted or there was some engine effect at play.

The elevator doors opened again and Nok entered, his golden armour moving smoothly and silently.

"I need to know what you intend to do to the Hegemony," Rhees said.

"There are too many variables at play to be able to say for sure."

She tried again. Perhaps Nok wasn't being deliberately vague. Maybe it was a cultural thing. "What are you hoping to happen?"

There was a pause. "You mean the optimal outcome?"

"I suppose," she said.

"Gather our forces. Optimally we will all meet and agree on a course of action, which can then be implemented."

"And by course of action, you mean?"

"The Hegemony is a blight on the galaxy," Nok said.

Which didn't bode well for the agreed outcome. She had to try to explain. Make Nok see.

"Can you sit down?" she said. "Can we talk about this?"

There was an assortment of chairs in the room, arranged in a loose arc. The seat surfaces looked metallic and uncomfortable. Did the Jantri shed their armour to use them or did they often carry non-Jantri passengers, Rhees wondered. She sat on an armchair. Despite the metallic cover, it felt like soft suede. Nok took two steps towards her and the suit locked into its chairless sitting position again.

How to explain to an alien the consequences of deep-seated cultural mores, pressures and historical events on an entire species? Rhees thought of how the Hegemony conducted itself as a sort of madness; a shared psychosis that grew from what humanity had suffered at the hands of the K-Chaan. All life in Sol system had been on the brink of extinction in the Battle for Earth. What followed had been a logical response to begin with. It had just gone too far. Of course, insanity was an illness and maybe that was the key ...

"Okay. The Hegemony is a blight," she said. "I agree with you. But the Hegemony is not synonymous with humanity. I'm human, but I don't agree with the methods the Hegemony uses. You can see that?"

"I can see that. But the Hegemony appears to be humanity's default operating paradigm."

"Not everyone thinks that way though. I can't justify what the Hegemony does, but I know how it came about. Do you understand about diseases, illnesses of the body?"

"We understand," Nok said. The visor still glowed golden, giving nothing away.

"The Hegemony's 'operating paradigm' is like a disease that infected humanity. We weren't always like this. Something caused it. If you understand illness, you know about medicine. You don't need to destroy humanity. There must be a way to cure it."

Again there was a pause that lengthened into silence. Rhees tried to think of some other way of explaining this to Nok, but she came up empty.

Finally Nok said, "And do you know how to cure this disease?"

"Not yet," she admitted. "And I'm stuck right now. I can't access Hegemony comms. But I want you to promise you'll give me a chance."

"That will be for the others in the fight to decide."

"And just who are they?"

Another pause. She had the feeling he was holding something back, but maybe she was anthropomorphising again.

"That's still fluid. It's safe to assume there will be Kresz involved. They are fragmented now but an opposition will emerge."

The Kresz would be disinclined to listen to reason from a human, Rhees thought. Or to cut humanity some slack.

"There are many other species across the Lenticular," Nok continued. "Not all are capable of participating in a fight. But the Telsans are certainly advanced enough, and the Svestans too. They also have a strong aggressive instinct."

Again, not very encouraging. She wondered if she was up to the task.

There was a flash through the curved window and their progress slowed as they neared the lip of the tunnel they'd travelled through. Rhees stood and pressed her face against the warm transparency. It was a Voss chamber, a junction filled with pale light. They hovered for a moment at the tunnel's edge somewhere towards the top of the chamber's irregular dome. Ships were scattered across the main volume below.

Rhees recognised the configurations. "Those –"

"Are Hegemony ships," Nok said, beside her now.

She quickly counted ship types, matching them with what she'd learned in her ship-deployment analysis. This was the attack group stationed at the Kresz end of the Lenticular. She assumed they were tasked with holding this junction to facilitate Fleet movement through the Lenticular to Hanloi space, and a similar withdrawal if things didn't go so well. On the space side of this chamber, the Hegemony were killing and enslaving the Kresz. A joint Fleet–HDC campaign sanctioned by Troels Volmar and her father.

The Jantri vessel began to sink towards the battle group.

"What are you doing?" Rhees said.

"They cannot detect this ship. And we have to pass through this chamber to get to our destination."

Rhees's body tensed as the Jantri ship swooped down to level out alongside a Storm Class gunboat and followed a path through the main concentration of ships. But they *were* completely unseen. They'd have drawn fire by now if they hadn't been. It didn't stop her holding her breath.

The Jantri represented the Hegemony's worst nightmare, she thought. An advanced species with inertialess and invisible ships that could pass through Earth's tightest defences unobserved. This was what kept Fleet admirals – her father included – awake at night.

When the Hegemony moved on the Lenticular, they'd started a war they didn't know existed with an enemy who – if left unchecked

– could kill every last human in the system. By ridiculously dumb luck she'd landed right in the middle of it. Leaving wouldn't stop what was coming. But if she stayed … Just possibly, she could make a difference.

Of course, the Hanloi could still come over the top of everything else and annihilate them. Always look on the bright side, she thought.

"You'll excuse me," Nok said and left.

Rhees sat again and watched the Fleet ships passing by. Fleet had once been her home; more of a home than her father had given her. After the K-Chaan killed her mother, Rhees had been passed from relative to relative while her father signed up for tour after tour. It had made her strong. Independent. But as distant as her father had been, she couldn't reconcile her few memories of him with someone who was a willing part of the Hegemony's war machine.

The last time she'd seen her father in the flesh, she'd been on the vast hangar deck of the *SCB Nimitz*, waiting with the other combat pilot cadets for a commencement speech from Admiral Ten Vargas. Petar had been sitting beside her and she'd felt the space between them like static electricity. They'd only met a couple of days before as they settled in for the trip to the Neptune Base training grounds. She'd thought he was cute from day one and it was clearly reciprocated.

Then the commander was at the podium and the sergeant-at-arms called them to attention.

"We have a slight change of arrangements," the commander said. "Admiral Vargas has been called away unexpectedly, but we're very fortunate to have his adjutant, Fleet Admiral Lowrans, in his stead."

"Fuck," Rhees whispered.

Petar looked at her sideways. "Lowrans. Is he any …"

The look on her face must have made the answer obvious.

Her father took the commander's salute and stood at the podium. He was a big, stocky man with a ruddy complexion, red hair, thinning on top, and a bushy red moustache. As he looked over the assembly Rhees tried to shrink into non-existence, but then their eyes locked. She couldn't guess if he'd known she was part of the intake. But he sure as shit did now.

She broke their gaze, but every time she looked back, his eyes seemed to be on her. Whatever speech he was giving passed by in a dream and then it was over. People were rising to their feet, clapping. And then, as the assembled cadets broke into small groups, she realised he was heading directly for her.

She grabbed Petar's hand. It was the first time they'd touched; she hadn't even thought about it. "Stay with me," she said.

Then her father was there. "What are you even –" he began. Then he exhaled loudly and took her in a strong hug, his stubble rubbing against her forehead. She didn't remember ever being held by him like that.

Finally, he stepped back. "You've grown."

"That's what happens when you haven't seen someone for twelve years."

She hadn't meant it to sound so accusing. It couldn't have been easy being widowed with a small child, but even so.

"Aye. I know." He'd looked at Petar. "Is this your young man?"

She'd thought about decks opening and swallowing her whole. Her father reached out and shook Petar's hand. He was looking a bit dazed.

"We just met on intake," Rhees said.

"But you'll look out for one another." He was still looking at Petar, expecting an answer.

"Yes, sir," Petar said. "I've got her back."

Her father nodded. "I've never been much for words, but … I'm proud of you, Rhees. Take care." And he turned to leave.

"Wait," she said. "That's it? Can't we meet later?"

He'd grimaced. "There are too many reasons why that's not a good idea."

Then he was gone, and she'd thought how stupid she'd been to hope for more after all the other times she'd reached out to him and he'd pushed her away.

∞

They'd left the Hegemony ships behind hours ago, running down Voss Space channels faster than Rhees had thought possible. But she hadn't been aware of time passing. She hadn't even been thinking in any conscious fashion. She'd already defined the big questions and they didn't have answers. Not at the moment anyway. Her eyes felt heavy and she was about to give herself over to mindless sleep when the view changed. There was no feeling of transition; no chamber or stabilising Voss bridge. And nothing of the tidal forces that should have ripped the ship apart entering space this close to a planet.

The world below looked prehistoric. It was wrapped in dirt-coloured clouds that glowed with hellish light, and through gaps in the cover the surface burned red and amber. She could see a lot of ships in orbit, but nothing threatening. Most of them looked like heavy freighters.

"Meet me in the hangar."

Nok's voice made her look around, but the lounge was still empty.

The elevator took her back to the ship deck, where Nok was waiting beside an open dolphincraft.

"Where are we?" Rhees asked.

"In the Telsans' home system."

So the Telsans were one of Nok's potential allies, she thought.

"The planet below is Telsus IV, and on that planet is Emba, senior ambassador in the xeno trade and relations branch of the Telsan government. You want to know everything – Emba is a good place to start. He has an intimate grasp of the political situation."

The dolphinship looked ready to leave, but it was the only one open and it wouldn't hold them both.

"You're not coming?" Rhees asked.

Nok was silent again.

"I get it. 'Facilitators' not 'doers'."

"I have other matters to attend to. The ship has Emba's coordinates."

"Don't you think he might feel a little threatened by one of the murderous Hegemony turning up at his door?" Rhees said.

"I've told him to expect a visitor. And assured him you'll present no threat."

Facilitator indeed. She felt bone tired, but the ship was here and the planet lay below. There was no reason to delay.

"You'll need this." Nok held out a gauntleted hand, the palm open. On it sat a black metal device about the size and shape of her pinky tip. "It's preloaded with all Lenticular and Hegemony languages."

A trink. "I put it in my ear?"

"If that seems sensible."

She looked at him, wondering if he was gently fucking with her. But she placed the device in her earhole, where it flowed – a little disconcertingly – to fill the available space. She tugged at the end and it came away easily enough. So she put it back in place.

The inside of the craft cocooned her. She felt her senses extend and understood the course, destination and flight plan. In under ten seconds she was in open space and arrowing towards the inferno below.

If Emba had clout in the Telsan government, she needed to convince him that not all of humanity was like the Hegemony. It seemed an impossible task, knowing what was happening to the Kresz. But she had to try.

6

I activated the vuscreen set into the wall in front of us in the small cabin and saw that we were in space, but it was nothing like the space around Homeworld. Above us, spreading right across the screen, was a haphazard array of orbital platforms, transports, cargo vessels, cruisers small and large, comms rigs, satbots, power collectors and other structures I didn't recognise. The ship designs varied wildly: lots of Telsan ships of course, but Aphsan, Svestan and Gen'sh ships too. Over to the left of the screen a large Jantri ship sat in orbit with smaller vessels dancing around it. It was hard to gauge its size, but if those smaller ships were singletons then it must be bigger than a city.

Then I saw it. A Kresz ship. One of the small manoeuvrable cruisers. Unlike the other craft, it was coming straight at us.

Our ship heeled over and accelerated viciously, and I felt the couch soften around me as I sank into gel. I pushed against the acceleration, reaching for the screen control on the armrest. There had to be an aft view. I flicked through options, frantic to see what was happening. Finally I hit on a split-screen combination: an aft and forward view. The Kresz ship was following and gaining on us, but it couldn't fire its missiles – assuming it wanted to – because the front view showed we were threading a path through the dense pack of ships. It slowed our progress but kept us safe for the moment.

We accelerated again as the ships around us thinned a little but our pursuer kept pace. Still they didn't fire. Rojen was a good pilot and had steered us straight towards the large Jantri vessel. The Kresz pilot couldn't risk a missile going wide and hitting it.

Our ship leaped forward, the Jantri ship seeming to jump to meet us.

Atalna groaned beside me. "The pressure."

The Jantri ship filled the whole screen. We were going to crash.

Then our course slewed around. More pressure. I heard Atalna gasp and felt the air hiss sharply through my spiracles, expelled by the crushing acceleration. We were flying straight across a vast expanse of Jantri hull and still gaining speed. Locks, sensor arrays, weapons bays flashed by below.

To the rear, the Kresz ship was almost on us. They still couldn't fire. We were too close to the Jantri ship. How many tricks did Rojen have left?

Despite our speed, the cruiser leaped forward again. Rojen's voice came over the comms link. "Get ready for impact."

I gripped the armrest uselessly.

The Kresz ship filled the aft part of the screen. There was a flash. The Kresz ship spun, suddenly out of control, dipped, and smashed into the Jantri hull, exploding in a fireball. We flew on, the flare shrinking in our aft view.

"What –" I began.

"They must have hit something." Rojen again. "A mast maybe. We're clear."

The acceleration eased off. I looked over at Atalna.

"I'm all right," he said. "Your luck is holding. I'm glad. From a purely selfish point of view."

I didn't feel lucky. More people had died, even if they were my enemies.

Rojen's gruff voice came over the comms. "Emba's not paying me enough for this. He's not paying me at all." He sighed. "At least we're safe for the moment. Speaking of money, Emba's sent me a ridiculous amount of credit for you. Once we get to Maelstrom, you'll be able to buy passage on a ship anywhere you want to go."

"Thank you," I said. "You've saved us."

He grunted again and the comms link went dead.

"Typical Telsan grace," Atalna said. "I'll miss it. But Rojen is right. It's probably best to put some distance between us and the Kresz right now."

No more ships pursued us and we moved away from the massive Jantri vessel, accelerating at a more comfortable pace and making for a transit point. A couple of ships were travelling out-system with us, which wasn't unusual. There were few regions near the Telsan system where transit into the main tenspace channel was possible. If the same ships continued to track us all the way to Maelstrom ... Well, that would be a different matter. The important thing was that they weren't firing on us.

Both ships were Jantri in design. One was similar to the contact ship Isza had piloted to meet the Hegemony. The other looked more suited for hauling cargo. It had a large drive section curving out wide from the main body of the ship, and markings on the rear. I didn't read Jantri but they looked a little like the Kresz ideogram for water. I looked at the other Jantri ship, the courier or whatever it was. It had a symbol too, near the curve of the drive. But this was something different: a spiked ball that didn't mean anything in Kresz.

I thought about my meeting with the Inner Council. Nok from Jantri'va had at least seemed open to my words, but he could just as easily have been playing with me. There was no point travelling to Jantri'va anyway. Even if I hadn't been a fugitive, few people were ever allowed to land there. The planet was too radioactive.

"What do you know about the Jantri?" I asked Atalna.

"They're the secret ones."

"What do you mean?"

"I haven't had much to do since I came to Telsus. Not until you arrived. I filled my time reading, watching the casts, searching for any mention of the Hegemony, and learning all I could about the goings-on in your Lenticular. There are eleven species living in this part of space, so lots going on. Petty disputes, territorial expansion, elections, mining and manufacturing. I got to know quite a lot about ten of those species just by watching the daily news. But nothing about the Jantri."

"Well, no external reporters could go there. It's deadly."

"True," Atalna said. "But no outsiders are allowed on your Homeworld either, but Kresz still make the news. You have your own reporters who feed into the Lenticular datastream. The Jantri don't appear to have any, or at least none that link up with the broader news networks serving this area of space."

"A cultural aspect of their civilisation?" I said.

"Or, like the Hegemony, they understand the importance of controlling the flow of information."

The Jantri contact ship disappeared from the aft view and reappeared in the forward view of the screen, its gravity drive making better time than our more conventional propulsion. After a while the cargo ship passed us too. There were no other ships behind.

"It's quite a trip to Maelstrom," Atalna said. "We should rest."

∞

Transit woke us both. My body felt ripped open, as if the ship had exploded. I think I screamed. And then we were in tenspace.

The screen in front of us still showed a split view. We were running down a corridor edged in swirling blue, which soon joined into a larger space – a proper junction. The volume was shot through with twisted columns of energy at all angles that dwarfed the ship and looked impassable. But the seemingly small spaces between them were big enough to fit a fleet of ships.

I knew the tenspace route from Kresz space led into this network, which curved through the Lenticular from end to end with many local branchings. I'd travelled only a small portion of it. Maelstrom was at the farthest point just outside the local network, at the start of the main route to the inner arm. Trade passed through there to the civilised worlds beyond. The Lenticular had felt vast when I travelled to Telsus the first time, but it seemed too small to hide me now.

Atalna had offered a choice. I could run and keep running – become a refugee like he was, never to see Homeworld again, reliant on the charity of others far from anywhere that held any memories for me. Or I could turn back towards the enemy. Every day that passed, more Kresz were excised or killed and I couldn't see a way to help them. Did the Hegemony have a weakness we could exploit? I didn't know, and it felt as if there were no answers. Perhaps it was madness to think I could stand against the Hegemony's vast instrumentality. They'd almost killed me once. The next encounter probably would. I had no idea what to do, and no energy left to fight.

We were accelerating again, going as fast as tenspace would allow along a corridor that twisted and spat pure energy. We didn't have access to charts on the screen so I had no way of knowing how far it was to Maelstrom. I would have gotten up, but Atalna was reluctant to move, so we connected with the flight deck through the screen.

"Any signs of pursuit, friend Rojen?" Atalna asked.

"The usual traffic, but nothing that's taking an unnatural interest. Or not an obvious one at least."

"How long till we make Maelstrom?" I asked.

"Two crew sleep rotations."

"And when we get there?"

"That's up to you. You'll have Emba's money. Use it wisely."

"It's not ideal," Atalna said. "We're still leaving a straight trail between Telsus IV and Maelstrom."

The Telsan harrumphed. "Well, I don't have a network of ships waiting to take fugitives on board in tricky tenspace transfers. Sorry. You'll have to make the best of it."

"Is there some way to hide our arrival at Maelstrom?" I asked. "A Kresz and a Betlaan walking off a Telsan freighter is going to attract some attention."

"Maelstrom's not your ordinary station," Rojen said. "I doubt you'd raise that much curiosity. But I'll see what I can do. Anything else?"

I thought for a moment, but the screen had already blanked. I sank back into the couch.

"Are you hungry?" Atalna said.

Despite the feeling of uselessness that weighed on me, I was. The cabin had a dispensary to the left of the screen. I freed myself from the couch and stood carefully. The only things to eat were tubes of a single flavour of paste.

I passed a tube to Atalna, who began sucking at it hungrily. I uncapped mine and extruded a small line of the greenish goo. My feeder mandibles picked at it tentatively, passing it into my mouth. There was no chewing involved. It melted away, leaving a taste that was inoffensive but not much more.

"So we get to Maelstrom station with a fortune in Telsan money," I said. "Then what?"

Atalna stopped slurping at his tube. "It's vital we keep moving. Direction's not important. There are a number of options. We buy passage on a commercial cruiser; we pay a captain much like Rojen to take us onboard. We buy a ship … Or we steal one."

"Steal one?"

"It's my preferred option." Atalna looked completely serious. "The commercial cruiser is out. Ships like that carry many passengers, most of them with too much time on their hands to be incurious about their fellow travellers. There's also the chance that the Hegemony has spies aboard. What better way to gather intelligence about local species than on a long journey with nothing much to do but make small talk? We'd be out in the open and trapped onboard. Not recommended."

I could see that. And I thought I could see why buying passage on a smaller ship would cause problems. "If we charter a ship, there'll be flight plans, details of passengers lodged with the station and checked periodically as we pass into different regions."

"It's part of the ship transponder information," Atalna agreed. "And if we find a captain willing to take us without filing the paperwork, someone who operates outside the law and is happy to take a bribe, there's no guarantee that they'll stay bribed. They're as likely to kill us, take the rest of our money and dump our bodies in space. Or, seeing as we obviously want to avoid attention, they could torture us to find out who's interested in a couple of travellers like ourselves and earn a bonus by delivering us right to Homeworld."

"I suppose buying a ship leaves a trail through open records as well," I said.

"It's as bad as the charter option, yes. Which leaves us with stealing a ship."

"But stealing it in a way that no one knows it's been stolen," I said.

"That would be preferable, yes."

Which meant it was very likely we'd have to kill someone.

Atalna saw my hesitation. "It doesn't have to mean that. A murder can leave as much of a trail as anything else."

"Kidnapping has its own drawbacks," I said. "And that's the only other way I can think of to keep a ship owner quiet."

Atalna sat forward, pulling against the restraints of the crash-couch. "Udun, sometimes we will have to do things that may not sit well with you. I agree that killing to steal is different from killing in the heat of battle or to save your own life."

"We're talking about killing an innocent being for a 'greater good' they've never heard of. That makes us as bad as the Hegemony."

Atalna shifted in his couch to face me. "Things change, Udun. We have to adapt to circumstances. We compromise ourselves, break old promises that no longer serve, but we do so to save those we love. That is the difference between us and the Hegemony."

"And what if that's their motivation? What if they act to preserve what they love? Look how far it's brought them. Look at the evil they do for that cause."

"Life isn't black and white," he said. "It's all grey. I can't convince you to go against your nature. Only you can decide whether it's worth it." He lay back against the cushioning and resumed sucking at his ration tube.

Could I do what Atalna was suggesting? More importantly, was it right?

Sakat had set up conditions on Homeworld to place Kresz on the path to perfection. That's what the Priests believed. Looking back on the march of history, I could see that the story of the Kresz people had been a progressive one. The civilising influences that brought about the end of the House Wars were evolutionary, leading to the Emergence of the communion that created an empathic link between all Kresz. The social structures that came next, like the council of hierarchs and then the lodges, gave order to a world in which we were forced to live in peace with one another. Those institutions had worked and brought us to our modern-day civilisation where cooperation was the linchpin, albeit with a persistent undercurrent of tribal rivalries. The next step was to break the monopolies of the houses and lodges – another logical evolution, and Czerag had been a tool of that. There would have been upheaval of course, but the communion would have prevented any large-scale violence and after a while things would have settled. The new order would have brought increased freedom of choice for the individual, building on the house/lodge split loyalties of the old regime even as it made them irrelevant. The Hegemony had stopped that natural progression. They had altered things. They had given Kergis a means to disrupt progress.

When Isza and I escaped the battle around the Point, we'd wondered how Kergis had been able to keep such extensive treachery a secret. It was easy for a hierarch in his shielded room to dole out limited orders to others who wouldn't see the whole picture, but Kergis had engineered a massive betrayal. The Defence Force had suddenly split, with Kergis ships breaking formation and killing other Kresz. How had they done that despite the full force of the communion? It wasn't possible. Which meant the Hegemony must have had a hand in making it possible. Did that justify any and all actions to change things back to the way they were?

When I'd hidden from Erdjis among the suicides in Cz'kras

Park, I'd felt so angry hearing him speak about the new Kresz society that was to emerge. It was easy to act out of anger. But now all these questions felt too big for me. When the Hegemony took my mantle, it had changed me on a fundamental level. I couldn't pretend otherwise any longer. Telsus IV had been my last chance to rally the Lenticular to help Homeworld and I'd failed. I couldn't trust my judgement any more.

"You're suffering the effects of trauma," Atalna said after a particularly long silence between us.

"Am I?"

"You've been physically injured, terribly so. You've witnessed a war and killing on a scale unknown on your world. You've been tortured, beaten, pursued and now you've been forced to stop. There's nothing to do but confront the horrors inside."

So I was traumatised. So what? That knowledge didn't change how powerless and confused I felt. How hard it was even to think about what came next.

"Let me take the burden for a while," Atalna went on. "You don't have to make any more decisions. Just come with me. Trust me. And take the time to heal. You may not believe it now, but you will heal. You know, when I finally escaped Betlaan I think I went mad for a time. But I came back to my senses. You're stronger than me. I can see that, though you probably don't believe it now. But it will get better."

I thought for a long moment.

"All right. I'll do what you say. I'm not sure I can kill though."

"I won't ask you to do that," he said. "Just come with me. That's all. Give yourself time."

7

Rojen's estimate was correct and we dropped out of tenspace on schedule. There was a lot of inbound and outbound traffic, but the vuscreen was dominated by the station: an elongated cone with a rounded top and a disc at the tapered end wider than the whole structure – that was the extra shielding it needed. Where the cone tip met the disc, there was a clear flattened bubble extending above and beneath the shield. It was the strangest station I'd ever seen.

"You want to see the Maelstrom?" I asked Atalna, my claw already on the screen control.

"No. Let's wait and see it from the station. It will be more impressive there."

So we were to play tourist. Not much of a cover, particularly as I was the only Kresz "tourist" in recorded history.

Rojen's voice came over the intra-ship. "Gather your things and meet me on the flight deck. I'm not docking for long."

We were both stiff getting out of the couches, and I stretched and bent my knees and back a few times.

"I think my body needs a gentler reintroduction to movement," Atalna said, then added, "Your appearance is problematic, Udun. Mine only less so. No one here will have seen a Betlaan before which is enough to draw comment. But some will know what a Kresz looks like. Of course … you look less like a Kresz without your mantle, but that –" He stopped, searching for a diplomatic way to say it.

I saved him the trouble. "But that's only a minor difference. To others, if not to me."

We collected our belongings – I only had my travel pouch, empty now; Atalna had a small cloth pack, which I carried for him – and walked along the corridor leading forward.

"We'll conceal what we can," Atalna continued. "You will be my travelling companion, my assistant. There will be no need to speak. I should be the centre of anyone's attention and you will be a mildly interesting addition." He stopped at the end of the corridor and turned to me. "That's the plan anyway."

I wanted to show that I appreciated what he was doing. "That sounds workable. I can be the quiet helper."

"Good."

He walked stiffly onto the flight deck and I followed him like a servant. Rojen was alone though the deck held stations for others. His seat swivelled to face us.

"All ready to go? We'll perform a touch-and-run. It's not so unusual out here with all the tourists coming and going."

"Udun will need a cloak," Atalna said.

"You'll find something in the port storage by the lock." He reached into one of his flight jacket pockets. "This is from Emba." It was a credit film. "It's not traceable, and you could buy this ship a couple times over with it."

I took the film and tucked it into my travel pouch. We stood there awkwardly until the flight board chimed.

"Better get to the lock," Rojen said and turned his chair back to the controls.

Out by the lock, I found a long, hooded robe inside a bulkhead cabinet. Tall as I was, it dragged on the ground and I wondered what use the much shorter Telsans had for it. The hood covered my head and sat well forward so my face was in shadow. It was perfect.

"Hang onto something," Rojen said over the intra-ship. "We're docking. There'll be some vibration."

Knowing his habit for understatement, I held tightly to a vertical pipe set beside the lock door. The other arm I wrapped around Atalna's shoulders and pulled him close to me.

"Thank you, Udun."

"Just looking after your safety, sir. But I need another name, just in case."

"Have you any suggestions?"

"Call me Reka."

Somehow it seemed fitting. The last time I'd seen my divide he'd been mad and screaming, just before Czerag excised and banished him. I wondered if he was still alive.

The hull rang and I shuffled to keep balance, holding Atalna tight. The ship reversed direction. Another clang, then a hiss and the sound of servos latching onto the outside of the ship. The lock readout showed a series of characters that meant nothing to me, but there was a shrill tone when they stopped changing and the mechanism hissed again and opened inwards.

We exited through the lock vestibule into a metal corridor that was well-lit with rungs set into the side walls. The station lock sealed behind us and the whole room vibrated. Rojen wasn't hanging around.

Atalna went ahead. A few paces along the corridor, gravity shifted so we were now holding onto ladder rungs near the bottom of a deep shaft.

"You all right?" I asked Atalna.

"I'll be fine. My leg is a little stiff for ladders."

"Wait," I said. I stepped back and my sense of up flipped again. From this perspective Atalna was clinging to the side wall like an insect. Ready for the shift this time, I walked forward again, grasped the ladder and stepped onto the rung below him. "This way, if you fall, I'll catch you."

We made slow progress up the shaft, stopping halfway as the ladder shuddered violently, perhaps with another nearby touch-and-run. At the top of the ladder was a round port set into the ceiling. I had to push Atalna through, and I scraped the carapace on my arms as I followed him.

Atalna lay on the hard deck beside the port hatch, catching his breath.

The sound of voices came from above. I helped Atalna to stand and we took a short flight of steps, emerging onto the main concourse of the cone section.

Crowds pressed us from all sides, some of the most outlandish beings I'd ever seen.

"This would appear to be the cheaper part of the station," Atalna said, his voice straining above the roar of conversation. "Artificial gravity only used in the docking area."

The outer wall of the station stood below us, the sense of down generated by steady rotation. Spinwise through the crowds the floor curved gently uphill until the view of it was cut off by the low ceiling.

Apart from the cacophony of voices, some translatable by voder but still unintelligible in the hubbub, a high skirling music added to the frenetic feel of the place. I shielded Atalna from the crowd, and felt bodies scraping against my plates through the cloak.

"No entry checks," Atalna said.

He was right. I couldn't see any security staff or customs officials.

"Easy to enter and leave," I said. "Good for us. But I'm sure there must be someone watching somewhere."

Atalna gestured at a pole with an illuminated symbol on top. "We need to go that way."

When we reached the marker I saw a broad set of steps running down to a lower corridor – just as crowded – that ran alongside a set of tracks. A transit car pulled up, and as its doors opened the press of the crowd moved us inside. The car jolted, then travelled downhill along the thickening body of the cone away from the Maelstrom. After a few stops, a tone sounded and the gradient increased. It felt like we were going down, and then, just as suddenly, the car was climbing then levelling out. The doors opened as it stopped. I saw that this part of the station had generated gravity. That sensation of moving uphill had signalled the change. The walls were walls again and the floor was comfortingly flat.

We exited the car and stood at one side of a broad circular plaza. Large display boards were dotted around the curve of the outer bulkhead, most showing advertisements or different databands from the Lenticular feed carrying the news from near space, but one or two displayed rows of information.

"Docking allocations," Atalna said. "We'll check those later. But first, a place to rest that's comfier than a crash-couch."

He activated a processor terminal set into the floor beside a bank of drop tubes. I gave him the credit film and he placed it against the terminal. It spat out a clear rod, which he pulled fully out. "Our room is just above here," he said.

The drop tube deposited us on the next floor, which was crammed with corridors radiating off in all directions, branching and re-branching, each lined with doors. The rod guided us to our room: a wide but low-ceilinged suite. The external wall was a large window. Outside the stars spun slowly around us.

"Is this expensive?" I asked.

"A little, but it's worth it for this." He gestured outside. "The accommodation in the spin section below is communal. Too many ears and eyes. The rooms above this level increase in price the higher you go. This level gives us the privacy we need without showing us to be more than moderately well-off and consequently of comparatively little interest."

It seemed logical. I sat in an armchair and looked out the window. I was finding it hard to think, let alone make decisions. Space was black and endless, but tenspace twisted unseen through and around it. Just like the Hegemony. If I was to fight against them I needed to shake off this feeling of uselessness. Start thinking like Atalna. Start acting. But I felt hollowed out. I was a fugitive. And Kergis and the Hegemony were free to do whatever they wanted on Homeworld.

Atalna flicked through data on a vuscreen. The symbols and figures mirrored the large screens I'd seen in the concourse.

"What now?" I asked.

"Rest," he said. "Then a little sightseeing."

"I need to know the details. I can't just be a passenger, no matter how I feel."

He looked at me with his black, black eyes. "You're sure?"

"No, but I have to."

"These are the docking allocations. Above the level where Rojen dropped us off are longer-term docks for low-end commercial cruisers, cargo haulers, sole traders, and service and maintenance ships. The large cruisers dock in a ring around the plaza below us. The longer-term docks in the spin section are where we need to look. We can't see what ships are there through this interface – that's secure information. But we can see when the dock is going to be vacated. Incoming ships need that information so they can configure their approach."

"So you're looking for docks whose ships will be leaving soon?"

"Yes, in the next day."

"But if we can't see any information about the ship currently docked, how do we know it's the type of ship we can use?"

"That's where the sightseeing comes in. The Maelstrom's not the only thing you can get a good look at from the bottom of the station."

Atalna spent the time until station night checking docking information. After that we lay down to sleep. The room had two beds like the one I'd recuperated in at Emba's house.

I watched the stars moving past our window until the pattern of their transit repeated and repeated and repeated. I didn't want to, but I couldn't help thinking about what was happening on Homeworld. The excisions. The brutality. The alien occupation.

There was no way Kergis could ever make the Hegemony leave. Without them, it would only be a matter of time before the other houses gathered strength and struck back against House Kergis. Then I remembered what Erdjis had said: "In time there will be only one house." That meant the excisions and killings would continue until there was no opposition.

∞

The trip down to the Maelstrom was the reverse of our journey the day before. It was early morning station time but still there was a reasonable queue for the transit car: a jumble of species, some travelling alone, but most in small groups, some with younglings.

We boarded the car, and immediately there was that sense of vertigo as it passed through the artificial gravity screen and into the spin-born gravity of the lower section.

Beside me, Atalna was holding a metal lozenge and pressing at small buttons recessed along its central spine.

"What's that?" I asked.

"Something I brought from Telsus IV. An image processor. We are sightseeing after all."

Sightseeing. It sounded so innocent, so normal. I looked at the people around us in the car: they probably still inhabited a world where they could be certain their home and loved ones would be there each time they returned to them. I knew that certainty was fragile, even though it seemed solid right up to the moment it was shattered.

Atalna played the tourist, quoting facts about the Maelstrom. "… one light-year across, it consumes the power equivalent of this entire station's yearly output a thousand times over in less than one-tenth of a second."

I didn't know what time or number scale the information was written in so it didn't mean much to me, other than it was considered an obscene amount of energy.

I wondered how long we had before a call for my arrest reached the station. There could be spies here already, alerted and watching, seeing instantly through our pathetic attempt at disguise. Even Atalna's in-character chatter seemed false and forced to me. I glanced at a Svestan sitting a few rows down. He was watching me. I pulled the hood of my cloak further forward. It wasn't fooling anyone, but I was trapped in this crowded carriage.

Then the transit car seemed to flip – another gravitational barrier pierced – and we were stopping. Doors opened and everyone in the carriage stood, eager to get out to see the Maelstrom and not at all interested in an old, crippled alien and his quiet travelling companion.

Atalna and I stepped out tentatively, because the landscape around us seemed to defy reality. The "floor" was transparent, at least to visible light, and shaped like a giant dish. Beneath it, the bulk of the station turned slowly, narrow where it met our dish but thickening out quickly, a curved cone dotted with ships.

"Ah, the station," Atalna said and lifted the image processor to capture the view.

The rest of the passengers walked to the outer rim of the dish where it curved sharply round the opaque ceiling above our heads. The gravitational mechanics of this area were intricate and seamless. The station engineers had succeeded in cancelling the effect of the station's spin, ensuring that "down" always pointed to the crystal floor no matter how acutely it curved.

Atalna walked around the dish taking more images of the station. When he was satisfied, he took my arm and we made our way to the outer rim and walked slowly round the curve and past the opaque ceiling – now an edge-on disc – until the station was above our heads. Below were three stars in a triangular formation: a fat red giant, a silvery smaller star and a blue dwarf. We were close enough to see the churning photosphere of the giant, the dark sunspots progressing across its face, the looping solar flares exploding from its surface. But that wasn't the focus of everyone's attention. Each star was a teardrop shape, with long tails of superheated gas – red, silver, blue – streaming from them, arcing back, twisting inwards, forming concentric lines round and around, spinning, drawing closer together, seemingly receding, forming the sides of a deep funnel. The Maelstrom.

To stare at it was to lose yourself in a headlong fall light-years deep, a lifetime-long, a silent plunge into the dark eye, darker still than the space around it. The terminating edge of that inner space sparked and flashed hungrily, sucking at the individual atoms of light and gas, drawing them into a final, crushing acceleration to oblivion.

I felt alone, stripped raw and bare, beneath that glowering eye. The others around me were silent too, taken into a private universe where nothing but the Maelstrom existed. A dark and hungry god.

The energy there was unthinkable. The radiations, instantly deadly. My body itched, recalling the feeling I'd had shovelling atomics for the Hegemony troops on the spaceport landing field at Aktiuk. But the glassy enclosure surrounding us was solidly opaque to any radiations that managed to escape the Maelstrom. It had to be or the entire station would be a deathtrap.

"Magnificent," Atalna said, the word no more than a breath. "Nothing can stand against that. No being or force is so great that it would not be brought low and humbled by what we see here. Our private hopes and fears pale into non-existence."

I could see what he was trying to do. Placed against this, even the Hegemony was weak and vulnerable. But I still couldn't see how I could hurt it. It was likely that when I became nuisance enough it would swallow me whole, just as easily as if I'd fallen into the Maelstrom.

∞

Back in our room Atalna loaded the images onto the vuscreen processor and created a split screen with his pictures beside the docking schedule. Most of the ships would be bound for destinations in the Lenticular. Some would travel further toward galactic centre, but a few may journey back through the Lenticular and out the other end, travelling perhaps as far as the region of space containing Atalna's planet. Beyond that lay the Hegemony and the other planets it controlled.

I realised where we needed to go.

"Do you remember we talked about the Hegemony in Emba's garden and how it must contain dissenting voices?" I asked him.

"Yes. The group called the Inclusionists, though I have nothing more than their name."

"I think we should find them."

Atalna stopped tapping at the processor and turned to look at me. "I've been waiting for you to suggest that. If we could make contact with the Inclusionists, they may have a way to help us."

I'd thought he would say I was insane. But maybe we were as insane as each other.

"There's another reason to go to Hegemony space," I said. "If we can find out why the Hegemony needed to invade Homeworld, it might point to something we can use against them. I know it's a slim chance."

"It's a chance," Atalna said.

"When Isza accompanied Kergis to meet the Hegemony, they showed her a map of their part of space near the tip of the galactic arm, but I suppose it might have been a lie. What do you know about the space they control?"

"It's many times the size of your Lenticular. It has been steadily expanding like some living organism for longer than I can say. A disease taking over the galaxy. One that has proven too virulent for the worlds it encounters to resist. Most of the outer part of the galactic arm is infected with it now. But while the Hegemony comprises many species – some willing members, others not so – its core is a single species. You've seen them: the ground troops that invaded your world. They're a constant wherever the Hegemony operate. So it's logical to assume –"

"That they're the leaders, or at least the members with the strongest voice?" I finished.

"It amounts to the same thing."

"There could be another reason," I said. "Their physiology may be the most adaptable – the best suited to spaceflight and battle. Or they're simply the most aggressively cruel. I saw enough of that on Homeworld. They may be the 'tool of preference' for the Hegemony, with some other species controlling things in the background. We may not have encountered the real rulers, if there are any."

Atalna thought for a moment. "Perhaps. What was your sister's impression of the one she met?"

I remembered the sense of the alien Isza had shared with us in Czerag's chamber. Troels Volmar didn't strike me as anyone's subordinate.

"So if they are the leaders, where is their home system?" I asked.

"That I'm not sure of. I have a name: 'Sol'. But I haven't been able to find it on any star map. Or not the ones I have access to."

"If the Hegemony originated in a single system, there are limited ways expansion can occur," I said. "I've read the early histories of many of the Lenticular species, and expansionist civilisations follow two main patterns. It can be outward but equal on all sides, like a growing sphere. Or it can expand from the same single point but progress in one general direction. In the first case, the originating system would be somewhere in the middle of the current space occupied. In the latter, the system would be at the inner or outer edge. Unless the origin point is at the extreme tip of the galactic arm, their expansion is more consistent with the first scenario. It means this Sol may be at the heart of the space they hold."

"And therefore much more difficult to get to," Atalna said.

"It's something. It's a start."

A tone sounded and the image on the vuscreen changed abruptly to show the corridor immediately outside our room. The single figure there wore the unmistakable golden body armour of a Jantri.

"It looks like he's alone," I said, crossing to the door. I pressed the screen. "Who are you?"

"It's Nok. You might recall we met at the Lenticular Inner Council meeting."

"Bring him inside before anyone sees him," Atalna said.

The door slid aside and the Jantri entered. He was like every other Jantri I'd ever seen in my – admittedly limited – exposure to them: the angular suit, as tall as a female Kresz, with only a pale glittering glow at the faceplate.

"I'm glad to see you survived your abrupt exit from Telsus IV," Nok said. "I expected no less of course."

"What are you doing here?" Atalna said.

I stepped aside and the armoured body turned smoothly, walked over to Atalna and locked into a sitting position at the Betlaan's eye level.

"No one saw me if that's what you're worried about. In fact none of the station systems are even aware my ship has docked."

"That's ridiculous," Atalna said.

"And yet it's the truth. Don't underestimate our instrumentality."

Sitting on a chair opposite Atalna, I repeated his question. "So why are you here?"

"I'm here to offer my assistance."

I felt sudden anger. "The time for that was at the Inner Council meeting. You could have helped me convince the others to save Homeworld."

"Is the timing of the offer so important?" Nok said. "Surely it's enough that I'm here now?"

"You can't trust him," Atalna said to me. "I told you, they are the secret ones."

His black eyes focused on the glowing faceplate. "Tell me, Jantri, would you fight alongside us?"

If Nok was offended, he didn't show it. "A direct fight is not always the best course of action. Here and now or with the Inner Council."

Atalna's cheek flaps vibrated dismissively.

"What I do offer are resources," Nok continued. "Help and support, Udun, for you to act as you see fit. You are an unusual individual. No other Kresz would leave his planet to seek help from outsiders. That alone makes you worthy of investment."

Other than giving me an army, I really couldn't see what use the offer was. "So you'll help me, but only so far? You want to remain in the shadows?"

"We prefer it that way."

"You *prefer* it that way," Atalna said. "While innocents are tortured and killed. What kind of people think like that?"

"Accepting our assistance does not require your understanding," Nok said calmy. "Clearly you want a fight with the Hegemony. Our analysis shows that direct action against them now would only result in both of your deaths."

"So what do you suggest?" I asked.

"Gather information, plan, and wait until the time and events are right."

But the longer I waited, the more Kresz died.

Atalna reached over and grasped my claw. "They're no better than the Hegemony, Udun. They have power, but will they use it to defend the weak and innocent? Will they make a stand and risk their own safety? We can't trust them and we don't need them. We can find allies who will fight at our shoulder, not lurk behind us in the shadows and disappear when they're most needed."

I thought it over. Nok said he was offering help, but it seemed that what he really wanted was for us to wait rather than act. Could the Jantri be working with the Hegemony? Or worse still, were they trying to play me and the rest of the Lenticular against the Hegemony for some other goal?

"I think you should leave, Nok," I said. Atalna was my only true ally apart from Emba.

"As you wish," the Jantri said, standing. "If you change your mind, my offer will be open for as long as you need."

When he was gone, Atalna sighed and sank back into his chair. "We'll win without his help," he said. "All we need is a ship off this station."

He pulled the vuscreen towards him and looked again at the docking information. "A small ship. Less crew to contend with. But it needs to be capable of a long journey now we know where we're going. A merchant ship." He split the screen and flicked through the images he'd taken, one finger tracing the lock number on the schedule. "A single trader, small, high-price commodities."

I kneeled beside him. His finger rested on a ship that looked like a thin pyramid. The lock had a character beside it.

Atalna tapped on the same character in the schedule. "No. Won't be leaving for quite some time. Possibly a charter ship, waiting on a rich passenger."

He scrolled through more ship images. Midway between the concourse and the viewing platform a dark, dome-shaped ship clung to the side of the station, smaller than the surrounding vessels. Smaller even than the pyramid ship.

"What about that one?" I said.

Atalna checked the schedule. "A new arrival is assigned to that port tomorrow morning station time. Early. It's the right size – room for a pilot and one other. Look at those farings along the curve of the dome, where it meets the station."

"Engines," I said. "Fairly large. But it's hard to know if it could make the trip."

Atalna sat back. "It's hard to know anything, but it's our best option. If we take it and it's not suitable we'll take another one somewhere else. At least if we manage this quietly we can throw off anyone following us."

Manage it quietly. That meant killing the pilot and anyone else with them.

"I'll handle that part," Atalna said, and his look slid off me towards the window.

8

It was a short slidewalk ride from Denev's dormitory to Rhees's apartment block. The elevator doors opened onto a narrow corridor lit sporadically by bioluminescent sconces. The last time Denev had been on Earth was the last time he'd seen his brother, Petar. They'd argued and now Petar was dead. Rhees was dead too. And Volmar had reassigned Denev to his personal staff.

He'd been happy to accept the posting – not that he'd had any choice in the matter. On Herakli he'd learned there was a file, sealed by Volmar, that held a clue to his parents' deaths. No information in the Hegemony was beyond HDC's reach, and Volmar worked in the HDC Datahive. Wherever that file was, the Datahive connected to it. Denev just had to find it.

He reached apartment 916-34Q and the reader acknowledged his HDC override. The door clicked open and he pushed it wide, green-blue light from the corridor spilling past him.

"Lights. Half-strength," he said and closed the door behind him.

This was where Rhees had lived. There were no windows. The light from the overheads was flat and cold, making the one-room apartment look stark. Like a hospital room. Or a cell. Single couch, low table, desk by the far wall, door slightly open beside it showing a modest plastic bathroom, and – on the other side of the couch – the unmade bed, sheets rumpled as if the woman who'd lived here had just gotten up, might turn on the shower at any moment.

Denev sat on the mattress. The pillow still held the impression of Rhees's head. He picked at a long blonde hair lying across the fabric. Last night he'd dreamed he was back on that ship, captured by the Maagba, waiting to be executed. And then Volmar came to tell him Rhees was dead. She'd either been killed by the Maagba when she escaped her cell, or Volmar had murdered her and lied to him about it.

Nothing Denev could have done would have changed the outcome, but he still felt guilty. After all, he was part of the HDC machine she was so opposed to. Not a willing cog perhaps, but the Corps had offered him security and a chance to create a safe place for him and his brother. Petar had other plans of course, but it was only when he'd been killed that Denev really started to think about the things he'd done in the service of the Hegemony. And whether they were worth it. By the time he first met Rhees at the spaceport on Herakli, he'd been well beyond making arguments for the greater good to excuse what he did for the HDC. He just followed orders. It was Rhees who had reminded him there was such a thing as decency and the right thing to do. She'd made him question again.

A small holo sat on the bedside table. Rhees and Petar. The image flickered as he picked up the projector disc. They both wore Fleet Academy flight fatigues. Petar's arm was around her shoulders, holding her tight. No shadow in their smiles. Nothing that spoke of how little their hopes and dreams had mattered in the end.

He turned off the image and placed the disc in an inside pocket.

∞

The picture window in Volmar's office gave a vertigo-inducing view of the steeply terraced banks of HDC dataminers, all the way down to the holotank at floor level. The image in the tank displayed the galactic arm, giving Denev the sensation of leaning over a precipice that ended in infinity.

On the other side of the room, Volmar flicked through reports on his deskscreen. "You're ready to go to work," he said, not looking up.

"Yes," Denev said.

"Good. There's a great deal of intel coming in from the Hanloi attack force and I need you to keep me ahead of it."

He beckoned to Denev to come stand beside him at the wallscreen. Volmar swept a hand over the display and it zoomed out from the holotank feed until the full length of the curved galactic arm was visible from its tapered tip to the bulging central mass crowded with suns. Sol system and the borders of Hegemony control were clearly labelled. In towards the centre was a curved line that marked the arbitrary border of Hanloi space. The territory they controlled was beyond belief – it spanned the width of the arm.

"You see now why we have to act," Volmar said. "The Hanloi may be so far away that under the normal pace of expansion we won't butt up against their borders for centuries, but that's beside the point. That border is a concrete limiting factor to our ultimate control of the arm. We penetrate that: everything belongs to us. It stops us: we wither on the vine. We stagnate."

"The diplomatic mission failed," Denev said.

He was referring to the negotiators the Hegemony had sent to Hanloi space. The Hanloi had destroyed their ship; which, Denev thought, was definitely the right thing to do. The Hegemony never negotiated in good faith.

"Our analysts believe that was a show of strength on the part of the Hanloi," Volmar said. "If we give them a bloody nose in return, they'll be more inclined to talk next time." He looked at Denev, one corner of his mouth turned down. "I know what you're thinking. A military solution – what would Lowrans have said."

Denev looked back at the screen. He didn't want to think about Rhees with Volmar so close.

"It's true that Fleet has its uses, but only insofar as they support the aims of the HDC. See here and here." Volmar pointed at two locations beyond the edge of Hegemony space. "These are mustering points for the two biggest Fleet concentrations in the history of the Hegemony. It's another reason why we used the Maagba instead of

Fleet to deal with the rebels you and Lowrans discovered in Cygnus Sector. The bulk of our ships had already left local space."

He indicated the lower point. "This force is making best speed direct for Hanloi space." Then he touched the edge of the screen and the tenspace corridor network showed in overlay. "But this force – the larger of the two – is taking a more circuitous route. We've already secured a staging point here." He indicated a fuzzy ellipse of stars sitting in the centre of a major tenspace junction, with a large branch corridor that reached all the way to the left-hand flank of Hanloi space. "The local species call it the Lenticular and, as you see, we're making use of its unique Voss Space topography."

Denev studied the map for a second longer. "You're attacking on two fronts."

"Classic military strategy, but from what we know of the Hanloi we believe it will be unexpected."

"And if they decide they don't want to talk afterwards?"

"Then we'll destroy them and take control of the entire galactic arm. There will be no one left to stand against us."

Denev doubted it would be that easy. But Volmar wasn't stupid.

"And what's my part in this?" he said.

"There's a lot of data to keep on top of. You'll coordinate the analysis effort and provide me with oversight briefings. But I need your instincts as well. You've proved yourself in the field. Attack scenarios against the Hanloi are being constantly updated. I want you to break them. If there's a weakness in our strategy, we need to find it before we engage the enemy."

"I'll do my best."

Volmar turned his cold blue gaze on him. "I expect nothing less."

∞

Denev descended to the top gallery and slid into a datanook's dark embrace. The autonomic shunt engaged and configuration data sprang into sharp focus. The output of three analyst teams was slaved to him and he felt the operators' shadowy presence like pressure on the back of his neck. He set them to feed in summary analyses all the way back to initial Fleet commit and let the dataflow take him where it would.

The Hegemony attack force was impressive by any measure, rivalling everything they'd thrown at the K-Chaan twenty years ago after the Battle for Earth. The primary battle group was well on the way to Hanloi border space. The secondary was split in two. An advance force had secured the key Voss Space junction in the Lenticular and occupied the nearest planet – called Homeworld by its inhabitants – through an artificial Voss bridge the dataflow designated as the Point. The remainder of the force was still en route there.

If the attack forced the Hanloi to the negotiating table, that would be when the real battle began. An invisible war, waged not with guns but words. Under the guise of diplomacy, HDC would infiltrate and subvert the Hanloi power structures as it had done in countless systems. And eventually Volmar would have his prize – the entire galactic arm under Hegemony control. Then no one would be free.

But nothing was certain yet. Denev still wore an HDC uniform, but he didn't have to actively support their plan for galactic domination. The data could still present something unexpected.

Tactical scenarios queued and he ran through them, watching loss projections, risk vectors and supply logistics. Any way you cut it, a lot of people were going to die. But any loss was acceptable if it brought the desired result. At least that was how the mission parameters had been arranged.

Finally, he had enough to prepare an initial briefing with options for further analysis. But that wasn't all he needed from the Datahive.

Twenty years ago, when Earth was losing the war against the invading K-Chaan Empire, Denev's father – a diplomatic consul in EarthGov – somehow convinced the K-Chaan to agree to peace talks. He and Denev's mother – a xenolinguist – had travelled to

Talos III to negotiate a treaty. History recorded that the talks were a K-Chaan trap and his parents were killed, but details of their deaths were classified. Growing up, Denev had never asked what happened, but after Petar died he started digging and came up against a brick wall. It was through a contact on Herakli that he discovered all material was sealed under Troels Volmar's authority.

It was a universal truth that the only way to keep a piece of information safe was to never enter it into a networked system. Security algorithms, black ice, AI watchdogs, encrypted access keys – all these tools made a system more opaque to datamining. But a system that was one hundred per cent secure was useless – because it would, of necessity, bar authorised access as well. Denev – trained by the best security analysts in HDC – was a master at this type of penetration. And he already had legitimate system access. The trick to not getting caught hacking a secure system was to make any access enquiry look innocent – or innocent enough that the threshold for a security alert wasn't breached.

While the attack scenarios continued to play in the dataspace, he ran a comparative search on historical conflicts and strategies. This opened pathways into military engagements with the K-Chaan. The data architecture shifted around him to accommodate this new area of enquiry. He accessed a few records at random – as if following a hunch. Just enough to leave a log that he'd been there. A footprint that would help him find his way back.

That was as far as he dared go. An HDC datanook was a state-of-the-art analysis tool, but it also analysed everything he did, as well as his brainwaves, pituitary output, skin conductivity, breathing and heart rate. It was better to make further enquiries elsewhere.

He shifted back to compose his briefing for Volmar.

9

Denev was dead on his feet, the massive resi-blocks of the conurb barely registering as he made the slidewalk trip from HDC Datahive to the dormitory complex. Sunlight slanted across the strip, finding its way through an unlikely gap in the urban sprawl, and he stopped to lean on the rail and feel the warmth on his face. Even this early the slidewalk was filling up, the morning commuters walking or standing in twos or threes. As he looked at them, he registered a sudden awkward movement in his peripheral vision. It was almost fifty metres back. A halting figure that grabbed the rail as if to stop from falling, then disappeared behind a group of orange-suited chem-workers headed for the cracking station on the coast.

Denev faced forward again. Just a trip and a stumble? Or someone following him and trying not to be seen? Admittedly not a very good someone. The clumsy move was bound to draw Denev's attention. He closed his eyes. Male – Denev was sure of that – medium build. Movements fluid. Not old then. Caucasian definitely. Ah. Blond hair? He couldn't risk another backward glance, but he was sure the man was blond.

He sighed, feeling deeply body-tired. He wasn't up for subterfuge. He just wanted his bunk. After he'd gotten up to speed on the Hanloi campaign there'd been an intense few hours of comms exchanges with HDC operatives embedded in both attack forces and on the Kresz Homeworld, and he had a mountain of data to assess as well as deep analyses of every contact with the Hanloi for the last five years right up to the failed diplomatic mission. He hadn't slept for thirty hours.

He moved across the deceleration strips to the ramp that spiralled down to the dorm entrance. As he descended he looked up at the sky, rubbing his scalp and yawning. The blond was on his way down too. Really not very good at this at all.

The wide entry hall was quiet. There'd be lines for the showers soon and then the servery would open for breakfast. Denev's room was on the second floor, up a short flight of stairs and almost to the end of the central corridor. The light activated as he slid the door open. A single bed on one side, desk and dataport on the other, storage cabinet opposite the door. Nothing on the walls and certainly no holos on the bedside shelf. Denev lay on his bunk, too tired to undress.

There was a smart rap on the door. A man stood there, young, tousled blond hair, open face. The man from the slidewalk. He was shirtless.

"Sorry," he said. "Just shipped in. You wouldn't have any depilatory gel? Commisary's closed."

Denev sighed and pushed off the bed. His washbag was on the desk. He picked out a spare tube and handed it to the man.

"Thanks," he said, holding out a hand. "Beloc."

"Denev," Denev said, shaking.

"I just got back off a rotation to Arcturus. Ever been out that way?"

Denev shook his head, but he knew what was expected. "I've been stationed out at Prox until recently. Then I did a short spell in Cygnus Sector."

"Ah, I've been pushing to get out to Prox. Maybe I could buy you dinner some night – repay you for the gel and get an inside line on Prox?"

Denev looked at him. He seemed friendly enough. "That sounds like a fair trade."

Beloc smiled and raised the tube. "Later." The door slid shut.

Denev sat on the bed again. Volmar was keeping a close eye on him – standard procedure for HDC. Beloc had introduced himself so they both knew they knew. Nothing personal – just following orders. It was a complication, but not a serious one. Sleep first.

Two hours later Denev woke feeling sharper. He pulled his travel bag out of the storage cabinet, moved aside spare shirts and underwear and released the false bottom in the lining. The snow suit inside looked like an ordinary worker's hooded onepiece, but it ran stealth software that would alter his physicality for any nearby visual surveillance monitoring, tricking the biometric algorithms.

Denev dressed quickly, then activated the dataport. He'd backdoored it almost as soon as he'd arrived and now he synced it with the dormitory's security system, slaving it to his band. He'd be invisible to sensors on the way out and his band location would show he'd never left his room. He just needed to make sure Beloc or anyone else didn't physically see him leave.

He was along the corridor and through the fire exit in seconds. At street level he pulled the hood close around his face. The snow suit would mask his identity as long as he stayed clear of sensitive areas and didn't draw the kind of attention that would raise his ranking in the security algorithms.

He stepped into the plaza and immediately stepped back to avoid being totalled by a group of gyropods whizzing by. They passed in a blur but through one of the plas-shields he caught sight of a kid's startled face. Bored teenagers tearing through the city, pretending to be free.

Denev had just over six hours before he had to be back at the Datahive. He'd need all that time. The subway system was quicker but the stations were security hotspots. He couldn't fool them all. He took the nearest accel strip to the slidewalk away from the city.

The bands ribboned through chasms of residential housing, their outsides festooned with vertical crops tended by drones. The strip was quiet, but there were enough riders that he didn't stand out. He walked a little, but mainly stood and let the scenery pass by. A person who lived on basic income didn't have much reason to hurry. It was an hour before he left the towering skyscrapers behind and the cityscape took on a humbler perspective. This was the second- and third-tier commercial apron. Beyond it spread low-density CA housing, then the green belt, and finally the coastal residences, all tastefully screened from the cracking plants and other heavy industry reliant on the ocean.

He took branchings from the main strip seemingly at random, but he'd already scoped his destination. The monitoring station was a nondescript cube, fifty metres on each side, huddled between a warehouse and a local courier hub. There were thousands of these cubes spread across the city – tertiary sensors for light, heat, water and recycling systems. Backups for the backups, which was why they were unstaffed. But they were still networked, and that's what he needed.

The locked door presented no challenge at all. Inside was dim blue, filled with the susurration of machinery. The interface was a simple keyboard station and dataport. No immersion. The city maintenance logon was an open book for operatives with Denev's clearance, and the user ID matched one of the local inspectors'. The program Denev loaded through the dataport was his own creation though, masking his keystrokes to a set of pre-arranged maintenance queries. He waited for the connection to HDC, watching for the telltale of discovery. Then he was in.

Denev knew the protocols. His access point was masked, but that wasn't unusual for a covert agency. And the user access he'd chosen was valid with a clearance that wasn't enough to raise alarms. He dropped through the checkpoints, taking a circuitous route to the huge records database cluster. The footprints he'd left while he was in the Datahive led him to the directories he needed. He still couldn't hack them. He didn't have the keys, and blunt force would get him locked out and scooped up almost as fast as if he was sitting in the lobby of HDC.

Instead, he accessed the K-Chaan archive, scanning the file tags quickly until he reached the period when his mother and father had been killed. Many of these files had been declassified with the passage of time, but there was a cluster that remained locked. The time tag was right. Something in there was still vital enough to the security of the Hegemony to keep them classified. At least he could access some of the files' metadata if not their contents. Two carried his father's ID. They had to be the ones that Ix'la had told him were locked on Volmar's orders.

Denev checked the security settings. The file locks were unusual. One ID he recognised as Volmar's, but these files were locked under multiple IDs that had to be submitted simultaneously. No single ID could unlock the contents.

He ran a search on the other IDs in the main directory. Then he ran it again because he couldn't quite believe the results.

Three highly recognisable names came up. Ruiz Rejak, the Secretary of Security and Defence and Chair of the Central Administration Security Review Subcommittee; Admiral Ten Vargas, Chair of the Joint Chiefs of Staff of the Combined Hegemony Forces; and Antonus Breslaw, Permanent Head of the Central Administration and the most powerful man in the system. It was only under their leadership that Earth had survived when everything went to shit with the K-Chaan. They were the founders of the Hegemony. And they were all linked to the locked file containing details of his parents' deaths.

Denev focused again on the data architecture. The longer he was in here the more likely he'd draw attention. He had to use what time he had left productively. The metadata also carried a ship ID. The registry extract identified it as the *Lincoln*, a destroyer in the old Earthforce, the pre-Hegemony Fleet.

He jumped to the full registry section. The ship had been destroyed in the Battle for Earth – like so many others – but every detail of its service up to that point was here. He sorted through the time stamps until he got to the right spot. The destination was classified of course, but other parts of the record were available, including the passenger manifest. There were his parents. He scanned the other names quickly, stopping at *VOLMAR, Troels*. He was listed as a diplomatic aide, and there'd been only one diplomat on that ship. Volmar had been working with Denev's father when he died.

Denev had as much as he dared for now, and worked quickly to leave the archive without tripping any alarms. He had to process this – work out where to go next.

He ran a final check as the port returned to standby mode. Nothing had tracked him back. Nothing he could detect anyway. He had two hours to get back to the dorm and be ready for his next shift.

At the door, he hesitated. Best not to leave the same way he came in. He skirted along the external wall, ducking pipework and heavy cabling, and rounded the corner. There was another exit here. He opened the door a couple of centimetres, then pushed it wide. A man was standing with his back to him at the corner of the building. Blond hair. Beloc.

Denev grabbed the man's shoulder even as he was turning, punched hard to his kidney and kicked viciously to the back of his knee. Beloc dropped, but he had a blaster – the muzzle arced round towards Denev's head.

Denev caught Beloc's wrist with two hands and twisted, flipping him onto his back. He wrenched the gun free and pointed it at the prone man's head.

Beloc held his hands wide, fingers spread in submission. "Okay, just calm down," he said.

Denev ripped Beloc's band from his wrist. But what was he going to do? He couldn't shoot him here.

That hesitation was all Beloc needed. A foot came up, kicking Denev in the chest and knocking the blaster wide. Then he was on his feet and around the corner.

By the time Denev recovered, Beloc was running towards the strips. He pushed the blaster into an inside pocket and ran after him.

He had Beloc's band. The man couldn't call for help, not unless he made it to a public comm. But how much had he already reported?

Beloc was racing up the accel strips, dodging between other travellers. Denev followed but he wasn't getting any closer. He put his head down and sprinted. He had to finish this before they reached the main band and drew attention.

He made it to the top of the spiral and saw Beloc still running about fifty metres ahead, now on the fastest strip. Denev leaped onto it, nearly losing his footing, but he didn't break his stride, closing the distance. Beloc risked a glance behind, eyes widening as he saw Denev gaining.

They were coming up on a junction, a three-way split, two arms peeling off the main band to loop into the next suburban centre. Beloc was tiring and Denev could see he was favouring the leg he'd kicked. The junction rushed towards them. Denev pushed harder, almost there.

He reached out, his fingers brushing Beloc's elbow. Beloc swerved for the left branch of the junction, skipped to the next strip over, then feinted, dodging right. Denev had followed left and his momentum still carried him that way. Beloc was going to get away.

Beloc jumped for the main band, but his leg betrayed him, the knee giving way. He stumbled, hit the barrier and flipped, sailing over it and dropping out of sight.

On the looping downward spiral now, Denev stopped and looked over the side. Beloc lay on the ground, arms and legs twisted like a broken doll, a pool of blood spreading out from his head. Denev broke the clasp on Beloc's band, wiped it and dropped it over the barrier to land near the man's body.

He had to get back to the dorm and change before his shift.

10

Maelstrom Station / Lenticular

The following day, Atalna made sure we were awake early, well before the ship's docking port was due to turn over. The station's corridors were dark, but lights flared and dimmed with our passing. The drop tube was empty, and only a few shopkeepers were on the main concourse, pushing back barriers and arranging displays.

We pushed open a bright orange door in the bulkhead that ran alongside the transit car station. A long flight of stairs led down, then angled strangely as if some giant had wilfully twisted them out of shape. I went first and Atalna came behind me, holding my arm.

After a turn we came to the strangely shaped section, painted the same orange as the door. This was where generated gravity ended and spin gravity took over. Down became "along". I stepped onto the marked area. It looked like my hoofs should slip off and leave me hanging from the handrail, but the transition in forces was smooth, just like the viewing platform. The stairs were now a horizontal platform with guide rails ending a short distance at another door, again unlocked.

We walked through into a narrow corridor. A low rumbling noise above us quickly faded.

"That's the transit car starting up," Atalna said. "Our ship is a half-turn that way and towards the Maelstrom end, then down closer to the outer skin of the station."

The corridor twisted and turned at regular intervals, with hatches set in the floor – entrances to the ships docked on the outside. Finally we reached our destination: a circular hatch with controls set into the floor beside it.

Atalna kneeled slowly to activate the caller, one hand behind his back holding a blaster. I stayed in the shadows. Surely he wasn't going to simply blast the pilot in the hatchway? Sensors would register the discharge. Security would be alerted.

But what was the alternative? Take the pilot hostage, force him to take us with him, and when we were in space … I didn't want to think about what would happen then.

Atalna pushed the caller again. Nothing.

As he straightened, holding the blaster out of sight, we heard footsteps in the corridor behind us. I turned. A Chirrik was staring at us. Shorter than me, it was insectile, with a bulbous head dominated by compound eyes. It wore only a pouched belt and its body was thin but hard, chitinous like my own shell. Long transparent wings hung from its shoulders.

A rasping from it was translated by the voder. "Can I help you?"

Atalna pointed the blaster at it. "You can open this ship, and then we're all going inside."

Whip-like, the Chirrik grabbed Atalna's gun-hand, pushing it wide as its other hand caught him by the throat. It kicked at his legs and the Betlaan went down. I was shocked by how fast it moved. It squatted on Atalna's chest, choking him and bashing his gun-hand against the floor until the blaster skittered away.

Atalna was unarmed now, but still the Chirrik was choking him. I stared, frozen. The Chirrik was only defending itself. From two robbers. Then I moved, chopping both claws down on the Chirrik's neck. It dropped to the side and rolled onto its back. Legs came up, twisting around mine and pushed, and then I was falling heavily.

The Chirrik leaped on me. It held a long baton I hadn't seen before, which it swung hard against the side of my crown plate. My head rang with the impact. I brought my arms up and pushed with my legs off the deck, trying to throw the Chirrik off, but the baton connected again. Atalna grabbed at the Chirrik from behind, but it shrugged him off and kept hitting me. I heard the chitin of my crown plate crack.

Then I saw Atalna again. He had the blaster. The Chirrik saw him too. It twisted while still straddling me and hit Atalna a vicious blow to the head. He went down. Then it turned back to me and continued the beating. I lifted my arms to protect my head, but it knocked them away easily.

And then it was off me. Two bulky figures, big as Svestans but dark-skinned, were dragging the Chirrik back. A knife flashed. Flashed again. One of the attackers grabbed at the Chirrik's belt then stood. The other poured a thin stream of liquid from a bottle onto the body. Then they were gone.

I collapsed back, then remembered Atalna and rolled on my side. There was a hissing noise. The Chirrik's body was disintegrating.

I got my hoofs under me and stood, holding the wall. By the time I was upright, there was nothing left of the pilot. Not even any marks on the floor.

Atalna lay by the hatch. I skirted the deck where the Chirrik had been, not wanting to touch whatever chemical had been used.

When I reached him, Atalna groaned. "Udun. You saved me. I knew you would."

"I'm not sure I did. The Chirrik almost killed us both. But someone came – thieves, I think."

Atalna raised himself up on his elbows. "They attacked you?"

"They attacked the Chirrik. I wasn't a threat by that stage. And then they poured a chemical on it. The body's gone."

"They did us a favour," Atalna said.

I helped him to sit. He seemed no worse for the fight. My head was still aching and I touched my crown plate gently. I could feel a crack running to the edge from the centre, but the plate was still intact.

"We still need to get into this ship," Atalna said. "It's almost time for it to vacate. If that doesn't happen on schedule, someone will come looking."

There was no body left to search for a code or a key for the hatch. I cast around and spotted a small object against a turn in the wall. A crystal. "This might be it."

Atalna passed the crystal over a grating beside the hatch. The cover hissed, recessed into the floor and slid aside, revealing a short tunnel with handholds leading down.

"Are you all right to move?" I asked.

"Yes, yes," Atalna said shortly. "It's not my first brawl."

I climbed down first. The section at the bottom of the tunnel was marked in the same orange as before. I let one hoof dangle. Sure enough, gravity was different here. I eased out of the tunnel and stood, now upright, in an entry vestibule with the ship's hatch in front of me. I helped Atalna make the transition and he swiped the crystal on a patch of the ship's hull. The hatch behind us closed over and the ship's hatch opened.

Inside, the walls were padded and the air was cold. We walked a few steps then stopped as a voice said, "Where is pilot Krrt?"

I looked behind us. No one.

Atalna said, "Pilot Krrt is gone. We are your new owners." He held up the crystal. To me, he said, "Ship AI."

We walked into a circular control room: one couch at the controls, a cot in a cabinet to the left, vuscreens wrapped around the walls. I expected the AI to say more, perhaps raise an alarm, but Atalna rested the crystal in a recess on the couch arm and the overhead lights brightened. There was a hum and the deck plate began to throb.

"That's a deepsleep cabinet," Atalna said, gesturing at the cot. "Good. It means the ship's outfitted for long runs."

He sat in the couch, keyed the armrest controls and brought up data on the forward display. "Krrt was a trader. Dealing in pharmaceuticals. Small cargoes, but they probably fetched a good price. Hmph. Controls are fairly standard. Realspace and tenspace propulsion. If he made long runs the tenspace signature should be well-damped. The ship's quite new."

The ship we stole, I thought. Krrt may have been a good person or a bad one, certainly an unlucky one. We were fighting for survival.

"Can you fly it?" I asked.

"I think so. And you will too. I'll teach you. I can't fly all the way to Hegemony space by myself."

"Incoming transmission." It was the AI again.

"Voice only," Atalna said.

"Port five-el-gira, your purge clock is coming up on zero. Confirm purge." On a side screen a semi-circle appeared, the shape filling with black.

"Purging now," Atalna said. "End transmission. Ship, disengage from the station and take us clear."

There was a sharp "clack" from the external hatch and the ship juddered. I felt us begin to drift, then accelerate gently forward.

"We're away," Atalna said. "And without any undue interest from the station, it seems."

The forward vuscreen showed space ahead of us, with a tile in the bottom showing a rear view. A bright red band arced through the centre of the screen and the ship turned to follow it. Our flight path out of here. We briefly caught sight of the ship coming in to take our place at dock: long and thin with tapered vanes at both ends. It passed out of the display as we banked further right and accelerated.

"You can't stand there safely," Atalna told me. "The ship's manoeuvring."

There was nowhere to go except the cabinet. It had a clear top, which slid into the wall at the touch of a contact. The cot below looked like any other ship's cot I'd seen. I'd heard of deepsleep, but Kresz ships didn't use it, even the deeprange ones. I rolled onto the mattress expecting tubes and contacts to snake out of the cabinet walls, but nothing happened. I had to pull my legs up to fit inside, but it was comfortable for all that.

The cabinet lid slid shut above me and I panicked for an instant.

A voice spoke softly in my ear; the AI. "Deepsleep functions cannot be activated while the ship is close manoeuvring. Would you like the vuscreen function activated?"

"Yes," I said.

A section of the clear cover above my head darkened and then I saw the same feed as on the main screen. We still followed the red band.

"Are you okay, Udun?" Atalna's voice came through a speaker in the cabinet wall.

"Yes. I have a vuscreen here to watch. It's comfortable."

"Good. We shouldn't have trouble getting to the edge of the Hegemony. There's a good set of charts here. And the AI is useful."

I wondered again if this was the right thing to do. The heart of the Hegemony's power seemed impossibly far. And the Hegemony's troops would continue to act unimpeded on Homeworld all the time I was away. But there was no other course I could see. Atalna and I were alone. Our only weapon was information and we had none, or none convincing enough to mobilise any sort of response from the rest of the Lenticular. I'd seen that at the Inner Council meeting. We had to find the Hegemony's weakness; or, failing that, at least some information we could use to rally an attack. If we made contact with these Inclusionists and they were willing to help, all the better. All of which meant we had to infiltrate the Hegemony, no matter how dangerous that might prove to be.

"How long to make the crossing?" I asked.

"The AI is still calculating," Atalna said. "As fast as we can without blowing up in tenspace. It's a balancing act. We can push our speed, but that will mean regular transits to realspace to shed field potential, which adds to the journey." He paused. "We'll make the best time we can."

We were clear of the station now and the ship gained speed, heading for the transit area, which, given the relative proximity of the Maelstrom, was another gravitationally balanced part of space similar to the Point. I hadn't seen it on our inward journey, but our approach now gave us a good view. The satellites were much larger than those in Kresz space. They had to be. This part of space was crowded. It hadn't been like this on the way in, but then our ship hadn't been part of a scheduled rotation of docking ports.

The ship slowed, joining an irregular queue of vessels waiting their turn to enter the globe of satellites and transit.

There was a Svestan ship in front of us, its ovoid hull bristling with spines like the beings inside it. Other vessels strung out ahead, some large, others small, many I didn't recognise. Then the aft-view tile caught my attention. There was a commercial cruise ship right behind us, sleek with lots of observation bubbles, and behind it another ship-type that looked familiar. It was a cargo ship, Jantri design with its curving drive section. As it manoeuvred into the line, I saw the mark on its rear. The symbol that looked like Kresz for water.

"That ship behind us. After the cruise ship. Do you recognise it?" I asked Atalna.

The display capture on the cabinet lid changed, enlarging the rear view and focusing in. I was sure it was the same ship.

"I don't know," Atalna said. "Where have you seen it before?"

"Right after we escaped Telsus IV."

"Hmph. You may be right. But Rojen didn't mention any ship following us in tenspace."

"Maybe it tracked us at a distance," I said.

"Not possible in tenspace. The raw energies there scramble any tracker signal."

"Any we know of. You said the Jantri were the secret ones. And I've seen some of their technology on Homeworld. Or at least the tech they've cast off to others. Nok offered to help. Perhaps he already has."

"I don't follow."

"That Kresz ship in Telsan space nearly had us until it exploded near that Jantri transport."

"Yes," Atalna said, stretching out the word as he thought about the implications.

"And two Jantri ships 'escorted' us out of there, one of which has turned up here."

"I suppose, although it could be –"

"Coincidence. I know. But just now, when the Chirrik was beating me to death, two thieves attacked and killed him, dropping the crystal for this ship. Another coincidence?"

"You think the Jantri are helping us?"

"Not directly maybe. If they're fighting the Hegemony …"

"If they are, they're doing it for their own reasons," Atalna said. "Which may or may not include liberating Homeworld. We can't afford to make mistakes, Udun. Every offer must be weighed, every option scrutinised. If the Jantri really want to help us, let them prove themselves. Lurking in the shadows leaves all the risk on our side of the equation. That's not the basis for a true alliance. You know you can trust me because I would gladly die to destroy the Hegemony. Make sure others you enlist will do the same."

The vuscreen relay returned to normal. We'd progressed in the queue. The Svestan ship was between the network of satellites now, and I heard the familiar sound of our ship's tenspace drive charging.

The Svestans disappeared into transit and Atalna accelerated us into the central space between the satellites. The sound from the tenspace engines jumped in volume and I tensed, holding on. Transit hurt. I would have preferred to be under whatever artificial sleep this cabinet provided.

The transit effect hit. It felt as if my body was torn away from me, shredded, then crushed. I hovered on the edge of pain for an instant, then it all came crushing back and I was still in the cabinet, the pain in my nerve ends fading out almost immediately.

Tenspace crackled around us. This was a large opening and on the vuscreen I could see the other ships heading away into a cavern of light, towards tunnels leading where I did not know. Our ship moved clear of the transit point, but without a destination as yet it floated in the centre of the space.

I activated the stud to open the cabinet and climbed out to

crouch beside Atalna. The screens showed multiple views of the cavern around us.

"Look at this," Atalna said, bringing a feed from a peripheral screen to the central one. "It's below us. Thankfully a long way below."

It was a lightning storm, greater than any I'd seen during the season of Kareee at home. Bolts of blinding purple and red crossed and recrossed, forming temporary spans at the mouth of a pit that spun with smoke shredding and forming, shredding and forming. The lightning built and built and then there was a flash of … Nonlight was the only word I could think of to describe it. For a moment it appeared realspace had broken in – I could see stars. Then the clouds closed over and the lightning came again.

"The Maelstrom," I said.

"Not only does it devour realspace," Atalna said. "It rips apart the subdimensions of tenspace."

"Let's get away from here. There are too many ships."

"Agreed."

We followed the same path as Rojen, looping back through the centre of the Lenticular, back past Telsus. We didn't see any other ships going our way once we were on course, though we passed plenty going in the other direction. But no Kresz ships.

∞

Atalna gave me some basic lessons in piloting, and after that we took turns in the pilot's couch, the other sleeping in the cabinet. The AI anticipated any problems. It even identified the optimum transit nodes to let us shed excess energy and get back on course with the minimum of delay.

The ship's databanks were open to us and the AI helped me find navigational data. The charts were good, especially of the Lenticular. I'd spent enough time studying that part of space to know that. They became less certain the further along the arm we travelled. Tenspace wasn't a simple linear affair, and what appeared to be the right tunnel could just as quickly loop back or strike off on a completely different heading. Some days it seemed we were making no progress at all. But it gave me time to learn to pilot the ship, and the AI provided a lesson plan on the basics: engine management, navigation, close piloting, tenspace hazards. Udun the tenspace pilot. Isza would have laughed.

We reached a branch in the tunnel we were following and I directed the AI to take the right limb, but some time later found myself staring at a darkly tapering dead end. With fore and aft views clear, I manoeuvred the dome of the ship in a tight turn, avoiding the walls, and then applied minimal thrust back the way we'd come.

As the tunnel widened, I moved the ship from side to side, practising close piloting, and imagined Isza commenting on my progress. "Not too close, Udun. Feather the thruster more. That's better."

The dead never really left us. Out here, away from anyone I knew – except Atalna – that thought was more of a comfort than a sadness. Physically, I had mended. The mantle wound no longer pained me and the scar had healed over. Mentally, some areas were still raw, and would remain so. Some pain I never wanted to fade. Like losing Isza. But I kept that at a distance for now, using the memory of the Hegemony on Homeworld and what I had to do to fight them to stop me getting lost in grief. That and the hatred I carried for Kergis and Erdjis. A red hot fury that had cooled and hardened.

Had Kergis known what the Hegemony planned for Homeworld before he met with them? Certainly Erdjis knew nothing because Isza would have sensed it. But she was only with Kergis for a short time and his presence was overwhelming, a distraction from anything that might be below the surface. And if Kergis hadn't joined the mission with the express purpose of securing the Hegemony as an ally, what had Troels Volmar said to convince the hierarch to side with them? The Hegemony diplomat had been full of lies, talking of peace and treaty, of sharing information, and Kergis had not been impressed – or that was the sense Isza had gathered from the meeting. Then, when Kergis rebuffed the Hegemony's advances, Volmar had resorted to veiled threats about a hostile universe. It didn't seem likely that would have swayed Kergis. The Kresz were careless about such things. Too careless as it turned out.

I rememberd then that Volmar had another message. At the time Isza thought it was meaningless rhetoric. What was it? That "each species had to follow its own path to achieve its full potential" and the Hegemony worked to support that. Volmar already knew some of our language, which showed he also knew something of our religion, about Sakat's plan, and about the political and social situation on Homeworld. I'd already suspected the Hegemony was behind the missing deeprange ship *Might of Gnow* and I'd tried to warn Czerag about it. Surely this proved it. I'd seen for myself that the Hegemony was capable of the cruelty and torture necessary to extract information from the Kresz aboard that ship. It had been crewed by House Kergis pilots. I wondered if Kergis knew his new friends had murdered his people to get to him. And whether he cared.

The tunnel we were flying through took a sharp left. I followed the inner contours of the curve, watching the forward vuscreen closely and glancing at the proximity sensors – mostly useless except for the closest approaches – when my eyes caught a flash of movement. It could just have been a plasma flash ahead but I stopped the ship immediately. My instincts saved us.

I killed the navigational lights and woke Atalna.

"What?" he said.

I helped him to sitting, then returned to the pilot couch. Most of the vuscreen was covered by a thick curl of plasma wall, but part of the tunnel beyond was visible. And there was movement there, lots of it. Hegemony ships. I'd recognise them anywhere.

I spoke to the AI. "Magnify the forward image and compensate for motion."

Atalna recognised them too. "They haven't seen us?" he asked.

"No. I was backtracking a dead end. We're at full stop and running dark. Unless their sensors can penetrate tenspace ..."

Ships passed the mouth of the tunnel at regular intervals. Some were the small manoeuvrable attack ships that had beaten us at the Point, but there were larger ships too, some much larger than the Hegemony cruisers I was familiar with. If I'd gone left at the branch we would have run right into them.

We watched in silence. The ships kept passing for a long time.

"Where are they going, do you think? The Lenticular?"

Atalna's dark eyes looked at me. "Perhaps."

It was clear this was a large attack force and I felt sure it was headed for the Lenticular. I couldn't see the Hegemony conducting multiple major offences in this part of space. It was hard for me to spare a thought for the other species who had proved so uninterested in helping the Kresz when the Hegemony overran Homeworld. But I worried for Emba.

"This is the instrumentality that controls your planet and mine now," I said eventually.

"Are you religious?" Atalna asked.

The question startled me. "No. But most other Kresz believe. Our creator god, Sakat, is also god of death. He steers our path by weeding out the imperfect – the 'non-Kresz', whatever that means. Imperfection seems to be in the eye of the beholder, depending on what house you talk to."

"I wonder what your Sakat would say about what is going on on his world."

"Would he disapprove, do you mean? His views – at least as expressed by the Priests – are polarising. Not all Kresz are worthy of survival. But if Sakat does exist, he hasn't intervened to save his own. Personally I believe I'm nothing more than the sum of the neurochemical reactions contained within my physical form. There is no 'me' outside of that."

"It's a bleak view."

"Not at all. It means I have to make the most of what I have, be the best I can. Because there's nothing else beyond what I can see."

"On Betlaan," Atalna said, "our god was the planet. Everything that sustained us sprang from it and for that we worshipped it. When we died, our bodies were interred within the soil to break down and return the life they contained back to its origin point. I'm not sure how much of our world remains now. When the Hegemony came, they opened up strip mines. Factories moved across the surface, eating into our world, and nothing grew where they'd been. If god was our planet, the Hegemony killed it."

We waited for a long time after what looked like the last of the ships had passed, then I piloted us out into the branch. There was no point pursuing them. There was nothing we could do against such a force. I turned the ship to the right. At least we knew now we were headed towards the seat of Hegemony power.

11

When Rhees's dolphincraft hit the Telsan planet's atmosphere, it was like plunging into the upper layers of Jupiter: shredding through murky vapour tinged red-brown, sulphur yellow and all shades in-between. The cloud deck extended to the surface, which made the visible spectrum useless for navigation. But her augmented senses shifted to a composite overlay that provided an information-rich view. Not just surface topography but temperature gradients and chemical and atomic composition. A slight shift in focus and she could "see" the sub-surface and plot magma flows and thermal circulation patterns. The planet's mantle was shattered, completely submerged in some places or just not there in others. She sensed thermal vents further down that extended all the way to the core.

Her destination tugged at her consciousness like a silent alarm. The ship levelled, skimming through thick fog just above the lava seas. Fifty klicks to starboard she registered some kind of floating manufactory – there and gone as she accelerated towards the small islet that was her target. It floated on the molten liquid, a rough disc of planetary crust five hundred metres deep and less than half that in diameter. Most of the above-surface landmass was covered by a habitat dome with a single structure inside.

The dolphinship broke out of the fog, decelerating across an angry expanse of lava and making final adjustments on approach to the pressure lock in the dome's circumference.

The outer door opened and the ship floated inside, waited as the external atmosphere was replaced, then moved through the inner door and along a curved path to settle beside the glass wall fronting the structure.

A creature stood beside the wall. Something like a small bear with longer limbs, except its hairy face was definitely unbearlike.

The dolphin peeled back around her and Rhees stepped onto firm ground. A shout and another Telsan appeared, a blaster in its hand rising towards her. She hadn't thought to bring a weapon.

The ship made a snapping noise and the Telsan yelped, dropping the gun and flapping its clawed fingers as if stung.

"I'm not here to hurt you," Rhees said.

The first Telsan – who must be Emba, she thought – said, "You've made a poor start then." He looked at his companion. "Thanks, Ketan. That will be all for now."

"Nok said he'd told you I wasn't a threat," Rhees said once Ketan had gone back inside.

"I'm not predisposed to trust the Jantri."

Interesting. Was that because the Jantri didn't like to get involved, or some other reason?

"I only met Nok recently," she said. "I don't know him that well."

"Yet you travel with him. You fly a Jantri ship."

"It's complicated."

Emba's snout crinkled and she saw a flash of sharp teeth. "You're here now. You may as well come inside."

She followed him into a long room as wide as the house, with a big dining table at one end and couches and easy chairs at the other.

"Are you here with a message from the Hegemony?" he asked.

"What? Fuck, no. I'm not part of what's going on here."

His eyes narrowed. "But you are Hegemony."

"I'm human. There's a difference. I want to stop them. Free humanity from Hegemony rule."

Emba scratched at a hairy ear point. "Words like that are best backed up with action. You must command a vast army. We know how strong the Hegemony is. How many in your insurgency?"

"Me," she said, then thought about Denev. "Possibly one other."

"You and Udun should meet."

"Udun?" The trink hadn't offered a translation.

"A Kresz. An outcast. He wants to bring down the Hegemony too."

"I'd like to meet him. You've helped him?"

Emba's snout wrinkled again. "I've tried. My government's too scared to act and they certainly won't fight unless things get a whole lot worse. But I know the Hegemony is infiltrating Telsus and other worlds. I hope the information I'm gathering on their activities will change minds."

"Anything you can share with me?" If she couldn't break Hegemony comms, perhaps Emba knew enough to help.

He emitted a growl-bark which she took for laughter. "Why should I trust you?"

She sighed. "It's a long story."

"Then you'd better sit down."

He indicated a low lounge – lower than she was used to so she had to fold her legs under her. He sat opposite, grabbed a crystal bottle and a glass and poured a ruby red liquid. He raised the bottle towards her invitingly.

"Better not," she said. Even if it wasn't poisonous to humans, she needed a clear head.

She told him everything. Petar's death, working for Volmar, meeting Denev. The betrayal and slaughter of the Cygnus Sector rebels. Not just facts, but how it made her feel. The change in her that meant she'd accepted Nok's offer. Which had led her here.

When she'd finished, Emba looked into his empty glass for a long time. Then his dark eyes settled on her. "It's hard for an old cynic like me to be confronted regularly by people who insist on doing the right thing. It makes me wonder whether it's *me* who's out of step with the universe."

Rhees guessed who he was talking about. "Udun?"

Again the growl-bark. "He's safe at least." He looked past her, maybe past the clouds outside. "A friend, Fa'ar Rojen, took him to Maelstrom."

"I don't know what that is."

He shook his head. "It doesn't matter. The point is, I'm not stupid enough to ignore the evidence of my own eyes. It's clear your Hegemony isn't content to sit on Homeworld. I may be in the bad books with my government, but you meet a lot of people working in the Xeno Trade Office. Haulage captains, lading clerks, customs agents, entrepreneurs and business types. Information is currency to these people. Especially if it points to a new player in the market."

"Someone's investing?" Rhees said. It made sense. Hegemony personnel couldn't show their faces around here without causing a panic, especially after the invasion of the Kresz world. They'd need to operate through intermediaries.

"Certain businesses are becoming more active," Emba said. "Here and in the Aphsan system so far. People with funds that can't be explained by the trades and deals they've been part of."

"It's how the Hegemony works."

Emba showed his teeth again. "Oh, I know. I helped a refugee from your part of space whose planet had been occupied by your kind. I won't let that happen here."

"Do you have enough information to warn your government?"

"I'm not sure I can trust them. I'm hearing worrying things coming out of Telsus Prime."

"Can you –"

A sharp crack and Rhees's ears popped with a sudden pressure change. A flurry of light debris fell from the ceiling between Emba and her. They both stood quickly, stepping back and away from each other instinctively.

With a deafening roar like a forest collapsing, the floor split open between them – a ragged tear the length of the room and opening wider. The walls at either end broke apart. The floor tilted inward. Rhees cried out and scrambled back.

On the other side of the widening chasm, Emba clawed his

way uphill, dodging chairs sliding past. The air smelled wrong and Rhees started coughing.

A gout of lava broke through the floor, cascading along the trench between her and Emba. The temperature in the room soared.

Rhees reached back as the floor tilted more, hooking her fingers onto the edge of the glass wall they'd entered through.

Emba shouted as the floor on his side swung away sharply. He reached for the wall, struggling to stay upright, but there were no handholds. Then he lost his footing, screaming as he slid towards the molten lava.

Rhees – hanging from the opening in the glass wall – looked away. When she looked again, he was gone.

She swung and, despite her shoulder feeling like it would pop out its socket, managed to grab the opening with her other hand and throw her leg up. She was coughing hard now, fighting for breath. She crawled onto the glass surface – hot to the touch – and hoped it wouldn't break beneath her.

The landscape around her refused to make sense. The dome was broken, letting the heat and deadly atmosphere rush in. The garden around the house was leaning on its side and on fire.

A flash of silver and the dolphinship scooped her up, closed over her and shot through the collapsing dome and into the angry sky.

She could breathe again, but it had been far too close. And Emba … What a horrible way to die.

∞

Rhees's ship rendezvoused with Nok's vessel near the heliopause of the Telsan system. She'd fallen into a fitful, exhausted sleep on the way back, but she was still angry when she climbed out of the peeled-back dolphin onto the hangar deck.

Nok was waiting for her as usual.

"Where the fuck were you?" Rhees said.

His faceplate revealed nothing. "I had other tasks to perform. But I've reviewed what occurred on Telsus IV."

A window opened between them and she was staring down at Emba's islet. Three holes opened in the dome and the house inside started to collapse. The image froze then ran in reverse, pulling back and up to focus on three sleek black cylinders. Clouds closed around them, then grew tenuous, and Rhees almost lost sight of the cylinders as they entered open space. The image pulled back again then focused and froze on their point of origin. It was an HDC clipper, disc-shaped with a tubelike spine running through the middle.

"The craft's still in orbit," Nok said.

Rhees pulled at the image, expanding the view. The ship had no registry markings, just the silver infinity symbol set into its black hull.

"Did they see me?" she said.

"You haven't been followed. The Hegemony had other reasons to kill Emba."

"He said he was spying on them. Tracking their infiltration."

"He paid the price." There was no emotion in Nok's voice.

"That's it? He's dead; we move on?"

Nok was silent, and an extremely paranoid part of Rhees wondered if the images he had shown her were counterfeit. Had Nok fired the missiles and killed Emba, and prompted the dolphinship to rescue her so he could manipulate her in some fucked-up way? Or had he seen the missiles – Jantri surveillance systems were equal to HDC's, that was obvious – but done nothing because he didn't want to get involved? Like some careless deity watching the insects below struggle and die.

And then there was what Emba had told her.

"He said he didn't trust you."

"I'd given him no reason to," Nok said. "Trust is useful, but it's not a requisite for joint action. But I didn't betray him."

She realised she was judging him by human standards again.

"I need to take my ship out again," she said.

"It's obvious you're upset, but destroying that vessel is going to alert the Hegemony."

Rhees bared her teeth. "They deserve it. But I'm not out for revenge." She nodded towards the HDC ship image. "They're going to give me access to Hegemony comms."

12

We followed a main conduit, possibly still backtracking the Hegemony fleet that had passed us. There were branchings, but narrower, so we held our course. Our next transit allowed sightings in realspace. Atalna and I were both awake and we looked keenly out at the starfield. According to the AI we were oriented towards that part of space that held Betlaan and the Hegemony's ever-expanding border.

"The stars don't look any different," I said.

"The stars are implacable, but that segment there …" Atalna toggled a switch on the couch arm and a thin sliver of space was overlaid with a pink shape. "That is the border of Hegemony space. We'll be encountering their border outriders soon. We should be ready."

He activated the tenspace drive. I climbed back in the cabinet feeling the tension jump inside me. After so long travelling we were fast coming up on a moment that could decide our fate.

The shift to tenspace gave me something else to think about for a short time. It was almost a relief. But then we were running down a tenspace corridor heading straight for Hegemony space. We weren't an obvious threat and our hopes of infiltration rested on that. And on our anonymity. By good luck our cargo – many types of pharmaceutical – furnished what seemed a convincing reason for our journey. We'd decided to play the part of entrepreneurial traders in medical drugs looking for new markets.

Atalna had reworked the databanks to insert information on us as rightful owners of the ship and created identity documents that looked official. There was no way they could be checked, or at least we hoped there wasn't. I was Reka from a random planet we'd found on the ship's charts, well outside the Lenticular and close to the outer edge of the galactic arm. Atalna was Min'tak, obviously from Betlaan. There was no way we could hide that. We'd met trading far from here and had become partners, sharing our knowledge to open new markets. I may have been fooling myself, but it felt like a convincingly detailed lie.

The AI jolted me from my thoughts: "There is an anomalous energy signature immediately ahead."

"What kind –" Atalna began, and then blackness.

We were dropping out of tenspace and realspace crashed through my consciousness. I pushed at the edge of the cabinet, my claws slipping on the glass, and somehow pulled myself to sitting.

"Atalna?" I said.

"Fine, Reka," he replied, using my false name. Were we being monitored?

I looked at the screen. A silver ovoid hung directly ahead, suspended between two weapons nacelles that were obviously open.

"Some kind of field," Atalna said. "The ship didn't see it until we were almost on it. It dropped us out of tenspace. I'd say we're at a border."

"Good," I said, in case we were being monitored. "Customers. Hopefully friendly."

"Transmission," the AI said.

"Accept," Atalna said.

The central vuscreen switched to show the interior of a spaceship and a face that didn't look like one of the Hegemony troops. Its skin was green and lined in a diamond pattern; its eyes like an ah'lok, made of many small surfaces fitted together. What I thought was its mouth moved, but all we could hear was a high-pitched trilling the voder couldn't translate.

I was beside Atalna now, so we both saw a section of the controls light up. We were transmitting.

"Ship, what's happening," I said.

"The vessel has nominal control over my systems. Language files have been requested and despatched."

"It's all right," I said. "We expected an encounter at some point."

"All right?" Atalna feigned anger. "They tore us out of tenspace and now they've taken over the ship."

The alien spoke again and this time our voders could translate its speech. "State your business."

"Who are you?" Atalna said.

"State your business," the alien repeated.

"Min'tak," I said to Atalna, "I think we should tell this being our business."

"Very well. We are traders. We seek to open new markets. If you're interested in purchasing –'

"Prepare to be boarded," the alien said.

"We don't want you onboard –"

"Prepare to be boarded."

"Ship," I said, "activate our hatch lights and rotate so the hatch is pointed at that vessel."

The screen kept the ship in view as we moved. Our own ship shuddered as docking rings engaged. We heard the outer door open on the lock.

I activated the inner lock and we heard a scraping noise in the short corridor but no green-skinned alien entered. Instead my eye caught movement near the floor. It looked like a tentacle, but then I saw a glowing red sensor at the tip as it rose to waist height on an articulated body.

It was joined by another. Both waited on the threshold, red eyes swaying, taking in the room. Then their long bodies undulated inside. They split up, moving left and right, dipping into recesses in panelling, sliding along and briefly into the deepsleep cabinet, under the crash-seat, nudging at the vuscreens and control surfaces.

They finished their sweep and both took up position in front of Atalna and me. They reared back, rising until each red eye looked at us from head height, then shot forward, coiling around us and pulling tight.

In an instant, my arms were trapped against my body. I tried to flex and push the thing from me, but it pulled tighter.

"Don't resist," Atalna said.

We heard footsteps in the lock and the green-skinned alien appeared. It was short, barely coming up to my waist, and wore a close-fitting vacuum suit, the helmet hanging from its shoulders. There were no Hegemony insignia I could recognise. It barely glanced at us before sitting in the crash-seat and running its hands across the controls.

"Is this necessary?" I said, and felt the robotic serpent coil tighter around me.

"Look at the size of you," the alien said. "It is necessary. You would be surprised by the kind of desperate individuals we find trying to get into Hegemony space."

And there it was. Confirmation.

"Well, we're not desperate individuals," I said.

"That is what all the desperate individuals say."

On the centre screen a trip log appeared, tracing back to the Maelstrom and then further again. The Chirrik had been crisscrossing the galactic arm in and out of the Lenticular for what looked like a long time. The screen blanked and then our ship manifest appeared. But there was nothing there to worry us.

"What is your destination?" the alien said, finally looking at us.

"Whatever civilised planet we can find with money and a need for our commodities," I said.

The alien hissed and the machines relaxed their grip and rolled off. But they stayed close, coiled on the floor in front of us.

"You have no charts of this sector," it said.

"No," I replied.

Its segmented eyes surveyed me. "That is an infringement. You have precious metals onboard."

"Yes," I said. It had seen as much from our manifest.

"We'll pay whatever fines are necessary," Atalna said. "We weren't able to purchase charts beforehand."

"You can pay with this." The alien brought up an atomic diagram on screen. The computer labelled it as gorundium. Or at least that was what it was called in the Lenticular.

"Two hundred grams for the infringement," the alien said. "We can sell you charts and language files for another fifty grams."

"That's over half our gorundium," Atalna said. "You're not leaving us much. We could trade some pharmaceuticals?"

"Do I look sick? I don't want your drugs. The gorundium. Now."

Atalna moved slowly, shadowed by one of the tentacle machines. I heard him opening the locker where the metals were kept.

"Where do the rich people live?" I asked our captor.

"There are rich people all over."

"Yes, but there are more of them where the power is. Can you tell us which planet rules this area? We want to get a good price for our wares."

The alien stood and hissed again. "I am not a tour guide. Keep out of trouble and we will not have any problems. We have placed a transponder on the hull of your ship. Do not try to remove it."

Atalna returned with the gorundium and gave it to the alien. "We're not criminals. We'll do what we're told."

"They all say that too," the alien said. "Obey the laws and you will have a safe trip." It left, taking its guardians with it.

Atalna and I stood in silence until we heard the dock ring disengage.

"Incoming transmission," the AI said, startling me.

On the screen a series of charts unfolded. A glowing cursor showed our position.

"They were costly," Atalna said. "Let's hope they're worth it."

I sat in the crash-couch and studied the charts. There was a sector overview and then grid maps in more detail. They even had a tenspace overlay.

"So where are we likely to get the best prices?" I asked.

We knew we'd acquired a tracker, but not if our visitor had left behind any listening devices. We had to stay in character, at least until we were back in tenspace where any signals would be effectively blocked.

"Look at the overview," Atalna said. "We seem to be in this boundary area."

We followed the line that marked what had now been identified as Hegemony space. Going on what we knew about the Hegemony, we'd theorised that the seat of power would either be in the centre of the space they controlled, or at the edge closest to the outermost end of the arm.

Picking up that earlier conversation, I said, "So we go for the centre?"

Atalna nodded, and I called up the grid for that section. There were a number of systems in the general area. Increasing the magnification, we studied the tags. The names meant nothing to us, the words too alien: Luyten, Tau Ceti, E Eridani, Wolf 359, Sirius. And then we saw it – Sol.

"We have a general heading," I said, still in character. "We'll work out the details once we're underway."

On the vuscreens, the patrol ship was nowhere in sight and it no longer registered on our sensors. I brought the tenspace engines online. Atalna went to the deepsleep cabinet and climbed in slowly.

Transit bludgeoned through me.

As soon as we were back in tenspace, Atalna left the cabinet and perched on the side of the crash-couch. "First things first," he said. "Ship, scan the interior and exterior. Are there any energy signatures that were not here before our last drop into realspace?"

We waited.

Finally the AI spoke. "There is a device attached to the hull emitting a regular series of harmonics."

"The Hegemony transponder," I said.

"Anything else?" Atalna asked. "Anything on the inside?"

"No," the AI said. "Nothing registers."

"Just because we can't see it doesn't mean it's not there," Atalna said. "There could be any number of nano-scale devices, shielded or cloaked in other ways. But while we're in tenspace there shouldn't be a problem. We need to be careful what we say inside the ship in realspace."

"Agreed," I said.

We were travelling down a wide, gently sloping corridor. Field activity was low. It was as safe as it got in tenspace. I called up the charts again, selecting the one we'd been studying.

"You're sure it's Sol we want?" I asked.

"Fairly. It's a place to start. And it's right in the middle of things."

"It's a lot of space to cover if we're wrong," I said.

"Let's look at them more closely."

I toggled the controls and we focused on each of the stars in turn. It was a tactical view with tagged symbolic representations of each system, showing planetary distribution from gas giants down to planetesimals, comets, significant concentrations of asteroids. The tags carried names – again, meaningless to us – and a great deal of data: on atmospheric content, mean surface temperature, orbit, axial tilt, rotation. But we had no information about Hegemony planets to compare it with.

"Maybe we're not looking at this correctly," I said. "A power base is defined by the interactions it has with the planets surrounding it. Think of how the Lenticular works. There are major routes connecting the main planets in the Lenticular: Telsus and Svesta, Homeworld and Telsus, Aphsus Prime and Jantri'va. And then within some of those systems there are minor realspace routes, say between Telsus Prime and Telsus IV. Tenspace corridors lead elsewhere in the Lenticular, but they're rarely used because they don't go anywhere worth visiting. Because the Lenticular is a collection of worlds where no one world dominates the others, usage of those routes is fairly balanced. Even Homeworld has a large number of visiting ships for trade, although their destination is the Hub rather than the planet. But this is the Hegemony we're talking about: a power base that dominates all the systems in a large part of the galactic arm. What we need to do is look at the navigation routes."

I searched the chart interface, saw what I was looking for and selected that view. A complex web of connections overlaid the stars on the chart.

"This may be skewed by where the tenspace corridors give out on realspace," Atalna said.

"Yes, but even if the power base isn't well served by tenspace transit points, I don't think it should make that much difference. Ships would still have to go there a lot. They'd just have to do it in realspace."

All the stars seemed well-connected though. No one system dominated.

"There must be something that differentiates the ruling system," I said.

"Perhaps the power is shared equally between these central stars," Atalna said. "Sol could just be one of a network of ruling worlds."

But that didn't feel right. The Hegemony was driven by a single species that exercised its might to bring other species in and control them. Isza's memories confirmed Volmar was a representative of the ruling species. And the force that had taken over Homeworld had all been Humans.

"If Sol is the seat of the Hegemony's power, where the driving force of the Hegemony originated, the stars nearest it would have been the first to be conquered and under the Hegemony's rule longest," I said. "They may not have been connected with each other before, but as part of the Hegemony connections between them would have grown just as we see now, effectively hiding the source of their domination. But if we take our view wider ..."

I expanded the vuscreen image, still keeping the navigational overlay active, and watched the connections grow between the planets.

A pattern was forming. I edged the magnification wider and wider until it suddenly jumped out at us. The paths from single stars twisted together to form thicker paths heading into the centre from all sides of Hegemony space until there were three main routes all leading to one system in the central cluster. Sol was where the Hegemony's might was focused, where their empire was controlled from.

We would go to Sol.

13

Denev couldn't tell if Beloc had reported in before he'd died. But when he finally got back to his room in the dorm, there was no one from HDC security waiting for him.

He deactivated the security hack, sat on his cot and clenched his hands into fists to stop them shaking. He just had time to shower and put on a fresh uniform. Appearance mattered. It spoke of internal discipline and put a barrier between him and the outside world. It was the only defence he had left. Security could still be waiting to arrest him at the Datahive.

He entered the Datahive foyer with five minutes to spare before shift start. His imaginary shield almost crumbled when he saw Volmar striding towards him flanked by two armed corpsmen. He took a breath and waited for the inevitable.

"You're early," Volmar said, stopping a metre away. "That makes things easier. Come with me."

Volmar continued past him. The corpsmen waited until Denev turned and followed, then fell in behind. Volmar's boot clicks on the hard floor rang in Denev's ears and he wiped a trickle of sweat from the side of his face. Even if he *could* run there was nowhere to go. Earth was a prison.

He followed Volmar to a bank of elevators at the far end of the foyer. Volmar entered an empty car and Denev followed. Their escort stayed behind as the doors closed. He was alone with the comptroller.

"It's tiresome that we have to do this in person," Volmar said.

"But it shouldn't take long." He looked at Denev. "You got the recall?"

Denev glanced at his band. A group of pixels glowed orange. "I overslept," he said. "And then I was rushing to get here for my shift."

"No matter. We're going to the CA Security Review Subcommittee. It's simple oversight, just ticking the boxes."

The elevator opened onto a hypertube station. The platform was polished black concrete, the walls incised with a repeating line of HDC infinity symbols. Clearly it wasn't part of the public network.

A car was waiting – a sleek turbine, the smooth casing split by a gull-wing door revealing a four-seat cabin. Denev sat beside Volmar in one of the thickly padded chairs. The armrests adjusted automatically, the seating folding along his sides and across his shoulders to hold him comfortably.

The gull-wing glided shut and there was the sound of an outer door sliding across the car, accompanied by the hiss of expelled atmosphere. There were no windows. There was nothing to see. And nothing much to hear as they moved off smoothly and in pure vacuum, hovering over a superconductive track. The car angled slightly, moving from the station loop into the main tubeline, then accelerated to cruising speed.

Volmar was flicking through screens on a pad. "You're settling in at the dorm?" he said, not looking up. "It must be like being back at the academy."

Was Volmar toying with him? If he hadn't been informed already, the report of Beloc's death would show up soon enough on his pad. Would Volmar know Beloc had introduced himself to Denev? There had been enough time for Beloc to log the contact and a lot more besides – like following Denev while he broke into a monitoring station. So why didn't Volmar confront him? Perhaps he suspected Denev was working with others and hoped he'd reveal them. Perhaps, perhaps, perhaps. Perhaps nothing.

Volmar was still waiting for a response.

"It's a place to sleep and eat," Denev said. "I spend most of my time in the Datahive."

"I know. And your efforts are appreciated. You were wasted on Proxima. But too much desk work can dull your edge. We must find you something to do in the field as well."

Bait and trap? Or an innocent offer? As far as anything from Volmar could be said to be innocent.

The car barely felt like it was moving now.

"Where's the meeting being held?" Denev asked.

"Close to CA Headquarters."

Which meant they must be well into the transcontinental tubes that burrowed beneath the mantle. There was an entire network kilometres below the surface – transit tunnels, power grids (both geothermal and fusion), military installations, entire cities. All built as a last resort or a final resting place for humanity if the K-Chaan war had been lost. All of it mothballed now, or that was the official story. Denev had no doubt the CA used it to conceal any number of secret operations.

"I'll need your updated status report when we're done here," Volmar said.

A spare pad was sitting recessed beside the arm of Denev's chair. He activated it and slaved it to his band so he could access his working directories in the Hive. He and Volmar worked together in silence for almost half an hour until the car started its deceleration.

There was a slight swerve into a side loop, a hiss of depressurisation, and then the door gull-winged open. The room beyond was as large as it was empty. A vast concrete space supported by closely spaced concrete columns, each easily fifty metres tall. The air was damp and cold. Pools of light picked a pathway through the columns to an opening in the far wall that glowed cold blue like a glacier. The floor was wet from an uneven almost-rain falling out of the darkness – from condensation or broken pipes Denev couldn't say.

Passing through the blue entrance, the space became noticeably warmer. This room was as long as a hangar in one of the Fleet destroyers. The ceiling was ribbed with thick supports that curved and tapered towards the far end so it looked like they were inside something organic – a giant whale instead of a vintage bunker.

Sitting incongruously in the centre of this vast room was a white-walled cube. A door stood half-open at one corner and the sound of voices came floating across to them.

Denev followed Volmar across the hangar, their footsteps echoing and re-echoing in syncopation. The voices stopped abruptly as Volmar opened the door fully. A number of people were seated round a large oval table that took up most of the space inside. Denev noted the lack of any security detail.

"Volmar, we'd almost given up on you."

Denev recognised Ruiz Rejak, Secretary of Security and Defence. He was of a similar age to Volmar and they could have been brothers, Denev thought. They shared the same sharp nose, angled cheekbones and high forehead, but Rejak's features were softer, the lips fuller, and his eyes, behind simple wireframe spectacles – no doubt an affectation – were brown instead of piercing ice-blue.

"I hope I haven't missed anything of consequence," Volmar said.

Rejak's smile was gone as soon as it appeared. He glanced at Denev and seemed to pause, then he raised his voice to address the room. "Let's continue."

Denev sat on a chair near the door as Volmar took his place at the table.

Undersecretary Cerise Laneaux sat beside Rejak. She headed up Sol System Security – SolSec. Denev had seen her countless times on the feeds and she was no less striking in the flesh – pale skin, deep-set eyes accentuated by high curving eyebrows, and a severe buzz cut greying naturally at her temples.

The other three men at the table, Denev didn't know. He thought one with large ears and curly brown hair swept over half his face might be Representative Eon Baxter, a member of the popularly elected Senate, which was heavily pro-CA.

"Horman here," Rejak said, indicating a dark-haired man in a colourful business cape, "was reporting on a review of the Voss bridge passive scanners."

"Which seems to be an exercise in data collection for its own sake," the third man – blond with a tanned complexion and thin lips – said. "I mean, what practical use is all this?"

Horman looked pained. "I would have thought it was obvious. It's important to keep track of alien elements."

"What, *all* of them? Are they *all* security risks? Is the security and defence budget so large we can just piss it against the wall tracking and harassing people who are just getting on with their lives?"

"Not people," Horman said. "Aliens."

The blond man glared at him.

"It's no more information than we already have on every human living in-system, Minch," Laneaux said.

So this was Alder Minch, Denev thought. The Inclusionist and also a member of the Senate.

Minch gave a short laugh. "And look at how the rights of our own citizens have been eroded as a result."

"Safety has a cost," Volmar said. "We can't afford what happened to the Brell colonies to happen here."

"And there it is," Minch said. "The same arguments we've been fed since the K-Chaan. But for all your security and spying, Comptroller, are we really any safer? It seems we're still surrounded by enemies. Why is that, do you think?"

Rejak cleared his throat. "We're not here to debate Centralist policy. Thank you, Horman."

"Thank you, Secretary," Horman said, pulling at his cape. "I move that the trial be extended."

"Seconded," Baxter said.

"All in favour?" Rejak asked.

Five hands were raised around the table.

"Against?"

Minch raised his hand.

"Carried," Rejak said.

From the look on Minch's face, this was a regular occurrence. Why did he even come to these meetings, Denev wondered. The committee was stacked against him and it would never be any other way. It took a certain stubborn fortitude to ignore that fact. Or maybe stupidity, but Minch didn't strike him as stupid.

Rejak turned to Volmar. "I believe congratulations are in order. You've brought the system-killers to heel."

Volmar inclined his head slightly. "Thank you, Secretary. It was a combined effort: HDC operatives working with local militia forces to track down and engage the raiders. The fighting was fierce but the Maagba who were behind the attacks were finally subdued. There's peace in the sector again."

"Yes, we've all read the report," Minch said. His eyes narrowed. "It's short on detail and long on rhetoric."

Denev had prepared that report and knew it for the fairytale it was. There was no mention of the secret rebel base and the ships they controlled. Or how Volmar had betrayed the rebels to the Maagba forces and subsequently entered into an alliance with the Maagba to police that part of space.

"Some details must remain classified even to this committee," Volmar said. "To protect the identity and safety of our operatives."

"Another familiar argument," Minch said. "But I'm more interested in what's been happening in the Lenticular."

From Denev's position behind Volmar it looked like the comptroller's shoulders rose a fraction of a centimetre.

"Another classified operation I can't say too much about, Representative. We've established a secure base of operations on a world close to a strategic Voss Space corridor as part of a joint operation with Fleet."

"And the world you occupied?" Minch asked.

"It's standard practice to enlist and work with indigenous factions. It provides us with valuable local knowledge."

"And helps you to divide and conquer." This was from Laneaux. Denev noticed a faint smile lurking at the corner of her full red lips.

"You could put it like that," Volmar said.

"But it's safe to say this faction did not represent the majority of the aliens on the planet," Minch said.

"We use what we can," Volmar said. "In all cases our aim is to apply the minimum of force to achieve our ends."

Minch sat forward. "That's an interesting way to put it. I've heard reports that when the fighting was done and the enemy elements were subdued and captured, a systematic operation was carried out to remove a particular organ from the aliens, rendering them unable to fully communicate."

"This is a common practice in the alien culture. Removal of the Kresz hood is mandated for criminals," Volmar said, still appearing calm.

"It may be common for these aliens but why was it carried out by Hegemony troops?" Minch asked. "Is this your idea of 'minimum force' – mutilating an enemy after they've already been neutralised?"

"There are nuances in any alien society that may not be evident when reading field reports, Representative Minch. I have met with these aliens, and HDC has analysed thousands of hours of their broadcasts and texts to assess them socially, politically, culturally and historically. These aliens were captured, yes, but in the long term we can't resource a garrison there to keep the peace. Our actions may be seen as extreme if your perspective is constrained to the current moment. HDC *must* look beyond that, and what we did has fundamentally changed a volatile situation for the better. There will be no opposition to the Hegemony-backed government now or into the future. The anti-Hegemony forces have been completely neutralised, but most of them still have their lives. *That* is what I call minimum force."

"Do you have any more questions, Representative Minch?" Rejak asked.

"I'll reserve my right to question this action further later. This isn't over."

"Of course. Then, gentlemen, lady," Rejak smiled at Laneaux but she didn't return it, "we are adjourned."

Minch stood and nodded to Denev as he passed, any trace of anger gone or hidden away for next time. Laneaux and the others left too. Volmar raised a finger to Denev and pointed. Denev closed the door behind them. Only Volmar and Rejak remained.

"Let me introduce you," Volmar said. "Secretary Ruiz Rejak, my aide for the Hanloi Campaign, Operative Denev Antwer."

Rejak was extending a hand towards Denev but hesitated as he heard his last name. He glanced at Volmar, but grasped Denev's hand warmly enough.

"Of course," Rejak said. "Your father was a great man."

"You knew him?"

"Only by reputation."

So why is your name attached to the file on his death, Denev wondered.

"Please, sit for a moment," Rejak said.

Denev took Horman's chair.

"That was more difficult than expected," Rejak said, sighing.

"Unpleasant," Volmar said. "But nothing to worry about."

"Are you sure about that?"

"Nothing surer."

"But his source?" Rejak pulled a cloth from his pocket and removed his spectacles to rub at the lenses.

"It's Laneaux," Volmar said. "I could see it on her face as soon as Minch started in. She'd never feed him anything truly damning. But … she wants to be the next comptroller."

Rejak snorted. "Then she's badly misread the situation."

"To put it mildly."

It was rare to see Volmar smile. There was clearly a bond between these two that transcended the usual backstabbing within CA bureaucracy. Denev wondered when it had been forged.

"Minch is a smart one, though," Rejak continued. "Our polling suggests he'll do well in the elections. All the Inclusionist candidates will." He looked at Denev briefly, then turned back to Volmar. "It makes me think the Inclusionist experiment is at an end."

Experiment? Denev didn't know what Rejak meant.

Volmar nodded. "Time to reset the board."

"I'll confirm with Breslaw, of course," Rejak said. "But you might want to start planning an exit strategy."

Volmar pulled briefly at his lower lip. "I already have. And Denev here will have a part to play."

Rejak glanced again at Denev but his expression was carefully neutral. "Excellent." He shook Volmar's hand and nodded to Denev. "A pleasure."

∞

Back in the hypertube car, Volmar asked Denev for his latest report and studied the detail on his pad. There was a lot of data to absorb: basically a rundown on the current status of every ship in the two attack forces, plus tenspace squirts from long-range scanners focused on the Hanloi borders. All the information in that respect was negative. No ship sightings, no energy signatures, no variance in local tenspace. It was data, but data at the lowest information state possible. Nothing could be derived from it. The Hanloi may be oblivious to the Hegemony advance, or they may be completing final preparations on their defences just out of range. Hell, they may have already launched an unseen counterattack directly on Earth and were moments away from striking for all Denev knew.

Volmar put the pad aside and seemed to stare into infinity. "This is good work," he said. "But you understand the situation with the Inclusionists now."

"I do," Denev said.

While Volmar was reading, Denev had considered the exchange with Rejak. From what Rejak had said, it seemed likely the rise of the Inclusionist movement had been manipulated by the CA, perhaps to give the appearance of democracy. But that didn't mean the Inclusionists knew they were just pawns. Their message had certainly struck a chord with Rhees. Perhaps their ideas had caught on more widely than intended, which meant their popularity would also be their undoing.

"I promised you some fieldwork," Volmar said. "Minch is going to Mars soon. Part of his re-election campaign. We must be ready."

Denev could have probed for more information, but Volmar would tell him when he was good and ready. Instead he said, "Did you know my father, Comptroller?" It was an innocent enough question since Rejak had already mentioned him.

Pale blue eyes considered Denev for a moment. "We met only once, when I was a callow youth in the diplomatic service, not much older than you are now. I doubt he was even aware of my presence."

The answer was short on detail, like Volmar's report on the Lenticular, but Denev knew now it was a lie. Volmar had worked with his father on his last mission and must know exactly what had happened. The only way Denev would find out was by breaking into that sealed file.

14

Atalna was sleeping when we encountered the first ship I'd seen since the border patrol. It was coming out of the mouth of a tunnel that opened in the roof of ours. I slowed our vessel to let it drop down in front. It was a strange design. A thin wedge, curved like a wing, with long tube sections hanging below it. There was no acknowledgement we were behind it; it didn't vary its speed or heading at all.

A movement in the aft vuscreen distracted me. Another ship, a different design again, was dropping behind us out of the same tunnel. I was instantly uneasy. There was no room in the corridor to manoeuvre or let the ship behind us pass. We were caught. But as we came to an arcing twist in the corridor and cleared the curve, I saw more ships ahead of us. The traffic was becoming heavier; there needn't be anything sinister about it.

The tenspace corridor was also registering the energies moving through it. Flares rippled along the wall surface, pacing the ships. Everyone was moving at a slow, steady pace, no doubt hoping – like me – it would be enough to prevent a spike. Or if there was a discharge, that it would pass over harmlessly or, at worst, hit some other ship.

Atalna woke, and moved stiffly out of the cabinet to stand beside the crash-chair. I offered to let him sit but he waved the suggestion away, preferring to hold the back of the chair and stretch his stiffened muscles.

"It's getting quite crowded," he said. "That's a good sign."

"As long as tenspace doesn't obliterate us, yes," I said.

The line of ships drifted apart as the tunnel widened and we were able to pick up speed. I was still monitoring the local field, but it felt good to put some distance between us and the walls. Then I noticed our companion ships were disappearing into a dark chamber.

I brought our ship to a complete stop when we'd cleared the entrance. Some sections within the darkness were lit by glowing columns of plasma, seemingly stable, like vast energy conduits running at all angles. The other ships appeared here and there as motes lit by the glowing columns. Despite the dark, our course was clear on the charts. We passed over one of the energy columns and then another. Their light made the darkness between even more impenetrable, but we kept going – and then, in the distance, so far away I thought I was imagining it at first, I saw a tenuous patch of light.

"What is that?" Atalna said.

"We're at the limits of magnification," I said, checking the controls. "But it doesn't shine like part of tenspace. The colour's wrong."

"Look at the map." Atalna indicated the side display with the tenspace overlay. "It's right where we want to go."

There was nothing to do but join another line of ships heading towards the light. As we got closer it became obvious what it was even if it was entirely unbelievable. Tenspace didn't take kindly to ships passing through it, but as long as the energy expenditure didn't tip the field potential and the ship didn't stay in the one place for too long, it was relatively safe. No species I'd come across had the technology to establish a permanent base inside tenspace. But that's what this appeared to be. It was a station, shining with light. An immense ball with arms – docking arms, weapons arms or living quarters, I couldn't tell; maybe all of those things – projecting out from the central mass at regular intervals so it resembled an instar's toy. It rotated slowly, standing astride the tunnel that led to Sol system.

"The ship is being scanned," the AI said.

"And?" I said.

"Scans are passive but penetrating. My encrypted records have been opened."

I looked at Atalna. This couldn't be good.

"There is an energy increase," the AI said.

"Where?" I asked.

"From the transponder device on the hull. Scans have ceased."

We were closing on the bottom section of the station. The only way to get to the tunnel was between the slowly turning station arms.

"We go on," Atalna said. "Perhaps if we didn't have the transponder it would be a different matter."

We passed under the central orb of the station and curved around one of the slowly turning arms. The thing was massive. The power signature equally so.

"This is no passive sentinel," I said. "It must have weaponry. How can it exist here without being destroyed? How can it use its weapons without tenspace hitting back?"

"Look at the tunnel mouth," Atalna said.

I magnified the view. The usually irregular opening had a structure set into it. Metal flashed in the light from the station above us.

"Ship, analyse the devices in the tunnel opening," I said.

"Electronic device. Operation unknown."

"Helpful," I said. "What's it made of?"

"Composition unknown," the AI said.

We entered the tunnel, passing close to the devices set into the living plasma. As we accelerated I watched the controls, but there was no effect on the field potential. It seemed the Hegemony had tamed tenspace. Or this part of it at least. Even conquerors bring benefits, I thought.

"Do you know what your world is like now?" I asked Atalna. "So long after the invasion?"

"I was hungry for information after I'd fled to safety. I stayed as close to Betlaan as I could for a long time, like an insect circling a flame. The official broadcasts were infuriating, painting a picture of new-found harmony and freedom after the 'recent unpleasantness', a new age of connectivity with the wider galaxy, reaping the benefits of their 'alliance' with the Hegemony. It sickened me, so much so that I considered striking back on my own, planning vainglorious and ultimately fruitless acts of sacrifice, something that would create a rallying point for my people to rise up and throw out the Hegemony." His cheek slits rippled. "It was pathetic. Then I made contact with some friends still on the ground. Communications were dangerous for them, but they were loyal. They hoped I would return some day. I guess they were as misguided as I was, for in reality there was no chance that we could ever defeat the Hegemony. We were too few and they were too strong. When I finally admitted that to myself it made the snatches of real news I got all the more depressing. My friends were starving to death, and suffering other deprivations and humiliations that I could not describe. I realised then how weak I was. I broke off all communication – I couldn't bear any more. And I fled the area and kept running until I came all the way to the Lenticular and felt that I'd run far enough. Another irony."

I touched his arm. His eyes, focused on the painful past, looked at me once more. "There's no guarantee our fates won't be identical," I said.

"I won't lie to you. It's true. We may both be exiled for the rest of our lives." He nodded at the screen. "Or die soon in the heart of the Hegemony."

"My sister believed that as long as you're breathing you still have a chance."

He could have reminded me Isza was dead, but instead he indicated the vuscreen. "Let's look at our next move."

We both sat on the crash-couch and I brought up our charts again, focusing on Sol system.

"There's the transit point for our route," I said. It was within the system, between the orbits of two gas giant planets. "Neither of those could be the origin worlds for the Humans. Nothing smaller than a Svestan could survive in that type of environment."

The map showed a lot of orbital facilities near the gas giants that were designated for mining. Past those planets was a ring of asteroids studded with more habitats. Not all of these were labelled, which suggested some must be military in function. Then came four smaller worlds: the closest one labelled Mars; a blue one, Earth; and two hot planets nearer the sun.

"Their homeworld must be one of the rocky inner planets," I said. "I suppose we'll have to check all of these once we get there, assuming we're allowed."

"Once we get there it will be obvious which planet holds their leaders," Atalna said. "You can't hide that much power."

I returned to the cabinet and slept for a while. When I woke, the devices set into the tunnel walls were far more numerous. In places it was impossible to see the underlying plasma. I wondered if, as well as dampening the tenspace energies, these things were also able to shape it, diverting the natural tunnels to align them more closely with a preferred transit point.

"Coming up on transit," the AI said.

I braced myself. But even transit was different. Almost like hearing an echo far away. The intensity had been bled out of it.

I climbed out of the cabinet. Atalna was staring at the vuscreens.

"They've tamed tenspace all right," he said. I could hear the quiet respect in his voice. "Look how close we are to that."

On the screen was a giant of a planet. Bigger than Svesta. Its surface was covered with swirling streams of brown, red and yellow, a large red spot shredding the clouds close to the south pole. It filled nearly half the screen, frightening for its size and the violence of its atmosphere. And yet even this place bore the marks of the Hegemony. A thick band of something, black but glowing dully, girdled the planet from pole to pole. It bulged at regular intervals and at each bulge a thin spike drove down into the clouds.

"What do you think that is?" Atalna said.

"I have no idea. Some kind of mining operation?"

Other screens showed the space away from the gas giant, and it seemed crowded in comparison to the Lenticular. A string of ships – cargo freighters from their shape – trailed away from the structure circling the planet. A pale yellow star gleamed faintly in-system. Sol, I guessed, as there were no other stars as bright. We were so close now, right in the heart of the Hegemony. Surely no other system could contain such wonders. There was a station off to our side bigger than some moons I'd encountered. Certainly bigger than Maelstrom station. And the ships – they were everywhere around it, their motions impossible to follow as they wheeled and dodged like startled flocks of ah'lok. Beyond these was another station just as big, and as my eyes grew accustomed to the sight, I realised that what I'd thought was part of the starfield was actually a chain of these stations, stretching further than I could see.

"The device on the ship hull is active again," the AI said.

"What's it doing?" I asked.

"Incoming transmission," the AI said.

"Voice only," Atalna said.

"They insist on vision."

There was nothing we could do.

"Very well. Vision," Atalna said.

The main screen cleared. A face appeared and I knew we were in the right place. It was a Human, though this one was brown, not pink, and it had black curly fur on its head but none on its face.

"This is Jupiter control. You are cleared for the trade compound on Mars. Your flight plan is being transmitted now. Do not deviate from that course. Out."

In hindsight it was too much to expect we'd have the run of the Hegemony's home system. But we'd been cleared to land on one of their planets. That device on our hull had been more of a help than a hindrance.

"AI, you have the course?" I asked.

"Yes."

"Then follow it exactly. And show us the path onscreen."

The ship accelerated smoothly and on the vuscreen a curving

green line extended past the nearest station on an oblique. We moved along it, still accelerating.

"How long till we get there?" I asked.

"Enough time for a meal and to get our merchandise ready," Atalna said.

"Do you feel rested enough?"

We'd been confined on this ship so long, Atalna was moving more stiffly than usual. And he looked tired.

"I'm ready for this," was all he said.

I supposed I was too. We'd talked enough about it. Having travelled so far, having endured so much, I wasn't afraid to die any more. If we succeeded and – a long way from now – were able to reclaim Homeworld and drive the Hegemony out, the dead would finally be at peace. But if we failed, if we died, so be it. We had done all we could. We continued to do all we could every second we were awake. Failure would not be for want of trying.

We ate some rations from the chest and watched our progress along the path the Hegemony had provided.

We entered an asteroid field that surrounded the entire system between the inner and outer planets, and the green line made small adjustments, taking us around rocks large and small and affording us good views of the activity going on there. Most of it seemed to be automated. Robotic ships moved among the rocks. Some were attached to larger asteroids, with probes extracting minerals or other commodities. One large asteroid – composed almost completely of frozen liquid – was being herded up and out of the ecliptic by small, embedded drive units that flared around it, nudging it along a pre-programmed path.

The entire planetary system seemed to be under the control of the Hegemony. No rock moved without their permission, and everything was required to yield its value to their will. It was what they were doing on Homeworld; what they planned for the whole galaxy perhaps. Every single atom owned by them. Nothing free ever again. Anywhere.

We cleared the asteroids and the ship accelerated again. The overlay indicated Mars's position even before we could see it against the starfield and we gained quickly on it. The planet was in night when we closed on it and from near-orbit it was easy to see just how populated it was. Strings of lights sprinkled across its surface so the whole globe seemed to shine in the dark.

"Prepare for close manoeuvring," the AI said.

The view on the screen tilted as the ship adjusted its orientation to the planetary horizon. Then the first tenuous layer of atmosphere chafed against our hull and the ship vibrated gently. The curve of the planet filled our view. Illuminated cities passed beneath us, giving me a sudden appreciation of just how fast we were moving.

The terminator rushed towards us and the screen blanked for an instant as it adjusted to the sudden glare of full sunlight. It was a shock after being so long in space and my secondary eyelid flicked over, darkening the view. It retracted slowly and then I saw the face of Mars: rolling hills swathed with forests that were a patchwork of greens in more shades than I thought possible. The trees flashed by and then we were flying over fields planted with ranks of crops that extended as far as we could see. Machinery was plainly visible in the fields.

The ship lost altitude and speed. We left the fields behind and grasslands took over, slowly rising as we dropped. Then the ship changed course, following a broad river with steep banks. We saw more fields dotted with large pylons, and over to our left something like the skystalk at Atktiuk. And then came something that was physically painful to see. Rising above the green was a line of red rock that thrust up from the land like the escarpment stronghold of House Czerag.

It was only when I saw wisps of cloud clinging to the edge of the cliff top that I realised the scale was wrong. This was bigger than any rock formation on Homeworld. Above it the ground was inclined, slightly at first then rising further to a peak that almost seemed to scratch at the thin layer of atmosphere between it and space. It was the largest rock I'd ever seen on a planet and we were headed directly for it.

"There's something at the base of that rock," Atalna said. "A settlement, I think. Ship, magnify those structures."

We saw a wide, dark field at the end of what appeared to be the landing strip, with low buildings surrounding it and, closer to the foot of the mountain, a tall ring-shaped structure, open at one end. A collection of ships were parked on the field, and towers stood at each corner of it; possibly controls for traffic management into and out of the field, but I had the feeling they were something more ominous. I watched them on approach, expecting to see weapon snouts converging on our position, but there was nothing, even as we hovered above the landing ground and slowly descended to what the ship informed us was our allotted bay.

Atalna unstrapped from the crash-couch and we looked at the multiple views of the ship's externals. The other vessels crowded around us were an eclectic mix of form and shape. There was nothing I recognised – how could there be? – but from the general configuration they looked like cargo vessels: small cockpits, wide and high sections for holding goods, no weapons ports that I could see, some with larger engines, presumably for longer hauls. Beings moved about the ships, entering or leaving or performing maintenance. I couldn't see any Humans, at least not in this part of the field. Everything seemed peaceful enough.

"We should go outside and see what reception we get," Atalna said.

I helped him stand and we moved along the short corridor to the hatch. The ground outside was compacted and sealed over with a hard, transparent covering. But beneath that it was red-brown. The air smelled of dust and the sky was a deep mauve above us. Despite the sun, it felt cold.

Over to our left there was a flash. A tall alien, far taller than a Kresz, or a Svestan even, but very thin with limbs like sapling endar trees, was welding the top section of its craft. Its head was covered with a darkened dome.

I went back up the ramp and gathered our things in a carry pack. "Secure the ship when I leave," I told the AI. "No one to enter except us."

"Acknowledged," the ship said.

Atalna's leg was stiff, and he leaned on my arm as we passed between closely packed ship hulls. The air was heavy with a mixture of lubricant, machinery and propellant residue.

"So many ships and all of them here to trade," Atalna said.

"It doesn't matter," I said, feeling my way into the character of Reka the trader again. "What we have is unique."

"I'll be fine now." Atalna released my arm and walked ahead through a gap between two ships, one like a mirrored pyramid, the other a tall, thin needle.

I followed him to the cracked and ragged lip of the field where it gave way to hard impacted dirt. After the quiet press of ships we'd passed through everything here was in loud motion. Two squat aliens, bulky with thick grey skins and long arced tusks protruding from their mouths, were bent over a low wagon piled with some round orange organics. Fruit maybe. They were straining at the cart, its wheels caught in a deep rut in the dirt. A beast was being tied to the front by another alien, this one like the tall mechanic we'd seen near our ship. It bent low, pulling at the beast, which gave a loud bellow.

A large ground transport, thick bulbous tyres suspending a glass bubble cab, spun in the dirt in front of us, kicking up dust, then shot off around the stuck cart, careless of another group of aliens nearby. One leaped out of the way and fell, and its companions shouted at the receding vehicle as they helped it to its feet. They were fur-covered beneath the loose robes they wore, but the fur was tightly curled and their faces were far from Telsan, shaved on each cheek beside their long snouts to show carved markings pierced with long chains of bright metal.

Low buildings on either side of the broad plaza led to the broken ring structure we'd seen from the air. The space between was filled with people. The breach in the ring wall was wide and a broken transparent dome covered the back half of the structure. Clearly the whole place had been enclosed at one time. Stalls set against the walls were doing reasonable trade, some selling cooked food or raw produce, but the majority of the beings under the broken dome were milling around with little purpose.

"What are all these people doing here?" Atalna asked.

"I don't know, but look around." The broad crowded plaza we'd walked through was enclosed on either side by newer buildings packed close together, and backed by a tall unbroken fence that ran all the way to the landing field. "It looks like they're trapped in here."

"As are we for the moment," Atalna said. "We should find somewhere to stay."

We pushed through the crowds to the ring wall and entered the first opening we came to: a narrow passage lined with doors. There were drifts of dirt accumulating where floor and walls met, and torn scraps of paper and other rubbish blown in from outside. The corridor opened up to something like a dormitory. Beds in rows, some of them occupied, others covered with bags or junk. The smell was overpowering.

"Not here," I said.

Back out under the broken dome, we followed the curve of the wall and paused at the next opening, looking into the semi-darkness. Halfway along the corridor a hunched shape lay on the floor covered in a ragged blanket. I was turning away when the shape spoke.

"If you're after a place to stay, it's not as bad as it looks. And the inside is cleaner."

I looked again at the alien who was unfolding its limbs to stand. It was short, about half as tall as Atalna, with spindly legs and too many arms. Its skin was black and shiny and sparsely covered in coarse hair. Its head looked too large for its thin neck to support. Large yellow eyes sprouted from the top of its skull.

"I'm Ephes Dreh. I can introduce you to the host if you like."

The daylight had faded. There was a loud crash and angry

shouting started up somewhere through the crowd.

"Thank you," Atalna said. "I'm Min'tak and this is Reka."

"You traders?"

"We are," I said. "Do you see many?"

"Most who come here. The lucky ones sell out quick and leave."

"And the rest?" Atalna asked.

But Ephes was walking ahead of us into the gloom. "The Hall of Industry is back near the left-hand break on the ring wall," it said. "That's where you'll trade. There's one entrance for us and one for the Humans. Don't try to go through the wrong door. Here we are."

Ephes stopped in front of a narrow pressure door and pressed a relay set in the wall. There was a grunt from inside.

"Customers, Patro. Open up."

There was another grunt and then nothing.

Ephes looked up at me. "He's coming." It turned back to the door, which remained resolutely shut. "Any moment now."

We waited. Ephes began fidgeting, its clawed hand tapping on the wall in what I took to be a nervous movement, darting towards the contact again, then drawing back.

"Of –" Ephes began, then broke off as the door slid up. "Patro! Look. Paying customers!"

Patro came up to my chest plate. Thin strands of long fur clung to the top of his head. His hide was mottled purple, his eyes sunk beneath folds of skin, and a single tusk protruded from the middle of his mouth and curved up to eye level. A white plastic tunic stretched across his body, which was as wide as he was tall. There were stains on the plastic; some looked to have been there a long time. The eyes swivelled beneath their fleshy coverings and he grunted. The voder didn't translate.

Ephes followed him inside, beckoning us to do likewise. "Patro's place is the best in the enclave – clean, reasonably priced, fantastic location. Whether you're a tourist or here on business, you won't find a better, homelier –"

"Ephes shut up now," Patro said, stopping at the bottom of a narrow flight of stairs. "Up here your room. You follow. You," he glared at Ephes, the eyes swimming out of their fatty resting place for a moment, "stay here. Better still, out in hallway."

Ephes backed away to let us enter.

"Thank you for your help," Atalna told him.

"Good luck." Ephes pushed past me in the narrow space and was gone.

Patro manoeuvred his bulk and started up the stairs sideways. His breath was whistling loudly through his short snout by the time we reached a landing. He stopped in front of a metal door with half the plastic covering peeled away, brought out a stubby piece of metal and pushed it into a hole in the door, turned it and pushed the door open.

The room was small, with a sleeping mat in each corner at the front of the room, either side of a large window that looked onto the ring courtyard below. A table stood against the back wall and two plastic chairs. The walls were worn but overall the place was clean.

"For evacuate waste," Patro said, pointing at another door past the table. "If no good your body type there is facility downstairs."

"It looks fine," Atalna said. "How much?"

"Twenty-seven hecs a day. How long you stay?"

"We're not sure," I said. "A little while."

"We don't have 'hecs'," Atalna said, "but will this do?" He held out one of our last ingots of gorundium.

Patro took it in his stubby-fingered hand and fumbled in the front pocket of his apron, pulling out a small scanner of some kind. The device lit up as he passed it over the ingot. He grunted. "Is good. But too much."

The scanner was put away and out came a pair of pincers. He snipped a corner from the ingot. "This you stay a tenday. Stay more need more." He handed the ingot back to Atalna.

"That sounds very fair," Atalna said.

Patro grunted again and shuffled past us towards the door, pausing only to place the stub of metal on the table.

He turned back to us. "This Ephes. You know him?"

"We just met outside. Our ship only just arrived."

Patro grunted and left, pulling the door closed behind him.

I looked out of the large window. Much of the crowd had thinned as night fell. Out among them it had been confusing, but up here it was possible to see them more clearly. There were so many different species – large, small, fat, armoured, with snouts or beaks, trunks, many eyes or none that were obvious, hands, claws, tentacles.

A line of Hegemony soldiers entered the courtyard from a door at the far end of the ring wall and spread out across the emptying space. It seemed we were all strictly confined to this ring settlement.

"I've never seen so many different aliens in the one place," I said.

"All citizens of the Hegemony," Atalna said.

I could tell he was thinking the same as me, but we had to assume our room was monitored. The diversity of species here represented a large number of planets, and there were many more aliens than Humans. And yet they all looked completely beaten down. Were the Humans so much smarter than the other species that they were able to dominate them? Or just more ruthless? I supposed some of those species might also be willing accomplices. Weak or complicit, it wasn't an attractive picture. But it was a familiar one.

If we could show that the Hegemony was vulnerable, would other species – even those who claimed loyalty to it right now – exploit that weakness and tear it apart? But to hurt the Hegemony even a little, to show to the universe at large that it could be hurt, we needed information.

∞

By later that night, the courtyard was empty and quiet. I opened a ration pack from my satchel and we switched on the vuscreen set into the wall. Its surface was as scratched as everything else in the room, but it was still functional, though there was only a single channel which appeared to be government-run.

The screen showed a line of blocky buildings beneath a blue sky with a single sun. A group of aliens clothed in dazzling robes stood with a group of Humans clothed in black Hegemony uniforms.

A disembodied voice spoke. *"The successful end of treaty negotiations with the planet Aleph-Kat in the Ophicus System was celebrated today at a ceremony held in Vigilance Plaza. Present to sign the official declaration of Hegemony Induction was Diplomatic Corps Comptroller, Troels Volmar."*

I stared at the screen. "That's the name of the Human Isza met."

The image cut away to other stories: the commissioning of a battleship; a missing ground transport on Mars had been found with all passengers safe; a new soil microbe had been released on Mars and this season's crop yields were the best on record; Senate elections were only days away and inner-system candidates were visiting major centres on the planet. It seemed so commonplace and so comfortable.

"Is there never any bad news?" I said.

"This is a government-controlled channel. I doubt we'll learn much from it." Atalna flicked the control and the screen blanked.

Perhaps, I thought. But we did learn what the government wanted its own people to know. And that seemed to be that there was nothing to worry about. It would be ironic if the Hegemony government lied to its own people as much as to those it intends to conquer.

Atalna used the waste room, then climbed onto one of the sleeping mats. I arranged a blanket over him.

"Thank you, Udun."

"Reka," I said.

His black eyes glinted. "Reka, yes. We'll need our wits about us tomorrow."

I dimmed the lights and climbed onto my own sleeping mat. From Atalna's breathing I could tell he was already asleep. The room felt cold and I pulled the blanket up.

Through the window I could see a misshapen moon, or maybe

an orbital station. Everything was still and quiet. It seemed safe but that was an illusion. We were in the heart of the Hegemony. It was unlikely we'd be able to leave as easily as we'd come.

15

Rhees's dolphincraft slid in behind the smooth saucer of the HDC clipper just as it broke orbit and accelerated straight up out of the system's ecliptic, heading for open space. The clipper was fast but she had no trouble keeping up, especially as it had no way of knowing it was being followed. If it transited to Voss Space that might be more difficult, but that didn't seem likely. Her ship had marked three easy access transit chambers already and the clipper wasn't headed for any of them.

The dolphinship's weapons interface expanded and she realised it had been reading her – either her thoughts or some telltale body chemistry that signalled a precursor to aggression.

The HDC operatives onboard the clipper certainly deserved to be blown to atoms without knowing by whom or why. It was what they'd done to Emba. Did they even consider the life they were snuffing out, or was he just a nameless target? A codestring embedded in a set of missile coordinates. It was senseless. All of it.

She was gaining on her quarry, so she pulled back. It was possible she'd been a little optimistic telling Nok she'd get access to Hegemony comms this way. It depended on a lot of things working out exactly right. But at least she was acting, not reacting.

Long-range sensors brought up a contact – several contacts, right on her course setting. The clipper started its deceleration and she manoeuvred closer.

The contact was a small ship group dominated by the chunky weight of a System Class Battlecruiser carrying the comms array for a Voss Space relay immediately behind its forward battery. Step one, she thought. The clipper trimmed its course to head straight for it.

The battlecruiser's hangar deck was open to space like a giant maw. Having passed the ships around Telsus IV without challenge, Rhees knew the stealth covering of her dolphincraft made it invisible to sensors. Even so, she flew under the curve of the clipper's disc, keeping it above her as they crossed the vacuum curtain at the edge of the hangar and manoeuvred onto the nearest landing area.

She held her breath as the dolphincraft touched down, her augmented vision showing every detail of the hangar around her. No sirens. No rush of armed troops.

A ramp extended from the clipper beside her and two HDC-uniformed figures descended – oblivious to the dolphincraft – walked to the nearest bulkhead and exited. The hangar was plunged into darkness, system lights studded along the walls providing pools of illumination.

Rhees's vision returned to normal as the dolphincraft peeled open. She made her way to the same door she'd seen the others leave by. It opened onto an empty corridor.

Fleet and HDC may have been cut from the same Central Administration cloth, but they exhibited very different characters. HDC was hyper-paranoid, checking personnel and access logs repeatedly and at every step. Fleet installations and vessels were just as impregnable as anything HDC operated; getting in was – normally – impossible without proper clearances. But once inside a Fleet ship there were very few checks. You were part of the Fleet family and trusted to do the right thing.

By the lighting in the corridor Rhees could tell the ship was in night mode. That should work in her favour. There were no deck maps on the walls but she didn't need one. There was a single logic to Fleet ship layouts that was religiously replicated regardless of size and type. It made sure you wouldn't be disoriented during an attack even if you'd just come onboard a new ship. She'd entered by the port hangar. There would be an auxiliary comms room – one of four on a System Class ship – up two decks and forward.

She found the elevator and entered a waiting car. The door closed and the elevator started up, but stopped at the next deck and opened on a young red-haired flight tech. He'd been looking at his deck boots as the door slid aside, but seeing the car was occupied he lifted his head, his expression shifting to a smile of greeting. The smile froze when he saw Rhees.

She felt a moment's panic but realised his gaze had locked on the HDC infinity symbol on her uniform breast pocket. She nodded to him as his eyes climbed to her face, but he ignored her, turning to stand a little in front of her, staring at the doors. She exited on the next level. There were times, she thought, when an HDC uniform was useful.

She tensed outside the door to auxiliary comms. If someone was inside, she could ask them to leave, claiming she needed the room for classified HDC comms. But the operator might insist on calling upstairs to check her authorisation. Which would quickly get awkward.

But the room was empty. She sat at the desk and linked to the array. If she was religious she'd have said a little prayer, but she settled for a slow, deep breath. She set up her own shielded channel, then built up several authentic-looking layers before adding Denev's unique codestring. She'd avoided contacting him since hooking up with Nok. HDC thought she was dead, and it was better that way. But Denev would be in more immediate danger if her communication was intercepted by the Hegemony. Unless he reported it immediately to his superiors. But after what they'd been through, she knew she could trust him not to do that.

There was a brief flash of Fleet insignia on the screen, then the HDC infinity symbol as the signal completed a series of handshakes.

And then she felt she must be doing all this in a dream because Denev was looking out at her. A little thinner, but alive. As if they were in the same room.

He stared at her for a moment, then said, "I knew Volmar was lying."

"Oh, yeah. That's his default. He gave me to the Maagba for execution. They let me go instead." Feelings so strong rushed through her that her throat almost closed over. "It's good to see you," she managed.

His eyes focused on the bottom right corner of the screen where the privacy icon glowed. "How are you even doing this? I thought Volmar was calling, so I climbed in a booth and invoked full HDC encryption."

"Are you safe?"

"I think so. Volmar's keeping me close, but I can't be sure he's not just waiting for me to screw up so he can jail me."

"That good, huh?" she said and he smiled.

"You were right though. The Central Administration – fuck, the whole political system – it's rotten to the core. And Volmar's at the centre of it all."

"All the more reason you need to be careful," she said. "Look, I don't want to waste time. I've found allies. We're running our own op against the Hegemony in a place called the Lenticular."

That sounded better than the reality of, *I'm up to my neck in shit with aliens I don't know if I can trust.* Still, Denev looked incredulous for about two seconds before he focused on the logical outcome of her statement.

"I've heard of it. Volmar's got me liaising with the ship groups there. Among other things."

It was Rhees's turn to be surprised.

"What do you need?" he asked.

"Access to Hegemony comms, but my band ident's been cancelled."

"Okay. Your band's already configured for HDC protocols, so loading alternative ident codes is standard for field operatives. Wait a minute." He looked down. "Your band's linked?"

"Yep." She waited. Her band vibrated.

"You've got access now. I gave you a promotion to HDC sector chief, but unattached on special ops. Your name's Elna Darrow."

"You just had that lying around?"

"I always carry spares. Just had to change the gender. Need anything else?"

"Teleporter?"

He smiled. "Fresh out."

But there was something else she needed. Though she didn't want to put Denev in any more danger, especially if Volmar was watching him.

"I could use the comms protocols for the Lenticular campaign."

"Those I can get."

She paused. "I wish I was there with you."

He smiled again. "It's really probably best that you're not."

She couldn't argue with that. "Look after yourself. I'll be in touch." She broke contact. Fuck. She hoped he stayed safe.

She should leave, but since she was here, she decided to download the ship's log – see where it had been recently, and the basics of any action it had been involved in.

Information scrolled across the main console screen. Course and heading details, sightings of non-Hegemony ships. The clipper she'd followed had rendezvoused with the battlecruiser's ship group two weeks ago and the group had changed course shortly after.

She could read all this later. She stepped up the download speed and cast a glance over her shoulder at the door. When she looked back, two words jumped out at her from the rapidly flowing data. She kept the download running but scrolled the screen back up, scanning for what she thought she'd seen. There. *Fa'ar Rojen.* Emba had mentioned him as one of his network. She read the entry.

"Fuck." The word came out in a strangled whisper that should have been a shout.

The download finished. She should leave. The hangar and her ship was two decks below; the surgery was one level up. Back at the elevator, she pressed for the deck above.

The surgery smelled: a complex mix of animal musk, astringent chemicals and blood. It was dark, but there was enough illumination to make out something lying on the trolley in the middle of the room.

Rhees switched on an overhead lamp and swallowed the bile that forced its way into her throat. She knew that before protein was synthesised from plant material or grown in vats, animals had been bred, slaughtered and butchered. It was a thing she understood intellectually without really considering the implications. Now her mind skittered over the evidence of her eyes, trying to make sense of the senseless.

The Telsan was still alive, breath shallow. His legs were gone, ending in flesh-welded stumps above the knee, his fur shaved in rough strips around the wounds. He only had one eye; the other socket a scorched absence. His left paw was missing, and the skin and fur had been peeled back along the inner forearm where wires were attached to the muscles and tendons laid bare.

The log said Rojen was being interrogated by HDC. The rest of his crew had also been questioned and "eliminated". Emotionless words for vile, inhuman acts.

"Evil fucks," she said.

She heard a grunt. Rojen's single eye was looking at her, wide and terrified.

"I'm not here to hurt you," she said, desperately trying to bring him some comfort. "Emba sent me. He told me you saved Udun."

Rojen groaned. "They picked us up right after we dropped him and the Betlaan off." His voice was little more than a whisper. "He's not safe."

No one's safe, she thought. But some part of her mind worried at what the Telsan had just told her. From what Emba had said, Udun was an enemy of the Hegemony. Rojen had helped him escape, but if Rojen had been scooped up as soon as he dropped Udun, it meant HDC was following him. Why? Why not just kill him like they did Emba?

Rojen coughed, His breathing was ragged. There was no way she could get him down to her ship without being seen.

"You're one of them," he said.

"I'm human. But I'm nothing like the bastards that did this to you."

"Prove it."

"What?" What could she do?

"They're not finished. I've told them everything but they keep going and the pain …" His eye was wet and glassy. "Prove it. Kill me. Free me."

"I –"

"Free me!" He lifted his head as much as he could to glare at her, then dropped back as his breath came in sobs.

She stared at the burns, the ripped flesh and surgical wounds. It was horrific to look at, but to live through … Fuck. She had no weapon, but … On the wall near the door was a familiar cabinet.

The heavier weapons were under lock and key, but the cabinet held four standard-issue stingers – flechette pistols – in case of boarding action. She took one and stood over Rojen, levelling the pistol at his chest. But she couldn't shoot him. They would find the dart and know she'd been here.

"Please," he said, misinterpreting her hesitation.

She was doing this, but how? She tucked the pistol into her pocket and took a deep breath. Let it out. "I'm sorry," she said, and closed her hands around his throat and squeezed.

Would this even work on a Telsan? But Rojen's breath wheezed and she pressed harder, pushing her thumbs down. His body bucked once, twice, then relaxed. She held her grip and counted off seconds. Finally, she stepped back. Rojen was dead.

Footsteps in the corridor. She switched off the overhead and rushed to the far end of the room behind a med console. The lights came up. Two sets of feet entered.

"Crap," a male said.

"He didn't know anything else." Another male. "Saves us the trouble. It stinks in here. You want to clean up now?"

"Fucking aliens. I'm in the middle of my meal," the first man said.

"Yeah. He's not going anywhere."

A laugh. The light went off. The door closed behind them.

Humanity had become the worst nightmare of sentient species everywhere – a perfect fusion of cruelty and cunning. And it couldn't all be blamed on the K-Chaan war experience, she thought. Those characteristics had been present in humans for a long time. Maybe back to the caves. Maybe longer. The K-Chaan just offered an excuse to cut loose and do what came naturally.

It wasn't all of humanity, she reminded herself. But enough. Enough for the majority, who just wanted a comfortable life, to go along with it and not ask too many questions. But what about those who *could* see how wrong this was? Did the Inclusionists have the numbers to turn the tide? So far it didn't seem likely. But that didn't mean *she* should give up.

Time to get the fuck out of here. She looked at Rojen's body on the way out. She hoped he was at peace now.

She met no one on the way back to the hangar. The vast space was still in darkness, open to the stars beyond the force barrier.

The dolphincraft folded over her and her vision expanded again as systems came online. She'd like to pick a distant star, aim for it and just keep going. But when she'd passed through the barrier, she brought her craft to a complete halt. Nok's ship was hanging a few hundred metres aft of the battlecruiser's main drive. No one on the Hegemony ship had noticed.

She flew the short distance to the Jantri hangar and parked the dolphincraft near the bulkhead door. Nok was waiting for her.

"We have comms access," she told him.

"There's no sign they detected your activity." It was a statement, not a question.

"They had a Telsan prisoner. They were torturing him."

Would Nok have given Rojen a merciful death? Maybe that was a step too far beyond "facilitation". Nothing stirred in the golden haze of his faceplate.

Finally, he said, "Regrettable."

There was no point being angry with him, Rhees realised. "Both Emba and Rojen mentioned a Kresz called Udun. I'm pretty sure HDC is tracking him, but I don't know why."

"Udun is changing the course of history for his people," Nok said. "If he lives, he will rid the Lenticular of the Hegemony and he will help you stop it completely."

"One person can't do all that." Even to her own ears she sounded tired and cynical.

"They can if they inspire others."

Nok's armour moved fluidly to the bulkhead door. As it opened, he said, "I picked you up in Maagba space because you are another such individual around which the universe turns. You challenge the status quo, and everything you have ever done has brought you to this point. You can change things too."

He left and Rhees stared at the door for a long time. Maybe this Udun *was* special. But she wasn't the saviour of her people. At best she was an idealist who'd come to her convictions too late to do anything about them.

It had been simpler when all she'd wanted was to be with Petar and to fly. They'd talked about how – centuries before – the real heroes were those who'd risked their lives on wooden ships, exploring and extending the boundaries of the known world. That would be their life. They'd see what was beyond the edge. Now this was all Rhees had left.

Nok might be on some messianic quest, but she wasn't going to be a part of it. Besides, messiahs had a habit of getting sacrificed.

16

The small pale sun had only just crested the broken ring wall but the courtyard was already crowded and the market stalls we'd seen the day before were busy.

Outside, I looked around for Ephes, but couldn't see him. "Well," I said, "we're here to trade. Let's go see what it's like."

Halfway to the Hall of Industry, a loud noise sounded. A ground transport parked at the opposite end of the courtyard and an armoured Human figure climbed onto its roof.

Most of the crowd converged on the vehicle, individuals pushing hard at each other to get to the front. Human soldiers lined up either side of the transport, conspicuously armed.

"Today's details," the Human on the roof said. "Twenty to the south pastures, grid kay-pee-ay, sorghum harvesting." He held his arm out to the left.

People moved in that direction, leaving a smaller group in front of the soldiers.

"Forty to grid zed-ell-ess, ploughwork and planting," the Human said, and this time he pointed right. More of the crowd broke off to form a work gang.

"Twenty-five for orange harvest, grid wy-ex-gee." He pointed left again, and again a smaller group formed and followed two of the armed soldiers towards the perimeter buildings that surrounded the field.

"I wonder what they get paid," Atalna said beside me.

"I don't expect it can be much. It's basic manual labour. Don't they have machines for this kind of thing?"

More groups were called for and led away until less than half of the original crowd remained.

"That's all for today," the soldier said, and climbed off the ground car and got inside.

What kind of existence was this to wait on the Humans' pleasure and trade labour for a few coins? I looked at the strange faces around me and could see no dignity in them. It had been stripped away by whatever had happened on their homeworlds or here. The Hegemony was a giant machine for breaking people's souls.

Now the crowd had dispersed, the entrance to the trade hall was visible. Part of a door remained, but the opening had been widened by breaking into the wall on one side and above the doorframe.

Inside, it was clear the space had once been living quarters like those at Patro's place, but corridor and room walls had been broken through and removed. Guards stood at regular intervals around the perimeter of the hall, and rows of low tables filled the rest of the space, many of them already occupied by traders. The far wall – what must be the outer wall opening to the world outside this compound – had a ship's lock set into it.

We chose a table near the middle of the room, beside a short alien covered in long yellow hair that poked through the gaps in the equipment harness it wore. I greeted it, but the alien turned away and began rearranging the small but perfectly clear stones it had laid out on a dark cloth on the table.

I got some of the pharma-phials out of my satchel and placed them on our table, and added a portable scanner and data library with information on their chemical composition.

"When do the Humans come, I wonder," I said to Atalna.

"It must be soon. There aren't any more traders coming in. We were the last."

We sat there for what felt like a long time, watching the sun swing around the courtyard, but no one came.

Finally – it must have been past the middle of the day – the airlock at the end of the hall opened and in strode a small group of Humans and then a line of them. They were dressed in a variety of styles, some with body armour, others in travel cloaks and tunics. All were accompanied by aliens of different species, covered in hair, scales or bright or dull coloured hides, but with a common trait. They moved always a little behind their companions, picking up trade goods for the Humans to inspect, speaking to the traders before turning to consult with what I now came to think of as their Human masters.

I began to doubt the effectiveness of our plan. We'd hoped to meet with Humans over our trade goods, perhaps strike up a conversation to gently prise information from them about the Hegemony. But we hadn't figured on the conditions that existed here. The fact that aliens were at best second-class citizens, with no freedom of movement and very few rights accorded them.

Suddenly we had company. There was a Human standing back from our table, its head turned away from us, looking perhaps at the sunlight outside. Its pink features were soft and shapeless, the fur on its head long and yellow. Its alien companion was the colour of an instar, bright red, and its skin shone with the lustre of shell. It was so short that its spindly arms could barely reach across our table. Nevertheless, it snatched up the scanner and looked at me with pink eyes set tight against a long, wet snout.

"What we have here?" its voder croaked.

"Our catalogue of pharmaceuticals," Atalna said. "I doubt you will have seen anything like them in this part of the galaxy."

The alien turned to proffer the scanner to its Human. The Human took the device as if it was covered in dirt and held it up. It still didn't look our way or acknowledge our presence.

It said something to its alien, but too quietly for me to hear.

The alien spoke up. "Have been tested against the Human genome these?"

"Yes," Atalna said.

The alien snuffled, gripping the table edge. "Then where your results?"

"My friend misspoke," I said. "We —"

"Misspoke!" the red alien said. "Non-Humans to possess Human genome illegal." It indicated the other Humans and their escorts in the room. "That why none come. Goods untested. They know."

"So why are you here?" Atalna said.

The alien indicated the Human who was still ignoring us. "My associate. He possess genome data. We test samples you. Check compatibility and efficacy. For a fee. If test safe, you sell many as you like."

It looked up at us with its pink eyes. If what it said was true, no Humans would trade with us and there'd be no chance for interaction with them. I couldn't see an alternative.

"What do you need?" I said.

"Access to samples. Get results. One day."

"And what will it cost?" Atalna asked.

"Less than you sell for." It produced a flat square, which it placed on our table. "You have niprocian? Five hundred grams according this planet gravity."

Atalna looked at me. We had some of the metal it asked for, but I felt a sudden caution.

"You can test half the samples," I said. "If we are happy with the results you can test the other half."

"Cost what it costs. Half or all, it still five hundred grams."

They had us. I could see that. But still I couldn't give up all the samples.

"Half the samples." I kneeled, pulled out a block of niprocian and placed it on the alien's device.

It assayed it, then sheared a corner off with a small laser cutter. I looked at the figures on the display but I couldn't tell if they were correct.

Atalna bundled up half of our samples and gave them to the alien.

It bowed. "Till tomorrow. You not disappointed."

The Human had already walked off and the alien ran to catch up. We watched them disappear through the airlock door.

"There's not much point waiting here any more today," I said, and we packed up our goods.

"I suppose it hasn't been too bad," Atalna said as we walked out of the hall into the afternoon sunlight. "We've made a Human contact of sorts, if at a remove. Tomorrow it may actually speak to us."

The courtyard was busy again. Most of the work crews must have returned from their jobs.

"Look, there's Ephes," Atalna said.

The short alien had seen us and was pushing past a small knot of aliens towards us. "I was looking for you earlier," he said. "I got caught up with a friend. He was injured in the fields back a ways and he still doesn't get around too well. I tried to get him a job in a work gang this morning, standing in for him at selection. But it didn't work. They pulled him out as soon as we swapped. What have you been doing?"

"A failed attempt at selling our pharms," I said. "We didn't know they had to be tested against the Human genome before anyone would buy. One of the Humans took some samples to test for us. For a price."

Ephes cocked his bulbous head to one side. "Took your samples?"

"They wanted to test them all, but we only gave them half."

"For the same testing price," Atalna added.

"Ahh," Ephes said. "You won't see those samples again."

"What do you mean?" Atalna said.

"They'll use those samples to synthesise exact copies of your drugs. Sell them themselves, assuming they're safe."

"But the drugs needed to be tested," I said, feeling stupid. "How else could we do that?"

"There's a government testing facility in the ring wall. They certify all goods for safety and give you the proper data authorisation.

Buyers can pick up the signal in the hall. That way they know your goods are safe. You've been tricked."

I felt Atalna's hand on my arm. "It doesn't matter," he said. "Ephes, can you take us to the testing place?"

Ephes gave a brief chitter. "I won't even charge you." He looked at me. "Just think of it as a valuable lesson learned. Trust no one."

"Not even you?" I said.

The chitter again. "Especially not me."

Atalna was right: there was no use worrying. The drugs were of no value to us really, apart from providing a convenient reason to be here and to interact with the locals. Still, it was galling to be so easily tricked. I felt again that we were out of our depth.

I heard a shout and a head appeared above the crowds, blue skin, large ears sticking out at both sides, a thick line of fur standing up from the temples. The head disappeared but I could see the crowd rippling, getting out of the way. The group near us broke apart and the alien shot through the gap, arms flailing, long legs pumping. Two Hegemony guards came after it. One stopped near us, levelled its rifle and fired at the running alien. The bolt caught it full in the back and it lunged forward, hitting the ground face first.

All around us, people were picking themselves up, staring at the downed alien. I was sure I saw anger reflected in many eyes. Not fear. Not spiritless submission.

The guards walked through the crowd, seeming oblivious, or at least impervious, to the anger. They picked up the alien, manacled it, and loaded it on the back of a ground cart that drove up. Then they climbed aboard and the vehicle moved off slowly.

"Why do you think they were chasing him?" Atalna asked.

A shiver ran up Ephes's body so he seemed to shake from spiny-haired feet to bulbous head. "Anything can set them off – it's no way to live. They're not all like that though. The Humans. Ack, don't worry. Let's get you sorted."

Ephes led us through another airlock-type door into a white

room divided from floor to ceiling by a large glass partition with an opening midway up. Behind the glass stood two aliens, both dressed in the black Hegemony uniform. One of them regarded us with a single green eye.

"Smek," Ephes said, "my friends here need some goods certified." He turned to me. "Give him the samples."

Smek looked at them briefly then handed them to his colleague. "You can pick them up when we open tomorrow," he told me. A plastic strip extruded from a reader and he passed it to me. "This is your receipt. Bring it with you when you return."

Outside again, the ground was vibrating and the tall ship we'd seen the day before rose slowly on a column of smoke. Ephes stopped to watch it.

"Do you mind waiting for a moment?" I asked him.

His yellow eyes focused on me, then turned back to the departing ship. "There's nowhere else I have to be."

I walked Atalna to the side of the testing lab entrance.

"What is it?" he asked.

"Ephes knows how this place works. He could tell us so much."

I could see he thought the idea was risky. But every moment we were here was dangerous and if Ephes could help we could leave a lot quicker. Still, he hesitated. Then, finally, he said, "All right."

I gestured to Ephes and he came over. "Is there somewhere we can talk," I said. "In private?"

He took my question in his stride and simply said, "Follow me."

He led us round the ring wall to a narrow door set between two food stalls, then into a vestibule with stairs leading down.

"This is my favourite place," he said as he started his descent. "Not everyone is welcome down here."

There was another hall at the bottom of the winding staircase, badly lit with a single door at the end. Ephes placed one long finger on the door lock. The door slid in and up with a hiss.

Inside was dark and cramped. Then an inner door, unseen in the darkness, opened onto a long room lit in dim red. Figures moved about in the gloom or sat at tables. It appeared to be a bar. We followed Ephes to a table set into an alcove. He left us and returned with a bottle of something and three glasses.

"Just water," he said and sat. His voice was pitched lower when he spoke again. "We can talk safely here. The Humans never come down, and those aliens that do prefer to keep to themselves." He took a drink of water. "So why are we here?"

I paused and looked at Atalna who nodded.

"Whether we sell all our goods or not, we're leaving soon," I said. "But there's one more way to turn a profit before we go."

"Go on," Ephes said.

"This is the first time traders from our part of space have come here. What we've learned is useful information for those who come after. People would pay for it, to help their trip here go more smoothly. You know how this place works and you've helped us. That's why we want to repay you."

Ephes didn't say anything, but waited for me to explain myself.

"We've watched the government channel but it's not very informative."

Ephes grunted agreement.

"If we could find an alternative data feed – something that would provide mapping data for a start. It would be useful to know where other markets are on the planet. And anything else that would provide background on the place, perhaps suggest what goods are scarce. Anything to give a trader a foothold. A point of difference that could help them turn a profit. That would be profitable to us. And to you."

Ephes's yellow eyes regarded me. "You could really make money on this?"

"I believe so. And it would help us too, for when we come back."

He took a sip of water, considering. "I can see that. But you've seen the way we live here. We're not exactly free to roam around. The kind of information you're after involves risks."

"We don't want to endanger you," Atalna said. "Much less ourselves. If it's not possible –"

"I didn't say that," Ephes cut in. "But it might cost a bit."

"We look at it as an investment. In this place. And in you."

"It'll take time to organise," he said, standing. "I'll come to your ship after sunset tomorrow."

"We'll be there."

We waited long enough for him to clear the exit before we made our own way out.

"He could betray us," Atalna said.

"If he does, we'll find out soon enough."

17

The next morning I went to check on the ship. The AI reported no attempts to gain entry.

I walked to the testing facility and sat outside, waiting for it to open. The ring wall was still mostly in shadow but the sky was brightening. People emerged slowly from whatever dormitories or hostels they'd spent the night in and crowded round the few vendors that were trading at this time. I imagined they were savouring a few more moments of respite before facing the reality of life in the Hegemony. A life of fear and uncertainty. The same life that was taking hold on Homeworld. Millions of beings across the galaxy were growing up without any idea of what they'd lost when the Hegemony came for their world.

When the sun rose above the tallest ship in the field, Smek opened the airlock. I followed him inside and handed him our receipt and he gave me the samples. Each phial had some writing inscribed on the side now, and a plastic ring with a small data crystal set into it around the neck.

"That's the registration data and health safety clearance," Smek said. "The red phials are not safe for Humans."

I met Atalna outside the Hall of Industry. As we made our way to our table, I now recognised the registration crystals attached to each item our neighbours were displaying.

When the Humans and their aides or slaves or whatever they were entered by the airlock door our table became the centre of attention. The registration transponder clearly did its job. But it was still the aides who picked up our goods or enquired as to the price of this or that pharma; the Humans stood back, feigning indifference. I saw that our plan to connect with a Human through trade was pointless.

Atalna, however, was in his element: haggling with the aides over price, suggesting other pharmas that may complement the one being studied. By the afternoon our table was empty. Even the Human poisons, it seemed, may have some use. The hairy, eyeless alien at the next table said something to us as the final buyers drifted away. The voder couldn't translate, but it didn't sound unfriendly.

Atalna handed me the small pile of metal we'd made for the day.

"You missed your calling," I said.

"Not at all. Politicians are good at selling. They sell ideas. And, ultimately, they sell themselves. By contrast, selling some chemicals is child's play."

We left the hall and returned to our ship for our meeting with Ephes. Atalna sat on the crash-couch and I activated the vuscreens, setting them to watch all around the ship's exterior.

"It's strange," I said. "We've spent so much time in here already, but I'm almost looking forward to getting underway again. To going home ... Well, you know what I mean."

"Yes," Atalna said. "But I won't believe we can get back to the Lenticular until we do. And I'm not sure what we do once we are back."

I spotted Ephes on the vuscreen and activated the lock as he approached the ship. He didn't alter his pace, just walked straight in, and I closed the lock quickly behind him. Then he was in the control deck with us.

"Ah," he said, sitting on the couch beside Atalna. "That's one walk I'd rather not make again."

I waited until he got his breath back. "Did you manage to get –"

"I got it all right. Not easy, but here." He held up a data crystal. "This is a particularly elegant little program, but you need to get it loaded now. It holds the scramble codes for the next four hours of datacasts. Load it in your AI and let it get to work. Every second you delay means a second of data you'll miss recording."

I placed the crystal in the arm of the couch. "Program accepted and running," the AI said.

"Can you explain what we're doing?" I asked Ephes.

"You wanted access to datastreams other than the government service we get in here. That program will do it – for four hours. The reason we don't receive other datacasts is because there's a scrambler effect at the perimeter of the shield wall that turns any coherent signal into static. To be effective the scrambler changes every few seconds so that even if someone were to work out the scramble code it would only work for a short period of time. What we have here is the next four hours of algorithm changes, so you get four hours of uninterrupted, decoded external datacasts."

"Why only four hours?" Atalna asked.

Ephes gave Atalna a hard stare. "Min'tak, it was hard enough getting this much access. Anything else would have cost more than you could afford and would have drawn too many awkward questions."

"Is the program traceable?" I asked.

"That's the beauty. It's passive. All your AI is doing is translating the scrambled signal that everyone can receive. Let's take a look at what we're getting. I'm as curious as you are."

I switched the vuscreens to play the signals the program was decoding. The screens split into multiple panels. There were a large number of datacast channels, each one a small mosaic. Most of them were blank, or showed a random pattern. The room filled with overlapping sound but the AI cut the noise into the background.

"Those will be encrypted communications," Ephes said, pointing at one blank mosaic. "Private calls, that kind of thing. You'd need the encryption key to read them."

"Ship, display only unencrypted channels," I said.

The blank mosaics started to wink out, the remaining channels expanding to take up more room on the vuscreen. There were still a lot of mosaics left.

"Sound sample," I said.

Each mosaic was highlighted for a few seconds accompanied by a burst of sound. The content was puzzling and I wondered if the voder was working correctly.

"Those sound like private conversations, but unencrypted," I said.

"Ah," said Ephes. "They would be the dramas."

"Dramas?" Atalna said.

"Representations of things that haven't happened and perhaps never will. The Humans enjoy them."

"Why invent something that hasn't happened and pretend it's real?" I asked.

"Perhaps it helps them anticipate the unexpected," Atalna said. "A species trait?"

"But the content wouldn't carry any true information," I said, touching the tiles that were obviously "dramas" so they winked out. There were a lot of them.

Other mosaics depicted physical challenges: Humans using spheres or clubs, Humans in water, in strange-looking flying machines. Ephes called them "sports". There were a lot of those too.

There weren't many mosaics left now. The AI began to cycle through their sound feeds.

Available on the transweb and in stores right across in-system, the new T — but the naughty little puppy just kept on eating and didn't — these ruins now some five thousand years old show a remarkable — oh lord, we beseech thee in thy infinite mercy —

I discarded these channels too. They were just another form of entertainment. We were running out of options.

The next mosaic was highlighted and the sound cut in.

" *— Inclusionist representative addressed members of the Chamber of Commerce at the Tranquility Basin Assembly Hall.*"

I looked at Atalna. An Inclusionist. The Human stood at an elevated desk in front of tables filled with other Humans.

"We've been lucky so far," it said. *"But that luck cannot and will not hold. The sheer number of what the CA laughingly calls "member species" is vast and continues to grow. We can't hope to control them all. In fact, the effort put into information manipulation in all its forms means HDC is the single largest government bureaucracy we have. The biggest that has ever existed in the history of our civilisation. Think of the resources it expends; resources that could be put to much better use in our hospitals and welfare organisations, and to improve our infrastructure. And yet those vast resources HDC wields won't keep us safe in the end. They're like a wall of sand against an encroaching tide, because the fundamental policy on which the Hegemony was formed is flawed. We can't beat the universe into loving us. The Central Administration uses HDC to fool us just as much as the aliens. But all they're doing is papering over the cracks and one day soon we'll find that what we built is falling down around our ears. That's why we have to act now, before that happens. I'm not talking appeasement or capitulation. I'm talking about a different ethos for working with the aliens we encounter. A more constructive one. One that builds positive relationships for them and for us. It's not too late. But it soon will be. That's why the Inclusionist party needs your votes on polling day."*

The scene changed to another Human with long fur and a red mouth. *"Representative Minch is now on Mars attending a number of speaking engagements, including a visit tomorrow to address the alien enclave at Olympus Mons. And now we continue our program of light music from Renaissance Europ—"*

I muted the mosaic.

"He's one of the Humans that don't think we're dirt," Ephes said.

I didn't respond. The remaining mosaics looked like the government news feed we had in our rooms. So much for spying on the Humans' broadcasts. The information they held was worthless.

"The ship is recording all the streams," I said. "We'll look at the rest later."

Ephes shifted on the couch. "Not what you were looking for really."

"Any information is useful to us," Atalna said. "You'd be

surprised what some people will pay for."

"Ah, yes. Payment," the little alien said.

"I have it here." I handed him a block of metal.

Ephes took it and weighed it in his hand. "Thanks. Will you be leaving now?"

"We'll stay one more day to rest," I said.

Ephes stood. "I may see you tomorrow then."

Atalna waited until the external hatch had closed. "You want to see this Minch when he comes here," he said.

"It's a chance to learn more about the Inclusionists. It's worth the risk."

"We trust to fate?"

I placed a claw on his shoulder. "We trust to fate."

∞

We slept in our room at the hostel that night and woke late. It didn't take long to pack, and after breakfast we took what things we had to the ship. I filed a departure plan with flight control.

Towards the afternoon, the atmosphere in the settlement took on an expectant air. The crowds in the courtyard were a little quieter, the majority of them waiting near the Hall of Industry which had been closed to trading that day in preparation for the visit. Our ship was ready for take-off by then, and with the AI there wasn't much a living pilot needed to do. So Atalna and I joined the crowds waiting for the doors to open into the hall where Minch would speak.

The sun, though setting, was still hot and to save Atalna we pushed through to stand in the shade near the broken ring wall. A narrow door opened slightly behind us and I heard a familiar voice. "Reka." It was Ephes. He lifted one clawed hand and beckoned.

Atalna and I walked through the door into a dusty corridor, the wall cladding scored and broken in parts.

"What are you doing?" I asked Ephes as he closed the door behind us.

"Getting you more information. Minch is keen to meet aliens

on his tour. I got asked by his people and I suggested they might want to talk to you too, since you're from so far out."

I felt suddenly light-headed. After the disappointment of the last few days this was a real chance.

"Ephes," Atalna said, "you've earned yourself a bonus."

"Then we're all happy," Ephes said. "He's preparing for his speech, but he has a few minutes to talk."

We didn't have much time. We had to tell Minch enough so he'd agree to meet us later.

A metal door ahead stood slightly open. Ephes indicated we should go first. I pushed the door wide.

18

"Head for the Voss bridge," Volmar said. "We already have the necessary clearances."

"The Voss bridge?" Denev asked. "I thought we were going to Mars?"

Volmar sighed, indicated with a nod the bridge structure gleaming brightly in high Earth orbit, then settled back in his crash-chair and closed his eyes.

That morning, they'd taken the private hypertube to the secure HDC field on Bathurst Island and picked up a scoutship almost identical to the one Denev and Rhees had used to follow the Brell diplomat, Delegate O'Dran, to the secret rebel meeting. Except this time Denev was the pilot and Volmar the only passenger. They'd lifted as soon as pre-flight checks were complete, their flight path arcing over the ocean. Below, the parallel lines of the trans-Pacific hypertube glowed like hot wires running across the face of the water.

Volmar had been quiet for most of the trip and it was making Denev edgy. Piloting the ship was a welcome distraction. It seemed they had priority as other ships queuing for the Voss bridge moved aside to let them pass. Transit was instantaneous. The artificially induced chamber on the other side was vast. It had to be to cope with the traffic.

"Move well away from the transit point," Volmar said, eyes still closed.

Denev knew better than to ask for clarification.

When Volmar opened his eyes and sat forward they were well

into the central space of the chamber, far from the other vessels following the main tunnel connections.

The comptroller touched the controls and a section of the chamber wall was highlighted on the screen. "This tunnel will take us to Mars. It's no quicker than conventional flight, so it's seldom used. But it has the advantage of evading SolSec scrutiny. For all they know we're off to some completely different star system."

Which was exactly the way Volmar liked it, Denev thought as he steered the scoutship into the narrow, nondescript tunnel. Deception and lies were Volmar's defaults. He'd lied about Rhees escaping and being killed by the Maagba, and he'd lied about knowing Denev's father. And now it seemed the whole CA leadership was somehow implicated in covering up what had really happened to Denev's parents.

It was entirely possible Volmar knew about Denev's own investigations – and his part in Beloc's death – but chose not to confront Denev about it because he still had a use for him. He'd seen how Volmar had manipulated the rebel forces in order to sacrifice them to the Maagba. Denev could be another unwitting pawn to be killed when Volmar got what he wanted. Or Volmar might believe Denev was still loyal. Either way, he was trapped. He had to keep going.

This deep into the complicated gravitational straits between Earth and Mars, the tunnel was studded with Voss stabilisers that kept the field potential low and prevented a random collapse. Denev could have set the ship on auto-pilot it was so safe, but he preferred to stay occupied.

A little over five hours later they transited to Mars orbit. The Voss bridge exit tracked the vacuum end of the Deimos space elevator in an elegantly complex marriage of orbital dynamics and multidimensional mathematics. Mars's second moon, Phobos, had been disassembled and the raw materials used in part to fabricate the elevator. Its lonely sister moon, Deimos, had been rudely shunted to an areosynchronous orbit to act as the elevator's space tether.

"Deimos Terminus to HDC craft. Transmit your authorisation."

SolSec would be aware that an HDC craft had entered Mars space, but as they'd lifted from a secure HDC facility there was no record of who was on board or why they were here. HDC didn't need to explain its actions to anyone except the CA Executive, and Denev knew after the meeting he'd attended that whatever the mission was, it was sanctioned by the highest levels of government.

He transmitted the authorisation codes, which pretty much amounted to: we're HDC, don't fuck with us.

The terminus operator answered immediately. "You're clear to dock at the HDC entry."

This was another way HDC could operate without oversight. It occupied a secure area of the terminus and had a dedicated elevator car.

The terminus station was a flattened sphere, pierced by the monofilament tether that extended to Mars surface below and the captured Deimos above. The scoutship screen highlighted their entry point with a green circle. On approach, Denev matched velocity and let the automatics take over for final adjustments. He heard a low rumble as docking clamps engaged.

Volmar was first out of his seat. Denev followed him through the lock and into the entry vestibule to the terminus. Two men waited for them. One was large and muscled, black-skinned, bald and with a thick black moustache. The other was shorter, barely up to his partner's shoulder, skinny and pale with thick stubble on his chin. Both wore blue SolSec uniforms with the golden sun badge on the breast pocket.

"Don't let the uniforms fool you," Volmar said. "This is Operative Drenn." The black man nodded. "And Operative Finn."

"A pleasure," the thin man said in a thick Irish accent.

Drenn held out two neatly folded bundles of clothing coloured the same SolSec blue.

Volmar took one and handed the other to Denev, then started stripping off his onepiece. Drenn's and Finn's gazes wandered to the walls, clearly not sure of the protocol for watching their comptroller get semi-naked. Under his onepiece, Volmar's skin was pale with a yellowish cast, stretched like parchment over his thin frame. Any muscle he'd had as a younger man had melted away with age. He looked held together with sinew.

"Are we impersonating SolSec?" Denev asked as he changed.

"Not in any significant way," Volmar said. "It simply makes travel on the surface easier."

Drenn and Finn led them to the HDC elevator car, which was ready and waiting. They saw no one else on their way. The HDC section might have had a small staff complement, or it might have been cleared to hide the fact that Comptroller Volmar was visiting Mars.

The doors to the car closed and the opaque window cleared, though Denev expected it was still opaque to any surveillance equipment looking in from open space. The car felt stationary, but looking through the window he could see they were already plummeting to the cloud deck.

Another few seconds and they were through it, with all of Mars laid out before them. The base of the elevator was anchored at Airy-0 crater, sitting on the prime meridian and just five degrees south of the equator in the foothills of the mountainous southern hemisphere. The flatter plains to the north were given over almost completely to agriculture, and the contrast of rich red Martian rock meeting vast rectangles of green and yellow fields cordoned by irrigation channels was striking. Closer still, Denev could see the kilometres-high atmosphere processor stacks – mothballed now – strung in a chain across the fields, their long shadows progressing like timelapse sundials towards the receding terminator.

Another few seconds and suddenly they were in the landscape rather than looking down on it – the peak of Olympus Mons at eye level, thrusting above a line of lesser mountains between it and the elevator. The view cut off as the car entered the base superstructure and, without any sensation of coming to a halt, the door behind them opened.

Denev followed the others down a short ramp to a broad concourse filled with light from an atrium window. A row of ground cars were parked to the right opposite two ornithopters. The nearest car was already opening gull-wings.

Drenn took the pilot seat, while Denev sat in back with Volmar and Finn trotted around to the other side. Denev still had no idea why they were here and it was getting harder to maintain a calm exterior.

The car moved off quickly and down a ramp, merging with the traffic in the undergound highway. Finn looked at his band.

"Everything in order?" Volmar asked.

"He's just arriving," Finn said. "Should be in place as arranged."

Denev glanced at Volmar, who was staring at the blank tunnel walls. Asking what the fuck was going on would only show how nervous he was and stir Volmar's suspicions.

The car peeled off from the main tunnel, up a ramp and into a large parking garage. They got out and entered an elevator, just four SolSec men doing … what?

The elevator opened onto a twisting corridor. Drenn and Finn took the lead, walking like they knew exactly where they were going. A few turns and they came to a plain door guarded by another officer – dressed as SolSec but definitely HDC. He nodded and left. Drenn palmed the door and they entered.

A man turned, alone and surprised by the interruption. It was Representative Minch.

His eyes latched onto Volmar. "Comptroller, what are you –" He stopped as his gaze took in Volmar's SolSec uniform.

"It's over, Minch," Volmar said. "You were useful for a time, if irritating. Now you're just irritating."

Finn crossed to a side table. Whatever the room was being used for now, it looked to have once been an engineering station judging from the tools scattered across the tabletop. He picked up a long metal bar, hefting its weight.

Minch tapped at his band, then looked from Finn to Volmar. Denev had seen that look before: disbelief mixed with dawning terror.

"Your band won't work," Volmar said. He sounded disappointed, as if explaining something to a child. "We control everything. We've *been* controlling everything since we allowed you to be elected."

Finn took a step towards Minch.

"Wait!" Minch said, raising an arm to ward off the blow.

Finn swung. There was a sickening crunch. Finn's arm rose again and again – a series of dull thuds interspersed with sharp cracks. Then he stepped away, panting, and dropped the bar to the floor. Blood was sprayed across his uniform, looking black against the blue. Minch was a crumpled bloody mess, almost unrecognisable as human.

"Go and get cleaned up," Volmar said. "Drenn can look after the rest."

Finn gave a ghastly smile and left.

If Volmar had ordered Denev to kill Minch, would he have done it? Denev had killed for HDC before. That P'Len diplomat on Eaphesus VI, and an entire terror cell on Dekalia. He'd killed for himself too. Beloc's blood was on his hands just as surely as if he'd pushed him over the barrier. But this was the cold-blooded murder of an elected member of the Senate. Minch was no more an enemy of Earth than Denev was.

Denev was sure now there was nothing Volmar would not do if he thought it expedient. Even kill a diplomatic consul and his wife that he'd been assigned to help. But the question remained. Why?

Drenn looked at his band. "They're coming."

Drenn and Volmar moved to the other side of Minch's corpse. Denev followed them, avoiding the thick blood pooling on the floor.

The door opened and three aliens entered. They couldn't be more different in appearance, Denev thought. One was a Kresz, big and covered in a deep red exoskeleton. He recognised the species from the reports of the Lenticular occupation. The smallest alien was a Remander, wearing a dirty and torn cloak. The third was vaguely humanoid but its skin was mosaiced and highly reflective. It stood bent over and Denev got the feeling it was old.

All three looked at the bloody remains of Minch.

"Run, Ephes," the Kresz said, tensing to do the same.

"No need for that," Volmar said, now levelling a blaster at them. "Thank you, Ephes. You can shut the door behind you."

The Remander left. It was hard to read alien expressions at the best of times, but Denev thought the Kresz and its friend looked defeated.

Volmar – as always – was two steps ahead of anyone else in the room. "It's good to finally meet you, Udun," he said to the Kresz. "Even without the transponder our border patrol fitted to your ship, we've been following your exploits since your rather dramatic escape from Telsus IV. Your every move has been anticipated; the things you've 'discovered' here all stage-managed. You learn what we want, you think what we want, you do what we want."

"Don't listen to him," the old alien said.

"You think you're our enemies," Volmar said, ignoring it. "But everyone serves us in the end."

"We'll never serve you," the Kresz said.

"You do serve us. You have no say in the matter. And you must know by now there's nothing you can do to save your planet."

"What do you want, animal?" the other alien hissed.

"From you?" Volmar said. "Nothing. Your time is almost up. But Udun here ..." He glanced at Minch's body. "Unlike you, this man was dangerous. Because he believed in an idea. An idea that, if planted in enough minds, could grow to harm us. You have no such ideas. Because you know nothing. That is why you are my perfect instrument."

"Just kill us and get it over with," the Kresz said.

"You don't get to decide your fate. Minch had to die, but killing him won't kill his idea. That's how dangerous he was. No, to counter the Inclusionists we have to show the people of Earth just what happens when you treat fairly with aliens. Tragically," Volmar raised his voice slightly, "while preparing for a speech to the alien species he had championed throughout his campaign, Representative Minch was accosted in his private rooms by one of those very aliens and brutally murdered. Minch's assailant escaped capture and is still at large."

"What?" the Kresz said.

The alien clearly didn't understand, but Denev did. This was straight out of the HDC playbook.

"You killed him," Volmar continued. "Of course the guards could have gunned you down afterwards. But I think an alien killer still roaming free in-system will do much more to convince the general population that the Inclusionists are tragically misguided. We shan't meet again, Udun. And for the sake of economy, I won't be needing two aliens to escape."

Volmar's blaster hissed and a bolt struck the second alien. The Kresz grabbed at it, laid it down on the floor. But it was already dead.

The Kresz made a noise. Was it anger or anguish, Denev wondered. Perhaps both, or some emotion humans didn't have a word for.

Volmar levelled his blaster at the Kresz's head. "Run."

The Kresz stood slowly, hesitated for a moment, then pulled the door open and left.

"So ends Alder Minch," Volmar said. "And so begins the end of the Inclusionists. Of course, this won't be enough to destroy them. But it's a start. And you, Antwer, will play a part in phase two."

"What about the Kresz?" Denev said.

"He's an interesting one. Heaven knows what he hoped to achieve here. But he's served his purpose. I expect him to crawl into a hole somewhere and die."

19

I ran down the corridor and crashed through the door into pale sunlight. Startled aliens, still queueing for Minch's speech, stared at me, their conversations falling into silence.

Run. I heard the word again. But it wasn't Volmar's voice inside my head. It was Isza's.

I pushed through the crowd, heading as fast as possible towards the landing field. I felt sure I'd be shot in the back at any moment. But better to be killed running than to just give up. Atalna would never surrender. He'd fought to the end.

The door to our ship – my ship – seemed to open in slow motion. There was a piercing wail from somewhere. An alarm.

I was inside the ship before the outer door was fully open and fell into the crash-chair. "Ship. Emergency lift-off. Now!"

"Complying," the ship said. A roar filled the cabin and I was crushed into the chair.

On the screen the sky looked so peaceful – careless of the violence and suffering beneath it, and of my friend lying dead where I'd left him.

"Maximum acceleration," the ship said as the pressure eased.

"Cycle up the transit engines."

"Transit inside a gravity well is –"

"Do it," I snapped. "Scan for ships on intercept."

Orbital space was crowded, but there was nowhere to hide.

"Four ships on intercept."

The screen tagged them. A side window showed a magnified

view of one: a sleek dart. There was no way I could outrun them. And I'd left whatever help the Jantri could provide far behind. The ships would either capture me or blow me out of the sky. Transit was the only option.

Isza had done it at the battle of the Point, but she'd been tracking a region of flattened spacetime – a remnant of the Point satellites' destruction. A desperate move. But I was more desperate still.

"Transit!" I screamed. The scream went on, longer than my spiracles could sustain it. My body was fire. The ship screamed in response, an atonal accompaniment. Or maybe it was space that screamed. Something slammed me sideways. I couldn't see a thing, but I could feel the couch straps holding me. I was upside down for an instant, then the ship righted. The scream ended. Silence.

When I opened my eyes I was amazed to see the flight deck still intact around me. The screen showed black space and stars. Were we still in-system?

"What's our position?"

"Computing," the ship said.

I couldn't see a planet, but we were in realspace. How far had we come?

"Are there any ships nearby?" I asked.

"No."

That didn't make sense. I unstrapped the couch bindings and sat up. The other screens showed the same. Realspace. There was a star in one of them, about as far away as Sol was from Mars. But the colour seemed wrong. More orange.

A chart came up on the main vuscreen. Our position blinked in green.

"Where is Sol system?" I asked.

"Here." A marking showed in blue to the left of our position. "We have travelled the equivalent of fifteen light years."

"That can't be right."

"A statistically low outcome of a transit deep inside a gravity well," the ship concluded.

Statistically low but still possible. Though I wouldn't want to chance it again. But it had given me an advantage. The Hegemony pursuit ships would either suspect my ship had been destroyed, or they'd search the local tenspace corridors.

Then I remembered the Hegemony tracking device attached to the hull. "Scan the hull."

"Minor damage. Some scarring near the left engine port. Hull integrity optimal. All systems functioning."

"Can you pinpoint the Hegemony tracking device?"

"It is on the underside of the ship near the rear vent ports."

"Is there a moon nearby we can put down on?"

"The system has no planetary bodies."

It may already be too late, but I couldn't leave the transmitter in place.

"Where are the pressure suits?" I asked.

A hatch opened in the hall near the lock. Two suits hung inside. The first was custom-made for the ship's owner, the Chirrik who'd died on Maelstrom. I'd never fit that. But there was an emergency suit, designed to fit a wide range of body types. It was little more than a large clear sack, with a breather tank attached to the back and adjustable straps that would cinch the material in around head, claws and hoofs. I could use it if I kept my upper knees folded. The air supply showed full.

I pulled the suit on in the airlock. The less I had to walk in the thing the better. The breather activated as I fastened the main closure, and the suit's sensor node, just above my pectoral plate, chimed as it linked with the AI.

I took a tool pouch from the locker by the outer door and tied it round my waist. There was a safety reel on the other side of the door. It was awkward, but I managed to secure the end of the reel to a ring at the top of the breather.

The inner lock door closed. The suit inflated as the pressure dropped, but rigid sections and the strapping meant the inflation didn't impede my movement. The outer door opened on nothing. I stepped off the gravity plating of the deck, held onto the side of the lock door, and floated round until I was in contact with the hull.

From here I could see the weak sun, lonely and planetless. Not even a rock to keep it company. I thought of Atalna lying dead on Mars. Isza lying dead on Homeworld.

No time. I had to find the device. I had to live a little longer so I could remember those who had changed me. It was as good a reason as any.

I moved round awkwardly to the ship's underside. The surface was laced with conduit and component systems, so I was able to get a good grip. I knew the general location of the transmitter, but it would be hard to see among the cabling, pipework and ducting.

"Ship?" I said.

"Yes." The calm voice sounded inside the suit.

"Can you move the hull so the underside is illuminated by the sun? Gently so I'm not thrown off."

The ship vibrated slightly and what light there was out here spilled across the underside until the whole area glowed a warm orange.

"Tell me when I'm near the tracking device," I said. "I'm not sure I'd recognise a transmitter even if I was looking right at it."

The clear fabric of the suit was stretched around my lower knees. I'd have to rely more on my arms to move. I reached along the underside and gripped a hold, pulling myself along. It was hard without proper gloves. I knew I could reel myself in on the tether if I drifted off, but I couldn't afford to waste any time.

The air seemed to rasp loudly through my spiracles as I pulled myself along the hull, searching for something unusual. Was the breather running low?

I stopped close to the vents, moving my body so the suit sensor node pointed at the hull. There were some dark marks and scarring here. A deep bright score ran down alongside the exhaust.

"What is this?" I asked the ship.

"I recorded a plasma strike when we transited near Mars. This scarring is consistent with the energy I registered. It is surface damage only."

I started back along the hull, aiming the sensor node to sweep the centre line of the ship.

"Stop," the AI said.

I did, and looked at the hull immediately below me. There were a number of projections – fuel lines, part of the landing gear assembly, some cowling that was a little melted and blackened.

"The tracking device is beneath the cowling," the AI said. "Move the sensor node back so I can see."

I angled my body and reached my claws beneath the cowling to prise the thin metal up a little.

"That small circular projection at the base of the cowl, to the left."

I pointed at it. It was partially melted and covered in black scoring.

"Yes," the AI said.

I pulled at it and it came away, showing a bright patch of unbroken hull beneath it. It wasn't part of the ship, wasn't connected to anything else on the hull. I put it in the tool pouch drifting at my side and made sure it was secure.

"How much air do I have left?" It hadn't occurred to me before to simply ask the ship.

"You should return now," the AI said.

"Wait. Is there anything else that looks unusual?" I turned this way and that, trying to cover the whole area with the sensor node.

"No," the AI said.

"Well, keep looking as I come in. Stop me if you see anything."

I started forward again. And, startled by a high-pitched whine, almost lost my grip. It was the breather.

"Ship, how long until the breather ceases to function?"

"Five minutes."

I hoped it was long enough.

I reached for handhold after handhold, pulling forward as fast as my muscles and the suit would allow. It was almost my undoing. I reached the entry and grabbed the thin rim, but my body kept moving forward. My claws were wrenched from the ship and I tumbled as inertia carried me away.

My body jerked around and the strap pulled hard against my face as the safety line reeled to full extension. For an instant I thought it would snap or the suit would tear. But it held.

I reached behind my back, clumsily groping for the end of the line attached to the breather. The whine was rising in pitch. I got it and started pulling, my body spinning round until I was heading for the open hatch. And then I was through the outer door and slapping the closure mechanism.

Air hissed into the lock and I stood, spiracles rasping, until the suit collapsed around me as the air pressure equalised. I pulled at the main fastening and the breather alarm stopped. The silence was startling.

I left the suit in the lock and carried the tool sack with me into the flight deck. I rested on the couch for a moment, then brought the strange device out.

"Can you scan this?" I asked the AI.

"Yes. It's not part of the ship. High band transmission components. Inoperative."

"You're sure?"

"Yes. The transmitter is melted. The power supply has been breached. The damage is consistent with a tenspace plasma strike."

So the device had been destroyed escaping Mars. The Hegemony had no idea where I was. Maybe they thought I'd died in transit.

I'd managed to live while Atalna died, but I'd gained nothing from our visit to Mars. Everything we'd learned and experienced was part of some plan of Volmar's. Atalna's death was for nothing.

"I need to get back to the Lenticular," I said. "Can you plot a route? One that gets me there as quickly as possible?"

"Working," the AI said.

And when I got back to the Lenticular, what then? What could I do to defeat the all-powerful Hegemony that anticipated my every move, bent my actions to suit their goals?

"Course plotted," the AI said.

I climbed out of the couch and folded myself into the deepsleep cabinet. I could ask the ship how long the trip would take, but that would be meaningless. I could ask how safe it would be, but nothing was safe. If I got there, I got there. If I died along the way or the Hegemony found me, so be it.

"Wake me when we're approaching the Lenticular," I said and reached to activate the deepsleep field.

"A ship has dropped out of tenspace," the AI said.

So they'd found me anyway. There was no way to escape the Hegemony.

"Show me," I said.

An image appeared on the cabinet interior. It was a Jantri vessel, the gracefully sweeping curve of it unmistakeable. I was out of the cabinet and strapping into the crash-couch a moment later.

"Receiving a transmission," the AI said.

"Onscreen."

A golden-armoured head appeared, the faceplate dancing with light. Nok? Had he followed me all the way from Maelstrom?

"Are you ready to accept my help now?" he said.

Atalna had warned me not to trust the Jantri. But there was nothing left.

"I'm ready," I said.

The ship spun smoothly as it approached, the curved nacelles turning away from me and a section of the ovoid main body slipping aside.

"You'll have to stay in your ship, I'm afraid," Nok said. "This vessel isn't rated to accommodate non-Jantri."

"How did you find me?"

"It wasn't difficult."

The walls of the Jantri ship slid past me and closed over. The AI landed the ship on the deck and powered down the engines. I was in a large, empty bay, unremarkable except for the glowing atmosphere.

"Where are we going?"

"The Lenticular. There are some people I want you to meet."

The screen went blank.

I refused to feel hope. Too much had gone wrong. Too many had died. Atalna and Isza had both died because of me.

No, Atalna was down to Volmar. And he'd known the risks of engaging with the Hegemony better than me.

With nothing to do and no indication of how long the trip would take, I re-entered the stasis cabinet and a dreamless sleep.

I felt far from rested when the AI woke me.

"Another message," it said.

On the vuscreen, I was still in Nok's cargo hold. The Jantri appeared on a side screen.

"Our first rendezvous," he said. "I need to transfer your vessel to a larger ship. I'll meet you in person there and you'll be able to leave your own craft."

"How long have I been asleep?"

"Four days."

Which told me little. Atalna and I had travelled for two zero days from Maelstrom, but this ship would be much faster.

I sat in the pilot's chair as my own ship vibrated and lifted from the deck.

"I'll guide the transit," Nok said.

Perhaps it was safer this way, but it reminded me how powerless I was.

The hull opened onto a dimly lit tenspace chamber, like one of the many junctions we'd traversed on the way to Mars. A bolt of plasma struck for an instant far off and I could see movement closer in. Another ship. It disappeared in the darkness again.

Slowly I became aware of a deeper blackness moving towards

our position. But as navigation lights suddenly blazed on I realised I'd misjudged size and distance. It was another Jantri vessel, the same configuration as the one I'd travelled on but easily one-zero times the size.

My ship passed out of the hold, manoeuvring gently. Tenspace was quiescent; the only illumination was strobing guidelights coming from the other ship – for my benefit, I supposed, certainly not Nok's.

The hull opened and I saw that this hold was far from empty. Lines of small grey, elegant ships – curved like a physical expression of speed – were ranked across the full length of the bay. My ship glided above them, then changed course to descend to a gridded pad beside a wide bulkhead door that must lead into the rest of the ship.

As I touched down, the door opened and a Jantri stood waiting for me. Just who did Nok want me to meet? More Jantri? I felt some of that old fatigue settle on me; the feeling of hopelessness that made it hard to think. This time I didn't have Atalna to pull me out of it.

The Jantri still waited, so I opened the ship hatch and walked down the ramp to the deck.

"This will be more comfortable for the rest of your trip," the Jantri said.

I looked at it. Same armour. Same blankly glowing faceplate. "Nok?"

"Of course."

I wondered again why I was so important he'd follow me all this way.

"Come," he said.

I followed him down gently curving corridors until we arrived at another bulkhead door.

He turned to me. "I hope this will help."

The door swept open and I saw another Kresz. A youngling. Same body plan as me. Intact. We stared at each other, both doubting the evidence of our eyes.

Before I could speak, he turned and shouted, "Agik!"

Through the doorway was a large partitioned room. I could see other Kresz sitting or standing. All now looking my way.

There was a blur to my left and I was almost knocked off my hoofs.

Strong arms enfolded me and I heard her voice. "Udun. You're alive! Are you all right?"

I couldn't sense her without my mantle, but I could touch her, smell her, hear her ragged breath. She was Isza. She was alive.

20

The Vault, Novy St Petersburg, Earth / Sol System / Hegemony

It was impossible to tell exactly where the sterile white meeting cube was located beneath Novy St Petersberg. Denev and Volmar had landed at the spaceport along the coast at Vyborg and entered the bunker tunnels through the same hypertube. But the concentration of power in the room was at odds with the dank surroundings outside.

Volmar obliged with the introductions although for the most part they were completely unnecessary; a callback to a more mannered age where political assassins and the upper echelons of society rarely mixed. Or if they did it was only briefly and with catastrophic results.

Rejak was first, greeting Denev warmly as if they'd met more than just once. He stepped back after shaking his hand and Volmar turned to indicate two men dressed in Fleet uniforms ascetically devoid of medals or rank insignia.

Vargas was instantly recognisable but he was accompanied by another man Denev didn't know.

"Fleet Admiral Vargas, Chair of the Joint Chiefs of the combined Hegemony Defences Forces," Volmar said. "Admiral Vargas, my assistant Denev Antwer."

Denev extended his hand to Vargas, who was completely bald with a hawklike nose and sunken eyes, and the older man took it in a firm grasp.

"And this is my adjutant," Vargas said, his head inclining towards his companion.

Both men exuded quiet strength and authority but where Vargas was shorter than Denev – but broad and muscular – his adjutant was a bear of a man, a head taller and with a craggy face, ruddy complexioned with thinning red hair and a bushy moustache.

"Fleet Admiral Gart Lowrans," Vargas finished.

Denev looked more closely at the man as they shook hands. Of course Volmar had known he'd be present. Was he testing Denev again?

"Admiral," Denev said," I served with your daughter for a short time. I'm sorry for your loss."

Lowrans remained stony-faced, but frown lines bunched between his eyes.

"Thank-you," Lowrans said. "Life was difficult for her since her mother died. I have to believe she's gone to a better place."

His voice was heavily accented. Scottish Denev thought and realised there had been echoes of that in the way Rhees sounded some vowels.

"I heard about your brother too," Lowrans continued. "I met him once. He struck me as a fine young man."

Denev was surprised by this, but it made sense Lowrans knew his name. His brother would have figured heavily in Rhees's trial after Petar was killed. But he'd had no idea Lowrans and Petar had met.

"And Antonus Breslaw, the Permanent Head of the Central Administration," Volmar said, reclaiming Denev's attention.

Breslaw took Denev's hand in as firm a grip as Vargas, but the skin of his hands was rough and weathered. He was a strong man, with an air of friendly confidence that seemed the hallmark of the truly powerful. He also had the eyes of a killer. Denev had seen that look many times and he had no trouble recognising it now.

"Let's convene," Breslaw said, sitting at the table before acknowledging the only other person in the room. "We thank Undersecretary Laneaux for joining us in this special meeting of the Executive.

Laneaux nodded to Breslaw and looked round the table as the others took their seats. Denev again sat on a spare chair by the door. Volmar said she wanted his job, perhaps that was why Denev thought he saw a certain satisfaction in Laneaux at being invited to join a meeting of – what was this exactly? It wasn't a meeting of the full Executive or even the Inner Cabinet. But all of the people connected with his parents' sealed file were here.

"I understand Representative Minch is no longer a problem," Breslaw said.

"I think it's safe to say he won't be winning any more elections," Volmar added.

Rejak chuckled but Breslaw merely smiled.

"His supposed alien assassin is still at large," Laneaux said.

It was clear from the way she said the words she had a good idea of what had really happened on Mars, despite Volmar's subterfuge. But she had no proof. Denev was sure, however, that the others around the table knew exactly how Minch had died.

"We've found no debris from the ship after its jump, either in Mars orbit or corresponding Voss Space," she said. "It would have been far better if this alien had been captured at the scene or killed."

"An alien murderer on the run is better optics. It gives the public something to fear and plays against the Inclusionist message," Volmar said.

"Optics?" Laneaux said, her voice rising. "The optics are incredibly bad. But I'm talking about the safety of Sol system. It seems to me HDC does not share our security concerns, and this is not the only example."

"Look, Laneaux, you were –" Rejak began, but Breslaw's voice cut across him.

"No. Let her go on."

Laneaux leaned forward, eager now. She wanted Volmar ousted, this was the place to make her play.

"I'm talking about the deal you made with the Maagba raiders out in Brell space. That agreement was a unilateral action made without proper consultation. SolSec should have been involved and, more importantly, so should the Combined Hegemony Forces." She looked pointedly at Vargas who remained stony faced.

But from his vantage point, Denev noticed Lowrans frowned for an instant. What was going on here?

Denev didn't know the others around the table, except by reputation, but he knew Volmar. The worse things got, the quieter he became, and he was now almost preternaturally still. But even so, the dynamic in the room seemed off. Denev had been with Volmar during the Maagba mission and the Comptroller had sailed very close to the wind. Laneaux had a point, but the feeling in the room was more embarrassment at one of their number being caught out than any real feeling of censure.

The Undersecretary was winding up for another volley but Breslaw held up one hand, stopping her in her tracks.

"We hear your criticism," he said. "Troels."

Volmar turned slowly to regard the Permanent Head. If Breslaw was expecting Volmar to mount a defence he was disappointed. Volmar said nothing.

"I know how much of yourself you put into defending the Hegemony," Breslaw said. "Sometimes it's hard to keep sight of all the moving parts when you are focused on such vital outcomes for all of us." He looked at the table for a moment, pursing his full lips. "This can't happen again," he said finally.

The silence across the table lengthened until Volmar said, "Of course."

Rejak rallied to move the meeting forward past the embarrassing interchange. "The question –" he began, but Volmar interrupted him.

"The question is what we do now to finish off the Inclusionists. Minch's seat will most likely go to the Centralists. There's no time for a replacement candidate to gain significant traction." He regarded Laneaux with half-lidded eyes. "For the sake of inter-service cooperation, I admit we had a hand in Minch's death. Our actions may have been ... outside standard protocols, but they've sown the seeds for the Inclusionists' destruction."

"How so, Troels?" Rejak asked.

Laneaux was staring at the table, the red nail of her right index finger deepening a long score in the surface. Denev thought she had the air of someone who had finally realised the club she aspired to was permanently closed to her. Twice now she'd sought to damage Volmar – through Minch at the Security Review Subcommittee meeting and now here. What should have opened up a frank discussion of Volmar's faults had elicited no more than a faint slap on the wrist. Most groups of powerful people jockeyed for relative status, using any transitory weakness in another member to gain advantage. But not this group. Something they shared meant more than any internal politicking. And as as result, key decisions were being made without her.

His attention snapped back to the meeting when he heard his name.

"It was having Antwer with me on Mars that made me think of it," Volmar said. "The Inclusionists are smart enough to know Minch didn't die because of some random alien attack, but they have no proof. Many of them will be angry and with the right push, we can make them use that anger publicly. That's the way they'll lose popular support for their party."

Laneaux stopped scraping the table and made a fist. "You're talking about radicalisation."

"The Inclusionists become a terrorist organisation," Volmar said. "One act – carefully managed – and no matter how much their leaders decry it as the work of outlier factions their brand will be irrevocably damaged. There's an immediate and broad-based public safety investigation by SolSec and their licence is suspended. They'll be tied up in inquiries for years."

"Death by a thousand cuts," Breslaw said.

"And where does Antwer come into all this?" Laneaux asked.

The ghost of a smile cantilevered Volmar's lips open a fraction.

"Antwer here is a very accomplished undercover operative. He's worked on dozens of worlds. But more importantly, he's completely unknown on Earth."

"This is clearly a SolSec matter," Laneaux said, bristling again.

But it was obvious to Denev, even before Breslaw cleared his throat that she knew this was another argument she could not win.

"It's broader than SolSec," Breslaw said. "The political aspect puts it squarely within HDC purview. So, a joint mission under the aegis of the Security and Defence Secretariat."

Rejak smiled and nodded.

Breslaw turned to Denev and considered him for a moment that seemed to stretch to infinity. His eyes were deep watery pools, but lifeless and cold as space. "Your father was very good in difficult situations," he said. "The apple does not fall far from the tree." He turned back to Volmar. "You have a green light, Troels. Let's call it a day."

Laneaux clearly wanted to say more, but she also knew when to cut her losses.

Volmar leaned towards Denev as the others stood. "You'll start on this immediately, Antwer. Your current duties will be reassigned. We need a target and a plan by the end of the week."

Denev nodded, watching the others as they filed out of the room. He'd accused Rhees of talking like an Inclusionist on Herakli. She'd be shocked to find out they were a creation of the Hegemony. It seemed there was no real opposition to the Central Administration. On Earth at least. By helping to sweep the Inclusionists out of the way, he'd reaffirm his loyalty to HDC. But for what? What was his endgame? He was powerless on his own and still no clearer on how his parents died. The only thing he could do was to keep digging around the edges of the data. Track forward and backwards and focus on the movements of the four men who had shared something so fundamental it had brought them together and kept them together for over twenty years. He had to hope that something would shake loose.

The room was empty when Volmar said, "We share none of this with SolSec, of course."

Of course. Enemies were countless when you were Troels Volmar and even colleagues were held in suspicion. How long would it be until Volmar saw Denev as "problematic"? At least Rhees was alive and far from his grasp. Helping her was the best thing he could do right now. But first, he had to give Volmar an Inclusionist target that would bring the whole party down.

21

Slowly Isza released me. I felt her claws brush the edge of my mantle stump. "They did this to you," she said.

I pulled away to look at her. There was a long scorch mark down her left side just below the upper torso plate. The chitin was rough and pitted along the edge, and near the middle was a lighter-coloured jagged star shape.

"I thought you'd been killed," I said. "How –"

"Not here." Isza glanced behind her and I saw we were the centre of attention.

Maybe two-zero Kresz stood watching us: Cultivators, Adepts, Priests, Merchants; house colours of red, white, blue and brown visible.

Isza's hood trembled across her shoulders as if it meant to rise, then hung at rest again. "Let's find somewhere quieter," she said.

Nok was still standing in the doorway. "I'll leave you to get reacquainted with your people," he said and left.

A tall Adept, chitin a deep burnished brown, stepped forward. He held a gaszti by his side. "He is outcast," he told Isza. "He can't be here."

"This is my brother, Udlade," Isza said, her voice low and dangerous. "He belongs with us."

Another Kresz – Cultivator caste – stepped forward and placed a claw on Udlade's lower arm. "It will be as Isza says."

Udlade turned in disgust and walked away.

"Come," Isza said, and led me to a partitioned space hard up against the curved bulkhead. A thin sleeping mat lay rolled on the deck. We sat together on it.

The tension I'd been holding inside for so long fell away. I still couldn't believe it. Since the last time I saw her my life had been full of death and fear and running. Now, even with so much still uncertain, I didn't think I'd ever felt such happiness.

"I'm glad you weren't killed," I said.

I heard her familiar rattling laugh. "I'm glad you weren't killed too." Then her voice tightened. "So many were. Or worse, like ..."

"Like me," I finished. "My mantle's gone – there's no point worrying about it. I'm still me. I feel the same."

"A lot of them weren't as strong as you," she said. "We saw the suicides."

"I know. I tried it myself. I wanted to die. I just couldn't." It wasn't something I wanted to talk about. Instead I asked, "How did you get away? Get here?"

She stared at the deck for a moment, picking through memories. "When I was shot on the steps ... I don't know. I must have been left for dead. I came to surrounded by bodies. I didn't know how long I'd been out. There was still fighting, but it had moved on. I couldn't walk. I still thought I was going to die. It was pure luck Agik found me."

"Agik?"

"The Cultivator who told Udlade to back off. House Ukat. He carried me away from the Mount. I kept passing out, but each time I woke he was there, carrying me, talking to me, telling me to hang on. If not for him ..."

"I need to thank him," I said. "If he'll talk to an excisee."

"They're not all like Udlade." She blinked. "But I'm telling you my great story of escape. Aren't you enthralled?"

"Sorry." My feeders folded in a smile. "Go on."

"Out near the outskirts of Aktiuk, Agik met some of his co-workers with a ground car and persuaded them to make room for us. It was night by then and I slept. They didn't expect me to live through till morning. I'm sure some would have left me by the side of the road, but Agik wouldn't let them. Dawn came and I was still alive. I was even able to sit up.

"We were in the foothills to the east of Aktiuk, just coming out of the tree line. There was a ship in a steep-sided canyon – with the sun so low, we didn't see it until we were right on top of it. It was a tekla freighter. One of Kergis's. But no crew. It was only when we got closer that we saw the mine. There'd been a collapse – the entrance was completely blocked. The crew must have been inside with the miners when it happened.

"Maybe I was delirious, but I told the others I could fly them all out. And they believed me. I guess they were desperate. They carried me into the ship and strapped me into the flight seat. I couldn't feel my left leg. I was worried the rusz flow to my leg had been cut off for good and it was dead. So Agik became my co-pilot. I could feel how terrified he was, but he did what I told him.

"We reached orbit without trouble. I suppose the Kergis transponder helped. And the traffic round the Hub was in chaos. No one had time to query an ore freighter. We just flew away. But we didn't know where to go, and we couldn't stay on the ship forever. We made it to Svestan space and hid out on a moon. It was riddled with mine workings, but Agik found a place with water. We even started cultivating the local fungus to supplement the supplies we had left. But at best we were looking at a slow lingering death from malnutrition. Then the Jantri turned up. They offered us sanctuary. Some of us didn't want to go. You know what we're like. But Agik agreed with me. There was no other choice."

"The Jantri again," I said. "I don't understand why they're doing all this. Helping but not *helping*."

Isza twined her claws in mine. "They're aliens. We can't know what they want. I'm grateful they saved us, but I don't trust them."

I looked at her, remembering the last time we were together. "What happened to the pupa you carried?"

"Czerag's hierarch? I was too injured in the fight. It was

reabsorbed."

"I'm sorry," I said. I knew it wasn't the first pupa she'd lost.

"I'm not. This is no world to bring a youngling into."

"What about Gurud?" Isza's mate had been caught up in a kind of battle madness with the other Defenders gathered on Treaty Mount.

"You saw what he was like when the Hegemony soldiers arrived. There's no way he would have allowed himself to be captured. And there was certainly no escape."

The youngling I'd seen first appeared by the partition. "Agik asks if you will eat with us."

"This is Sahi," Isza said.

"Hello," I said, but he just stared at me. It must have been strange for him, communicating without empathic sense.

We followed him into the main open area. The rest of the Kresz were sitting on the floor, passing round ration packs from an open pod.

Udlade stood as we approached. "I will not eat with him. He is outcast."

"Look where we are," Isza said, her voice rising. "We are all outcast. And Udun is not a criminal. The Hegemony – our enemy – did that to him. Everything has changed. And we need to change too if we're to survive."

She was right of course. I wanted to live, but I wanted my people to accept me even more. Me and the others the Hegemony had mutilated. Families and houses had been torn apart, divided into the war-excised and those who – on some whim – had been spared. We had to abandon our deep prejudice against imperfection.

"That is not the way –" Udlade began.

Agik cut across him. "Be quiet. We wouldn't be here if it wasn't for Isza. We'll respect her wishes." He looked at me, and even though I had no empathic abilities now, I could see no trace of revulsion, hatred or even pity. "Join us, please," he said.

"Thank you."

We sat, and Agik handed Isza and me a ration pod each. It split open and was instantly hot with the smell of potla – a popular spiced dish made with fungus. The Jantri had brought Kresz rations. What were they planning? Isza didn't trust them and neither did I.

Udlade moved away as soon as he was served, but the others stayed, watching me over their bowls. Strangely – but perhaps not so – it felt good to be among them. I could almost imagine we were home.

Now I had time to look properly I saw there were two-one in the group.

"Is this all that came with you?" I asked Isza.

"All that escaped. So," she added around a mouthful of fungus, "you know what I've been doing up to now. Where have you been since …" She hesitated. I guessed she was going to say "since your excision" but instead she finished with, "the battle".

I could see what she was doing. She wanted me to tell the others my story. To become Udun the fellow refugee, not some unknown excisee. It was a good plan.

"Across the galaxy and back," I said, and told them as much as I could about what I'd done or failed to do. Ultimately it was a tale of missed chances and personal tragedies, finishing with Atalna's murder. But Isza didn't see it that way. All through her attention was divided between me and the others sitting around us. No doubt she sensed their emotional reaction, the effect my words were having. When I'd finished, she put her mark on their opinion, to guide them to the conclusion she wanted them to make about me.

"You've done things I wouldn't have thought possible," she said. "Even for an intact. No Kresz here has even contemplated what you tried to do for us. I can't see that as a failure. You've learned so much."

"But achieved so little." I couldn't lie, even to make others like me.

"Now you're here we can use what you've learned. It will help us," she said. "I don't know how yet, but it will."

"There was a point, I think, where every one of us was sure we were going to die," Agik said. "We've certainly seen enough of death. We've had to struggle every step of the way. But we're safe now. No matter how strange the surroundings. If we never see Homeworld again that will be a sad thing, but we will go on. We have each other and that can be enough."

Agik was an optimist. No doubt that had sustained the group, but I wanted more than survival. I wanted to sweep the Hegemony from Homeworld. I wanted to see Kergis broken. Revenge was a powerful survival trait too, although perhaps not as sustaining. Especially when you didn't know how to achieve it.

Agik cracked another ration pod, dug a claw into the steaming broth and said, "Tell us more about this Hegemony world you visited."

"Mars?"

"Yes, Mars. Tell us about it."

So I did. It was a strange sight: an excisee talking to a group of intact who sat listening politely. Even Udlade stayed within earshot. But they listened like younglings, not like warriors. There was no strategic analysis of what I'd seen and what it might tell us about how Hegemony society was organised, what its strengths were, its potential weaknesses. They were farmers and technicians. What else could I reasonably expect?

22

After the meal, a female Adept in a dirty robe collected the pods. The others moved singly or in twos or threes to different partitioned areas until it was just me and Isza alone on the deck.

"Remember that night you came home?" she said.

"The night Reka attacked the female."

"Yes." She looked at me reproachfully. "But I wasn't thinking about that. I was thinking about how good it felt to be together again. I missed that. Nothing felt right when I thought you were dead. It feels right now."

I almost asked her how anything could feel right buried on an alien ship so far from Homeworld. I was glad she could no longer read my emotions. When did I get so cynical?

I reached out and held her claws. I could never lie to her. "I'm glad you're not dead, Isza. But I want more. I don't think I can settle for simple survival."

I thought she'd draw away from me, hurt. But she squeezed my claws tightly and her feeder mandibles spread apart. "Good. Now I know you haven't changed."

I looked down, not wanting to meet her eyes. "I thought maybe *you* had."

"Living with Agik and the others?" Her feeders stretched wide. "They're good at surviving but … It's like the fight's been knocked out of them. They're traumatised, I suppose. And, realistically, what can they do? Two-one Kresz, no Defender caste among them, who stole an antiquated freighter with no weapons and lived on a subsistence diet until the Jantri came for us. We're not much of an attack force."

I had to agree.

"But that doesn't mean we should stop thinking, stop planning against our enemies," she added. "Somehow there must be a way. We'll find it. Together."

"Together," I said. "No matter how long it takes."

The hold was quiet and empty now, and I became aware of the ship's own sound. An almost inaudible rushing noise, like water passing through a channel.

Isza helped me up. "It's quite peaceful here when you get used to it. The ship's noise lulls me to sleep, gives me something to focus on outside myself. And then next thing I know it's time to wake."

I followed her back to her partition near the bulkhead, no need for further words. She pulled the thin mattress from the corner and we lay down side by side. Despite my time in the sleep cabinet, I was tired. Deepsleep wasn't real rest. It was a simple off switch.

"Sleep well, Isza," I said, touching her delicate feeders.

She did the same. "I will."

In the entire time I had been away from Homeworld, I hadn't dreamt once. But that night I did. Maybe, even without my hood, there was something about being physically close to other Kresz, to some portion of the worldmind, no matter how diminished.

The wide rolling dunes of the deep desert lay before me, startlingly bright. The sky shimmered bronze beneath djel, ataz and sura, and a dry hot wind coursed over the lip of the escarpment, strong enough to be a constant pressure pushing me back from the edge.

Tzek was beside me, the folds of his robes flowing behind him, revealing the deeply incised swirls patterning his shell. Curves lay within curves, lines crossed lines, hidden labyrinths, channels, networks, shapes that looked like one thing but revealed an entirely different shape with a shift in perspective. Shapes that had been there all along if only I knew how to see them.

Tzek was talking to me. But I couldn't hear him above the wind. I told him so but maybe he couldn't hear me either.

I watched the patterns again, then looked out into the desert. The suns were setting. The sand looked like burnished metal.

Darkness fell and the wind dropped and I heard Tzek's voice at last. "We will go to the deep desert. The hides have been prepared."

I turned quickly, but he was gone. I was alone on top of the escarpment beneath a starless sky.

∞

When I woke the room was so dark I couldn't see a thing, only hear the breath in Isza's spiracles beside me. My inner eyelid slid across and I saw the smooth ceiling in muted shades of grey.

"Isza," I said quietly. She stirred, but not enough. "Isza," I said again and felt for the exposed skin below her skull cap.

She turned over to face me. "Udun," she said sleepily. "You're still here. Good."

She was quiet again and I thought she'd fallen back asleep. But then her eyes blinked open, the inner eyelid sliding across. "I had a dream about you," she said. Her throat was dry and she swallowed. "We were together with Tzek on top of the escarpment. Watching the suns go down. You were talking but I couldn't hear you."

"Really?" Shared dreaming was common, especially when sharing a bed, but without my hood I didn't think it could still happen. "I was on the escarpment in my dream. Tzek was there but you weren't."

Isza got up onto one elbow. "Maybe that means something of your empathic link survives, even if not at a conscious level."

"Perhaps."

"Let's see," she said. "Sit up."

She sat opposite me on the mat and took my claws in hers. She closed her eyes, but I kept mine open, taking the opportunity to really look at her. To see the changes in her face since we'd last been together. There was a small puckered scar above her left eye that hadn't been there before.

Isza's mantle rose, curving around and over the back of her head. I felt the muscles beneath my shoulder plates respond, pathetically trying to lift a ghost mantle.

"Anything?" I asked her.

"No. You?"

"Nothing."

She opened her eyes as her hood softened and relaxed onto her shoulders. "Still. Shared dreams," she said, not wanting to give up easily.

"Potentially shared dreams. Do you remember anything else from it?"

"No. Just the suns setting."

"Tzek was in my dream – he talked about the hides in the deep desert. And I remembered that last day, the evacuation of the house. Do you think some of them could have survived in the hides? Might even still be living there undetected?"

"It's been a long time," Isza said.

"But they were well-provisioned. And it would have been safer in the desert than in Aktiuk."

"It's possible. But if so, so what? We're here and they're there."

"But we're not alone. And perhaps neither are they." The feeling I'd had when Tzek spoke in the dream was still with me. I was sure it was important.

"I don't know what you mean," Isza said.

"The others here – how many houses are they from?"

"Well, Agik is House Ukat. So are Elra, Dakiut and Udir. Sahi, Czigrisz and Dikrah are House Dageru. And Elartu, Idhala and Bvakti are House Czerag, though I didn't know them before I got here. Did you?"

"No."

"Your friend Udlade, Azigur and Kale are all House Akczek."

"I thought Akczek was with House Kergis," I said.

"Not any more. When the fighting started it was only Kergis

Kresz that were safe. Most of the Akczek buildings in Aktiuk were destroyed in the first attack wave."

"Interesting," I said. "Akczek had strong ties with the Defenders Lodge and the Merchants Lodge. Maybe Kergis saw them as competition and took the opportunity to weaken Akczek as part of the attack."

Isza blinked. "It makes sense for that power-hungry czidak. We monitored the Lenticular feed as best we could from the freighter. Not that there was much from Homeworld. But last we heard, Kergis had been named Rector or some such thing. Supreme leader basically. His dreams of power must be complete."

"What about House Haketiug?" I asked. Haketiug had always been Kergis's lackey.

"That hasn't changed. Haketiug's so weak it's likely they'd all be absorbed into House Kergis and no one would notice the difference."

"Is that all that Kergis wants?" I said. "Supreme power over all Kresz? It doesn't seem enough to sell out your entire planet."

"Not to you. But you're not a megalomaniac."

"I suppose."

"You're not, are you?" Her feeders rattled.

It was a bad joke, but it felt so normal I couldn't help opening my mandibles wide. "What I was driving at is we have people from House Akczek, Ukat, Dageru and Czerag."

"I still don't —"

"All those hierachs had contingency plans. Hides, just like us."

"It goes with the normal paranoia," she conceded.

"So there may be caches of survivors dotted over the planet, well-provisioned and possibly armed."

"So?" she said again.

"We talk to the others. Find out what they know about their hide locations. How they were used. How many of their house might have made it there."

"House Czerag were preparing for trouble with Kergis," Isza

said. Czerag's trade war seemed so long ago now. "That's why our hides were prepped and our people were ready. The other houses wouldn't have had that kind of headstart. And even if a few of the hides were activated, what does it get us?"

"Knowledge of a potential force that's still free and inside enemy territory. It's a start, Isza. You don't want to squat here the rest of your life, and neither do I. A full-blown plan to restore Homeworld isn't going to land in our laps. That's a certainty. So we have to be smart and think about all the possible things that can help or hinder us. That's the only way a plan will come together. Once we see something that Kergis hasn't already exploited, we gain an advantage."

Isza sat back. "You've thought a lot about this, breach-brother."

The thing was, I hadn't. I was working on intuition and dreams. Still, it was the way Atalna had operated. He'd worked with what he had and used whatever he could.

"So let's start acting," I said, rising.

∞

The ambient light had increased while we talked, and the others were at their morning meal. When I said good morning, my greeting was returned by some. Not Udlade of course, but it was a start.

We ate, and afterwards Isza asked Agik if we could speak to him alone.

"Hides?" Agik said after I'd explained things.

"Yes. Do you know if Hierarch Ukat had any?"

"Well, it's not something spoken of with …" He hesitated, looked at Isza. "Outsiders," he finished.

Perhaps he was going to say excisees. Or perhaps I was being overly sensitive.

"That time's past, Agik," Isza said. "It's time to share our secrets."

"You know our lands across the southern shore of the Inland Sea?" he said.

"Not really," I said.

"Our house and outlying homes are built around the forests that follow the shoreline. I could see those trees burning from Aktiuk. The whole arc of the sea covered in flame and thick smoke. Nothing could have survived that."

Isza closed her eyes. I could tell she was experiencing some of Agik's remembered distress.

"You don't know that," I said. "Some might have got away. Where would they go?"

"Beyond the tree line. There's marshland there, where the sea drains and eventually becomes the Resiut River past the marsh. The river cuts a course through the hills further south, making a steep, curving ravine. There are some hides there, cut into the soft rock and covered from aerial view. There are others, but where they are I couldn't say."

"Were they provisioned?" Isza asked.

"Always. Though they hadn't been used for cycles. Maybe not since the last House Wars. But we're creatures of tradition, as you well know. Look, why do you need this information? What are you planning?"

Isza placed a claw on his lower forearm and Agik calmed a little. "We don't know. Maybe nothing."

The story was repeated with the others from Agik's house. Udir and Dakiut described the same hides as Agik, but Elra had once visited a different site beyond the hills in caves carved by an underground river.

With all of us congregated in a shared space, there was no privacy. By the time we spoke to Sahi, Czigrisz and Dikrah of House Dageru we didn't need to explain and they shared what they knew readily enough. Besides, I could tell that they liked Isza, deferring to her whenever she spoke and calling her "daha" which meant "to fly high". Between them, they knew of two-four sites. None knew if they'd been occupied when the attack came, but Dageru lands extended round much of the south polar latitudes, far removed from the main focus of the fighting, so there should have been time to evacuate.

I wasn't sure how we'd approach Udlade and the other two House Akczek Kresz. They were huddled together near the door, talking in whispers.

In the centre of the room, Agik was sorting through one of the podules the Jantri had provided. He followed my gaze towards Udlade, and came over. "Udlade isn't so bad when you get to know him." He spoke quietly, careful that his voice didn't carry.

"I don't think I'll get the opportunity," I said. "It's clear I'm not the kind of person Udlade wants to associate with."

Agik blinked. "It's difficult for some of —" He paused. His short feeders pattered together. "I was going to say 'them' but really I mean 'us'. I'm no different. It's strange talking to someone who looks Kresz but doesn't feel Kresz." He glanced at Isza. "I'm sorry."

"Just think of me as an alien," I said.

"That doesn't help. You don't look like one. But it's not your problem. It's ours – mine. It's a sub-rational reaction, something we can alter if we put our minds to it."

"Thanks," I said. I knew he was being sincere, but I was sure others – here or on Homeworld – would never be as enlightened.

"You want the same information from Udlade as you got from me?" Agik asked, shaking me out of my thoughts.

"Will you help?" Isza said.

Even without my mantle, I could feel the tension between Isza and the Cultivator.

"Yes," he said, "but I'm not sure I like where this is going."

"You care for us all," Isza said. "I understand that. We wouldn't have lasted in that cave if it wasn't for you. I wouldn't have lived if you hadn't found me. We're not going to do anything that puts the group in danger."

Agik stared at her, then blinked. "Not yet, anyway."

"We'll talk to the Czerag people," I said. "Thanks."

The three other survivors from House Czerag were lying

together on mats in a partitioned area against the far wall and directly opposite the door. Even with everything they'd been through, all stayed within their house groupings, only – it seemed – coming together for meals. I supposed I couldn't criticise them for wanting to cling to some kind of normality in all this strangeness. But, like Udlade's reaction, this was another facet of Kresz life that would have to change if we were ever going to get our world back.

One of the Czerag Kresz was carving a piece of white plastic with a gaszti, slicing thick white curls from it in long sweeps. The carving was already recognisable as a stylised luk'ah fish.

"How's the artwork coming along, Elartu?" Isza asked.

Elartu looked from Isza to me. His expression was hard to interpret, but I didn't think it was unfriendly. "Good enough," he said. "It passes the time."

He was an Adept from the incised markings across his chest plates. Looking at those patterns, the image of Tzek from my dream flashed into my mind.

Idhala – Cultivator caste with the beaded headband of a fisherman – sat up, making room on the mats for us. Isza sat, but as I squatted beside her, Bvakti, the Priest, got up and walked away. Something like me wasn't part of Sakat's plan.

Slowly, Elartu's and Idhala's stories came out, telling how they'd survived. Isza had heard them before, so really, even though both of them mainly addressed Isza, it was me – the excisee – they were telling their stories to. They'd both been in Aktiuk when the attack hit, and they'd both run, heading east to get out of the city. Idhala had used one of the lodge ground transports, picking up Elra and Udir on the way. But they'd crashed near the Academy and been forced to walk, first meeting Elartu and Bvakti and then joining up with Agik's group.

"I wasn't at all sure we should leave Homeworld," Elartu said. He was old, older than Tzek, his shell thick and almost entirely black. "It felt like a betrayal."

Idhala shifted uneasily. I could tell this was a conversation they'd had before.

"Most of those who stayed ended up like me," I said. "Or killed themselves. The spikes in Cz'kras Park were full of the newly excised."

"There was no way we could have got to the house lands," Idhala said. "We'd have been captured like Udun."

"But others must have," I said.

"The hides were already in use," Isza added. "As soon as Czerag's trade fleet took off."

"Anyone trapped in the city would have tried to make it to the deep desert," Elartu said.

"That's our thinking," Isza said. "There may be House Czerag Kresz – maybe quite a lot of them – out in the hides. Unable to move about while Kergis and the Hegemony hold power."

"We're building up a picture of where they might be," I said. "Them and Kresz from other houses that escaped the occupation."

I thought they'd ask why, which would reveal our lack of any solid plan. But perhaps they sensed something from Isza and chose not to. Or perhaps they were just relieved to have something to think and talk about during long days with nothing much to do.

We spoke about the caches and hides each of them knew about. Isza and I had heard of most of them, but there were some we hadn't known about or had forgotten. Elartu promised to corner Bvakti later to add to our store of knowledge.

We broke for dinner, and afterwards Agik joined Isza and me in our partitioned space to share what we'd learned.

Isza had found some parchment-like material and a stylus in one of the podules. She smoothed it out on the deck, then sketched the globe of Homeworld in two circles side by side. In the middle of the left circle she drew the gently curving diamond-shaped shoreline of the Inland Sea, with Aktiuk on the eastern shore and the marshlands and the Resiut River to the south. To the north-east was the escarpment and House Czerag, gateway to the deep desert. North and west, above the equatorial jungle that bisected the planet, were a range of hills that rose and rose to the stepped plains of House Akczek, all the way to the glacier-crossed pole. Below the jungle and to the east lay the rich arable lands belonging to House Haketiug, giving way finally to the rock-strewn south polar reaches of Dageru.

I took the stylus and marked the Czerag hides Isza and I knew about. Some in the tail of the escarpment; others forming an uneven line with one tip out from the eastern edge of the escarpment; and the rest sloping directly away from a line parallel to the shoreline of the Inland Sea far to the south.

"There's the tekla mines too," Isza said. "A lot of heavy machinery there, but probably under Hegemony guard now. Kergis wouldn't let a resource like that go to waste."

I placed a mark where the mines were.

"How did you go with Udlade?" I asked Agik.

"Slowly at first. He isn't given to sharing house information."

"None of us are," Isza said.

"There's a network of outposts through the hills below the plains to the west. One near the top of almost every rise. The plains themselves are too bare and flat for anything, but there's a series of deep ravines closer to the pole." Agik drew thick furrows near the top of the circle on the right. "Udlade described the pattern. Two sets of claws spread, one set pointing south, the other laid on top pointing to your escarpment." He pointed at the first and third "claw" of the set pointing south. "These ravines have hidden entrances near the tips which lead to underground caves. Big ones, Udlade says. And on the third claw of the other set, at the middle, is another bigger cave system." Agik marked the positions.

I added the Ukat hideaways, dotted among the foothills that rose up from the marshland heading south.

"Then there's the Dageru locations," Isza said. She marked them on the southern sections of the maps as best she could tell. "It's not accurate. But with the terrain and location descriptions, it's close enough. We'd be able to find them on the ground."

"Except landing on Homeworld would be insane if it wasn't impossible," Agik said.

Isza tapped her thigh plate with one claw. "Not impossible for a small ship. Even with whatever tech the Hegemony has, that's a lot of territory to monitor."

"You said you wouldn't endanger the group," Agik reminded her.

"I won't. But there's nothing to stop me and Udun taking a ship."

"That takes care of the impossible part," I said. "How insane are you feeling, Isza?"

The pleasure I took from the warmth in her eyes was diminished only slightly by the fact I couldn't sense the feeling in her.

Agik clearly could. "I don't want *you* endangered either."

She looked at him and I could only guess the emotions passing between them. He cared for her. Perhaps she cared for him. But that wouldn't stop her helping me.

"Assuming we get there, escape detection and make contact with these free Kresz," Isza said, gesturing at our map. "And assuming there are free Kresz to be contacted, what's the plan?"

"I thought we'd work that out along the way," I said.

"So when do we leave?"

"You're not serious," Agik said.

"I don't plan to hide on this ship for the rest of my life," Isza said.

"Is that what I'm doing? Hiding? I thought we were escaping –"

Isza cut him off. "There's no escaping this."

Agik stood. "I have to sleep. I'll see you in the morning."

"I don't need a hood to know he has feelings for you, Isza," I said after he'd left. "Feelings you may have bruised a little."

"I'll talk to him," she said, getting up.

Alone, I stretched out on the deck to look at our map. Going back to Homeworld *was* insane. The Hegemony soldiers were dangerous, but the House Kergis Kresz and those intact aligned to them were more dangerous because of their empathic ability. They wouldn't pick up anything from me, but Isza would need to be careful. And if we found and recruited others in sufficient numbers, the chances of being discovered would multiply.

That's where the hides would make a difference. They were empathically shielded; they had to be to avoid discovery. If we could make contact with enough of them, our plans could still remain secret. I just couldn't be sure what was possible until we knew how many of those hides were being used.

Isza came back round the partition.

"Everything all right?" I asked.

"He's fine," Isza said and her small feeders rattled. "We've never really talked about … his feelings for me. Then you arrive and he sees how close we are. He feels threatened, and scared for what you're getting me into."

She wasn't accusing me, but she wasn't dismissing how he felt either.

"How do you feel about him?" I asked.

"I'm interested. But now isn't the time. My brother's leading me into certain death."

"Almost certain," I corrected.

I rolled out the sleeping mat while Isza folded the map and stood it against the wall. We lay down side by side.

"That's a good map," I said.

"One of the benefits of studying navigation," she said.

The ambient light was dimming and I turned on my side. Isza turned too, her lower knee pressing against the back of mine.

"Do you ever think about Gurud?" I said into the darkness.

I thought Isza had been as happy with him as she could ever be with a mate. And the big Defender had been so open with me, so non-judgemental.

"I did," she said. "All the time." Her voice was robbed of all intonation by her whisper. "Now days go by and I don't think about him, and then I remember, and that gap when he was out of my thoughts makes me sadder even than the memory of losing him."

"I'm sorry. I've never loved anyone in that way," I said. "I suppose now I never will."

There was a rattle as she drew closer and rested one claw on my shoulder plate.

It was strange to think this way. I'd never missed the intimacy of a mate. "Out of the ordinary" was bad in Kresz society, so I'd never had the opportunity. And I wouldn't now, not with my hood gone. Even if I did find someone, it wouldn't be a true Kresz mating – that complete interconnection of personality that was so much more than a physical thing.

"Did you feel that?" Isza said.

I turned to look at her. There had been something. Like a vibration but more subtle.

"The engines on this ship work differently but I've been aboard long enough to recognise if we're moving or not," she said. "We just came to a complete stop."

23

Rhees stood at the observation lounge window with Nok. There was another Jantri ship waiting in the relative calm of the Voss Space chamber. But as Nok's ship continued its approach, it was clear to Rhees this other ship was much larger than the ship she'd called home for … Fuck, she'd lost count of the days.

She'd retreated to her cabin after Nok had spun her some bullshit about being the chosen one. Or "a" chosen one, alongside the Kresz, Udun. It had made her feel as if the world was tilting under her feet. Nok was powerful, one of a highly advanced species. Perhaps their leader, because although she'd seen other Jantri, none of them had spoken to her. He commanded amazing resources, technology and firepower. It was also possible he was fucking mad.

If the Jantri did eventually strike back at the Hegemony, it would be all-out war. The mainstream of humanity would support whatever action was necessary to avoid another Battle for Earth. Even those Inclusionists who wanted to live alongside aliens would be dragged into the fight or face being executed as species-traitors. Like her.

Nok was right. A full-frontal attack wasn't the answer. The loss of life on both sides would be unthinkable. What was the alternative? Use Udun as some sort of messiah to stir up a holy war against humanity? The result would be the same. They needed to be smarter than that. But time was running out.

There were no comfortable answers, so she'd dodged the question, instead linking her reactivated band with the Jantri tech to run a deep comms analysis on Fleet and HDC interactions across the

Lenticular. She didn't have the mission protocols – hopefully Denev would come through with those – so many of the codephrase labels were still untranslatable. But routine comms were open, and even encrypted comms carried information about the originating ship. She already had the Jantri intel on Fleet movements through the Lenticular and she used this along with the Hegemony battlecruiser ship's log she'd stolen to build up a more granular view of Fleet disposition. It wasn't definitive, but clearly there were many ships, just like the HDC clipper she'd tailed, that were busy about the Hegemony's business, not just around the Kresz Homeworld and the Telsan system, but surveilling other systems, tracking Lenticular trade or military vessels and generally information-gathering the shit out of local space. It was business as usual for these guys, she thought. Except they were being watched by invisible ships run by gold-armoured and heavily armed aliens.

She'd left off her analysis and opened the news band for Earth sector. Too much time had passed and she felt disconnected from the standard Hegemony news stories – mostly jingoistic or cautionary to keep the population in line. But a brief image made her pause the flow. The figure was blurred with motion but it was clearly a Kresz. She expanded the story, reading the tagged reports that spread out from the initial bulletin like the roots of a tree. The Inclusionist Representative Minch had been assassinated by an alien of "unknown origin" which was still at large. SolSec Undersecretary Laneaux was getting roasted for the huge security lapse.

Fuck knows how the Kresz had gotten there, Rhees thought, but it felt like Volmar had to be involved somehow. Did Denev know anything about it? And what did this mean for the action in the Lenticular? Was HDC building a narrative to support a more public invasion scenario? But they were already here and didn't need public opinion to support what they were doing. So – if Volmar was involved – the real reason must have been to kill Minch. But wouldn't that boost Inclusionist Party support?

"Fuck," she'd said aloud as she realised Volmar's play. An alien had killed Minch. How misguided were the Inclusionists that they'd support the very creatures that were a proven danger to humanity? It was the perfect result – if you were a sociopathic madman like Volmar.

The ship had vibrated then and she'd felt the unmistakeable shift to Voss Space.

"Nok," she'd said, "what's happening?"

"It's time to meet your new allies," Nok had said over the comm. "Come to the observation lounge."

And now she was looking at a huge Jantri vessel and wondering what the hell came next.

"That's where he is? The one you want me to meet?" she asked.

"Yes," Nok replied.

Rhees stared at him, but neither the Jantri nor the golden armour he was wrapped in gave anything away. Which was becoming the infuriating norm.

"So let's do it," she said.

Nok turned smoothly and entered the elevator. Rhees took one last look at the other ship – a graceful arc of patterned metal – and joined him. She'd expected to exit at the hangar and take a shuttle over, but when the elevator doors opened they walked down a curving corridor. At some arbitrary point she realised something had changed.

"We're in the other ship?"

Nok stopped beside a wide bulkhead door. "Yes. And the one you are to meet is behind this door. Don't be alarmed. You will be perfectly safe."

"That's not a reassuring thing to say." She was unarmed and wearing the same flimsy HDC uniform she'd worn since lifting from Herakli.

The door opened slowly and she heard a series of sharp clacking noises from inside. Saw figures moving in the dark. The lights came up and she was facing a room full of Kresz.

One of them, bigger than the rest – and they were all pretty big

– pointed a scarily clawed fist at her. "What is the Hegemony doing here?"

The Jantri trink in Rhees's ear translated the alien's hiss-click language. She hoped it worked as well in reverse. One mistake and she could quickly lose a limb.

"I'm not Hegemony," she said. Her voice sounded frightened. Fuck, she *was* frightened. Did Nok's suit carry some decent firepower?

"Rhees is a Human," Nok said. "And she is your ally."

"We don't need an ally like that," the same Kresz said.

"Isza, wait." Another Kresz stepped up and rested a claw on the big Kresz's arm. "This Human could help."

"The Hegemony does not help." This from another Kresz.

It was hard to tell them apart, Rhees thought. Until she looked closer and saw that some had longer arms, and the colours of their shells varied. Nok had shown her pictures of Kresz but that was different to seeing them in real life. Their mouths looked like a cross between a spider's mouth and a crab's, but their eyes looked almost human.

"She wants what you want, Udun," Nok said to the Kresz holding the arm of the big angry one.

So this was the Kresz's saviour. He and the larger Kresz – Isza if the trink was working as it should – spoke to each other too quietly for Rhees to hear.

The whispered conversation stopped and Isza looked around at the other Kresz. "This Human looks like our enemy," she said, dropping her clawed hand to her side. "But ... she's not very threatening."

Another Kresz with much longer arms said, "This could be a trap."

"A very elaborate trap," Udun said, "for no visible gain. She's dead if we will it."

Fuck, Rhees thought and edged a little closer to Nok. This could go either way.

"But," Udun continued, "if Nok is correct, she could be an important source of information. She could know why the Hegemony came to Homeworld."

"That kind of information is only useful if you want to fight them," the long-armed Kresz said. "I don't –"

"I know you don't," Isza said. "But you can't keep everyone safe, Agik. And more than that, you can't tell me what to do." Isza placed a claw on the long-armed Kresz's shoulder, almost as if to soften the harshness of her words, Rhees thought. "Udun and I are going to Homeworld. What she tells us may determine whether we make it back or not."

Okay, Rhees thought. Helping is fine. It beats dying.

Isza raised her voice to address the other Kresz again. "The Human will be safe with us."

The group was silent. Rhees hoped that meant they agreed.

Nok bent close to her ear. "I'll leave you now. But I will be monitoring. You have nothing to fear."

That was easy for him to say. When he'd gone, she folded her arms and stepped back until the bulkhead pressed into her, then squatted. She hoped it indicated "nothing threatening here".

"Not very threatening at all," Udun said, as if he could read her mind. Could he? Nok had said they were empaths not telepaths.

Udun opened a nearby crate and rummaged around in it. She could see he was different from the rest of them. There was a long scar where the others had fleshy capes. Oh, fuck. He was one of the Kresz the Hegemony had butchered.

Udun stood again, holding a small sphere and a bottle of what looked like water. He started towards her, followed by Isza. Rhees tensed as both Kresz hunkered down beside her. Udun pulled a tab on the sphere. It split open and he took off the lid, leaving a bowl. Rhees could smell strong spices, like a curry. Further into the hold she could see other Kresz sitting around eating out of the same things.

Udun held the steaming bowl and looked at her. They were

either going to feed her or marinade her in it. Rhees tried not to show how scared she was.

Udun extended his double-elbowed arm, which looked simply wrong, and offered her the sphere. "You should eat," he said.

"I don't know if —" she began, but Nok's disembodied voice cut through the air. *The food is edible for humans too.* At least he was watching out for her.

Rhees took the bowl and laid it on the ground between her legs. She couldn't avoid staring at the ridge of scar tissue across Udun's shoulders.

"You must hate me for that," she said.

He followed her eyes and raised a claw to the edge of his scar. "You didn't do this. You didn't order it. I don't hate you. I'm Udun and this is Isza."

"I can try to hate you if you'd like," Isza said.

It was hard to tell if the big Kresz was joking.

"Nok says you're our ally," Udun said. "Why are you not with the other Humans?"

Rhees laughed and shook her head. "You could say I don't agree with what they're doing."

"That makes three of us," Isza said.

"I won't lie to you," Rhees said. "I worked for the Hegemony. They tried to kill me, so I ran away." Hearing it out loud made her sound pathetic.

"That sounds like a reasonable response," Udun said. "Tell me, have you heard of a Human named Volmar?"

She laughed again and it sounded a little manic to her ears. "I don't know why I should be surprised by anything any more. Yes. He's the man who tried to kill me. He's the man I want to stop."

Udun shifted to sit more comfortably on the deck and Isza followed suit, the plates of their exoskeletons sounding like distant waves as they moved.

"I last saw Volmar on Mars," Udun said. "He killed one of your politicians, then he killed my friend."

Rhees remembered the image on the news band report. So Udun was the "killer alien at large". "Volmar killed Minch," she said.

"Minch, yes. And let me escape. I was to be blamed for the murder. He said it would convince the Humans not to trust aliens." Udun paused then asked, "Are you an Inclusionist?"

"No. Well ... I never counted myself as one. But, fuck ... I suppose I am." The enemy of my enemy, she thought. "I was part of the Hegemony. But the things I saw ... They made me question what they're doing. That's why Volmar tried to kill me. That, and the fact my death helped him seal a deal."

She relaxed a little, stretching her legs out. It didn't look like she was going to die today. "It's like I told Nok. Humanity's caught a sickness that's driven some of them mad. That's the Hegemony. It's made them do what they do to aliens. It's made them attack your world. But there are others like the Inclusionists who aren't sick, who don't automatically see aliens as enemies."

Udun looked at Isza. "We understand sickness and madness," he said.

"We need a cure and we need it soon," Rhees continued. "The Hegemony's picking a fight with the Hanloi, and it's one they might not be able to win."

"The Hanloi," Udun said. "Who are they?"

"Highly advanced civilisation towards galactic centre."

"How many wars does your Hegemony want to fight at the same time?" Isza asked.

"You mean what's happening here in the Lenticular?" It was time they understood just how much the Hegemony could fuck with them. "I only worked it out after I met Nok. The Hegemony wants to crush the Hanloi. But they're sitting in a highly defensible position close to galactic centre so a frontal assault is useless – unless it happens to hide the real assault force advancing from an unexpected direction, through your area of space. The Hegemony needs to control the main Voss Space junctions in the Lenticular so there's no chance of being cut off if they have to pull back."

"So the invasion of Homeworld ..." Udun began.

Rhees nodded. "That's a local action, run by the HDC with some Fleet resources and the help of indigenes."

"Kergis," Udun said, and he and Isza looked at each other for a moment. Then Udun's large golden eyes turned on Rhees again. "So all this is the means to an end half the galaxy away? There's nothing the Hegemony actually wants on Homeworld?"

Rhees fancied she could hear his hurt through the trink. He was finally getting it. The "sorry" she uttered seemed inconsequential.

"How can we use this?" Udun said, turning to Isza.

Rhees was impressed. She'd expected anger. Instead, Udun's reaction spoke of an underlying rationality to use what he learned no matter how unsavoury it might be. Both these Kresz were intelligent and articulate, and Isza had a dry humour Rhees could appreciate. She was inclined to trust them more than she felt like trusting Nok. After all, they were guests/prisoners/interesting specimens to the Jantri, just like Rhees herself was.

"Knowing this casts everything the Hegemony has done in a different light," Udun said. The small jointed claws around his mouth opening stretched wide, which Rhees found a little disconcerting. "It means Homeworld isn't as important to them as we thought. Different priorities guide them. So if the Hegemony became stretched in other key areas ..."

"It would shift resources from your world to compensate," Rhees finished. "Yes, that's what would happen. And the Hegemony's already focusing its attention elsewhere in the Lenticular. Emba told me —"

"You know Emba?" Udun said.

"We only met briefly. Nok took me to his world." She paused. There was no easy way to say this. "I'm afraid he's dead. The Hegemony killed him. They nearly got me too."

Udun was silent for a moment and Isza reached out and took his claws in hers in an obviously comforting gesture.

Finally, Udun said, "Will you help us?"

Rhees felt his intense curiosity, his focus.

"I want to show humanity that the Hegemony and the Central Administration – the ruling body – don't have all the answers," she said. "They keep the populace in line by spreading propaganda about alien threats. There's no room for discord or even an alternative viewpoint. That's not healthy. For us humans or the aliens we encounter."

"I understand," Udun said. "Minch spoke like you. That's why Volmar killed him."

"Volmar is like a tumour."

"Too-mur?" Udun said.

"An infected growth inside a body. It needs to be cut out before the body can heal."

"We have one of those," Udun said. "A hierarch – a leader – called Kergis. He and Volmar work together." He turned to Isza again. "We need intelligence from the ground on Homeworld. Once we get to where Nok's taking us, I have to go there."

"We're both going, remember?" Isza said.

"I've been thinking about that. It's too dangerous for any intact Kresz. Could *you* hide the fact you were on a spying mission if you were put under scrutiny?"

"I could try," she said. "I'm sure I could do it."

"You couldn't, Isza. No one here could."

"If you're alone on Homeworld with no mantle, you'll most likely get euthanised," Isza said.

"Not if I'm careful. They use excisees for manual labour. They don't necessarily kill them. Besides," he looked at Rhees and the small feeder claws around his mouth rippled, "I may be in the safekeeping of a Hegemony guard."

"I don't –" Isza began, then looked from Udun to Rhees.

"You want me to go with you?" Rhees said, surprised. "Most Kresz on your world would probably want to kill me."

"And many will see you as an ally," he countered. "Or at worst, too powerful to attack without reprisal. You'd be in a better position than me."

"Udun," Isza said, "you don't even know this Human. You can't do this."

"It makes perfect sense to me," Udun said.

Rhees could see the advantages too. Maybe she was as crazy as this Kresz.

"Look," she said, "I'm here to do whatever I need to bring Volmar down and get home. You think we can do that by going to the Kresz Homeworld, then let's do it."

Isza stood, drawing Udun up with her. "We'll talk about this later," she told Rhees.

Udun didn't look ready to leave, but he did anyway. Rhees was pretty sure he would get his way.

I'm back in the firing line, she thought. It felt good. She picked up the bowl and took a bite of alien curry.

24

Denev had been immersed in his nook for days now, tracking what HDC knew about the Inclusionists, looking for the right lever.

The Datahive monitored everything. Even those elements of the net that were supposedly protected by privacy laws. As for the spaces people or groups designed to be opaque or invisible to CA hacks – HDC monitored those too. Nothing was closed to them: virtual meetings, comment streams, datashares, and longforms. Everything anyone ever said or shared or received was open to their algorithms. Language and context was tested and sorted and categorised. People were labelled on the spectrum of loyalty. Deviating behaviour was flagged.

Denev sifted possible targets. He wanted someone who was young, rebellious, a fringe member of the Inclusionists – not a person to put the interests of the movement above their own desire for justice. A fellow traveller. They'd have a small group of friends. Be the one that others followed. A natural ringleader ripe for manipulation.

The algorithms never failed. Preem Renalds. Vocal on the comment spaces. More so since Minch's death. Regular trouble as a juvenile. Smart, but not as smart as he thought he was. Denev called up Preem's known associates: Medge and Torp. They'd do what Preem said.

HDC had many personas their operatives could use: seemingly real citizens who regularly interacted on the net, commenting, sharing, keeping the conversations going. Denev chose one now

– Alban Grenoble. Supported the Inclusionists. Pretty vocal about the lack of CA accountability. Short spell in Fleet but quit halfway through basic. Pretty vocal about that too. Alban and Preem had a couple of streams and datashare nodes in common. Denev took over the Alban persona and upvoted a couple of Preem's recent comments.

There was a virtual rally protesting Minch's death about to start. Preem was already registered. Alban registered too. Within a couple of minutes, Denev saw Torp had checked out Alban's persona.

The nook fed the stream directly through Denev's optical and auditory pathways, and as the rally opened to the datastream he dropped into virtual space. Perception warped around him, following the focus of his attention, filling in detail as he scanned the area. It gave the whole experience a dreamlike quality – people and things coming into existence as his perspective shifted.

Reality in this space was non-permanent but it still managed to convey a sense of things beyond his own thoughts and feelings. Even though he couldn't take it all in with a single look, the volume felt crowded. Snatches of conversation flowed around him and he could dip into a stream just by concentrating. People flicked in and out of focus, some less than shadows, many deliberately occluded to hide their identities – although it would be the work of barely a second to break through their encryption.

There was one group that persisted, larger than life and floating on a dais above the assembly that stayed in Denev's field of vision wherever he looked. He recognised Emille Kant, Secretary of the Inclusionist Party. This was her rally, which gave her an override on all inputs.

His target was somewhere on the virtual floor. He concentrated and the bodies and faces around him blurred and shifted until he was standing behind Preem and Torp. Neither of them would be using a rig like the datanook, but even the cheapest interfaces had haptics or visual prompts to alert the user when they were being observed. The nook let Denev bypass all that.

Comment substreams flowed above and around them – tagged news reports on Minch, CA statements heavily annotated (all of it anti-government), and commentary forums coloured by topic. Denev wondered how heavily infiltrated the crowd was with HDC or SolSec operatives. All the streams, substreams and encrypted chats would be analysed. Every possible datapoint would be extracted. No doubt there were multiple subversive events occurring all around him.

Both Preem and Torp were making the same "brave shouts from the crowd" that others were, in-between private chat that was as open to Denev as anything else.

Preem's other friend, Medge, coalesced beside them.

> Fuck, look at the crowds <Medge>

> Where you been, you lazy toss <Torp>

> Fucken your sis <Medge>

> She keep her eyes shut, yeah <Torp>

> What – <Medge>

> Shut it, Medge <Preem>

> No, really – <Medge>

All three were different from how they appeared in reality. Medge had green skin and a muscled, leather-clad torso, his face dominated by a pig's snout and tusks. Torp was all flickering shapes and angles, features melting and morphing where his face should be. Preem looked like a pencil drawing but was still recognisable as himself – dark curly hair framing a wide forehead, eyes with a slight Asian cast, and full almost feminine lips. Even the colour of the "paper" approximated his pale skin. Spatially they were in Cape York. Good area, good homes. They were just kids really. Privileged and bored, pushing against the constraints of the world. It didn't matter. Denev had to do this.

= If we can begin *Kant*

The comment streams froze for a moment as Kant's image expanded until it felt like she was everywhere – demanding their attention – then dwindled to a still imposing presence above the crowd.

= Thank you for gathering tonight. A very real blow has been struck against our collective freedom with the brutal murder of Alder Minch *Kant*

Images of Minch proliferated across the space and the streams picked up slogans and protests that were tagged and commented on and overwritten until it was hard to keep up.

= It's hurt us. We all feel that hurt. But none more than our first speaker tonight. He served with Minch on his first successful campaign for the Inclusionists, and has been a close friend ever since. Please welcome Kal Huberman *Kant*

Again the streams reacted and Huberman was everywhere for an instant. Hovering above the crowd, he looked like he'd barely slept for days, but he spoke with a quiet strength.

= My friend lies dead on Mars *Huberman*

The streams exploded with comments, but Huberman stood quietly, waiting for the first rush of anger to flow across the crowd and subside.

= The authorities would have us believe he was killed by an alien. Killed in one of the most secure enclaves on Mars. How could this happen? *Huberman*

THEY DID IT flashed across the official stream and was picked up by others.

In front of Denev, Preem pushed Medge in the shoulder and subposted.

+ What are we going to do about it? *Preem*

That comment too proliferated across the streams as it was upvoted.

= There are too many unanswered questions for this to be forgotten. But that's what the SolSec office wants us to do *Huberman*

There was another flood of comments as the crowd expressed just how they felt about SolSec.

= We're not going to let that happen! *Huberman*

Preem pushed Medge again and subchatted.

> This is what I told you. We're going to show those fuckers <Preem>

= We need your support. We need the CA to halt the election in Alder Minch's division so we can prepare a new candidate. And we need an independent investigation into his death *Huberman*

Preem's flickering image stilled and his hands dropped to his side. A new stream opened above him.

≠ We need to fight these fuckers #Preem#

Medge and Torp upvoted and commented.

√ Fight! Fight! Fight! #Medge#

√ Smash the State #Torp#

The stream expanded as it gained upvotes and comments. Some were real, but Denev was deploying multiple personas to add support, skewing the stream so it started to dominate the space.

> Fuck, look at that <Preem> Preem subchatted, and threw his papery arms around Medge's green pig man and Torp's flickering shadow.

> Yeah! <Medge>

Denev added his own subcomment.

√ They're killing us. We need more than an investigation #Alban#

The stream swelled again, but Huberman was still talking and Preem's stream flickered and shrank in on itself as the official stream expanded with a scrolling statement.

= This petition sets out our demands. We need you to sign it and get everyone you know to sign it. With your voices the Inclusionists will demand the justice Alder Minch deserves *Huberman*

Denev added another reply to Preem's stream, which had all but disappeared.

√ A petition. Are you fucking kidding #Alban#

Preem was one of the first to upvote the comment. But it was no use. The organisers had spiked Preem's stream just as Denev knew they would, and the main stream took over all the others with a running tally of signatures dominating the space.

Preem added a final comment to his stream even as it was shrinking to nothingness.

≠ Fuck this #Preem#

And then he, Medge and Torp winked out of existence.

Denev pulled out of full immersion and watched the rest of the rally via a simple vidfeed. Whatever party they represented, politicians used the same tricks to push people's buttons or shut down a dissenting view. The petition was in the millions by the time the rally was over.

Now Denev knew the Inclusionist Party was completely compromised, he wondered just how many of the upper organisers believed in what their party stood for. Minch had seemed genuine. Volmar hadn't given him the chance to die for his beliefs – he'd killed him like a dog. But that must mean Minch was a real Inclusionist, didn't it?

Half an hour after the rally wrapped, Alban got a request from Preem to swap privileges.

Two hours later, Denev sent him a message: *So do you want to sign a petition or actually do something?*

∞

Denev sat on an angled frame in a sea of mirrors ranged in concentric circles around a monolithic tower. The cloudless sky was reflected all around him, as if he were in the middle of a perfect blue body of water set like a jewel in the middle of a barren, red-brown plain. A light shadow – the apex of the mirror arrangement – hovered like a ghost above the partially dismantled top of the tower.

Preem and his cohort were on their way, but this disused power plant was quite a distance from the Cape York conurb. The satellite feed on Denev's wraparounds showed Preem, Torp and Medge approaching long before he heard them. Three dust plumes arrowing for the broken blue target, moving into single file as they followed the service path between the mirrors. He pocketed the wraparounds and swivelled on the frame to face them as the electric whine of their unicykes became obvious.

The cykes slewed to a halt, plastic windbreaks everting and folding into the combined seat/engine mounts.

"Why here?" Preem said as he, Torp and Medge stepped down on to the dirt.

Denev shrugged. "It's quiet. And you can see company coming for miles."

It was also completely open to every type of orbital sensor HDC had. As well as being – according to Volmar – a SolSec surveillance dead spot. Denev wasn't sure if that was due to negligence, funding or HDC interference.

Preem smirked at Denev. "It's all a bit 'holodrama' isn't it?"

Medge laughed. Just like his avatar, he was short and solid with small sunken eyes and a lantern jaw. Torp was thin and wore a dark grey coat that trailed in the dust. He was squinting in the daylight, as if he wasn't used to it, and puffing flavoured inhalant from a curved silver vaper.

Denev frowned and jumped down off the frame. "I'm not fucking around here. You and your little pals can piss off back to your mum's house if you're not serious."

Medge sniffed and took a rapid step towards him. Denev swivelled and thrust his arm out, palm flat, pushing the youth hard in the chest. Arms cartwheeling, Medge fell on his ass in the dirt.

Torp laughed as Medge scrambled to his feet, his face red with rage, but Preem placed a hand on Medge's shoulder. "Relax," he said to Denev. "We're all serious here."

Medge, still angry, swatted at the dust on his breeches.

"I backgrounded you," Preem went on.

"I'm flattered," Denev said, and Preem looked annoyed. "I did the same with you. You need to understand – I'm going to do something that will make a lot of people sit up and take notice. If that sounds too dangerous for you …"

Torp shifted his weight from foot to foot, puffing on his vaper. Medge just looked angry; he probably didn't have the wits to realise what he was getting into. But clearly Torp did.

"We don't fuck around," Preem said. "I've been working on something of my own to hit back. But you've got my interest. For now."

Preem took off his tinted goggles and Denev could see the calculation in his eyes. He was the leader of this little group. The alpha male. He talked big on the boards and in his subchats to his friends. If he backed off now, his friends might still follow him, but the narrative he'd constructed for himself would be damaged. He'd have a harder time believing in himself. Challenge and counter-challenge, Denev thought. Preem was hooked. The others would follow along.

"How much do you know about explosives?" he said.

Torp gave a startled half-jump, but Preem said, "It's okay. We're just talking."

"Talking can get you arrested," Torp said.

"There's no one out here but us," Medge said. He stood relaxed now, but ready.

Denev thought he'd be handy in a bar-room brawl where it was okay to give in to rage. But not in something more focused.

"Who do you want to blow up?" Preem asked.

"Not who. Not yet anyway," Denev said. "But this petition … It's not going to make any difference. We need something to make them know we're serious."

"And you can get your hands on explosives?" Preem said.

It was Denev's turn to smirk. "Already have." He looked around. "Since we're just talking, I have a safe place, not far away. Let's get out of the sun."

He walked through them, brushing against Medge on purpose, and retraced their path up the service road.

"You walking?" Preem shouted after him.

Denev held up his hand and a low-slung podcar turned out of a side channel between the mirrors, thick tyres spinning in the dirt as it accelerated then came to a halt. The curved roof split open and

Denev swung one leg inside, looking back at his co-conspirators.

"Are you coming?"

The cockpit folded around Denev as the pod sealed over his head and the car kicked up a plume of dirt behind. In the rear screen he saw the others step onto the wheel-plates of their cykes and take off after him.

They didn't have to go far. The dry, burned ground gave way to slick blacktop – a self-repairing nanostructure that harvested more energy in a single metre than the whole disused solar array they'd left could manage. The road was deserted but Preem and the others were hanging well back. Just three guys out for a joyride because they could.

Out here, the blacktop linked satellite town after satellite town. All CA-supplied housing, every unit the same: well-maintained, self-sustaining, with the same amenities and services. Basic income covered everything a reasonable person could need. Denev had read about people in the past dying of starvation and poverty or lack of medical care. They were free of all that now. But how could they be really free when their government kept everyone under continuous surveillance, rigged elections and conducted state-sanctioned assassinations? It was a facsimile of freedom. Even if most people were unaware of all this in their daily lives, it had to have some effect. A rat didn't need to know it was in a cage for its behaviour to change.

Denev turned off the highway at the sign that pointed to Conurb Town XT67#, slowing as he turned again so the others wouldn't lose him. The houses were utilitarian cubes with broad awnings and treed gardens to provide shade. There was no one on the streets, but that was hardly surprising. People worked from home or in local hubs and it was mid-afternoon.

He pulled the car into the driveway of a house like any other. The broad door to the attached garage tilted open and he drove in, followed by Preem, Torp and Medge. Denev stepped out of his car as the garage door closed behind them. The boys' cykes stood on their single wheels, defying gravity.

Preem looked around the garage. Neatly stacked pods covered the back wall. "Your place?" he asked.

"A safe place," Denev said. "Come on."

They followed him through an internal door into the kitchen, which opened into a main room. Forensics could be faked, but it was simpler and safer not to, which was why Denev had brought them here. They would leave skin cells on door handles, hair on the floor and tables, while their clothes soaked up the unmistakable chemical signature of bomb-making material.

Preem went to the window, looked at the lifeless, sun-soaked street outside, then set the glass to opaque.

Denev stood at the table. One half was littered with electronic blocks, wrappings and tools. The other half was clear except for a flat holoprojector.

Preem joined him, flanked by Medge and Torp. Preem had a hungry look in his eyes – Denev recognised it right away. It was the look of someone who had realised they were close to getting something they'd wanted for a long time.

Medge was looking at Preem, feeding off his quiet excitement. Torp just looked scared.

Denev activated the projector and buildings and streets appeared in miniature above the table. The egg of the Datahive hung over the open space of Vigilance Plaza, flanked by monolithic blocks that ran its length. Office blocks, businesses and retail outlets crowded the surrounding streets. Loops of pedestrian bands threaded paths through it all.

"This is where the CA spies on us all," he said. "They hurt us, so we hit them where it hurts." He pointed at a large cube of a building a few streets back from the plaza. "That's the power transfer unit that feeds the government buildings. We take it out and shut them down."

"They must have a backup," Preem said.

Denev nodded. "A small reactor in the basement of the Datahive." He pointed at the egg. "We take that out too."

"You can't break into a government building," Torp said. "They'll shoot you."

Preem cuffed him on the back of the head. "Harden up."

"We don't need to break into a government building," Denev said. "The power transfer unit is the easier target. It's civilian infrastructure, passive security. Torp …"

The young man looked startled at the mention of his name.

"You'll have the easier job. Stand on this corner and keep an eye out for security patrols."

Torp visibly relaxed.

"Medge lays the explosive. You don't need to get inside. The unit output runs along this wall before feeding into the distribution network underground. The charge will bring the whole wall down on it. By then you and Torp will be far away."

"How does it blow?" Medge asked.

"Simple timer that you'll activate once the charge is set," Denev said.

That wasn't quite true. Medge would be killed in the blast as soon as he set the device. A terrorist blown up by his own faulty bomb.

"Which leaves Preem and me to set the big one," Denev went on. The buildings lifted above the table top, revealing the basement under the Datahive and a tunnel running below that. "A hypertube station runs under the basement. We mine that and drop the reactor right through the floor."

"And blow up the city," Medge said.

"No," Denev said. "These things are built to fail-safe. But we black out the government sector for hours. They can't ignore us then."

"How do we get down there?" Preem asked.

He wasn't scared in the slightest. Denev couldn't decide if he was fundamentally sociopathic or just too stupid to see how this would all pan out.

"I've got maintenance uniforms and fake IDs. Placing the

charges will take time. There's a maintenance shelter right where we need to be. We place the charges on the ceiling, activate the timers and get the hell out."

Denev had toyed with the idea of leaving Preem to be crushed by the reactor. But two accidental terrorist deaths would raise questions. Once arrested, Preem and Torp would blame the mysterious Alban who put them up to it. But Alban didn't exist and his persona would disappear from the net along with all his interactions. This unit and all the materials in it would be traced back to individuals in the Inclusionist movement, who would be damned for radicalising impressionable youngsters. The Hegemony machine would swallow these kids whole. Denev knew it was wrong. Before Petar died, before he'd met Rhees, he might have convinced himself otherwise. Once this plan was in motion, there was no way it could fail unless Denev deliberately wrecked it. Which would raise too many questions with Volmar.

Preem and the others were waiting for him to say something stirring to commit them to act.

Instead he said, "You don't have to do this. It will be dangerous. You could be killed. Or go to prison for the rest of your lives."

But it was too late.

Preem clapped his arms across Medge's and Torp's shoulders and pulled them close. There was a glint of madness in his eyes. "Fuck that. We're going to be heroes."

25

Isza waited until we were out of earshot of Rhees to let me know how unhappy she was. "You can't do this. It's beyond stupid."

"It's the next logical step, you agreed so yourself," I said. "We've identified where the free Kresz might be. And now we know causing trouble for the Hegemony on Homeworld might make them think twice about how useful occupation is. All I need to do is find our people."

"But not with her. How do we know she's not still working for the Hegemony?"

There was that. Volmar had proved how devious and ruthless he was. He'd tracked Atalna and me all the way to Mars and used us for his own ends. The Hegemony had infiltrated the Lenticular – not just Homeworld – I was sure of it. Could this Human be another part of their trap?

"Why come with me to a place the Hegemony already controls when she'd be better off staying here to find out what the Jantri are up to?" I said.

"To find the hiding Kresz?"

"She doesn't know we suspect there are any."

"We don't know what she knows."

"Isza, we won't get anywhere if we suspect anyone and everyone."

"Not everyone. Just her. She's a *Human*."

"And not Nok because he's Jantri."

"You don't trust him either," she countered.

Our voices were getting louder and Agik and the others were looking straight at us. Even if they couldn't hear every word, they must sense Isza's growing frustration with me. And she *was* making sense. I could have accused her of preaching the typical Kresz worldview about untrustworthy outsiders. But that wasn't what motivated her. She was trying to protect me.

But the Kresz couldn't win this war alone. We needed – as a species – to seek and accept outside help. We needed the Jantri and we needed this Human. The inward focus of Kresz society had to be broken just as much as the taboo about excisees. I felt in a deeply intuitive way that I was a fulcrum for both of those fundamental changes. If I said it out loud it would sound as if I was full of my own importance and maybe more than a little delusional. But I didn't feel like that. I felt more like an Adept toiling in a laboratory and being the first to witness some new chemical reaction, something transformative, something that went against everything we understood about the world. I could be that catalyst. I could bring the unthought-of change. And it felt to me now that choosing to work with the Human, choosing to work with the Jantri, was the right thing to do no matter how many good reasons against it Isza threw at me.

Of course I couldn't tell her that. But there was another reason to take Rhees to Homeworld instead of Isza. I'd only just gotten Isza back. I wouldn't risk her life again if I could avoid it.

"I'll talk to Nok," I said. "See if I can find out more about Rhees. It makes sense to do that, whatever else we decide."

"I suppose," she said grudgingly. "You know I'm only saying this because I'm worried for you."

"I know. The others are staring at us. Let's go back to them."

No one asked us what the Human had said or about the unease they must have felt from Isza. They all sat in their own kind of silences. Udlade's sullen, Agik's concerned, Sahi's contemplative, Dikrah's exhausted, or so I imagined them.

Udun.

The voice was Nok's, sounding close to my ear gap, but even though I sat beside Isza, she hadn't heard it.

"What is it?" she said as I stood.

"It's Nok. He's talking to me."

Can you come up to the flight deck, Udun? Just you. Wear a suit.

A panel by the main door slid aside. Environment suits were hanging inside, made of clear film held together at the junctions and seams with silver bands. I walked over and pulled one that looked big enough off the rack. Isza followed me.

"Nok wants me to meet with him," I told her.

"Alone?"

"Can you help with this?" I handed her the suit. "I'll be fine."

Isza helped me pull the film over my legs and lower plates and sealed it along the side. I pulled a transparent cowl over my head and fitted the loose edges into the metal fastenings across my chest plates. As soon as I was completely sealed inside, the material pulled tight, moulding to me, but I didn't feel constrained at all and could breathe easily enough.

"Don't be long," she said.

Nok's voice guided me along the passage. *To your right and along the hall, there's a black door. It's an internal lock into our environment.*

The black door opened and I entered a short, narrow room. The door closed behind me and the room moved forward, stopped, then moved up.

Another door opened in front of me, but I hesitated before stepping through. The air, or whatever the Jantri breathed, sparkled. Golden eddies rippled across the door opening, just like looking into Nok's faceplate.

As I left the lock, I felt no more resistance than I would in normal atmosphere. From the control surfaces against the wall on one side of the room, it was clear we were on the flight deck. But there were no seats, and the curving wall in front of me looked like a window with tactical data scrolling across a view of the tenspace corridor. We were travelling down it at an alarming speed. This apparent motion in what felt like a stationary room made me feel unsteady. I looked away, wondering where Nok and the other Jantri were. Was the ship flying itself?

"No alien has ever seen what I really look like."

It was Nok's voice, but still I said, "Nok?" like some idiot youngling. Then I realised. "You're the glow in the air?"

"Most simply put, I am pure energy."

He was all around me. It was a strange feeling and I was glad of the suit.

"Other Jantri are here too?" I asked.

"There will always be secrets between us, Udun, but I can show you this much truth. I am the consciousness of the Jantri – combined when we left our mortal shells and became mind and energy."

"But I've seen you with other Jantri, all in your armour."

"All of them were me. My aspects. Some in the Lenticular would feel threatened by my true nature. The suits provide them with a comfortable lie."

And yet he – they? – was sharing this truth with me. But not every truth, he'd said.

"What is it you *can't* tell me?"

"Matters that do not concern you. Out of discretion not a lack of trust. But I can promise you we will never do anything to harm you or the Kresz. You have nothing to fear from us."

As I stood amid the glowing, pulsing flecks of the Jantri mind, spirit, essence – an entire species transformed – I wondered if that was what trust really was: to work side by side even if there couldn't be full disclosure between you. To take some things on faith.

But how could I know *this* was the truth? It could be another layer of deception. Atalna had said the Jantri were the "secret ones" and their motivations couldn't be trusted. I'd trusted Ephes on Mars and that had led to Atalna's death. Lacking any other solid fact, I had to trust my instincts. I heard Nok's words, but I still felt I should trust him only so far.

"What about the Hegemony?" I asked.

"We're agreed on that," Nok said. "They must be removed from the Lenticular."

"Did you know about what Rhees told us?"

"That the invasion of Homeworld is just a small part of a larger offensive? Yes. But even if they succeed in their war, I doubt the Hegemony will relinquish your planet without good reason. They are here to stay."

"How far have they spread?"

"Their ships are throughout the Lenticular. Rhees has been instrumental in tracking them and listening in to their comms. The Hegemony's presence threatens my position as the most powerful entity in the Lenticular," Nok continued, "even if no one is aware that I am. I am not doing this for altruistic reasons. *That* is why you should trust me. My motivations are purely personal, but aligned with your own."

These were words I could understand, sincerely spoken.

"So what's the plan?" I asked.

"I'm relying on you and Rhees for that. What I'm offering is the full and not inconsiderable resources of the Jantri'va."

There was a chime and the wall screen flashed briefly. The data scrolling across it vanished.

"In fact," Nok said, "one of those resources is about to be revealed to you. One of my most secret."

We were still travelling down the tenspace corridor. It was narrow now and tapering narrower still. The walls were shot through with purple flashes which, as I watched, turned from random flares to a regular pulsing – hoops of lightning running away from us. The terminus of the tunnel was approaching and still we flew forward.

I anticipated a shock when the ship hit the tunnel end, and there was nothing to hold onto. No shock came. The ship pierced the plasma channel, moving through it unharmed.

"How?" I managed.

"Wait till you see what's on the other side."

The view on the screen merged with the wall; the room

dimmed and brightened with that strange plasma pulse. Nothing else was visible, and then we were through it and into a seething conflagration.

"Tenspace fights it all the way," Nok said. "But still it's here."

"Here" was a space no living creature could survive in. Bruised walls of plasma churned around us, points erupting with streams of arc lightning, some strands thicker than a Kresz cruiser, all of them dwarfing our own ship. One hit would take us out, I was sure of it.

Somehow, there was a structure in the middle of the furious energies tenspace was hurling around this place. Illuminated in purple flashes, it looked at first like an uplink spire – a broad dome with a broadcast tower thrusting up from its centre. The spire was its most visible feature because it was being struck again and again by thick, twisting cables of plasma. Then, in a particularly bright flash, I saw another spire projecting downward at the end of a long tapering cone at the bottom of the dome. The end of that spire was taking plasma hits as well. Glowing ripples of energy coruscated down the spires and across the body of the dome, which was ringed in bulbous pods, hangars perhaps.

And there was another pod I could see now, bulging at the broad base of the lower spire. Our ship was heading for it. While the space all around us was filled with deadly shafts of energy, none of them struck us. Some came close, but twisted away to strike instead at the spires.

"Your station," I said, realising what I was looking at. "It stays here in tenspace?"

"Yes," Nok said. "It uses the tenspace energies for power. It's a fine balance, but we've achieved it here. Other parts of tenspace are less hospitable."

"I've seen something similar in the corridors leading to Sol," I said, "but tenspace there wasn't so … energetic."

"You and your people can rest in the station's lower pod. It was designed for cargo that can't withstand the high energy environment of the main dome. You'll be perfectly safe there until you work out what you need to do."

"I need to know about the Human," I said. "How do you know she's not a Hegemony spy?"

"You Kresz go to great lengths to hide secrets from each other: shielded rooms, careful doling out of small parcels of information so no one knows too much, especially if they come in contact with other houses."

"It's because of our empathic ability," I said. "We can feel lies and subterfuge."

"You feel the emotional temperature of others?"

"Yes, you could say that."

"I have something similar. Not a natural ability that has evolved over time, but a technological means to map and measure that emotional temperature. By analysing a person's words and actions and correlating that with the physiological reading, I can determine the emotional state of a being – even a non-Jantri – once I've established a baseline."

"You've used this on the Human?" I said.

"I've had many conversations with her. She's been badly used by the Hegemony. And while she doesn't want to destroy them, she does want to bring them to a halt. I know she means what she says."

"You're that sure of your device?"

"It's impossible to trick. No living creature can control their unconscious responses."

"Maybe she doesn't know she's a spy."

"Perhaps. That's what makes the game so exciting, don't you think?"

"I have enough excitement without adding to it unnecessarily," I said.

"And yet you are prepared to go with her to Homeworld."

So Nok did listen in on us continuously.

"What does your emotion machine say about me?" I asked. Could I even be read without a mantle?

"It confirms what I already know about you. Fear and pain

won't stop you. You'll do what you have to do. It's why we're both here."

I knew he was right. I was already committed. Despite Isza's fears.

"You'll give us a ship that can take us safely to the surface of Homeworld?" I asked.

"I'll give you a ship such as you wouldn't believe."

I looked out at the nightmarish space. Plasma flashes still shot to the spires, and I could see the energy rippling down their length. The Jantri had developed a way to tap the destructive forces of tenspace; different from the human station approaching Sol but just as daunting. They were, it seemed, full of wonders. Wonders they – or the entity that was Nok – had decided to keep to themselves until forced to do otherwise with the arrival of the Hegemony.

"I'll meet you below," Nok said. "I have to suit up for the others."

As I re-entered the moving room and the door slid shut on the sparkling atmosphere, it struck me how like the Hegemony Nok was. Both worked through others, unseen. I was the Jantri's equivalent of Kergis: a tool to be used to bring about a desired outcome. The Jantri didn't care about Homeworld for its own sake – Nok had told me as much. They just wanted the Hegemony out. So did I. But that didn't mean I wasn't being manipulated. Isza's reserve towards Nok had been right. I could trust the Jantri up to a point, but they were using us just as much as we were using them. We had to work with them. Trust, but not blind trust.

The room stopped but the door stayed shut. An AI spoke in reasonable Kresz. "Please stand still for decontamination."

The space was filled with light, painfully bright until my desert eyelid flicked across. There was no heat in the light, but it was accompanied by a low hum that ended with a chime.

"Please remove the suit and leave it on the floor."

I did as the AI asked, tossing the suit into the corner. The wall opened to the corridor and Isza.

"I was getting worried," she said.

"You shouldn't have. We're almost at a Jantri station in tenspace. We should get ready to leave."

She stopped me before we returned to the others. "You're going ahead with this, aren't you? You're going to work with Nok, travel with the Human."

"Yes."

"What did he say to make you believe him?"

"Isza –"

"Tell me, Udun. I want to understand. Maybe I'll worry less."

"I'm doing this because there's nothing else we can do. It's this or hide away forever."

Her claws were still on my chest plate. "What if there was an alternative?"

"Is there?"

The silence pooled between us. I could see her struggling to come up with another argument to stop me or come with me. There were none.

"No," she said, dropping her claws.

∞

Rhees was relieved when the bulkhead door opened and Udun and Isza returned. One Kresz in particular had been staring at her the whole time Udun had been away. She'd stared back at first, but when the Kresz hadn't looked away she'd tried hard to pretend it wasn't there.

If the HDC caught her on Homeworld she'd be up for mindwipe at the very least. Though maybe a mindwipe wouldn't be so bad. Life up to now hadn't been crammed with delightful memories. In the meantime, this Udun seemed okay. If she was going to share a cabin with an alien, she could do a lot worse. Like staring guy over there.

Udun was talking to the others. "We're leaving," Rhees heard over the trink. She stood up to get ready and then felt stupid. There was nothing to get ready with.

She thought about joining the knot of Kresz standing around Udun and Isza, but that didn't seem right either, not without being asked. Then Nok was back in the room, helmet faceplate glowing on top of his armoured suit.

"We're docking," he said.

Docking where?

The hull rang dully and there was a slight jolt, but not enough to unbalance her. The Kresz followed Nok out into the corridor and Rhees went with them, lagging behind. The lock was open at both ends; a hard connection then, not a universal collar. Another Jantri ship? But it didn't look like a ship. It looked like the inside of a hollow donut the size of a reasonably large asteroid.

The donut hole was filled with a large column extending up through the ceiling. As she crossed the threshold her footsteps echoed and re-echoed on the deck plating. While this entranceway was clear and open, cargo podules were stacked in walls lining out from the central column and she could see the irregular shapes of machinery and maybe even vehicles in the distance. It was too large a single space for a ship. A station? But where?

She walked over to join Nok and the others. "Where is this?" she asked, but it was Udun who answered.

"It's a Jantri station inside tenspace. I saw it on approach. I think it's powered by tenspace."

"We're not alone," Isza said and the small group instantly drew together, like a frightened herd, Rhees thought, all keyed to the same danger.

"What do you feel?" Udun asked.

"Surprise. Fear," Isza said. "They're close."

"It's all right," Nok said. "No cause for alarm."

Round the nearest wall of podules came the biggest Kresz Rhees had ever seen. It was quickly joined by others. They had the same crab-claw mouths and mantles – all raised – but they were taller and bulkier than Udun's group, and each had one preposterously large arm ending in a pincer big enough to snip a person's head off.

The group advanced, and Rhees saw it was interspersed with Kresz whose body types were more like Udun and the others.

Someone nearby said, "Haketiug Kresz."

There had to be over a hundred of them. Rhees saw that Udun's group were raising their mantles now, falling into a defensive line.

She moved closer to Nok. "What's going on?" she said, her voice barely a whisper.

"An experiment." Nok's voice was barely any louder. "Watch."

The new group halted about five metres away in a close semicircle. All those mantles, like fleshy microwave dishes, were focused right at Rhees and the others. It felt like the newcomers were about to attack.

"What are Haketiug Kresz doing here?" one of Udun's group asked. Agik, Rhees thought his name was. She saw now that all these new Kresz wore a yellow collar with a gold band as a kind of clasp. A clan badge or service insignia?

"What are *you* doing here?" one of the smaller Kresz on the other side said.

"The alien brought us," Agik said. "We fled the war that Kergis brought down on us. Kergis, the true leader of House Haketiug."

Some of the larger Kresz raised their pincers. Rhees thought they were about three seconds away from some real unpleasantness. And she wasn't at all sure Nok would do anything to stop it.

"Hierarch Haketiug is dead," the other Kresz said. "His ship was destroyed by the Hegemony in the first wave that broke through the Point. We are Haketiug Kresz but without a hierarch. And we do not count the traitor Kergis as a friend of our house."

Mantles were going down on both sides. It seemed to Rhees the tension had passed. At least until the newcomers noticed the presence of a human. She moved closer to Nok.

There was a sound of rasping steel. Another of the newcomer Kresz had pulled an evil-looking blade and was pointing it at the group. "You have a criminal with you," he said.

But he wasn't pointing at Rhees. He was pointing at Udun. Why?

"He's not a criminal," Agik said. "He was excised by the Hegemony."

"He is outside the communion," the bladed Kresz said. "You must clear the way."

"No," Agik and Isza said together. "You will not touch him," Isza added.

Things were getting ugly again. The mantles on Udun's group were rising. Isza pulled Udun down to a crouch and the others closed around him. More blades were pulled.

"They won't fight," Nok said.

Rhees wasn't so sure. She'd seen a lot of brawls, many from the inside. This had all the hallmarks.

But then mantles were folding down again, bodies relaxing their tense stance. Finally, to Rhees's disbelief, the knives were sheathed.

"The thing about a truly empathic race," Nok added, "is that they're always able to gauge the passion behind the words. When the opponent is bluffing and when they are not."

"You said you were conducting an experiment," Rhees said.

"I did. And it seems to be working."

26

Agik, Isza and the rest of our group had banded together for me and the Haketiug Kresz were backing down. I was grateful, but it wasn't enough. I stood and stepped forward.

Isza's claws wrapped around my arm, stopping me. "What are you doing?"

"I have to make them see, Isza. I appreciate what you've just done, all of you. But the Haketiug Kresz will still kill me when they get the chance. We haven't changed anything, and it needs to change."

Slowly I pulled my arm free. Isza didn't want to say it, but she knew I was right.

I walked clear of our group and stood in the space between us and the Haketiug Kresz. None of the newcomers were looking at me directly. Agik and the others had robbed them of their chance to "clear the way" so now they preferred to pretend I didn't exist. I felt my anger rising and hoped that would help.

Thankfully, the Kresz that had drawn the gaszti wasn't Defender caste. His body shape was the same as mine. I moved to stand directly in front of him, but his eyes didn't flinch, didn't acknowledge my presence. The space around us was completely silent. Outside, I knew tenspace was in uproar. But that was nothing to what I felt inside and what I suspected the Haketiug Kresz was feeling and broadcasting to every other Kresz here.

"What's your name?" I asked.

No response. Fine. He could listen then.

"Are you so stupid that you will help the Hegemony destroy us from within?"

That got a reaction. His eyes flicked to me, then over my shoulder, looking at the group behind me.

"What is this?" he asked them.

"*I'm* talking to you," I said. "On Homeworld, if you fought against the Hegemony, the chances are good you would have been excised, just like me."

His claws thrust against my chest plate, pushing me back a step. He held his claws up, looking at them. I couldn't be sure but I thought it was the surprise of pushing another Kresz and not feeling the emotional result of that action. His gaze moved from his claws to focus on me fully for the first time.

"The Hegemony designed the perfect way to break us and change our way of life forever," I said.

He gripped the top rim of my chest plate, pulling me closer. His eyes were on me, suddenly wide, but he was listening. He had to be listening.

"They excise those that resist them," I said. "With no mantle, those Kresz are instantly outside Kresz society. They have no voice."

He drew back his other claws and smashed them into my mouth. I would have fallen with the force of the blow but he still held me. The pain was intense. Isza was behind me but she didn't move.

"Those left intact are either Kergis Kresz or too scared to speak up," I said. It hurt to talk.

The claws smashed into the side of my cheek, the partial plate taking some of the force of the blow. I fell back this time, but he came with me, kneeling above me, still holding onto my chest plate.

"Those who fought are suiciding. The house spikes are choked with their bodies."

Another punch. My head rang, but I still heard the rasp of a gaszti being unsheathed.

"Loyal Kresz. Kresz who honoured their house. Who fought against an alien invader." I was shouting now.

My attacker placed the blade at the spot where my chest plates overlapped. His face was all I could see. I wondered if Isza would intervene. I wanted her to but knew that would undo everything.

"Go on!" I shouted. "Finish the Hegemony's work for them. End us all if you want. Give Kergis his final victory."

His eyes bored into mine, sharper than any gaszti. The blade point withdrew. "What's your name?" he asked.

"My name is Udun."

He bent and helped me stand. "I am Tzulak."

The other newcomers watched. I couldn't tell what they were feeling, but they were looking at me now. Really looking at me.

Now the immediate danger had passed, Isza came to stand beside me again, assuming the role of my Defender.

"Shall we sit and share?" I said to Tzulak.

There was hesitation in the other group. No doubt emotions were shifting as our recent clash was absorbed.

"There is a Hegemony with you," Tzulak said.

"She's not a Hegemony," Isza said. "She's here to help, like the Jantri."

"She's an alien but also a friend," I said. "She'll share with us."

Tzulak considered then blinked. "Agreed," he said and sat.

The rest of his group sat too, the lumbering Defenders seeming to fall slowly to the floor, their bodies rasping as thick armour plates slipped over one another.

I motioned to Rhees to join us as we sat and she sank to the deck at the back of our group. I wondered what she thought of our behaviour. Were we animals to her or was this something she recognised? Did the Hegemony fight and kill each other? I wasn't sure what passed as civilised behaviour with them.

Isza told her group's story: the flight from Homeworld, almost crashing on the mining planet and living in the caves before the Jantri found them. Then I told them something of my adventures and they listened. It was as much as I could hope for. I was changing the ingrained behaviour of generations. It would take time, but I'd made a start and I needed to capitalise on that quickly by showing them, at every opportunity, that I was more use to them alive than dead.

Finally it was their turn.

"We're from the heavy cruiser *Kareee*," Tzulak said. "Haketiug had few ships but we were part of the contingent, under the protection of Kergis, that moved to defend the Point when the Hegemony came through."

Were they also part of the force that had chased Czerag's trade fleet, I wondered. It seemed likely.

"Our other heavy cruiser, the one with Hierarch Haketiug on it, was the first to blow when the Kergis ships broke formation," Tzulak continued. "We were right alongside and the blast knocked out our drive and sensors and put us into a spin. We flew – uncontrolled – right out of the combat zone. All our flyers were gone, launched into the battle. There was nothing to do but wait, either for a rescue ship or some Hegemony cruiser to come finish us off. Instead there was a tenspace shift beside us and then the Jantri were knocking at the main lock. We didn't let them in at first. Some of us wanted to fight them. But that didn't seem very sensible. Our command deck had been ripped open when Haketiug's ship went up. There were no command crew left, just Defenders, techs and support staff. We let the Jantri in and they brought us here."

"How long have you been here?" Isza asked.

"We're not sure. A long time."

The Jantri had been working in the background since before the invasion, I thought. Gathering resources. Had I been part of their plan from the beginning, or was I just a useful opportunity that came along at the right time? I looked around for Nok, but he must have left during our talk.

"Do you know what's happening on Homeworld now?" Tzulak asked.

"I think I saw the beginning of it when I was there," I said, "and we've picked up more information along the way. The Council has been dissolved. Kergis has installed himself as planetary leader. The old balance between the houses has been broken. The lodges too. The Hegemony enforces Kergis's will and kills or excises anyone who opposes them. In a single generation Homeworld will be nothing like you remember. That's why we have to act. And soon."

"Act? If our Defence Force couldn't win against the Hegemony, what can we do?"

"The Defence Force was betrayed," I said. "But even now there must be Kresz on Homeworld who oppose Kergis and the Hegemony. We all had our secret places. Czerag certainly did and we've been pooling our information, identifying the same for Houses Ukat, Dageru and even Akczek. I'm leaving soon to see if we can make contact."

"Perhaps you know of Haketiug hides?" Isza said.

"Perhaps," Tzulak said. "You would go back there, into such danger?" he asked me.

"Kergis has to be stopped. I'm prepared to do what's necessary."

"And when you come back?"

I couldn't help it: my feeders rattled in laughter. I stopped quickly in case they thought I was a mad excisee. If I made it back alive, it would be a miracle.

"When I come back," I said, "those who wish to fight and kill the Hegemony should be ready."

"Would you tell us where your people might be hiding on Homeworld?" Isza asked. "And the safewords they use to find each other?"

Tzulak looked from Isza to me. "I never thought I'd say this. But then I never thought I'd be talking to an excisee on a Jantri station. Yes, I'll tell you."

"Then let's eat and talk," I said.

Nok must have been listening from the control deck because a podule detached from a stack and rolled towards our group. The lid hissed open; it was full of meal packs. Nok wanted his resources well fed and healthy.

"The Jantri provide," Tzulak said.

The food wasn't the standard Kresz fare we'd been eating on Nok's ship. But strange as it looked, it tasted good. We sat again and Tzulak talked about the hides. As he spoke, I dared to believe – assuming we didn't get caught and killed – that this might actually work.

∞

Rhees sat at the back of the group and ate the spicy cubes of whatever. Everyone seemed to be one big happy family now. The Kresz that had nearly killed Udun while Isza and the others watched was talking about secret locations.

Nok had said Udun and the others were tools for him to use. Rhees was certain Nok saw her in exactly the same way. Still, if they *could* break HDC's hold on the Kresz that would hurt Volmar. It would be a start. She had the ultimate goal figured too. It was just the part about getting back to Earth and changing the whole way the Hegemony operated that was a little hazy.

Udun was the key to the first part. If he could link up with the Kresz resistance on Homeworld. But Nok – despite his preference for sitting in the shadows – would have to bring some big guns to the table when they were ready. Because Udun's rebels wouldn't be enough against Hegemony forces this well dug in.

She finished eating and listened to the conversation some more, but couldn't keep her eyes open. The lights were dimming, giving a sense of encroaching evening. Her internal clock felt like it was later. She pulled a sleeping mat from a pile near the bulkhead and found a curve of wall to lie beside.

She woke to activity all around. She couldn't remember the last time she'd slept the whole night. It felt like she'd been on the run and on edge for so long. The lights were bright again and Isza, Udun and the others were already talking in groups of two, three and four and sharing meal packs. Rhees pushed up to sitting and rubbed the sleep out of her eyes.

"Here," a voice said – or rather there was a sound louder than the background hum of conversation that the trink picked up and translated. Isza tossed her a meal pack.

More cubes in plastic. "My favourite," Rhees said and shuffled over to join Isza.

"Quite a sight," Isza said, indicating the other Kresz. "Things aren't always so convivial between the houses."

"The enemy of my enemy is my friend," Rhees said, adding when Isza looked at her oddly, "Old Hegemony wisdom. Or rather old Earth wisdom – the planet I came from. The Hegemony doesn't believe anyone is a friend."

"And what do you believe?" Isza asked. "Would you be a friend to Udun?"

Rhees looked over at Udun, who was talking to Agik and one of the newer Kresz. He was easily distinguishable by the cruel scar across his shoulders, but Rhees thought his difference from the others extended well beyond the physical. The way his mind worked, the way he saw the world … He'd been prepared to accept her before any of the others. Yes, she thought, he could be a friend.

"You're going to Homeworld with him," Isza went on. "And if you betray him, you'd better not come back."

The trink wasn't good at portraying the emotion behind words. But it didn't need to be. What did Isza want her to say? They'd only just met. And Rhees didn't know what she might have to do on the Kresz planet just to stay alive. But that was no answer.

"If he's in danger, it won't be from me," she said.

Isza held her gaze, then plucked a cube from Rhees's meal pack and popped it between her feeder claws where it was quickly pulled apart and stuffed through her mandibles.

"What else do the people of Earth believe?" she asked.

The tension had passed. Rhees breathed again, unaware until then just how stiffly she'd been holding herself.

"To err is human, to forgive divine," she said. That had come out of nowhere. But it seemed apt. "Another piece of wisdom the Hegemony chooses to ignore," she added.

In fact it felt to her at that moment that the whole Hegemony structure humanity had built up as a protective shield ran counter to a lot of received wisdom that had grown out of millennia of Earth culture. What about "love thy neighbour"? We've really messed ourselves up, she thought.

The main door opened and Nok walked in, the suit moving smoothly, robotic and alien.

"Rhees, Udun," he said. "Time to go. Say your goodbyes."

Rhees stood, suddenly fully alert. She hadn't expected things to move so fast.

"We'll both come back," she told Isza.

"I wish you good luck for that," Isza said, then turned to Udun and wrapped her double-jointed arms around him in a strong hug. "Be safe," she said softly.

"You be safe too," Udun said.

"Come," Nok said.

Udun untangled himself from Isza, who was reluctant to let go. He – kissed her, Rhees supposed – those crab-mouth feelers touching gently together. It wasn't repulsive. It was something in this strange-looking species she could understand.

Then she and Udun accompanied Nok out of the cargo bay, following the corridor as it curved along the central access. They passed a number of doors on what Rhees thought of as space side. No doubt more cargo bays like the one they'd left. Finally, Nok halted at another identical door and turned. Gold mist sparkled in his faceplate. Why even have a faceplate, Rhees thought. She'd never seen a face through that mist.

"I promised you a ship, Udun," Nok said. "You may find what's inside a little unsettling at first."

The door sliced open and they entered, as Rhees had suspected, another cargo hold: wide and high-ceilinged with broad lock doors at the other end big enough for a medium cruiser. She'd been expecting something like the dolphincraft, maybe a little larger for the two of them, but apart from cargo crates stacked along the left wall, the hold was empty. Had Nok chosen the wrong hold?

"So … ship?" she said.

"Three more steps," Nok said. "But carefully. I don't want you to injure yourselves."

They moved tentatively closer to nothing.

"Hold out your arms."

Rhees and Udun extended an arm each. Rhees moved forward a little more to compensate for her shorter reach until she felt … something. Four darkly smudged marks appeared at her fingertips. She pulled her hand back. The marks slowly faded. She looked at the ends of her fingers. They were unharmed.

Udun's claws touched nothing and again a dark blur appeared around the contact. "It feels spongy and cool," he said.

"Cool to your touch, Udun, but at the exact ambient temperature of this hold. The skin is a mimetic multiplanar laminate, functional across the entire visible spectrum and beyond. But that's only part of its shielding properties. Heat, electromagnetic signature, sonic resonance, everything about it blends in with its surroundings. Its weight doesn't even register."

"Gravity drive," Udun said.

"Yes. What do you think, Rhees?"

"I was already impressed with the dolphincraft stealth tech. This is …" She couldn't think of the words. Fleet had nothing like this.

"Shall we go inside?" Nok said.

"If you can find the door," Rhees said.

"That's what you need this for." Nok held out a thin metal disc. "Hold it in your fist in front of you. The door hatch is open." He handed another disc to Udun. "You don't want your enemy to see the entrance of your ship. Let the discs guide you."

Rhees held the disc in front of her and immediately felt a pull to the right. It was a strange sensation being led by her arm. She took a few steps, eyes focused on her outstretched fist, then felt the pull shift forward. She took another step, then stopped as her knuckles disappeared. She pulled her arm back. Her knuckles were unharmed.

"That's it," Nok said. "But you wouldn't want to linger if someone was after you."

Rhees could see his point. She pushed forward, arm slipping into nothing, and then her head was through the shielding or whatever it was and she was climbing a short flight of steps into an unremarkable corridor. She waited until Udun and Nok joined her.

"Straight ahead," Nok said. "I'm afraid there's not a lot of room. Most of the hull is taken up with the drive and stealth tech. Rations are stored in the corridor panels along here. And this," he pointed to a door on the right, "is the sanitary disposal. Multispecies-functional you'll be glad to know. But you'll spend most of your time forward."

The corridor opened onto a tightly curved bubble with two crash-chairs and little room for anything else. Readouts and controls crammed the wall space around a central tac screen.

"Home, sweet home," Rhees said.

"This is what your home looks like?" Udun asked.

Rhees shook her head, then, not sure the gesture would be understood, said, "Just an old Earth saying. I'm full of them today."

"Most of the systems are automated or have intuitive interfaces. Nothing a pilot like yourself can't work out, Rhees," Nok said.

"Weapons?" she asked.

"No. Built for speed not combat. No blast shielding for the same reason. Don't get into a fight."

Rhees turned to Udun. "We're really going to do this?"

27

I hesitated for only a moment, then folded my frame into the nearest crash-chair. For once it was surprisingly comfortable. "Yes," I said. "We are."

Nok palmed a locker under the vuscreen. The space held a rack of devices, lozenge-shaped with green lights blinking. "These are shielded and encrypted comms devices," he said. "Tenspace-capable and slaved to each other. If you do find others of your kind, these will let you set up a communications network that should be undetectable by the enemy."

"Let's hope it's more than 'should'," Rhees said.

"Nothing to keep you here," Nok went on. "The ship's prepped and ready."

Rhees had an expression on her face I hadn't seen before. I hoped she wasn't reconsidering. But then she sat in the other crash-chair and the wall of instrumentation activated, the screen showing force lines that represented the tenspace architecture outside the base.

"I see," Rhees said. She touched something on the armrest and the image shrank to show more of tenspace – a tunnel leading from the wide chamber holding the base and linking to a broader channel. A line appeared, showing a path from the base out into open tenspace.

Rhees was looking at the other systems set into the chair and along her side of the curved wall. "Propulsion, transit drive, navigation. What about comms?"

"Functional through Udun's chair," Nok said, pointing to a series of simple studs on my nearest armrest. "Transmission is locked to the base. I'll hear you wherever you are."

"Secure?" Rhees asked.

"The same as the comms devices. Encrypted and packeted into microbursts through some exotic spectra that are non-linear. Never the same one."

"What fuels the ship?" I asked. "We wouldn't want to run out."

"You won't," Nok said. "It's self-replenishing."

"Perpetual?" I asked.

"No. But not so you'd notice."

"Let's go then," Rhees said and touched a plate on the armrest.

I heard and felt the ship powering up.

"I hope to see both of you again soon," Nok said. "Where will you head first?"

"The south polar region," I said.

It wasn't what I'd intended to say, and I didn't know why I'd lied – Nok may be able to track the ship even on Homeworld. But something in me didn't want him to know every detail. We had to have something for ourselves.

"May your respective gods go with you," Nok said, and turned back along the short corridor.

After a moment Rhees said, "Hatch closed. And ... he's gone." Then she breathed out noisily. "So where are we really going?"

"It was that obvious I was lying?" I asked.

"Not until you just confirmed it. But it's what I would have done – to maintain mission security if for nothing else. Though if the ship's bugged, or he can track our location, he'll know anyway."

"That's not the point."

"Some partnership we have here," she said, touching the wall panel.

I didn't feel movement but, as the screen changed to an internal view of the hold, the ship turned towards open bay doors. A crackling maelstrom waited outside.

"Let's hope this ship is tenspace-proof as well as invisible," Rhees said.

We moved out into the storm and the view changed, shifting to look above us at the massive bulk of the station and the walls of the tenspace chamber. Thick twisting arms of plasma lashed out from the walls and struck the distant tip of the station, which cleared the way for us.

I was departing on another journey accompanied by an even stranger companion. If it hadn't been for Atalna, I wouldn't have survived the last trip. Rhees had her own reasons for helping me but I didn't want her life to end the same way. I couldn't be responsible for another death.

A smaller image opened in the corner of the screen. It was Nok. "Rhees, Udun. Just checking the comms link. What's your location?"

"We'll be entering the main tenspace corridor soon," I said.

"Good. Travel well." The image was gone before we could respond.

"Maybe the ship doesn't have a tracker," Rhees said.

"Or he wants us to think it doesn't," I said.

"You're thinking like me again. We certainly are ungrateful after he gave us such a nice ship. Here comes the junction."

Our forward progress slowed as we rounded a bend and saw the small opening.

"Sensors say it's clear," Rhees said. "Though I have no way of knowing if they work any better than Hegemony sensors in tenspace."

I found screen controls near the comms studs and cycled through views as we emerged into the corridor. Nothing in line of sight, ahead or behind. We accelerated smoothly.

"So where are we really going first?" Rhees asked.

"My homelands. A friend said he'd leave a message for me there if I ever needed help. It should speed things up considerably."

"And if we meet this friend or a bunch of other Kresz?"

"I'll explain you. But it's best if I do that before they see you."

"And how's that going to work? The last group of Kresz you bumped into tried to kill you right off. They weren't in the mood for conversation."

"They were following their instincts."

"Because you're different from them?" Rhees said. "Your scar."

I settled further into my chair. "It's not simply a matter of difference. It's a religious belief."

"What do you mean?"

"Our Priests teach that Sakat, who created us, set us on the path to perfection. That path doesn't allow for the sick and crippled."

"That's really extreme. And it's going to make explaining me difficult."

"We'll manage," I said, though I wasn't sure how.

Rhees lapsed into silence, but it was a comfortable one and, despite our destination, I felt relaxed. Let what would happen happen. I'd already survived longer than I or anyone else had expected.

Rhees spoke again. "The thing you people do with the hoods – you can read people's emotions?"

"Surface feelings generally, unless there's strong emotions or touch involved, or we're in communion. Then it goes deeper."

"I wouldn't like that. People knowing what I was feeling, even on the surface, before I opened my mouth. And then knowing how much I'm lying when what I say doesn't match what they're picking up from me."

"You say that coming to the concept as an adult. You might think differently if you'd grown up feeling and doing exactly those things. It can cause difficulties, but it can also be quite wonderful. To know just how much you're loved and trusted by another and to have them know how you feel in return, without the need for words. To be among others in your house and know there's a place for you. That you're accepted without condition. It's natural for us."

"You're a romantic, Udun."

"I don't know. I didn't really appreciate those things when I was home. All I could think of was getting away. But now it's something I can't experience … It's something worth saving."

There was silence again, each of us lost in our own thoughts. Tenspace whirled past the screen, but the ship was moving smoothly.

"You know Nok's using both of us," Rhees said.

"Yes."

"He wants me to use you in the same way. He told me on the station that you're a means to an end for him and for me."

"We all use one another, Rhees." The name sounded strange in my mouth and I wondered if I was saying it right.

"But that's the problem." Her voice was suddenly louder in the small space. "Nok uses me, I use you, you use Nok. It's what the Hegemony's been doing for years. But if you keep using people as objects, pretty soon that's all they are to you. You had your empathic sense stripped away from you. The Hegemony – well, they removed theirs deliberately because it was inconvenient. By keeping the human race safe, we've lost our humanity. This started out for me as a way to get back at Volmar. It's so much more than that now."

"You fear for the spirit of your species," I said.

"I suppose. But I wouldn't put it so grandly."

"But I know exactly what you mean. It's why I chose not to kill myself. With Kergis in sole control, the Kresz will be moulded to his worldview. And it's such a mean-spirited one."

"There's an alternative to using and being used," Rhees said.

"Yes?"

"We could cooperate as partners."

I thought about that. "You mean our cooperation would go beyond the satisfaction of our own needs and desires? We'd make the other's goal our own?"

She moved her head up and down. "I think that's a healthier way to act for both of us."

"The Kresz are insular by nature," I said. "We don't make friends with aliens. Any external relations only existed to support trade."

"And how's that been working for you?"

"Not very well. It was never something I agreed with. But I'm not an ordinary Kresz – more so now."

"I'm not an ordinary human. Look at what I'm doing. Most humans would brand me a species traitor and kill me on sight."

I thought about the many Kresz that would kill me as a matter of principle.

"So what are we going to do about it?" Rhees asked. "Keep on using each other like Nok wants?"

"I think I'd rather cooperate."

Her mouth split wide, showing white bone teeth so much like Emba's. "If we don't get ourselves killed, what do you want to do?"

"I want my people freed and the Hegemony gone. Then I want to heal the damage done and rebuild."

"That's what I want for my people too," she said.

"And how will you do that?"

"I'd like to present a grand plan to you, but I haven't got one. I've been pretty much feeling my way on this since Volmar tried to kill me. Helping you is a start because it looks like it will really hurt Volmar and, by extension, the Hegemony. If I can show people the Central Administration isn't infallible then it may make room for other voices like the Inclusionists to be heard."

We lapsed into silence again. As I watched the plasma shapes twist and change on the screen my mind wandered, creating images in those shapes: a face, a claw, an ah'lok. I didn't know how long I sat like that but eventually Rhees spoke.

"We have company."

We were in a straight channel. The colours were muted, shifting pinks and purples. At first I couldn't make out anything on the screen. Then I saw two regular shapes among the shifting forms. Ships. The one on the left was a Defender Lodge light cruiser, sharply tapered at the front with weapons ports all too evident. But the ship on the right was quite different. I realised it was the Jantri ship Isza had used on the contact mission, or one like it.

"They're Kresz," I said.

"But that one on the right is a Jantri-design ship."

"We purchased a few of them."

"Oh fuck," Rhees said. I didn't understand the word, but I could guess her meaning.

"Could the Jantri ship detect us?" I asked.

"They haven't given any sign yet. But they could just be waiting for us to make the first move."

"Or Nok's shielding is working."

"That would be nice," she said.

"Where are we?"

"Close enough to Kresz space for them to be a border patrol."

"If they've been here for a while, most of their systems will be powered down to slow a field build-up. But they'd have passive sensors and line of sight."

"Well, it's a good test," Rhees said. "Let's see if we can sneak past in plain sight."

We moved forward again. Would the other ships be able to infer our presence by how our passing affected the local field strength?

Rhees was steering a path straight down the centre of the tunnel.

"You're going to pass between them?" I said.

"It's that or wait and hope for them to move on. That could be days."

We glided closer. Still neither ship moved. Flares of energy strobed along the tunnel wall, but I didn't think they were caused by our movement. They sped away behind us, hopefully distracting whoever was monitoring.

We were almost beside them now. More detail on each ship was visible, lit by the all-pervasive plasma glow and the occasional flash. The Jantri ship was smoothly organic. The Kresz ship was a far rougher prospect. Closer now, the hull plates were visible and the substructure clear in how the plating angled and joined together. I followed the line of rough and pitted plates up the central spine and almost ducked involuntarily. On the flank of the ship sat an observation bubble, immediately above a small cannon battery. And standing in the dome, staring straight at us, was a Defender caste Kresz.

On the vuscreen, he seemed close enough to reach out through the glass and touch us. In fact he moved forward as we watched, pressing against the dome's curve.

"Does he see us?" Rhees asked softly. I saw her hand was poised on the thrust control.

Our ship was level with the others, passing between them. The Defender was motionless, still looking right at us. Then he stepped back and looked in the direction we had come from. The ships made no move.

I switched screen views to see the ships passing by us, then a rear view, showing primary engine ports as we left them behind. I breathed again.

Rhees's hand moved away from the thrust control. "I think I just aged five years," she said.

"How much further?" I asked.

"That patrol was still quite a way from the Point. There may be others between here and there."

"We should transit while we're in deep space then. It won't be as fast though."

"It might be faster, depending on how many patrols we meet," she said. "We'd be in trouble if they blocked a tunnel so completely we couldn't squeeze past."

"Where do you suggest?"

She brought up a tactical overlay correlating our tenspace position with realspace. "There's a stable chamber up ahead according to the charts. It still could take a couple of days to get to Homeworld. I'm not sure how fast this thing can go in normal space."

"If I know Nok, it won't take that long," I said. "Speed and stealth."

The patrol ships we'd passed vanished from sight round a curve in the tunnel.

"We should be prepared to run when we transit," Rhees said. "It's unlikely but there may be ships on the other side, and I doubt even the Jantri can mask a transit effect."

We came to the chamber – a dark space that felt smaller than it probably was after travelling through bright channels.

"Let's do it," I said.

Rhees looked at the panel. "I've had some experience with Jantri ships. Which means this," she indicated a toggle at the end of the armrest, "should be it. Either that or it evacuates the ship's atmosphere."

"That's what passes for humour in the Hegemony?" I said.

"I'm funnier after a few drinks."

She pressed the toggle and I tensed for the painful non-being of transit. Nothing came.

"Are you sure …" I began, but the view on the screen confirmed it. We were in realspace. Instant transition with no physical effects.

"All right," Rhees said. "Let's see what this thing can do."

The starfield on the screen blurred as the ship leaped forward but we felt no acceleration inside. It was as if we were at rest and the universe was rushing past us faster and faster.

Rhees checked system readouts. "This is incredible," she said finally. "We're already at point two C and accelerating. It's like the ship is rolling space into an infinite downward curve that we're running along. But we're frictionless. The interstellar medium is being bent around us so there's no chance of colliding with an energetic particle. Meanwhile the space distortion is being masked. I'd expect a bow wave or aft turbulence at least. But it's smooth in front and behind. We're little more than a blip."

"Speed and stealth," I said again.

"Yes, but the tech here is beyond anything the Hegemony has."

"It's beyond what we've seen of Jantri tech in the Lenticular too."

"So, again," Rhees said, "are we really needed in this war, or are we protective cover? A distraction while Nok oversees whatever the hell the Jantri are really up to?"

"I honestly don't know," I said. "Kresz have lived alongside the Jantri longer than I can remember. If we had anything they wanted, it's obvious they could have simply taken it. We'd be powerless to stop them. For what it's worth, I think Nok's being as truthful as he can be. The Jantri want the Hegemony gone, but they don't want to be seen as the ones doing it, or not right away."

"That or there's some esoteric Jantri reason behind this we can't fathom."

"Or that, yes. Always that."

"Well, we're still accelerating. We'll be in Kresz space in less than a day," she said.

If we got through this and the Hegemony left, the Jantri wouldn't be able to hide their true selves any more. What would that mean for life in the Lenticular?

∞

There was nothing to do but sit and wait. Just like Fleet life, Rhees thought. Days of boredom broken up by seconds of sheer terror.

She glanced at Udun. He was still staring out into the black.

"I'd like to talk to a friend," she said. "He's on Earth, but he has information that will help."

Udun's feeder mandibles spread wide. "You trust this friend?"

"With my life. He's like me. He worked for the Hegemony, but now he knows how wrong things are."

"Nok said these comms were slaved to the Jantri base."

She knew her way around Jantri comms now. "I think I can fix that."

Udun blinked slowly. "Agreed."

She brought up the interface and linked her band. It shouldn't take long for her signal to find a Hegemony ship with a Voss Space booster. And the HDC identity Denev had given her meant her access wouldn't be questioned or tracked. Twenty minutes later, her link was confirmed.

"All clear," she said, and Udun shifted in his seat to watch the broadcast interface.

A square of grey projected on the wraparound. Rhees entered Denev's ident code and the window filled with numbers flashing through channels and hierarchies.

Finally Denev was there, seated in a small apartment, or maybe just a dorm room. She could see a bed and locker over his shoulder. He looked pale and tired.

"It's safe to talk," he said.

"Are you all right? You look slammed."

A half-smile ghosted onto his face. "Too much immersion. I'm trying to convince kids to commit domestic terrorism."

"Volmar's idea?"

He winced. "Mine. But it fits the brief he gave me and I have to keep him on side."

She sympathised. He was deep in enemy territory.

"And I was on Mars when Volmar killed the Inclusionist Minch," Denev went on.

"Fuck, you were with him?"

"Wait," Denev said. "You already know Volmar did it?"

Rhees glanced at Udun. "From an eyewitness."

Denev sat back and slowly shook his head. "It doesn't matter. He acted with the full backing of the Central Administration."

"Are you safe?" she asked. Maybe he should just get the fuck away from there. But if Volmar was suspicious it would be nearly impossible to leave Earth without him finding out.

"I honestly don't know. I'm alive for as long as I'm useful."

"So stay useful. Do whatever you have to do." She'd never seen him look so tired, but it was more than immersion fatigue. He looked defeated. "I mean it, Denev. I need you. If you have to kill to prove you're loyal, do it."

Again the weak smile. He leaned forward. "I have the campaign comms protocols. I'm still tracking down a full Fleet and HDC ship deployment in the Lenticular, but I do have troop deployment intel on the Kresz Homeworld. Sending now."

Her band vibrated.

"I'll put these to good use." She wished she was there to help him or that he was here to help her. It seemed unlikely they'd both survive to come out the other end of this.

He opened his mouth to say something then paused. Thought better of it. "I have to go," he said. "I'm due to make my report."

"Don't do anything stupid," she said.

"That's your area of expertise."

"Yeah. Don't remind me. Expect my call."

She broke the contact and stared at the empty frame for long seconds until Udun spoke.

"I saw him on Mars. He was with Volmar."

"I know. But Denev hates Volmar as much as I do. And he'll help us."

"Volmar's at the centre of all this," Udun said.

"It looks that way." She made sure the comms array was fully disengaged and checked their heading. "But even Volmar couldn't do what he does without the support of some very powerful people."

"Then they must all be stopped."

Rhees wondered again how she could stop the Hegemony without endangering billions. "It'll be hard," she said. "We have to keep the innocent safe. But Volmar and the others will use them as a shield."

"The innocent must fight too if they are to be free."

If only it was that easy, she thought.

28

Rhees reviewed the information her friend had sent her, then slept while I kept a watch on sensors. The ship was perfectly still and quiet even though we were now travelling at an appreciable fraction of the speed of light.

Seeing the Human – Denev, Rhees had called him – who had been there when Atalna was murdered had been a shock. But it was clear Denev and Rhees had a close bond, something like the one I shared with Isza. Now there were two Humans who chose to fight alongside us and against their own kind. Just as I'd discussed with Atalna back at Emba's villa, it seemed even the most aggressive species could not be completely evil.

By the time I next woke, we were decelerating into Kresz space. Our approach meant we were on the opposite side of the system from the Point, where I suspected most of the patrols would be concentrated. But vast as the space around Homeworld was, we did see two patrol ships. They were halfway in-system, in the shadow of A'ronn, the pink-belted gas giant. By the time our sensors saw them, we were already well past.

"Any contact?" Rhees asked.

I watched the tactical display. The ships were still following their course out past A'ronn. "Nothing obvious."

"I didn't think so. No offence, but if Nok's ships can evade Hegemony sensors, Kresz tech isn't going to present any problems. Still I'd rather not hang too long in orbit," she continued. "Just where are we going?"

"My own house in the escarpment north-east of Aktiuk city. It'll be under Kergis's control now but I have to get in there. It's the only way to find out exactly where my people are hiding."

"If they made it out," Rhees said.

"Most did. We'll put down on top of the escarpment. There are any number of ways in from there."

"And if we're challenged?"

"*We* won't be going in," I said. "I will."

Rhees made a rasping sound in her throat as she checked the escarpment's location.

The universe slowed as Homeworld approached. It looked the same as it always had, at least from this distance. On the tactical display we could see a number of ships, but our course took us well clear of them. Some must be on patrol, but others would be normal planetary traffic, probably going to or from the Hub.

Rhees had brought up a terrain overlay. "Here," I said, indicating the escarpment. "If we land far enough from the edge, I should be unobserved when I leave the ship. Especially if we wait for night."

"From the troop data Denev sent, that's pretty much Hegemony HQ right now. It's crawling with humans."

I'd imagined penetrating the escarpment would be difficult, but now … "Even with the Hegemony inside, there are many secret ways into the house," I said.

It was clear we were completely invisible both to the ships in orbit and planetary sensors, so Rhees manoeuvred us in close orbit until we were above Czerag lands and locked our movement with the planetary rotation.

The sky beneath us was cloudless and the line of the escarpment was visible even from this high up. The land was laid out like a softly rumpled sleep mat, shadows deepening in the folds of the dunes as sura, djel and ataz sank to the horizon. The play of colour on the sand shifted as each sun dropped from sight. Sura flared on the horizon, a final beacon, and then it was night.

"We should wait until whoever is at the escarpment is asleep," I said.

"Okay, but it doesn't prevent us taking a look around."

The view of the land below changed as our ship dropped towards the surface. Red beacons were dotted along the edge of the escarpment where none had been before, and between the oasis and the small landing pad were two long strings of yellow lights, arranged so one line crossed the other at their midpoint. Each light alternated on and off in sequence, the flashes leading the eye from the desert to the escarpment.

The image onscreen lightened as the view shifted spectrum. Ranged along the edge of where the lights ran were rows of ships. Small fighters like the Hegemony attack craft I'd seen at the Point. Figures moved among them. As the image panned, more figures became clear, stationed near the main entrance to the house and along the top of the escarpment where the red lights showed.

"No, you can't go in on your own," Rhees said.

"Why not? I just said –"

"Look. Do you see any Kresz moving around down there?"

The magnification rolled along the escarpment then swept across the desert floor. All we could see were blue uniforms moving in a way that was clearly non-Kresz.

"No," I said.

"And can you get to where you need to go without being seen?"

The chances of *that* were vanishingly small.

"Your house is under occupation," Rhees said. "I suspect any Kresz inside will either be loyal to your traitor –"

"Kergis," I said.

"Yes, or …" She hesitated. "Excised slaves."

She was right, of course. "So what do you suggest?"

∞

Rhees hadn't wanted to mention Udun's mutilated hood, but there wasn't room for sentiment in this kind of mission. Udun had seen the logic of her suggestion immediately, which Rhees appreciated. He would be her indigenous liaison. Little more than a slave really.

Now, of course, Rhees was terrified. It was that old pre-mission fear from her Fleet training days and it would vanish as soon as they got moving. Or she hoped it would. She'd gone over every detail she could think of, even getting Udun to sketch a layout of the house interior and their objective – Czerag's throne room was how Rhees thought of it. But there were still too many unknowns. What was the disposition of guards and checkpoints? How big a force? Were there even any Kresz allowed inside?

The house itself was another problem. She knew the main rooms and connecting chambers now, but if they got into a fight, or had to run, or – worse still – got separated, there were so many tunnels it wasn't certain she'd be able to find her way to safety. A Fleet-issue assault rifle would make her feel better, but HDC didn't use them. All she had was the flechette pistol she'd stolen from the battlecruiser. It was next to useless against body armour or heavier weapons. Udun would be unarmed. Anything else wouldn't fit their story.

Stay sharp and act like you're meant to be there, she thought. But it didn't do much to take away her nerves. Luckily Udun was hopeless at reading human emotional cues – the mounting nervous energy that made her fiddle with the tac screen focus or check the sensors, then check them again, and again – so he was probably ignorant of how she was feeling.

It was only when she took the controls to bring the ship down for landing that she finally calmed. The anti-grav drive was silent and responsive. They slipped slowly down through layers of atmosphere – no heat signature from re-entry friction; no visible image to track; and, she hoped, total transparency to any sensors deployed in their direction.

The chosen landing spot was well back from the lip of the escarpment in a natural depression in the rock. There was no sound as they touched down, no thruster wash kicking up rocks or dirt, nothing at all to see as the invisible ship settled on landing struts. The screen showed a 360-degree view around the ship. Nothing moved. Rock-penetrating radar showed the escarpment was solid for a hundred metres below with no tunnels nearby. Everything checked out.

Rhees powered down the systems and checked the flechette gun again. There was no more reason to delay.

"Time to face the music," she said.

"I don't understand," Udun said.

"Never mind. Let's go."

Rhees opened both lock doors, straining to hear any sound above the soft whish of the outer door opening and the muted hiss of the invisible steps deploying to the dusty rock floor.

She went first, the flechette pistol in her pocket. Stepping away from the opening, she turned to look back at the ship. All she could see was the gently curving rock floor softly illuminated by a star-filled sky. There was no moon tonight. A lucky bonus.

Rhees looked in the direction of the escarpment edge. It was almost a kilometre away and not visible from the depression the ship had landed in. She was standing in the middle of what looked like a natural amphitheatre which had been further shaped by hand – judging from the marks in the stone. Curving stone steps led down from the higher escarpment floor on either side. They were broad enough to carry large crowds. The side walls sloped gently down to meet the rock floor at the far end, which rose, Rhees could see as she turned, to – what?

"What is that?" she said, moving towards a broad and unnaturally flat monolith or some kind of stone table. Behind it, dark against a lighter sky, were what looked like a row of giant metal teeth, cruelly pointed and flaring down from the tips but then the shapes jumbled, suddenly irregular.

Udun moved past her, almost leaping on those strange double-jointed legs, and Rhees ran to catch up. Rounding the stone table she saw exactly what the irregular shapes were. Bodies. Kresz bodies impaled on the sharp metal. And not just one to each tooth. The broken carcasses were stacked one on top of the other, arms and legs draped over the body below in some loose death embrace. On the floor – not more bodies, but body parts. Armour-encased arms, legs, blank-eyed heads, unrecognisable broken pieces of shell, organs clinging to the insides, everything covered in a thick, glistening yellow ichor.

Rhees gagged but swallowed it back. She could hear Udun breathing beside her, that strange, almost machine-like respiration. She couldn't look at him. This was too much. These beings had been alive when they were impaled. She could tell that from the twisted claws, the wide open mandibles set in a final death scream.

Udun said one word. It sounded like "Bvak" but the trink offered no translation. He was kneeling by the second-last spike and its grisly stack of bodies, holding a lifeless arm. Its chitin was dark, thicker-looking, than Udun's own.

Rhees kneeled too. The body the arm was attached to was resting on top of two others and relatively intact. A face stared out, partially covered by the hood of the victim on top. Udun held the flesh aside to look into the face.

"Bvak," he said again.

"You knew him?" Rhees asked.

"They were all killed intact," Udun said. "They'd be lined up. Waiting. Feeling the metal pierce each body before them, hearing the death scream as if it was their own, experiencing that agony again and again and again until they felt it for real. Bvak didn't deserve that. None of them did."

It was brutal even by HDC standards, Rhees thought. Calculated to produce a precise effect.

"I'm sorry," she said. "I know that doesn't even begin to –"

"Your people didn't do this," Udun said. "Before the Emergence, before the Kresz became empathic, this is how battles were ended. The victors who overthrew a stronghold would put everyone to death, using the spikes and leaving the bodies unconsumed. It was the ultimate insult."

He straightened, and Rhees stood too. "Kergis's people did this?" she asked.

"Yes. Fully intact Kresz did this to other Kresz who also had their mantles. I can't understand how they could do it without being sent mad. But there's a lot I don't understand about how Kergis and his followers kept their plans from the worldmind right up until they turned on us at the Point."

"We'll find out," Rhees said. "But we should go now. We're too exposed here."

Udun didn't move, and Rhees thought he might be losing it. She was about to say something – though she didn't know what – when Udun let go the arm he'd been holding.

"This way," he said.

They moved around and past the spikes onto slowly rising ground. Thankfully there were no more bodies. At the lip of the depression, which was shallower here at the back of the amphitheatre, the ground levelled off and receded into darkness.

"This is the path excisees follow when they've been expelled from the house," Udun said, speaking softly. "They take the long walk, away from everything they've known. Though by this point they're probably mad. Loss of the mantle will do that."

Rhees looked at the ragged scar across Udun's shoulders as he walked ahead. He was far from mad, she thought. Somehow he'd been strong enough to keep going.

"There aren't meant to be any entrances into the house out here," he said. "But I found one a long time ago, exploring with Isza. I think the Defenders used it, maybe to make sure excisees kept walking."

A solid darkness in the starlight turned into a large boulder, almost as big as a two-person transport. They rounded it. Rhees couldn't see a thing in the shadows but she sensed Udun crouching.

"You see here, at the base?" he said.

"I can't see anything. It's too dark."

"You really can't see this?"

"No," Rhees said. "No augs."

"I'll guide you then. Give me your hand."

Rhees held her hand out, a pale blur, and felt hard claws close around it. The insides of the claws were ridged, perhaps to help grip things, and the shell was warm. Hot almost.

"Keep low and watch your head," Udun said. "The base of the rock slopes in and down over an opening in the ground. There's an incline, about as deep as you are tall, down to the tunnel floor. Sit on the ground and bring your legs forward. Can you feel it?"

Rhees sat on the dirt. Udun still had her hand and it felt like he was in front of her but lower. She extended her legs until she felt the hole, then pushed forward until she was sitting on the lip. She tightened her grip on Udun's clawed fist and slid down until her heels hit bottom.

"You can stand here," Udun said. "The tunnel slopes down into the main network."

Something dark moved across Rhees's field of vision. She realised it must be Udun and that the way ahead was lighter. The dark shape moved again.

"Wait," she said in a whisper. "What are we going to find here?"

"What do you mean?"

"Well, the outside is crawling with Hegemony. We didn't see one Kresz. Do you think there are any inside?"

"It's possible. If the Hegemony have taken this as a stronghold, there may be Kergis Kresz here too."

"I agree. But they'd be here as secondary personnel. The humans are in charge."

"That makes sense," Udun said.

"So I should go first. You're my indigenous liaison, remember. Just keep me pointed in the right direction and let's try to skirt what may be the busier areas."

The darkness moved to one side. "After you – master," Udun said.

Rhees stepped forward. Her skin was tingling and she wished she could take her pistol out of her pocket. Puny as it was, it would make her feel better. But no. She was an HDC sector chief and she had the right to go anywhere she damn well pleased. Walk like you own the place, she thought, and just hope you don't run into any more HDC.

She started along the corridor, Udun following. The floor still sloped down, which made walking in the semi-dark tricky. She could see a better-lit T-junction ahead and tried to extend her senses, straining to hear if others were there.

"Left," Udun said behind her.

No skulking, she thought, and barely slowed as she turned the corner. The tunnel was empty. Globes studded the walls at regular intervals and the rock arched overhead, tall enough for a fully grown Kresz. Ripples and indentations in the walls showed the stone had been worked, but a long time ago. These tunnels spoke of a long history of civilisation.

However the Hegemony justified its actions in near-Earth space, she had to believe that if normal citizens knew what was happening in the Lenticular, they'd protest against it. There was no reason to annexe the Kresz Homeworld. They weren't a threat to humanity or the mission against the Hanloi. And nothing could justify how the invaders had mutilated the Kresz that fought against them. But how could she cut through the misinformation the CA had been drip-feeding Earth for decades?

A hundred metres along, the corridor split, branching in four directions.

"Second on the left," Udun said.

As they passed the junction, Rhees thought she caught a glimpse of movement down the tunnel to the right. But she kept moving and heard no shout or pursuing footsteps.

There were signs that these tunnels had been more regularly used. Woven wall hangings were attached to the rock, and there were door openings with cloth draped over them, but the rooms were all empty. Some showed signs of a hasty evacuation. A satchel lay in one doorway, the cloth flap open, and Rhees saw it was half-full with what looked like pottery figurines. Further along, another room, which had lost its cloth door hanging, was piled with rolled-up mats made of reeds or some other flexible material.

Her attention snapped forward as they rounded another curve. A figure stood where the corridor branched again. Even in the dim light it was impossible to mistake the black body armour, the assault rifle slung at belly height.

As Rhees got closer, she saw the soldier's sensor helm was pushed back to reveal a young face. Younger than her, anyway. Walk like you own the place, she reminded herself.

She stopped three metres from the guard. "Bored, soldier?"

The boy held his rifle tighter when he saw Udun looming over Rhees's shoulder. "No, sir." The answer came smartly enough.

Present someone with a good enough approximation of what they expect to see and they'll go the rest of the way themselves, Rhees thought.

She held out her hand. "Check my band so I can be about my business."

The boy ran a standard reader over her band, looking intently at the small screen. From the look on his face, he'd been apprised of the fact he was detaining HDC Sector Chief Elna Darrow, the persona Denev had given her.

He stood a little straighter. "Thank you, sir. Your Kre—"

"It's with me," Rhees said, already moving forward and hoping Udun was following.

The guard stepped back, unwilling to press the matter.

The tunnel branched ahead, one path left, the other right. Rhees couldn't stop to consult Udun so she chose the right, and kept going until she judged the downward slope had carried them out of sight.

"Am I still going the right way?" she asked.

"Yes. At each fork now, bear right. It will bring us into the more central corridors, but we can't avoid that now."

"It doesn't matter," she said. "Our guard friend will have called ahead. I expect we'll be met further on. If our cover doesn't hold, we'll have to make a break."

"If that happens, follow me. I'm sure I know these tunnels better than the Hegemony."

She had no choice. She was deep in enemy territory now. She'd said they should trust one another completely.

They came to another branch and Rhees took the right corridor. Again it sloped down, but this one broadened out and had more light globes set into the walls.

She didn't falter when a group of three Kresz rounded the turn ahead, walking towards them. They were dressed in cloaks like Udun. Their talk stopped as soon as they saw Rhees, or – more precisely – Udun. Their eyes locked on him and Rhees could almost feel the aggression in the air. These Kresz wanted Udun dead. Perhaps all Kresz would because of his condition. But these had more reason than most to hate an excisee. Their clothing – even though it was like Udun's – was of much better quality, and spotless. Their shells were highly polished, almost shining in the brighter tunnel. The nearest Kresz had intricate whorls and spirals cut into the chitin of each forearm, the shapes inlaid with a brassy metal. The others wore metal armbands, torques, jewelled rings. To Rhees it was obvious: these were the victors enjoying their spoils, their new place in the world. Udun was an uncomfortable reminder of their treachery to their own kind.

She moved to the side of the corridor, Udun behind her, to let the others pass. There was a sharp slapping sound. Followed by another. And another. Rhees turned to see the group's retreating backs and Udun steadying himself against the wall. He waved a claw to Rhees to keep going.

Round the bend, the tunnel connected with a large, wide hall-like cavern, its roof arching away into darkness above floating glow globes. The room was set up like a mess hall with long plastic tables in three rows along its length, and what had to be over a hundred Hegemony troopers sitting at them in small groups.

As Rhees and Udun entered, conversation died. But Udun wasn't the cause this time. Eyes turned to Rhees and just as quickly slid away. It was the uniform, of course. Rhees had hated the reaction it caused among grunts even more than the grunts hated the sight of the HDC insignia on her breast pocket. But this time she was grateful for it. By the time they were fully into the room, conversations had started up again and she was being studiously ignored.

They headed for the continuation of the tunnel at the far end of the hall. Halfway there, it became clear their path wasn't to go unchallenged. A man wearing light armour and corporal insignia on his chest peeled off from one of the tables and waited for them, hands clasped behind his back. His dark hair stood straight up in the severe buzz cut favoured by zero-G warriors, and his lined face was deeply tanned. He threw Rhees a lazy salute as they approached and Rhees returned it. She was a good head taller than the corporal, but where she was slim and well-muscled, he was solidly built. Dense almost, with a broad chest tapering to a slim waist and arms that looked out of proportion the biceps were so thick.

"Perimeter advised us of your arrival, Sector Chief. Can I be of assistance?"

"Not really, Corporal," Rhees said in as bored a tone as she could muster. "This is HDC business. We can manage."

"I'm afraid I must accompany you, sir. Orders. I'm to provide you with whatever you need."

I bet, Rhees thought. Though she could understand it. Military command put up with HDC interference. They had to. But they took every opportunity to monitor their activities. Looked like they'd picked up a watchdog.

"My assistant and I are here to examine the hierarch's chamber."

Rhees saw the corporal's eyes sharpen. No doubt he was dying to ask the obvious question. But he knew better than to question an

HDC officer. Corps work was strictly on a need-to-know basis, and the way HDC worked, the military seldom needed to know.

"It's down this corridor," the corporal said, indicating the tunnel behind.

"We know," Rhees said, and the corporal's gaze shifted up and over her shoulder.

"Your –"

"My liaison with the natives," Rhees said. "Its local knowledge is useful."

"Certainly," the corporal said. "If you'll follow me."

The tunnel opened into a large chamber with two massive doors at the far end, which she figured must be the main entranceway to the desert. The corporal led them to the left and through another tunnel into a small vestibule ending in two thick wooden doors. There was another guard there. The corporal pulled at the doors and the metal shield wall behind rose into the rock above to reveal a softly lit chamber.

Before the corporal could lead them inside, Rhees said, "We'll go in alone."

The corporal clearly wanted to argue, but Rhees took the advantage and walked past him. "You can wait out here," she said, and then she and Udun were over the threshold. Udun pressed a small stud on the inner wall and the thick shield ground shut on the two soldiers.

There was a partition wall immediately in front of the door. They moved around it. It was clear to Rhees that this wasn't a natural cave. The vestibule outside had been naturally formed, but the interior was entirely plated in metal, bent and bolted together so that no gaps remained in the skin. The room was bare except for a bank of wall screens, a rough stone bench set across two stubby uprights.

"Now what?" she asked.

"Now I find out where my friends are hiding." Udun plucked a globe from the wall, lay on his back and pushed with his legs to slide under the bench.

With no one observing them, Rhees got down there too. Udun's claws were tracing a series of marks on the bench's underside – vertical lines incised into the stone. Three lines, a gap, two lines, gap, four lines, gap, one line, gap, five lines, gap, three lines.

"What does it mean?" she asked.

"Before I left the house for the last time, I met with Tzek, Czerag's advisor. Trouble was brewing with Kergis and he told me if the worst happened, he'd leave word on where to find him. This is a code we developed for my first trip to the Lenticular, in case I wanted to send a message to Czerag. I know where they went now."

A rumbling noise filled the artificial cave. The sound of the shielded door grinding open. Udun moved quickly, pushing away from the bench and standing upright in one fluid move. Rhees scrambled to her feet.

The door ground shut again, then a Kresz with the same body type as Udun, but in much better condition, strode around the partition. Its shell was burnished to a dark red with the metal inlay Rhees had seen earlier, and it wore a robe of very fine quality shot through with golden thread. It reminded her of the djellaba Denev had given her on Herakli. But that had been lost a long time ago.

"Well, well, well," the Kresz said. "Nomak said he thought he recognised you. I had to see it for myself."

Rhees's first instinct was to grab for her pistol and shoot. But flechettes wouldn't be much use against Kresz armour. Besides, their cover wasn't blown yet.

"I don't believe I know you," she said, sounding as pissed off as possible.

"Forgive me, honoured ally." This with a short bow, but Rhees couldn't tell if the Kresz was being sarcastic. "I am Erdjis, aide to Rector Kergis, whom I am sure you have heard of."

"Fine. But you're interrupting HDC business. You will have to leave."

"What business do you have with him?" Erdjis said, looking towards Udun.

"I don't have to explain myself to you," Rhees said.

Erdjis shifted to loom over Rhees. He wasn't a Defender, but he was still imposing enough. "Do you even know who he is? Udun, have you told her?"

"He's a slave," Rhees said. "Like any other slave, he does as he's told or he's punished."

"No, no, no, no, no," Erdjis said, shaking his head in a human gesture that spoke of long association. "He doesn't look like a slave. He's excised, yes, but in his eyes … He's not broken. Just why are you –"

Rhees pulled her flechette pistol and levelled it point-blank at Erdjis's eye.

"Don't move," she said, and for a moment Erdjis didn't. Then the Kresz grabbed for the gun.

Rhees fired, darts spattering uselessly against chitin, and leaped back. Suddenly Udun was on Erdjis, wrapping his own limbs around the other Kresz to bring them both down in a crashing heap. Erdjis lay prone on top of Udun, arms and legs trapped but struggling hard to get free.

Rhees aimed the pistol again, but didn't know where to shoot. Erdjis's armour looked impenetrable.

Udun had Erdjis's arms trapped with one arm now. With his free claws he reached around to grab Erdjis's skull plate and pulled the head back. "Above the neck ring," he rasped. "The flesh is exposed."

Rhees saw the spot and leaned over the two Kresz. Erdjis struggled harder, but couldn't get free. Desperate eyes met Rhees's and Erdjis screamed.

Rhees positioned the pistol and fired on automatic. A yellow line bloomed across exposed skin. The scream stopped. She moved the pistol from left to right, angling the firing pattern away from Udun. Yellow blood sprayed in her eyes.

There was a click as the magazine emptied, then a soft tearing sound like wet paper and the head rolled from Udun's grip and onto the floor. No blood came from the wound. It was as if whatever passed for Kresz arteries had self-sealed.

"Help me," Udun said. He was trying to pull free of the deadweight on him.

Rhees bent and pulled Erdjis's arm until the body slid to one side. Udun got to a crouch.

"Are you all right?" she asked. "I didn't hit you?"

"Just a scratch," he said and pointed to a deep score on his shoulder plate.

"Someone must have heard that scream, or … wouldn't they 'feel' his death?"

Udun blinked. "Not in here. Soundproof and shielded against empathics. The perfect killing room actually, though I doubt it's ever been used for that. We may still get out of here alive – if we can get past your guard outside. This room has secure comms facilities. Tell them Erdjis is communicating with Rector Kergis and mustn't be disturbed."

Rhees tore a strip of fabric from Erdjis's cloak and wiped the blood from her face. Then she took a deep breath, stepped around the screening wall and activated the stud.

The corporal was nowhere to be seen; just the guard, who stood straighter as the shield lifted.

"You couldn't stop that crab from disturbing us?" Rhees said.

"Sorry, sir. He insisted."

"He 'insisted'? Just remember who's in charge here. He's talking to his crab leader on the comms now. Leave him in there. That's all for now."

"Corporal Wagner told me to take you to see the CO, Major Gruder, sir."

Rhees laughed dryly. "I have more pressing tasks. I'll see your Major Gruder later. You can leave us now."

The soldier hesitated for a moment, then turned and left the vestibule.

"Back the way we came?" Rhees whispered when he was gone.

"It seemed quiet enough. But we'll avoid the hall where your kind were eating. I know a side tunnel."

"Good."

"One thing," Udun said. "What does 'crab' mean?"

"It's an Earth animal that has some of the characteristics of your physiology. Sorry, but I meant it as an insult. Fleet doesn't have much of a reputation for non-human tolerance."

They started back along the tunnel.

In the main entrance hall a group of Hegemony troops were filing through the massive doors into the desert, while another group filed in.

"Go right," Udun said.

"I know," Rhees murmured, striding forward with all the swagger of a high-ranking HDC official.

They crossed the entrance hall and entered the sloping corridor that led to the mess hall. Udun's claw brushed her right shoulder just as she came to an opening cut into the wall. She read his signal and pushed through the thin cloth hanging into a low room crammed with cargo crates.

She studied the manifest tabs on the nearest crates. "Rations, rations, toiletries, uniforms, comms gear. Shit. Not a single weapon."

"We need to keep moving," Udun said.

The opening on the far side of the room brought them into a corridor parallel to the one they'd left. Rhees started up the incline, moving as quickly as possible without seeming to hurry. Anytime now, Colonel Wagner was going to start asking –

A low tone sounded, rising steadily then repeating.

"Alarm," Rhees said and ran.

Rounding the next corner she halted so quickly that Udun almost ran into her back. A guard was standing in the middle of the tunnel, his rifle unslung and pointed halfway between the floor and where Rhees stood.

"They're behind us," Rhees shouted. "Get down!"

She ran forward again, Udun following her lead.

The guard hesitated and then they were on him, Rhees diving low and crashing into his stomach while Udun grabbed for his gun, ripping it out of his hands as they all fell.

There was a muffled crash. Udun rolled to one side as Rhees grabbed the man's shoulders, but he wasn't moving.

"Neck snapped," she said, rising.

Udun was holding the man's rifle.

"I'll take that," she said. "Any other guards we meet are likely to shoot first at an armed Kresz. Let's go."

29

Eagle Downs Mine, Cape York Conurb, Earth / Sol System / Hegemony

Denev had been waiting in the dark for half an hour. Don't do anything stupid, Rhees had said. This certainly qualified. Almost a kilometre behind him lay the tunnel entrance, raked into the side of a hill – the mouth to a road that went nowhere. Somewhere ahead was a gallery extending two kilometres straight down. This had been one of the last fossil fuel mines built, and it had never gone into production. Instead it was mothballed for over two hundred years, then used to store emergency equipment at the height of the K-Chaan war, then mothballed again. Crates of gear were stacked along the walls, unused and slowly rotting. Technology from a bygone era. The service road in had completely grown over, and the sweep he'd done had confirmed the site had been left untouched for years. Still, it was a risk. Everything was.

He heard the whisper-whine first – a cyke moving slowly – then saw a blue-white radiance dancing across the stacks. He stepped out of the shadows into the cyclops eye of the light. The cyke stopped with a squeal of gyros.

"Put that light out," he said.

The eye blinked shut and Denev shook an emergency lumen-stick to life. Preem stood in the sick yellow light, his cyke balancing peg-leg behind him.

He spread his arms wide. "I'm here. So what's the big secret?"

"I'm not sure you're the guys for the job," Denev said.

Preem's brow furrowed and his hands lifted higher, like he was surrendering. "What?"

"Torp," Denev said.

"Torp's solid. I vouch for him."

"You?" Denev's face cracked in a grin. "You *vouch* for him? This isn't some game of neobal. I need to know I can count on everyone."

"And I said Torp is solid," Preem repeated, his voice low and tight.

Denev folded his arms and leaned back against a crate. He knew Preem wouldn't be put off, but he could be delayed. Then he'd have time to figure out how to not get these idiots killed.

"I don't —"

There was the barest whisper of sound, but he'd been in the tunnel long enough to separate ambient noise from something else — something caused. He was pushing off the crate and reaching into his jacket for his gun when they swarmed him. Dark figures. Hooded. Three, maybe more.

One hit high, trapping Denev's arms as he fell to the ground. Another grabbed at his legs and the third stood above him — black hood, night scope, breather mask, assault rifle. The butt hovered above his head then came down —

∞

Denev woke slowly, keeping his eyes closed. It felt like he was still underground. Something about the low rush of air he could hear. There were voices too, but he couldn't make out the words. The place smelled damp, musty. Air circulation was natural. A cave?

He opened his eyes a fraction. Not a cave. But definitely underground. A square pool of green-tinged water lapped in front of him, constrained by broken-edged concrete and reflecting smooth-cut stone walls and an arched ceiling dotted with simple pendant floods. The far wall had four tunnels cut into it like the spots on a dice. Only one was illuminated.

"We know you're awake."

The voice came from behind, rich and deep. It carried no fear, no anger, no hatred. Denev lifted his head and craned around, but he couldn't see the speaker.

He was strapped to an old but solid cushioned metal chair. Not uncomfortable, but he was bound at wrists, elbows, upper arms, chest, waist, knees and ankles. There was no way he'd leave this seat unaided.

"Denev Antwer," the voice said in calm, measured tones. "Hegemony Diplomatic Corps, service number H59S12PX94. Graduated HDC Academy 2318. Postings to Lacuna B, Dekalia, Eaphesus and a bunch of other places. Three years at the listening post on Prox, then a short spell on Herakli just after the Brell massacre, before becoming an aide to the devil himself, Comptroller Troels Volmar."

Denev cleared his throat and spat. "I feel like I'm at a disadvantage."

"Get used to it."

There was a sudden noise then hands gripped the back of his chair, spinning it around until Denev was face to face with his captor. His skin was a deep black; his head shaved bald and tattooed with twisting black lines. A close-trimmed beard, barely a centimetre wide, followed the line of his jaw. A similarly thin moustache framed a full-lipped mouth. His eyes were large and slightly bulging and staring at Denev intently.

"So. Now you've seen my face, how do you think this is going to end?"

"We're still talking."

The lips turned up at the corners ever so slightly. "That we are. Tell me, Denev Antwer, what is the HDC Comptroller's aide doing subverting disaffected youth and turning them into suicide bombers?" He paused. "I assume this *was* a suicide mission for the poor lads."

"The CA wants to discredit the Inclusionists."

"We know that, but why are *you* doing it?"

Denev looked at the man. There was something about the way he phrased the question, the stress on "you". He didn't want the operational reasons, he wanted the personal truth. Perhaps there was a slim chance on offer here.

"I'm not. That was the mission, but I decided not to go through with it. That's why I called Preem out tonight, to put him off. Delay things until I could work out an alternative that wouldn't get them all killed or caught."

"And why is that?" The man squatted so he and Denev were at eye-level. "I need the absolute truth. I'll know if you're lying."

"Who are you?"

He shrugged. "Maybe we're HDC, or SolSec. Maybe we're the bogeyman. It doesn't matter who we are. Not when you get right down to it. The truth is the truth."

Denev answered the question. "Because it was the wrong thing to do."

"Hmm." The man tilted his head to one side. "We saw your little extracurricular trip to the monitoring station. And the fight you had with your HDC buddy. It didn't end well for him."

Denev was frantically trying to understand what was going on. Was this some elaborate trap by Volmar because he'd known about Beloc all along? How long had they been following him?

"Who *are* you?" he said again.

"Your mission was to bring down a puppet organisation the CA created to dupe the public. The Inclusionists have served their purpose for the CA *and* for us. Think of us as the *real* Inclusionists. We hide in plain sight. And we know what's really going on." He grabbed the chair, jerking it forward an inch. "What's a loyal HDC operative doing killing a colleague and subverting an operation?"

"I'm not loyal. Not any more."

The man let the silence stretch, studying Denev. "Sudden attack of conscience?"

"More like a few home truths made clear to me by a friend."

The man stood, pulled out an old recoilless projectile pistol, pulled back on the chamber and levelled it at Denev's eye.

"I can access HDC files for you. Systems." Denev spoke quickly, hating the pleading tone in his voice. His heart was hammering in his chest.

"Maybe we already have that." The man pushed the muzzle hard against Denev's brow.

"There's one file you don't have. Sealed by Volmar, Rejak, Vargas and Breslaw. All of them. Sealed twenty years ago."

"And what's in it?"

"I don't know."

The muzzle pushed harder.

"It has to do with my father's death!" Denev was shouting now, voice echoing against the hard walls. "It's something that could damage the CA, I know it. Nothing else I've come across is sealed that hard."

"But you don't know what it holds."

"I know it exists, which is more than you do. Together we could get it."

The pressure on the muzzle eased and the man laughed, but there was more exasperation than humour in it. "You want *us* to help *you*?"

"It's important to both of us," Denev said.

The man holstered his gun and stood back with his arms folded. "You still need to convince me you're not an HDC stooge."

"I can bring you any kind of information you want."

"Nice try, but that won't cut it. We need a more convincing demonstration. We need you to kill Cerise Laneaux."

"Laneaux," Denev echoed. That was as much of a death sentence as being shot in the head here and now.

"She's not so high in the CA that she's impossible to get to, but high enough to prove you're on our side."

What else was he going to do? "I don't really have a choice."

"No. You don't."

The man pulled out another, smaller pistol, this one with a

needle nose. He pushed it against Denev's neck, puncturing the skin. There was a hiss and a painful heat and pressure in the flesh beneath.

"This implant will monitor your location and your conversations. If you tell anyone about us, it'll blow your head off. If HDC moves against us, it'll blow your head off. If you do anything we don't like …"

"I get the picture," Denev said. "But this thing will be picked up as soon as I enter a government building. I'll be no good to you captured."

"You've still to prove you're any good to us at all. We've been hiding from SolSec and HDC for years. Their security isn't going to find that thing in your neck. Go kill Laneaux. Then we'll talk about this file of yours."

He started unfastening Denev's restraints.

"What's your name?" Denev asked.

The man glanced at him. "Call me Rapskel."

30

Rhees took the lead again as we continued up the incline. There were shouts and the sound of heavy hoofsteps, but in the corridors it was impossible to tell if they were behind or in front of us.

We came to the dark tunnel we'd first entered by and, finally, the covered exit. My desert eyelid flicked over and I could make out the opening. We stopped directly below and listened for any sound on the surface.

"I think it's safe," I said. "Let me lift you to the top."

She held the rifle in front of her and I stooped, holding her waist, and pushed her up to the deeper dark above. She felt for the edge, laid the gun on the surface, then scrabbled up and out of the tunnel. I waited until I heard her whispered "all clear", then joined her beneath the overhanging boulder.

The night air was cool and the sky was covered in thick cloud so the stars were invisible. The alarm was audible, but far away, sounding like the call of a night creature. We listened, but could hear nothing nearer, so we slowly emerged and looked around. Back towards the house the sky held four concentrations of light – small ships, though it was difficult to gauge distance. As we watched they were joined by another rising from the airfield.

"They're searching. But over the desert," Rhees said.

"They don't know about this exit," I said. "But there are other, more obvious tunnels to the escarpment roof."

"No ships over this way though."

"Maybe they haven't found the guard yet," I said.

"Maybe. But there's bound to be someone sent up here even if they're sure we're on the desert floor." She checked her rifle. "Half-full. I hope it's enough."

"I'll go first now," I said. The desert eyelid enhanced the contrast of the rocky landscape.

I strained to hear anything ahead and kept low, using whatever cover was available. Still I felt very exposed. The soft whine of turbines from the search craft grew sharper and then faded as the ships banked and followed pre-determined vectors to cover the desert floor.

Time seemed to stretch. It became an endless journey waiting for the inevitable burst of fire from behind this rock or the next. The cloud cover dissipated and the stars shone through – hard points of light. Were we being observed even now from orbit; ground forces being directed from above to intercept us? My skin itched across the excision scar. But still no shout came, no weapon fired.

After an age we came to the line of rocks that defined the edge of the amphitheatre where the house spikes were located. I hunkered behind the largest boulder and waited for Rhees to join me. She was breathing hard. Then I ducked out from behind the rock and looked quickly to the far end of the amphitheatre.

"Troops," I said. "Five of them. Against the steps and the far lip of the crater, looking back to the escarpment edge."

Rhees's head bobbed round the boulder and back. "A surprise party for anyone leaving by the known exits. There's probably teams on either side closer to the edge, ready to drive hostiles towards them. There's a lot of open space to cover to the ship. You're faster than me. Don't stop for anything and get in the ship. I'll expect a nice open hatch when I get there."

She held the rifle close, checking the charge again, and I understood she was going to create a diversion to let me get to the ship.

"No," I said. Rhees was more than a fellow traveller. She was a true ally, like Atalna, like Emba before him. They'd lost their lives for me. I didn't want that to happen again.

"What do you mean 'no'? We can't fuck around here."

"I'm not running while you fight."

"You've got nothing to fight with."

I picked up two large rocks. "Now I do. This is my planet."

Rhees said something under her breath that the voder didn't catch, but I got the idea. "Okay, where exactly are these troops?" she added.

I ran a claw through the dust to make the line of the far crater wall. "Can you see this?"

"Yeah, my eyes have adjusted."

I looked at her eyes more closely, but couldn't see a desert eyelid equivalent.

"These are the ramps to left and right," I said, marking them in the dirt. "There's a shelf that runs either side of them – the continuation of the crater rim. There's two soldiers on the shelf to the left. They're both in a break in the rim that gives them a well-covered view of the approach from the escarpment edge."

"It also means they can cover the ramps and the crater floor behind them if they turn," Rhees said.

"There's another soldier here." I marked the midpoint between the two ramps. "Again he has cover over the approaches, and if anyone does make it to the ramps they won't see him unless they look back the way they came."

"And by that time they'll have a hole in their head."

"The others are here and here." I marked both points where the ramps met the crater floor hard against the rim. "And low, using what cover they can."

"They're the most exposed," Rhees said. "And the slowest to bring weapons to bear on an attack from behind. This is the priority." She pointed to the crevice in the rim. "Concentration of firepower, protected position."

"I think I can hit this," I said, pointing at the crevice. "There's no space for them to dodge a missile easily."

Rhees's head bobbed. "I'll take the other three."

I picked up two more rocks, cradling them in one arm. Rhees held the rifle close to her body. We both stood, backs to the boulder.

"Remember to keep moving," Rhees said. "They'll be wearing combat helmets with motion-tracking. And don't run in straight lines otherwise targeting will lock onto exactly where you're going to be at the point of fire. If we get through this, I'm getting you a gun for next time."

"Ready," I said.

"Now."

We both rounded the boulder, already picking up speed. Rhees broke right, dodging past the spikes. I lost sight of her for an instant then saw her again as I leaped to clear a large rock in my path, keeping the jump low and short. I hit the ground, moved left then right, keeping my focus on the crevice. I could see the figures clearly, but I wanted to get as close as possible before throwing. I couldn't miss.

There was a single shot from off to my right. I hoped it was Rhees firing, but couldn't take the time to look. The soldiers in the crevice were both turning towards me. The space was narrow, which slowed them, but then one dropped to his knee and raised his rifle. The other was still turning, but I had no more time.

I threw the first rock, harder than I'd ever thrown before. It flew straight, smashing into the kneeling soldier's faceplate. He fell back against the other, dropping his rifle. I threw another rock immediately, still running. It clattered on the crevice edge uselessly.

The other soldier had his gun up now. He fired as I threw again. Heat washed over my head and I dived, rolling on impact, dropping my last rock. I came up on my knees, waiting for the next blast to sear me. When I looked again, both soldiers were lying in a tangle on the crater floor.

I stood and looked for the soldier stationed between the ramps. He was kneeling, rifle steady, pointing right at me. I had no more rocks. I was standing still and exposed.

The laser hissed. The soldier fell to one side, a single curl of smoke rising from his body. Rhees was walking towards him, shouldering her rifle. I could just make out the bodies of the other soldiers we'd seen, lying on the crater floor by the far ramp.

Rhees picked up the fallen weapon and jogged back across the crater. When she got close enough she threw the rifle to me. "For next time," she said.

She bent, hands on her knees, panting. "This gravity's a bit hard to take. I wouldn't want to be in an extended firefight."

I held out the small disc Nok had given me and let it guide me to the hatch, which opened invisibly at my approach.

Rhees sealed the hatch behind us, and checked the screens as I strapped into the crash-chair.

"Other soldiers," she said. "Coming this way."

She activated the controls and the ship lifted immediately on an oblique climb away from the escarpment. Once clear, we angled more steeply up. The display showed troops and ships converging on the spikes as news of our attack spread. But no ship followed us. There were no missiles or orbital laser strikes.

"They really can't see us," I said.

"A small fleet of these and you could neutralise a planet's defences in no time."

"Luckily the Jantri are our friends," I said.

Rhees bared her teeth. "So where to now?"

"Now I'm sure we're not being tracked, we head into the deep desert."

"The markings in the shielded room?"

"Yes. They told me Tzek was heading far past any oasis into the true deep desert. Nothing lives there, has ever lived there."

"Sounds attractive," Rhees said.

I tried to explain. "Traditions never die. No matter how collegiate the Council of Hierarchs became, no matter how strong the communion, preparation for war always continued. Each house had their hideaways, their defences, and kept them secret

– a particular challenge post-Emergence – using codes that were impenetrable to other houses and lodges. It just became something houses did. There was no malice or intent behind it."

"I'm trying to think of something similar on Earth," Rhees said. "Maybe sport."

I remembered the broadcasts on Mars that Ephes had described as "sport". "Physical contests, you mean?"

"Yes, but strictly codified to minimise physical harm. It had its origins as a replacement for battles against rival towns – decisions turned on which team won. But that reason eventually became lost as people started to enjoy sport for itself. They play for a token prize now, but that's a very small part of the whole endeavour."

"Yes," I said. "Building the hides and keeping them secret was our 'sport'."

"But the game's changed now," Rhees said.

"Well, the need for our hideaways has become desperately real."

"That's not what I mean. The excisees like you, they can't be 'read' any more. Which means no intact Kresz would even get a tingle that a nearby excisee had a secret or intended to do them harm. That's how it works, isn't it?"

"It's more than a 'tingle', but yes, you're right."

"And the intact Kresz shun the excisees, preferring to pretend they're not there."

"When they're not trying to actively kill them, yes."

"But no one tried to kill you inside the escarpment."

"I think that was more to do with being your property."

"Okay, we need more intel on how excisees are treated," she said. "But my point is: they could be useful. For carrying information, maybe even for sneak attacks."

It was possible in theory. But the excisees I'd seen after the Hegemony invasion were barely functional. It was hard to imagine them spying or attacking intact Kresz. Though with their hoods removed there was no longer an empathic barrier to violence.

The ship juddered, then levelled.

Rhees checked the flight monitor. "Wind's picking up."

"Look out for a marker – a group of stones, almost perfect spheres. The network of hides starts one-three-five measures from there on a line extending past that point from Treaty Mount in Aktiuk. If Tzek made it that far, that's where he'll be."

"And if he didn't?"

"Our job will be a lot harder."

"Is stoicism and understatement a species trait?" Rhees asked.

I thought of Isza. "Only in the best of us. I suppose I just picked it up from them."

The desert sand glowed a delicate pink and the shadows between the dunes were deepening. No, I realised, it was the reverse. The peaks were being lit up by the rising suns. I'd perceived one thing, when really it was the opposite. Could we trick Kergis and the Hegemony in the same way, by using the excisees – social outcasts – to bring them down? It would be poetic. Perhaps it would take away some of the pain and loss the excisees suffered. Perhaps it would transform them in the eyes of the intact. The reviled becoming the saviours.

As we flew on, the desert brightened, the pools of shadow evaporating as sura and djel rose together. The pinkish hues gave way to blues and browns, subtle variations spreading out to the horizon. And then the palette changed in an instant, paler but sharper with a golden cast as ataz rose into the sky. The sandscape grew steadily brighter, colour washing out as searing white heat took hold. The vuscreen filters dimmed so it was still comfortable to watch but I knew outside was becoming unbearably bright, and the scalding heat would bake the air until it was painful to breathe. No one would live here unless every other choice had been taken from them.

Sharp flashes leaped across the face of the desert, streaking into the distance. "Those are the glass pans," I said. "Catching the sunslight and throwing it back at us."

Finally, amid the heat rippling up from the glassy desert floor, I saw the marker.

"There it is," I said, pointing to the left edge of the screen.

"Okay." Rhees brought the craft forward until we were exactly over the stones.

The view shifted straight down. One of the stones was as big as the other two put together, but all were perfectly round. Cracked and pitted glass spread away from them, creating the incongruous effect of all three stones thrusting through an ice sheet rather than sitting within a desert furnace.

The ship slowly turned, orienting on a line back along the way to Aktiuk, and then we were moving forward again. The ground fell away from the rocks in a gentle decline, levelling out to form a vast flat basin with nothing to relieve the monotonous sameness except the smoky promise of mountains far on the horizon. The crazed glassy sand continued, until we crossed some invisible border where it was replaced by a single sheet of glass shot through with bubbles and streaks of colour: browns, yellows and reds. In some places it was clear and I could see the trapped sand beneath. Other areas were milkily opaque.

It took longer than I expected to travel across that unbroken plain. Finally, Rhees said we were approaching the coordinates, and brought us down to land gently on the surface. There was a flurry of cracking sounds as the ship settled but the glass held.

I was out of my seat before the hushed sound of the engines died. "It's best I go out alone. For all kinds of reasons."

Rhees looked at the screen and the glass desert rippling in the heat. "No argument here."

The heat hit me as the outer lock drew back. My desert eyelid reduced the glare, but even so it was almost too bright. The instant I stepped onto the glass I felt the suns burning my shoulder plates and skull cap. The glass floor burned the bottoms of my hoofs. I'd never been this far out before. There was no wind. Everything was still and lifeless, and the first intake of desert air in my spiracles was hotly sharp.

I stepped carefully forward. The heat rippled across my vision, making the landscape shift, elongating shapes, making me see movement where there was none. The noise all around was incredible: a thousand tiny ticks and splits as the glass expanded in the heat.

There was nothing to relieve the stark flatness. No entrance to an underground cave – even though I hadn't expected anything so obvious. I turned. The ship was behind me somewhere, though I could see nothing.

When I turned back, I was surrounded.

31

For Rhees, it happened with an almost dreamlike quality. There were no monitor scales on board that remotely related to Celsius, but the way the air shimmered off the glassy floor of the plain, the unbearable brightness that leached the colour out of everything outside the ship made her think of the hottest day she'd ever endured – on a training camp in Pan-Africa – and then double it. Maybe even triple it. Uncovered skin would crisp in an instant out there. And there was Udun, treading carefully – the ground must be really slippery – looking for god knew what because there sure as hell was nothing living in that furnace.

She was wondering how long Udun could walk around in that heat, and what they'd do if he couldn't find anything, when shapes came out of nowhere. She thought it was a trick of the light at first. Everything danced in the heat haze and it was all too damn bright, even with the filters. But there was definite movement, and once she realised that, it was as if the view on the screen shifted, like one of those kids' optical illusions. Figures. At least five of them, surrounding Udun. And they were armed with some kind of heavy poles, thicker at one end. Even with the heat ghosts she could see the business ends of all five poles being levelled at Udun.

She released the seat restraint and stood, cursing the lack of combat goggles. She should have stolen a helmet back at the escarpment. She grabbed up her rifle and activated the lock. The heat was a violent assault. The air burned her lungs. Her body instantly prickled with sweat, running in fast rivulets down her back and soaking into the onepiece. How long could she survive this?

She stepped forward, felt the soles of her boots burning on the hot glassy floor. Her eyes were slits against the brightness but her eyeballs felt like they were being coddled in their own juices. Still, she could see darker shapes against the brightness. One in the middle had to be Udun. She took a breath that hurt her throat and raised the rifle, shouting.

Something swung towards her. There was a shout in return, a string of words she couldn't understand. Had her trink failed in the heat? And then more movement. Her eyes were stinging and she was practically blind in this hellish sunlight.

Both her arms were grabbed and pulled behind. She lost the rifle. Then she was picked up and carried in arms that were too hard. They were running through the heat. Her eyes were closed tight against the glare, her vision pink-red. Her ribs bumped painfully against hard shell. Maybe she blacked out.

Then blessed darkness. Unbelievable coolness. And a voice.

"The deep desert is no place for a Hegemony. Your skin is as soft as a newborn nymph's."

Rhees was still blind and her mouth was dry. She worked what little moisture she had left into her tongue. "Where's Udun?"

"You care?" the voice asked in return.

"What house are you?"

There was a rattling noise, like rain on a drumskin. "You do well to ask. Hegemony are not popular with most houses."

Something shifted in the dark. Rhees's eyes were adjusting. She heard a rasp of metal and felt the sharp point of a blade against her neck. She tried to pull away but rough rock pressed against her back.

"If you're House Czerag, you won't do that," she said.

"You're sure of that?" Rain on the drumskin again. "They're brave, Udun. Or stupid and lucky."

The knife was gone. Rhees pushed against the rock wall to stand. Another figure moved in the dark, and then light flared. She blinked rapidly, but it wasn't as bright as outside.

Udun was there, kneeling beside another Kresz whose shell was almost black and incised with curling patterns inlaid with metal.

"So they weren't trying to kill you out in the desert?" Rhees asked Udun.

"No, they were. They would have succeeded if it wasn't for Tzek." He indicated the other Kresz. "Principal advisor to Czerag."

"Or I was," Tzek said. "Czerag was killed. Sorry, Udun – you wouldn't know. He was at the tekla mine when the attack came. They tried to make a stand, thinking they could escape into the mine workings if they had to. One missile and the entire area was vaporised. The crater goes deeper than the base of the main shaft."

"He might have escaped," Udun began.

Tzek raised a claw. "It's been too long. He's gone."

Udun looked at the stony floor. It was obvious Czerag had been important to him. Finally he said, "What happened?"

Tzek sat back on the bare rock, passing his claws across his skull plate. "We were ready for some sort of retaliation from Kergis for the tekla trade. I was with a small group directing operations from Czerag's chamber. As you know, everyone else had been sent to the hideaways close to the escarpment as a precautionary measure. We'd given them orders to go to the deep desert hides if things went really badly. Not long after Czerag and I talked to you and Isza about the strange readings inside the Point, Hegemony ground troops landed, backed by fast-moving air support. The house was attacked almost immediately. I managed to leave you the message before getting away – moments before the Hegemony took the escarpment. Anyone left was captured. Then the tekla mine – we heard the explosion from our hideout. We stayed put while we thought there was a chance to fight back. The hideaway had shielded comms and a newsfeed. From that we were able to work out the rest."

Tzek sat back. "But you don't want to hear this now. You need to rest, eat."

"No," Udun said. "I want to hear it all."

"Drink at least then."

The old Kresz had a skin with a wooden stopper at the tapered end. He offered it to Rhees first. It wasn't water but it tasted good. Cool and refreshing. At that point, it was all she cared about. She passed the skin back to Tzek, who offered it to Udun.

"Later," Udun said. "Tell us everything. Now."

Tzek took a drink, then stoppered the skin and laid it on the ground. "I sometimes wish I'd been in the mines with Czerag," he said. "It would have been a kinder end. I didn't expect to live past his reign." The air hissed in his spiracles, sounding like a sigh to Rhees. "What we learned later was that the attack on the escarpment and the tekla mine was a secondary front. The main Hegemony forces were attacking Aktiuk. It wasn't so much of a battle as a rout. Too many died that day. Those that survived were rounded up and excised. I see you know all about that. Many didn't, or couldn't, live past it."

"I saw them in Cz'kras Park," Udun said. "The family spikes were choked with the dead."

Rhees imagined something like the piles of dead and dismembered bodies they'd seen on top of the escarpment. But the dead Udun spoke about were suicides, unable to live with what the Hegemony had done to them. She felt disgusted and ashamed.

"Things quietened after that," Tzek said. "I think both sides were exhausted. Both Kresz sides anyway. I don't know what would affect the Humans." He looked at Rhees, but she felt no fire or hatred in his words, just tiredness and maybe curiosity.

"I don't know what it was like in the houses or the city," he continued, "but even shielded from the worldmind our sleep each night was punctuated by our collective fear and horror. The massacre of the remaining Czerag prisoners at the escarpment came next. We don't know what provoked it, or even if provocation was needed. Then we learned the Hegemony had taken the escarpment as their base of operations. Some with me wanted to strike back, using the secret tunnels into the house. I forbade it. I couldn't see the point of any more killing, any more death. I didn't have the strength any more, Udun."

Udun placed a clawed hand on Tzek's shoulder, a very human gesture to Rhees's way of thinking. But could the humans in the Hegemony really claim humanity any more?

"Then we heard about the younglings," Tzek said.

Oh god, Rhees thought. What now?

"It was a decree of Kergis, self-proclaimed Rector of the Kresz. All houses were disbanded save his. Kergis Kresz went to all houses, settlements and those hideaways they knew about or had discovered through torture, and they took the younglings away from their families. Those younglings have no families now. No house but Kergis. They're kept in camps and taught whatever Kergis thinks they need to know. They're told to forget their families. Forget the old ways. Those who don't obey are punished or killed."

"He's changing our way of life," Udun said.

Tzek's large eyes blinked in the dim light. "In the space of a single generation. When I heard that, I knew I hadn't had my fill of killing. To stop fighting now isn't simply to die. It means the end of everything.

"We were too close to the Hegemony in the escarpment, so we came here. To plan, I thought. To work out how to strike back. I've had reports of a renegade group of Defenders, led by a Kresz called Gatiku, that split from the lodge when their dean sided with Kergis. But there's no way to make contact even if they are still at large. I just don't know how we can win."

∞

Tzek was old. But he'd never looked so old to me as right then. Or sounded so hopeless.

"We're not just here for a friendly visit," Rhees said. She seemed to have been touched by Tzek's words too.

"She means we're here to help," I said.

Tzek looked like he didn't believe us. I could understand that. If the houses had fallen, what possible good could an excisee and a renegade Human be?

I helped him to his hoofs. "We'll talk later," I said. "First I'd like to see the rest of your hideaway, how strong your force is and what weapons you have. I take it I won't be attacked again?"

"You won't. The Kresz here still recognise my authority. Even with Czerag gone." He looked at Rhees. "You will be safe too, Hegemony."

"The name's Rhees," she said.

When Tzek tried to say it, it came out "Reeks".

"Close enough," Rhees said. "And I appreciate your help out there."

"If I've learned one thing in all these cycles," Tzek said, "it's that nothing is obvious. I see a suns-blinded Hegemony waving a gun around, I don't necessarily think they've come to kill me. Come, I'll show you around." He started down a sloping corridor. "We're quite deep beneath the surface here. About four heights, but it goes deeper."

"Where's the entrance?" Rhees asked. "We didn't see anything from the ship."

"Good," Tzek said. "It's a glass plug in the fused floor. The edges are hidden in the surface's natural imperfections."

I'd been in a few hides before, but never one this far out. All of them were different; by necessity they took advantage of the available terrain and formations. This one had a feeling of antiquity: this tunnel seemed to have been cut into the living rock with tools.

Lights were set into the wall ahead and we emerged from the relative dim into a corridor that could have been part of the escarpment dwellings. Doorways on either side at regular intervals were covered with woven hangings.

"It's cool down here," Rhees was saying.

"Breezeways," Tzek said. "Part natural and part cut by claw. There's a large underground lake at the far end of the complex. No one's sure quite how large but the main air inlet is on its other side. The air cools and moistens as it moves across the water."

It was then I noticed the ceiling. Not irregular cut like the walls, but smooth and dark grey-blue. Shield metal.

Tzek saw me looking. "Yes, we're shielded," he said. "Kergis's patrols do come out this far on occasion. We'd have been found long ago without it."

The corridor opened into a wide, well-lit area with a few Defenders mixed in with other castes sitting at metal tables and what looked like a kitchen and servery at the far end. I recognised some of the faces and was sure they recognised me. But they'd never have spoken to me when I was intact, and now ... I was doubly outcast.

On the left I saw comms gear and processors, even a plotter, although the screen was dark.

"We have power," Tzek said. "Shielded too of course. This is one of our main command areas. Not that there's much to command now. Still we listen in on comms and feed what intel we have into the plotter."

"It's good," Rhees said beside me.

"It'll be useful," I agreed. Czerag and his predecessors had kept the refuges well-stocked and prepared.

We walked through the common area and into a broader corridor with offices and small meeting rooms running off it.

"What about weapons?" Rhees asked.

"The armoury is this way. I think you'll be interested," Tzek said.

The corridor ran down and turned sharply left, then right. I caught sight of more common areas through side tunnels. The hideaway had been designed to be home to a large number of House Czerag Kresz in time of need. We'd seen other Kresz in the rooms and common areas we passed but the hide didn't seem anywhere near filled to capacity.

"Are other hideaways in use?" I asked.

"Two we're in contact with. There may be others who can't or won't answer our calls for whatever reason. There were two-four hideaways I knew of before the invasion, and I'm sure Czerag had more. Here we are."

Tzek pulled aside a patterned hanging to reveal a large room with weapons racks against two long walls. The racks held a few Defender Lodge blasters and rifles but most of the room was taken up with more traditional weapons: gaszti blades of course; tapered lances with a hooked end called czid-ga; heavy-weighted ha'ga and other clubs.

In the middle of the room was a collection of benches. At least two-one Kresz were sitting there working on weapons. They were all excisees.

"These are our foundlings," Tzek said. "Some we rescued when we were at the old hideaway near the escarpment. Others found their way across the deep desert. Including someone I think you'll recognise. Reka?"

Last time I'd seen Reka he'd been screaming, clearly insane. Now, as he joined us, I looked into his eyes for a flicker of recognition. There was confusion for a moment then ...

"Udun?"

I put my arms around him. We were numb to each other's true essence but still I felt something deep inside me unclench.

"We found him living here when we arrived," Tzek said. "Tending the machinery."

Of course. How else could he have survived in the deep desert.

"The voices are gone," Reka whispered in my ear. I pulled back so I could see him clearly. "All those years ... I couldn't unhear them." He seemed to shrink, as if the memory had physical weight. "I couldn't sleep. Couldn't think. Then the others took me and talked to me. Said it was a secret I couldn't tell. And I did ... did that to the female."

I looked at Tzek.

"It's as you thought," he said. "Kergis's people took Reka like they took you. But it broke his mind."

"They had him for longer," I said. "I would have gone the same way."

Reka stood straighter, shaking off the memory of his old life. "When they took my hood and sent me away, I slept for a whole day, a night and another day. Now I sleep whenever I want."

"You can go back to the others," Tzek said. "We'll meet them all soon."

"You'll be safe here," Reka told me and returned to his bench.

"How functional are those Kresz?" Rhees asked Tzek.

"Functional. Reka is the strangest of them, but that's because his problems stretch farther back. They've all been scarred by what happened, but they're useful. And they deserve to live as much as we do."

"And they live alongside the others? The intact?" Rhees said.

I knew where she was heading with these questions.

"There are many intact who would want to clear the way and finish them all off," Tzek said. "They're safe here because I order it so. Kergis may be trying to change our way of life by taking the younglings. But it's already changed."

Rhees looked at me. "This is just what we need."

"We have the location of other hideouts," I told Tzek. "Not just Czerag but Dageru, Ukat, Akczek and Haketiug too. We need them to join us to strike back at the Hegemony."

"We have communication devices shielded from Hegemony ears," Rhees added. "But we need a way to deliver them. Your excisees are perfect for the job. They can't be read for guilt and there must be a lot of them just wandering around homeless. What difference would a few more make? Maybe they could find these renegade Defenders too."

"It makes sense," Tzek said. "We need to organise the Kresz that remain free. But these messengers, they'd be travelling even to Dageru lands? That's quite a journey over difficult terrain. It's true what you say though – many intact will leave them alone. Especially in more populated areas where they're a common sight. But if they're not lucky, there's a good chance they'll be killed on the way."

"So we send more than one to the same location, but travelling individually," Rhees said. "We increase our chances they'll get through."

A cycle ago I would have objected to the casual mathematics Rhees used with people's lives. But this was war.

"What if they make it all that way and are killed anyway?" I said. "They'll be in foreign house lands, they'll be excisees *and* they'll be trying to enter a secret facility."

Rhees's pink flesh face wrinkled. "Fuck it. *You* think of something."

"Actually," Tzek said, "that part might not be so difficult. Even during the House Wars, rival groups needed a way to temporarily cease hostilities. Sometimes to talk, sometimes just to reclaim the dead. Emissaries were used. They carried a rod, carved and painted with intertwined house colours and threaded with ah'lok feathers. Anyone holding one was granted a hearing."

"I've never heard of it," I said.

"You were never interested in the finer points of Kresz history. Your head was already out in space by the time your shell had hardened. But we are traditionalists. Most would recognise the at'heka rod and it would stop them attacking long enough to deliver your message."

"I didn't have such a stupid idea after all," Rhees said.

"Perhaps," I said. "But a lot can still go wrong."

"Come to my rooms and tell me more about your plans," Tzek said.

32

We followed him to a small but comfortable chamber, with tsin to drink and cushions to sit on. There were no windows — any opening to the furnace landscape above our heads would have been madness — so there was no sense of time passing as we sat and talked.

Tzek was quiet for the most part as I told my story. He'd experienced the invasion in his own way and no doubt heard accounts from many others since then. My relationship with Nok prompted some questions, mainly about Jantri tech. It didn't seem right to reveal Nok's true nature to Tzek or to Rhees.

I was at pains to explain I didn't particularly trust the Jantri either. "But I do believe they want the Hegemony out of the Lenticular," I said.

"The problem is, what are the Jantri's plans for the Lenticular after the Hegemony are gone?" Tzek said.

"I don't know." Nothing was certain about what came next. "The Hegemony is the priority now. But there's always the chance the Jantri could be just as bad."

"Oh for the old days," Tzek said, "when we only had one planet to worry about. Our own."

"The old days never really existed," I said. "You can be as insular as you want. It doesn't stop a Hegemony coming along and destroying everything."

Tzek looked at me for a long moment. "We have a lot to be thankful for with you. Not least the way you've fought for us, even when your outworld views made you a target for taunts and worse."

I didn't know what to say. Growing up, I'd never had the chance to become accustomed to praise. Only Czerag had treated me as if I had some value. And Isza, of course, but close family were meant to say those things.

Tzek stood. "Come. It's time to eat. I think we have food you can digest too, Human. Or at least it won't kill you."

"Can't wait," Rhees said.

We followed the short tunnel back to the common area. This time, the tables were full of Kresz at their meal. The hum of talk faded.

Tzek led us to the serving area where various dishes were laid out. I picked up some dried lefa berries and stru and put them on my plate. Rhees was following my lead so I chose other foods she might like. Dried fruits for the most part that I thought wouldn't be too outlandish for Human digestion – whatever that involved.

As we turned, it seemed every eye in the room was trained on us. I didn't need a mantle to read the emotion in the place.

There was a small table near the serving area with three empty chairs. We followed Tzek to it, and the two Kresz already seated there stood and moved to another table where room was made for them. Rhees and I sat. But as soon as we had, Tzek stood again.

"Listen to me," he said, his voice ringing across the room. "This is Udun. Some of you will remember him. Whatever you thought about him then or now means absolutely nothing in this place. He was favoured of Czerag – that alone should tell you something. In the time since the Hegemony came, Udun has done more than anyone in this room – myself included – to fight our enemy and bring freedom to Homeworld again." He paused, looking over the gathering. "He will be safe here. And you will obey him as you obey me. His companion, the Human Reeks, will be safe here."

There was a murmur but Tzek's voice cut across it. "This is not a request. If anyone is to rid our planet of the Hegemony, it is Udun. While we have been hiding here, he has been acting. Personally, I am shamed by that. So think on what I have said, eat your food and get on with your work. We have a war to prepare for."

His last words were greeted with more talk, but rather than a tone of complaint, it carried a sort of vitality, an excitement even.

"Nice trick," Rhees said. "Tell them off and fire them up at the same time. They could use you in the Diplomatic Corps."

But I knew it was more than words that had passed between Tzek and the others. You didn't get to be a hierarch's chief advisor without knowing how to dampen "unhelpful" emotions and reinforce those that aligned more closely with whatever had to be achieved.

I looked at Rhees as she nibbled tentatively at a lefa berry. She'd been mostly silent during the recount of my adventures. Some she had heard before but others were new to her. She'd told me some of her own journey here and Volmar's part in it. She said she hated the Hegemony Diplomatic Corps. It could all be lies. She could still be lying. So could Nok. It was important to keep that thought at the front of my mind, and be ready for the moment of betrayal.

∞

Rhees took a back seat over the next few days, listening to the discussions with Tzek and other Kresz, chipping in where it wouldn't be too disruptive. After Tzek's speech in the commons, it seemed Udun was more welcome. Rhees thought that, perversely, her presence probably helped. She was clearly from the enemy, whereas Udun was one of them, even if he didn't have a mantle.

The first group meeting with the excisees was difficult. Just Udun, Tzek, Rhees and the thirteen excisees were present. No one else was to know the details.

None of the excisees wanted to talk, which Rhees thought she could understand. She'd seen how the intact ignored them and it reminded her of the bad old days in HDC headquarters. No one had befriended her. They all knew why she'd been dumped there, and the way Volmar treated her made them stay clear. So she'd gone quiet and kept herself to herself. These guys were the same. But at least they had each other. And Udun was like them – scarred. So he was the one to talk.

The story of his excision by the Hegemony was just as hard for Rhees to hear as the first time. When he finished speaking, none of the excisees said a word. They just sat like statues, making Rhees even more convinced that their plan wasn't going to work.

The next day, after the morning meal, they gathered again. Tzek made his excuses and left. Rhees couldn't blame him.

She looked around the group. Her time with the other Kresz on Nok's ships had taught her how to differentiate between individuals. Females were larger than males. Then there were the different body plans. Most in the room were the same as Udun, but there were a few long-limbed farmworkers. There were no Defenders in the group. They'd probably died fighting rather than being excised, Rhees thought. There were variations in shell colour too, which she knew was an indication of age, ranging from bright orange to all the shades of red, darkening to purple, brown and through to black. The skin or hide beneath the shell showed more familiar signs of ageing – wrinkles and deep folds around the eyes and mouth parts, and blemishes like liver spots. And then there were the personal differences – the colour of their house showing in their clothing or simple cloth braids, and some indication of lodge affiliation, whether it was a piece of jewellery with the lodge symbol, or a tool or piece of practical clothing dictated by function.

She realised she was being studied in turn by a female almost directly opposite. From shell colour she was similar in age to Udun, and she wore a tattered cloak pinned at one shoulder with a brooch in the triangular sigil of the Merchants Lodge. Rhees smiled at her, though what the Kresz would make of the expression was anyone's guess.

The female sat a little more upright and the cloth on her cloak shifted to reveal a long, ragged crack running diagonally across her chest plates. Seeing Rhees looking at the scar, she pulled at the cloak self-consciously. Two claws were missing from her left hand.

"Will no one share?" Udun asked.

The female's golden eyes were still locked on Rhees. She blinked, then turned to Udun, her mouth parts stretching wide as she spoke.

"I was ... am Djidka," she said, her voice barely above a whisper. "I lived in Aktiuk, keeping the rolls at the Merchants Lodge."

Rhees glanced around at the others. None of them were looking at Djidka. In fact most of them were staring at the floor. But they were listening.

"I didn't fight when the Hegemony came. I couldn't. I hid in the cellars, trying to block out all the ugliness. It was too much. I lost myself."

Udun tilted his head and Rhees saw the muscles across his back that had supported his hood ripple. She'd thought the mutilation cruel before. But here, listening to Djidka, seeing Udun trying to reach out to her in a way he could never do again because of what the Hegemony had done to him, to all of them – it was horrific.

"Go on," Udun said.

"Days passed. Maybe three. The feelings became ... bearable. I couldn't stay there. I had no idea what I'd find outside, or even if I could get out. But the way was clear, though mostly there was rubble where the lodge had once stood. Some of the other buildings were still on fire. I could see bodies crushed beneath walls. I didn't know where to go – where was safe. Finally I came to a market. People were queuing for food, all playing at being normal. But there was no normal any more. A ground car drove up and Hegemony troops got out. They started to take people out of the line – every second person. I could see I would be taken but I didn't believe it." Djidka looked at Rhees again. "I'd done nothing wrong."

Rhees forced herself not to shy away from Djidka's gaze. She owed her that much.

"But they took me, even though I told them I hadn't fought. That I wouldn't fight. They took me with the others to a waiting place. And we felt the little deaths. When they came for me, I told them I wasn't a danger. When they led me to the white room, I told them I'd never hurt them. When they strapped me to the table, I pleaded with them. I asked them to spare me. I'd do anything they wanted."

The breath was loud in her spiracles, and she took a moment to calm.

"It didn't matter. They took my mantle and I don't know what happened after that. I went away in my head for a long time." She lifted her damaged hand to her face. "I don't even remember how I lost these." Her feeder claws folded and unfolded. "Every morning I wake, I wonder why I'm still alive."

Udun wrapped her damaged hand in his own. "You're alive because you choose to be. Everyone here has the strength that you have. And I would know all of your stories because they honour all of us."

Rhees rubbed at her eyes. She couldn't believe the intensity in the room. She expected Udun to call a break, but then one of the others – a male with long Cultivator's limbs – started to talk.

The stories were hard to hear. But there was no stopping them now. Each of the excisees had a different experience but the result was the same.

How much of this suffering was down to Kergis, Rhees wondered, and how much had the Hegemony pushed for it? Though it sickened her, she could see the tactical advantage of breaking the empathic bond of these people. Even without Kergis's desire to unify the Kresz under a single house, the excisions meant an entire section of the adult population was severely traumatised, and an already fragmented social structure was fractured even more. It reduced the likelihood of revolt against the Hegemony forces to next to nothing. And yet, it had been a miscalculation. Even though these people had been horribly damaged, they hadn't been defeated.

She would help them. And some time in the future, Volmar would kneel before the aliens he'd tried to destroy and learn for himself what it meant to lose everything.

It felt like late in the night when the excisees finished telling their stories. Udun held out a clawed hand to the Kresz sitting on either side of him, and a ring was quickly formed.

Rhees was going to push herself back out of the circle, out of the way, but the female to her left held out her clawed hand. Rhees looked into those golden eyes, trying to decipher what she saw there. But it was impossible. She took the hand, feeling its ridged, warm shell.

On her other side, an old Kresz with shell turned almost black took her hand in his. The circle was complete.

Udun looked at them all, his feeder claws spread wide. "Tomorrow," he said, "we begin the journey to take back our home."

Glossary

Adjubon	Capital city of the main landmass on the planet **Herakli**.
ah'lok	Kresz small, feathered reptilian flying creature.
Ah'lokna (season)	Kresz season when the ah'lok swarm and mate in the desert reaches. Weather is dry and hot.
Aktiuk	Chief city of the Kresz Homeworld. The Treaty City where the houses made peace after the **Emergence**.
Aphsan	Lenticular sentient species, resembling cone shape mounds with a thick brow ridge of sensory tissue. Close trade partners of the Telsans.
ataz	Largest of the Kresz Homeworld's three suns; golden yellow in colour.
at'heka rod	Kresz ceremonial stick adorned with long braids and bleached and dyed ah'lok feathers, used to initiate peaceful parlay between rival houses pre-Emergence.
auto	Hegemony term for automobile or small, personal ground vehicle.
Battle for Earth	A pivotal moment in the Earth–K-Chaan war, when the enemy penetrated the Solar System and almost invaded Earth before being driven back.
Betlaan	A peaceful planet and home to **Atalna**. Due to political infiltration by the Hegemony, the rightful government was overthrown and replaced with a puppet government controlled by HDC.

Brell	Cygnus Sector alien species from the Brell Conglomerate. Bipedal but horse-like. Tall, covered in fine brown hair, long-necked and long-headed with long ears. Their home planet is **Brell Prime**.
Central Administration (CA)	The executive governmental body of the Hegemony.
communion	A full empathic sharing between Kresz.
compensator	Hegemony ship device that assesses the stability of a Voss Space chamber in three-dimensional space and selects an exit point out of Voss Space.
Cygnus Sector	A region of space that was annexed and settled by the Hegemony shortly after the defeat of the K-Chaan. Home to the **Brell**, **Sissilak** and **Totek**.
czidak	Kresz curse word, literally 'withered limb'.
czid-ga	Kresz traditional weapon: tapered lance with hooked end to pull at enemy, and sharp outer edge to slash between armour plates.
Cz'kras Park	An area of Aktiuk set aside for Kresz house funeral ceremonies.
Datahive	HDC headquarters and main surveillance and analysis facility, situated on Earth in Cape York Conurb.
datanook/nook	Immersive data conduit for HDC operatives. It connects directly with the operative's mind, establishing a **synapse link** that enables them to interface directly with the data architecture in cyberspace. The nook imposes a **neural brake** on the user during interface with the datastream to still any involuntary muscle movement while connected.
dean	Title for the head of a Kresz lodge.
Defence Force	The combined Kresz defence fleet, comprising all ships owned by Kresz houses and lodges and controlled by the Defenders Lodge when required.
djel	Second in size of the Kresz Homeworld's three suns; red in colour.
Elysem	A domed city on **Telsus IV**.
Emergence	The moment in history when the empathic link manifested between all Kresz.

endar	A type of tree on the Kresz Homeworld with blue foliage.
Endikar	A **Brell** colony in Cygnus Sector.
gaszti	Kresz traditional weapon – a long knife, carried in a sheath.
ha'ga	Kresz traditional weapon: long club with heavy weights at end, used for smashing through shell.
Hanloi	An alien species that inhabits galactic centre. A Hegemony mission to Hanloi space was lost, presumed destroyed.
Herakli	Hegemony-settled planet in Cygnus Sector.
Hierarch	Title for the head of a Kresz house.
House Akczek (Kresz)	House colour: white; house lands: the northern reaches of the planet. The Akczek hierarch controls lands with an abundance of gem stones and precious metals; consequently they have much to do with the Merchants Lodge and strong ties with the military.
House Czerag (Kresz)	House colour: brown; house lands: the escarpment and the deep desert. The Czerag are traditionally nomadic, producing much of what they need in hidden areas of the desert. Their main trade item is tekla, an ore which they mine and refine. It has good properties for spaceship hulls particularly for Voss Space craft.
House Dageru (Kresz)	House colour: red; house lands: the southern reaches. The Dageru lands occupy the southern pole and extend around a major proportion of the far southern landmass. Dageru lands produce textiles and electronics.
House Haketiug (Kresz)	House colour: yellow; house lands: plainlands to the east of the Inland Sea. The Haketiug are traditionally agriculturists.
House Kergis (Kresz)	House colour: green; house lands: the equatorial belt of tropical rainforests. The Kergis hierarch holds the title of Protector and commands the combined Kresz armies and fleets in war.
House Ukat (Kresz)	House colour: blue; house lands: the Inland Sea and the southern shores. The Ukat hierarch oversees cultivation and harvest of the Inland Sea.

Jantri-va	Lenticular sentient species. From a highly radioactive planet. Always wear radiation armour when interacting with other species.
Kareee (season)	Kresz season of rains. The drought breaks and, particularly over the Inland Sea coastal regions, there is heavy rainfall. Temperatures begin to fall. Planting begins for the growing season.
Kedisz Ocean	Kresz Homeworld's southern ocean.
K-Chaan Empire	Aggressive alien species in the Earth–K-Chaan war.
Kresz caste: Adept	Professional disciplines such as scientists, lawyers, technicians, pilots etc.
Kresz caste: Cultivator	Agents of agriculture and fishing. Cultivators have elongated limbs and are taller than most Kresz, except for female Defenders.
Kresz caste: Defender	Defenders are the tallest of males, despite lacking a second knee joint and mid-calf. Their armour plating is thicker and they have an oversized arm – usually the left – which ends in a massive pincer. Prior to the **Emergence**, Defenders were a warrior caste who fought for their house hierarch.
Kresz caste: Merchant	Agents of manufacturing and commerce.
Kresz caste: Priest	The priests are devoted to maintaining the teachings of the Kresz god, **Sakat**.
Kresz caste: Scholar	Academics, researchers and scientists, Their claws are thin and delicate and their feeder claws are similarly longer, used for manipulating delicate instruments as much as for eating.
luk'ah	Kresz fish and a valuable food source. Also the name of a Kresz-style singleship similar to a ramcraft.
Luk'ah (season)	Named after the indigenous luk'ah fish which is the primary food source from the Inland Sea. Luk'ah is the period when these fish are harvested. The cooler weather is coming to an end. Temperatures are rising as the rain ceases to fall.
luk'ri	Larval stage of the luk'ah fish.

Luk'ri (season)	Named for the larval stage of the luk'ah fish which develops along the shores of the Inland Sea at this time. The weather is hot but changeable and thunderstorms predominate.
neural brake	See **Datanook**.
podule	A standard-sized cargo unit used across the Lenticular.
processor	Kresz computer.
Prox Base	HDC intelligence gathering post, second only to the **Datahive** in importance.
raktaa	Maagba term for agreement by blood sacrifice.
realspace	Kresz term for space, as opposed to **tenspace**.
Resiut River	Kresz river running from southern shore of Inland Sea, between the marshlands and House Haketiug arable lands to the west.
rikla	An edible Kresz fern, the heart is considered a delicacy.
Rikla (season)	The season of drought. Harvest occurs during the first few weeks before the heat and lack of rain take their toll. The season is named for the rikla fern which withers at this time.
rusz	Kresz blood analogue. Thick and yellow.
Sakat	The Kresz 'god of death'. Also the name of the season at the end of the Kresz year associated with rebirth.
Sakat (season)	The season of rebirth. Crops benefit from cool days and mild nights and regular rainfall.
setzla	Kresz animal. A predator, the size of a large dog. Known for its cunning.
shield metal	A dense bluish metal that blocks Kresz empathic signals when of sufficient thickness. It is used to line the offices of house hierarchs and lodge deans and other sensitive facilities.
Sissilak	Cygnus Sector alien species. A reptilian analogue, resembling human-size snakes but with four arms. The scales that cover their bodies are thick like an armadillo's plate armour.
skystalk	A space tether and orbital elevator between the Kresz Homeworld city of **Aktiuk** and the **Hub**.
SolSec	Sol System Security: an arm of the Hegemony's Central Administration.

stinger	Fleet standard-issue flechette pistol.
stonewood	A type of tree on the Kresz Homeworld known for its strength.
sura	Third and smallest of the Kresz Homeworld's three suns; blue in colour.
Svestans	Lenticular sentient species. Methane-breathers, large, covered in thick bony skin bristling with spines. Aggressive.
Talos III	Barren world in neutral territory used as a ceasefire meeting place in the Earth–K-Chaan war.
tekla	An ore mined only on the Kresz Homeworld. It has unique insulating properties over a wide range of temperatures and is favoured in ship-hull construction and mining and other heavy industrial applications.
Telsans	Lenticular sentient species. Small, furry and sharp-toothed. Generally brusque in nature.
Telsus IV	A molten world in the Telsan system. The Telsans scoop the abundant minerals from its surface in floating manufactories. They have also constructed cities such as **Elysem** and other habitable areas on suitable floating plates of the rocky crust, covered with crystal atmosphere domes to keep out the deadly air.
tenspace	Lenticular word for **Voss Space**.
Totek	Cygnus Sector alien species. Look like walking kettle drums; communicate by rapping a beat on tightly drawn skin across the top of their body.
trink	Hegemony tech. A translator link, worn in the ear, that provides instant translation of programmed alien languages. See also **voder**.
voder	Ubiquitous Lenticular tech. A voice decoder that enables instant translation of Lenticular languages for the wearer. See also **trink**.
Voss Space	Also known as **tenspace** by the species in the Lenticular. A space that exists above/below/between space – dimensions other than the four dimensions of spacetime. Access to Voss Space enables ships to travel to other parts of space more quickly than by conventional means.

| vuscreen | Kresz term for visual display. |
| yoq | Kresz animal. A beast of burden similar to a buffalo. |

THE LENTICULAR

BOOK THREE

TRAITOR'S WAR

AN EXTRACT

RELEASE DATE:
1 JUNE 2024

1

"Udun!"

I woke, disoriented at the sight of the dull blue shield metal on the ceiling above me. Then I remembered where I was and rolled off my mat to push aside the door hanging.

Rhees – a human from the ruthless Hegemony, now a renegade who had returned with me to Homeworld to help us in our fight – stood beside Tzek, longtime advisor to Czerag, our house hierarch who had been killed when the Hegemony invaded.

Rhees and I had found Tzek and others from my house sheltering from the Hegemony invaders in this refuge below the deep desert – one of a network of hides that House Czerag kept as a place of last resort. It spoke to a lack of trust inherent in the hierarchs that, even after cycles of peace on Homeworld, places like this had still been stocked and maintained, their locations kept secret from rival houses. Now we were grateful for them.

"This is no time for sleep," Tzek told me. "You'll be leaving soon and I have to show you both something."

His staff thudded rhythmically on the stone floor as he led the way along the main corridor of the hide to a set of steps spiralling down to another level. Most of the lower corridor was filled with stacks of cargo podules, leaving just enough room for us to pass through.

"This is where most of the supplies are kept," Tzek said. "We have enough for our current complement to last three cycles. But

I'd rather not be here long enough to use them all up. In any case, we keep him down here, well away from the others."

"Him?" I asked.

Tzek stopped in front of a heavy door clad in the shield metal that covered the hide's ceilings. He operated the lock and the door swung wide to reveal a small room with a weak globe set into the ceiling. Inside sat a Kresz, about the same colour and size as me, but he still had his hood. He wore a finely wrought green torque around his neck.

"This is our guest," Tzek said. "His name is Amaroc."

It was clear from the colour of Amaroc's torque that he was House Kergis and a senior house functionary.

Hierarch Kergis had betrayed us all when he sided with the Hegemony ships as they invaded Kresz space. Now he ruled Homeworld with the Hegemony's support. It was still a mystery how he'd managed to keep his plotting with the enemy a secret, given the empathic connection between all Kresz who retained their hoods.

Amaroc's attention focused immediately on Rhees. "A Human." His voice was hoarse but gained strength as he spoke. "Something tells me you're not here to liberate me, Human. You could have brought some food though. I'm starving in here."

"You have to prove you're worth the rations," Tzek said.

Amaroc raised his claws and glared at Tzek. Even without my mantle I could see he was consumed with hate. If he wasn't restrained he would have attacked us as soon as the door had opened.

"When Kergis comes, he'll roast you slowly in your shell, old one," he snarled. "And I'll be there to watch."

"We get nothing from him," Tzek said to me. "Even on an empathic level. He hates us as much as we hate him. That's all."

"What do you know about him?" I asked.

"He was with the Defenders on the frontal assault of the escarpment and clearly in charge of his contingent, maybe more. The authorities he carried said he was part of a unit called the 'stek-la'. It's not clear what that is but the permissions were signed by Kergis. I'd know his mark anywhere."

Which meant Amaroc was close to Kergis and could be a good source of information. "We'll take him with us when we go," I said.

"Oh, you'll take me, will you, cripple? How fortunate for me."

"Not really," I said. "I don't think you'll enjoy our cargo locker. It's smaller than this cell."

Amaroc screamed obscenities at us as Tzek pushed the heavy door shut.

"He's a charmer," Rhees said. "Is it worth the trouble to take him?"

"He's no use to us here," Tzek said. "He's told us nothing. And not for want of trying on our part. He's been on subsistence rations for a season now, but he's still sure of himself, and full of fight."

Tzek may have had no luck, but my sister, Isza, could be very persuasive. "He must know information that could help us," I said. "It's worth a try."

As Tzek led us back to the upper level I remembered how tense things had been between us in the escarpment when I returned from Telsan space. I'd seen a different side to him here. He'd protected the excisees and led the other House Czerag Kresz to safety.

"Come. We should eat."

I thought Tzek meant just the three of us would dine, but when we got to the commons the room was full, everyone already seated. Even Reka, Djidka and the rest of the excisees – those, like me, who'd had their empathic mantles severed by the Hegemony – were present. Though I noticed that no intact Kresz sat at their tables. Still, the difference between now and our first day in the hide was palpable. No strained silence, no stares. The conversation level barely dipped as we headed to the servery, picked up our platters and selected preserved fruit and dried fish.

It was only when we sat at our table and Tzek remained standing that the talk stilled.

"You're leaving soon, Udun, and everyone wanted to join

together before that happens," Tzek said. "You may not fully realise it, but you've brought hope to us again. Hope that the fight's not over. And you've completed a change that our enemies started. I thought I was too old for lessons. I thought the excised were to be pitied. Many here wanted to end their lives. But you've shown us that even with the communion shattered we are still strong. And those that have lost the most are strongest of all. That's a hard thing to come to terms with after so many years of no change.

"I wish you could feel what I feel in this room, Udun. Because you'd know that what you and the other excisees have been through was worth it. Kergis and the Hegemony tried to break us. You've shown that they failed."

The skin beneath my chitin tingled as I saw the looks on the faces of the other excisees. I couldn't sense anything of course, but this simple act of coming together – sitting among the intact and hearing Tzek's words – was enough.

Tzek said I'd caused this change. Some of that may have been true – I'd certainly been changed by what was done to me, by everything I'd seen – but one change was more than anything else. This feeling of belonging. Of being Kresz.

"I'm just doing what I can to fight our enemies," I muttered.

"That's fine, Udun. Eat. Let us all enjoy this evening together," Tzek said, and sat down.

Rhees was looking at me with her teeth bared, an expression I'd come to associate with humour. "My friend, the saviour of his people," she said.

It was ridiculous and I stuffed some preserved fish into my feeder mandibles to avoid having to say anything else. Thankfully Rhees and Tzek turned to their own meals.

As I ate I thought about what Rhees had said. Were we friends? Was friendship even possible between two beings whose species were at war? I didn't think it was. But we'd agreed to cooperate and further each other's interests. And given what we'd been through together so far, I trusted her.

We finished our meal in silence. As Rhees and I rose, the others all stood too. It was a sign of deep respect that I would never have thought possible.

No doubt Tzek had influenced this change in the assembled Kresz more than anything I'd done. I could imagine him moving between groups, seeking out those with even a tiny amount of sympathy for me and the other excisees, using his influence and clever words like blowing on a warm coal until the fire sprang to life and spread.

Yes, if there was a saviour here, as Rhees put it, it was Tzek, doing what he needed to give his people a fighting chance. But next time I returned home, I wouldn't feel like an outsider any more.

∞

When I arrived at our final session with the excisees the next day, I was struck with how different everything was from our first meeting. Then, the only thing the excisees had in common was the thing that shamed them in their own eyes and the eyes of the intact. They'd been thrust together by the others in the hide who wanted nothing to do with them. But after sharing their struggles and acknowledging the simple triumph of staying alive, they'd found something that bonded them more closely than before. There was healing here.

Now they had a chance to do something that would show the intact Kresz just how valued they should be. That would be a kind of healing too. Not just for the excised but for everyone.

Djidka and the Cultivator Galok sat with Rhees and most of the others, studying maps showing the locations of the other hides we'd been able to discover. Djidka looked up at me as I entered and her feeders spread wide. I spread my own feeders in return. It wasn't exactly the common sending – I knew I'd never feel that again – but this would do. We excised were learning how to be together with others again.

I saw Reka in the corner in deep conversation with a female excisee. Sazu was her name and I knew they would be travelling together. It was good to see Reka had a friend. He'd always been quiet and withdrawn when we were growing up together and I hadn't realised that he'd struggled with the empathic link just as much as I had. I'd grated against the feelings of others who viewed me as odd and that had made me stronger. But Reka had blamed himself and turned inward. It would have been unthinkable before, but it seemed that losing his mantle had freed him.

I joined Rhees at the table. Djidka and Galok moved to make space for me to view the charts.

"I spent a lot of time working those marshlands," Galok said, pointing a claw at the region beneath the southern shore of the Inland Sea. "Once we get there it's less than a day to the hills."

"Sounds good," Rhees said and bared her teeth at me. "Groups are set, routes are clear."

I looked around the table at the faces of the others. How many would survive the journey or the fight to come?

"Gather round!" It was Tzek.

He dropped a basket on the floor, filled with what I guessed must be newly made at'heka rods. They were about the length of a lower forearm, painted with lines of twisting colour for each house, and topped with long braids threaded with bleached and dyed ah'lok feathers.

"One each," Tzek called as the excisees jostled to get close to the rods.

"It's like kindergarten," Rhees said, but the voder didn't provide a translation.

"At the first sign you've entered house lands," Tzek explained, "take the rod from your pack and hold it above your head like this." He lifted a wooden rod as high as he could despite his thickened shell. "And shake it continually so the feathers dance. Try it."

The excited talk among the group rose in volume as they all held up their at'heka rods and shook them vigorously.

"That's right," Tzek said. "As long as the feathers dance you will be given fair hearing by those who guard the house."

The plan was for the excisees to carry our communications equipment to the other hides we'd identified so we could make contact with the remaining free Kresz on Homeworld and – hopefully – coordinate a counterattack against the invaders. The fact the excisees had no hoods meant any intact Kresz they met wouldn't be able to sense their emotions or tell that they were keeping the real reason for their journey secret. But excisees were often euthanised on sight and it would be a dangerous trek across the desert and into other house lands, even with the at'heka rods.

The excisees had gained so much in the past few days and still they were willing to risk all of that for all of us. For all of Homeworld. I knew there were many more like them out there. Victims of Kergis and the Hegemony. Broken and lonely, just like these excised had been when we arrived. If I survived, I would do everything I could to make sure those others found the same friendship and love I saw here.

"All right, all right," Tzek said loudly and the group quietened. "Stow your rods in your packs and get ready. It's time."

I crossed to Reka, who was refastening the straps of his pack. He glanced at me then focused on his task again.

"You're happier now, brother," I said.

He paused, considering my words. "I am. And sometimes it puzzles me. That the worst things can happen, but time passes and one day there is something to be grateful for. That's how I feel now."

I placed my claws on his shoulder plate. "That's how I feel too."

I thought about asking him not to go with the others. To stay here and be safe. His life had already been enough of a struggle. But when he rejoined Sazu and the rest of the excisees and I saw how they were together … He wasn't a scared child any more. He wanted this, and who was I to deny him.

When everyone was ready, we walked together to the hide entrance. Two Defenders lifted the glassy plug above our heads, pushing it through the ceiling and sliding it aside. All the moisture in the room was instantly sucked through that hole and my desert eyelid slid into place to cut the sudden glare.

Rhees accompanied us onto the surface. No part of her skin was uncovered. She'd wrapped a thick cloth around her head and borrowed a pair of dark-lensed goggles from the workshop. She'd also tied thick slabs of leather to her boots to keep the soles from melting.

A baking wind pushed at us, shifting direction. All three suns were up and the sky was perfectly cloudless, glowing like an arch of molten metal.

"It's like standing in a furnace," Rhees said. "I don't know how they're going to make it anywhere in this."

The excisees wore their packs strapped across their shoulder plates. Each carried one of our communications devices along with the at'heka rod and a pathetically small stock of supplies. It was true that a Human couldn't survive crossing this desert. But what the excisees had was enough.

Tzek's voice rose above the wind. "If Czerag were here, I know he would be proud. You have proved your strength, and that strength will sust–"

He stopped at a loud cracking noise.

I turned back to the entrance to see more Kresz emerging. They walked forward to gather around the smaller group of excisees. No one spoke, but soon it felt like the entire hide had joined us. None of the intact Kresz knew what the excisees were doing, but it was clear they were going on some kind of mission. And they'd come to bear witness to their departure.

I felt suddenly proud. Here was a group of intact Kresz paying silent respect to a group of excisees who normally wouldn't be spoken to or acknowledged, and more than likely dispatched without a second thought by any intact with a blade. I caught Reka's eye and it seemed to me he stood a little taller.

Tzek spoke again to the small group now in the middle of a larger one. "The House needs you. Do well."

And that was it. The travellers, as Tzek called them, turned and walked into the blistering heat, already splitting up onto their separate headings. We all stayed to watch until their images broke apart into abstract pieces of movement in the rippling heat and were gone.

They would cross out of Czerag lands in three days or maybe a little longer, their paths diverging south and east. Then the going – while physically easier – would get more dangerous: skirting settlements, avoiding Kergis or Hegemony patrols, staying alive. Not all of them would make it. I hoped Reka wasn't among those who fell.

∞

Rhees hurried back underground as soon as the excisees had gone. I found her hunkered against the rough wall, unwrapping the bindings from her head and pulling the thick leather from her boots, as the rest of the Kresz streamed past us into the tunnels.

I passed her a water skin and she took a swig, tipping her head back and making a strange bubbling noise before swallowing.

"Are you all right?" I asked.

She took another drink. "I am now. How can anything live out there?"

Tzek appeared, leaning heavily on his staff. "It finds a way." He reached his claws down and helped her up. "You'll be leaving now?"

"We'll wait until nightfall," Rhees said. "I'm not setting foot out there again in daylight if I can possibly avoid it. But yes. It'll be easier to monitor the travellers once we get back to the Jantri station."

"And we still need to organise our forces off Homeworld," I added.

"They need more than organising," Rhees said. "Me, a small group of Kresz refugees and an advanced species that prefers to stay in the shadows isn't going to be enough."

She was right, of course. Nok of Jantri'va had brought us together, offered his station as a base of operations and fabricated the communications devices that would avoid Hegemony detection.

The instrumentality he commanded was far beyond any technology the rest of the Lenticular possessed, but he guarded his privacy. Partly to avoid undue attention, but partly – I thought – because he was so different from every other species in the Lenticular that his motivations couldn't be understood within a normal frame of reference. That made him difficult to trust. Still, he was the only ally we had so far.

2

Rhees and Udun emerged onto the glassy desert in full darkness. The ground was still hot, and a dry wind blew in from the north. The cooling glass pinged and tinkled around them. The other Kresz from the hide stood together, a deeper mass of black in the total darkness forming a path to the invisible ship. The whole scene felt surreal to Rhees.

Individuals spoke softly as they passed between the group of Kresz: "Sakat guide you." "Go safe to your destination."

Rhees recalled her conversation with Nok before they met up with the Kresz refugees. Nok had described Udun as someone who was changing the course of history for his people. She had to admit he'd been right.

Tzek held a glowing lantern and waited for them at the end of the line, just in front of where the ship sat, still invisible.

"We'll be in touch by comms," Udun said to him. "And we'll meet again."

"Count on it," Tzek said and clasped Udun's lower forearm.

Tzek did the same to Rhees. His armoured claws felt smooth and strong against the fabric of her onepiece. "Be safe, Reeks."

Rhees looked into his dark eyes and felt a mix of emotions. Gratitude that he'd accepted her so easily, concern for his safety and that of the others hiding out here, and shame for how the Hegemony had destroyed the lives of these people.

When she'd first encountered Kresz in real life, they'd been so alien to her. Taller than any human, covered in thick shell-like articulated armour, arms and legs that bent strangely with twice as many elbows and knees, and their faces … The eyes were human enough but their mouths were a mass of articulated claws like something out of a nightmare. And yet living among them she'd learned they were just like her or anyone. They all had dreams, things they regretted. They were people, no matter what they looked like, and they deserved to be respected.

Tzek turned and raised his voice. "Bring the prisoner. He'll present no trouble," he added to Rhees and Udun. "He was easily captured and didn't put up much of a fight."

Two of the largest Kresz Rhees had seen cut through the group, each holding Amaroc tightly by an arm.

His mouth parts rippled as he spoke. "You are all going to die."

"I'll show you where to stow him," Rhees said to the guards.

Guided by her disc, she walked up the invisible entry steps. The large Kresz hesitated for a moment then followed her with Amaroc. Inside the ship, Rhees palmed open a locker just past the internal airlock and the Kresz guards pushed Amaroc roughly inside.

She followed them out again. Udun and Tzek were grasping forearms one last time.

"Thank you, Tzek," Udun said. "For now and for all those cycles you were around when I was growing up. You've given me a great deal."

The old Kresz blinked. "I have a feeling you'll return whatever I gave you many times over."

Udun had told Rhees about how much of an outsider he'd felt growing up on Homeworld. It seemed he'd found his way back into his family. She was glad for him. But she couldn't see a similar path for herself. Her father, who'd been distant all the time she was growing up, had all but given up on her when she crashed out of Fleet in disgrace. Her time working in the Hegemony Diplomatic Corps had ended disastrously when Volmar tried to kill her, and she had no doubt that if she turned up anywhere in human space she'd be shot on sight.

She re-entered the ship and sat in front of the displays, prepping for flight. Udun sat in the crash-chair beside her.

"You're a hit," she said.

"Hit what?" he asked.

"I mean you're popular with your Kresz friends there. Hell, they were even nice to me because I was with you."

Udun ignored the remark. "Now all we have to do is get back to the Jantri."

"And hope our couriers do their job," Rhees added.

"They'll do it. Nothing but death will stop them."

"The Hegemony's going to regret picking a fight with you and Tzek."

What about her? It was all too likely she'd die alone, perhaps right here on Homeworld. At best she'd be forgotten by everyone who knew her. At worst she'd be reviled by humanity as a species traitor.

Fuck, she was getting maudlin. And anyway, Denev would care. He'd helped her when they were investigating the raider attacks in Cygnus Sector. And when he'd found out she was still alive after Volmar tried to kill her, he'd kept helping her. Despite the fact she'd killed Petar – his brother and her boyfriend – in a training accident. Another messy set of emotions she'd rather not look at.

She activated the drive and the ship lifted silently into the dark.

Safely out of atmosphere, Rhees negotiated their way past the shell of satellites and ferry craft in near-orbit. Far off to port they could see the beanstalk elevator decelerating in readiness for docking with the Kresz station – the Hub, Udun called it. A pretty standard spoke-wheel configuration of cargo bays studded around a central disc. The beanstalk cable passed straight through the centre of the station and kept on going until it met the counterweight asteroid a few more thousands of clicks above. A Hegemony Hurricane Class Corvette was docked at the Hub and a flight of singleships flew past it as she watched, heading for the planet. Their own ship had gone completely undetected and landed in plain sight in the middle of an arid wasteland. Volmar would freak if he knew.

She checked her setting and accelerated, leaving Udun's world behind. "I think we'll take the conventional route back," she said.

"You mean the Point? Is that wise?"

Rhees shrugged, but wasn't sure if he understood her gestures. "It'll be crowded, but they can't see us. And we'll get an idea of Hegemony deployment around the Point and on the immediate Voss Space side."

"The Point it is then."

With the Hub and everything else safely behind them she punched for maximum acceleration. She was almost used to the lack of any sensation of speed now. But if whatever generated the inertialess field failed, they'd be a colourful paste of human and Kresz insides smeared across the back of the cockpit.

She became aware of a steady thumping from the rear of the ship. Amaroc. They flew on for several minutes and the sound didn't let up.

"Is he going to keep doing that all the way back?" she said.

"House Kergis is known for its stubbornness," Udun said, unlocking his harness.

She laid a hand on the smooth chitin of his middle forearm. "No, I'll go."

She walked aft to the storage locker, opened the door and dodged as Amaroc's foot lashed out at her. She stamped on it, bringing her full weight to bear. The Kresz's other leg and arms were still bound.

"Are you going to be quiet?" she said.

He glared at her.

She used her arms to brace against the walls, lifted her other leg and kicked him hard across the feeder mandibles. His head rocked back, and she kicked it again on the rebound.

"Your face is going to wear out before my boot does."

She stomped on his lower knee joint and kicked his free leg

back into the locker.

"You're going to die," he said.

"Shut up or I'll break both your legs. We don't need you to walk where we're headed." She slammed the door, cutting off his response.

Back in the cockpit, she said, "Message from Amaroc: we're going to die."

"At least he's consistent."

"We could space him. He didn't tell Tzek anything. Maybe he's not worth the trouble."

"I've been thinking about that," Udun said. "It's hard to believe they got nothing out of him."

"He's tough."

"You don't understand," he said. "Empathic interrogation is about more than what you say or don't say. You have to be in complete control of your emotions. Even reactions to words spoken by the interrogator can give away vital clues."

She hadn't thought about that. "Is there any way to block being read like that?"

"Strong emotions, like hatred directed at the interrogator, can blanket the rest. But it's not something you can keep up day in, day out. Eventually something will slip past your guard."

"Maybe he's just a foot soldier and doesn't know anything."

"No. Tzek said he was part of the stek-la."

"But he didn't know what that meant," Rhees said.

"No, he said it wasn't clear what it was. But you see what 'stek-la' means?"

"I'm not getting a translation."

"Ah." Udun paused. "It's from a pre-Emergence dialect. It means a person or group that is special because it is close to the middle. Trusted by the leader so able to access more secrets."

"Not a foot soldier then. So how do we get him to talk?"

"Isza will think of something."

Rhees had to agree. Udun's sister wasn't the type of person to give up easily.

They were approaching the loose globe of satellites that balanced gravity for transit and she dropped speed.

"This is where Kergis betrayed us," Udun said. "The Hegemony came through the Point and our Defender ships were containing them. Then the Kergis ships broke ranks and started firing on our own ships." He looked at Rhees. "We still don't know how they did that without any warning."

"Sensors read increased radiation," Rhees said, "but nothing else. Fleet would have cleared the debris. Hazard to naviga–"

The ship shuddered.

"What was that?" Udun asked.

"We just launched something. Or the ship did." Rhees looked at the boards, trying to make sense of the readouts. "Nothing on the screens. Wait … I'm getting a signal. Fuck." The ship had launched something all right. Autonomously. "It's a probe. Cloaked, luckily. It just attached itself to one of the Point satellites. I'm getting data packets. But no alerts on any of the Hegemony channels. That I know of anyway."

"A surveillance device?"

"I guess it makes sense, but ships don't generally act autonomously. Is Nok operating this thing remotely?"

"That or …" Udun paused again. It was clear he knew something she didn't.

"You're scaring me now. Or what?"

He seemed to be considering what he should tell her. She bit down on sudden anger. The trust they'd spoken about was still problematic in practice.

"I don't think it's something to worry about," he said finally. "Nok can split his consciousness. He's not just in the armoured suit you see."

"He could be with us – in the ship?" Rhees looked around the cockpit, expecting some ghostly form to appear. *Come out, come out, wherever you are.* She almost laughed.

"Nok?" she said. But if Nok was there he wasn't answering.

"Or it could just be a protocol," Udun said. "To release surveillance drones at useful targets when it's safe."

"I'd class this as a useful target," she said, still spooked but relaxing a little. "Good thinking, ship. Or disembodied alien spirit." She keyed the transit drive. "Let's get out of here."

The satellites failed to register them as they slipped between them and gently into Voss Space.

The chamber on the other side displayed all the mind-bending architecture of a non-three-dimensional space where energy and matter swapped places in a chaotic dance. But still there were safe channels and it was here that two System Class Hegemony battlecruisers, three Planet Class destroyer escorts and a standard complement of singleships waited. There could have been more in the darkness.

The ship vibrated again.

"Son of a—" Rhees said. "Another cloaked probe. Fuck, it's attached to the cruiser. Nok, if you can hear me, it's *our* lives you're risking."

Of course if he could hear her he'd know they didn't trust him. And that they'd contacted Denev on the outward leg. The second didn't really matter, and the first … Well, it was pretty obvious given all of their backgrounds. Maybe it was easier to be upfront. At least about some things.

She moved the ship invisibly past the Hegemony vessels and into the network, making best speed for the Jantri station. They passed more sentry ships on the way out, but she was confident of their own ship's abilities now. Nothing could see them if they didn't want to be seen.

Once they were clear, Udun spelled her on the controls and she slept.

It was a dream she hadn't had in a long time. The training mission over Neptune. Fleet singleships flying in precision formation – Petar to her right, Jute to her left – wingtip to wingtip as they weaved a path through a sky too full of icy rock. Bogies on tac, centre screen and closing.

No. She knew what was coming.

Cannons cycling up. The sudden rattle of pellets on her hull as the bogies fired. Wingtips touched, the barest kiss of contact. And through the canopy Petar's face. Focused concentration turning to surprise, the first inkling that everything was going to shit.

She couldn't look. She pulled on the controls, her dolphincraft executing an inertialess turn that would have pulped a singleship pilot. But three of the bogies were in pursuit, following her out of Neptune's rings. Except she wasn't there. It was Voss Space. A spitting chamber of violent energies, like being caught in an electric storm dialled up to a thousand. The Fleet ships were still on her tail, somehow keeping up with her physics-defying moves.

A comms window opened on her forward screen. The face of her father, pale and drawn, clearly pulling heavy gees in one of the singleships behind her.

"Rhees." It was hard for him to talk, the word drawn out in a groan. "What are you doing?"

"You don't understand," she said. But his eyes said he did. She was betraying everything he stood for. Everything she'd believed in.

The transmission cut.

More dolphincraft appeared, flying out of the Jantri station dead ahead, angled towards the singleships.

Rhees brought her own ship to a complete stop, flipping over and back towards the Fleet ships. Towards her father.

She tried comms. "Nok. No! Call your ships off."

Nothing.

The singleships bunched closer, taking an attack formation. On the tac, the dolphincraft vectored down from both flanks.

Rhees dived directly at the singleships, but they didn't veer off. So she slewed her ship around, leading them now and placing herself directly in the path of the oncoming Jantri ships.

"Nok!"

The dolphincraft fired and the singleships erupted in flames as her own cockpit disintegrated.

∞

She woke with a start and looked quickly over at Udun, who was steering them down a Voss Space corridor. That had been a bad one. And it didn't take a psychoanalyst to work out where it had come from. She could keep telling herself she was doing the right thing, but sooner or later innocent people were going to die because of her.

But what was the alternative? She hadn't been able to think of one. Not since Volmar had left her to die on the Maagba cruiser.

"We're here," Udun said, and she realised they were negotiating the final twisting channels that led to the chamber holding the Jantri station.

It came into view like some storm-blasted lighthouse. Plasma raged around it, strikes concentrated on the two furthest points of the structure, like anodes in some long ago experiment. It was hard to understand how the station withstood such violent energies. Hegemony Voss bridges took advantage of the relative peace of stable transit nodes. Even the sentry installations in the channels approaching Earth had taken years of exotic engineering, incrementally dampening the local fields and slowly building a beachhead that could be extended. The Jantri station stood dead centre of untamed Armageddon. Not only surviving, but sucking hungrily at the energy expended. The Jantri hadn't tamed Voss Space, they'd harnessed it. It was a huge tactical advantage in a place that still claimed hundreds of Hegemony ships every year.

They docked in the same bay they'd left and Udun cut the controls. Rhees felt exhaustion close in. They still had such a long way to go.

About the Author

Keith Stevenson is the author of the science fiction thriller *Horizon*. His short fiction has appeared in *Andromeda Spaceways Inflight Magazine*, *Aurealis Magazine*, *Oceans of the Mind* and the Agog! Press anthology *Agog! Fantastic Fiction*. He's a past editor of *Aurealis – Australian Science Fiction and Fantasy Magazine*, hosted the Terra Incognita Speculative Fiction Podcast, and edited and published *Dimension6*, the free Australian speculative fiction electronic magazine.

WWW.KEITHSTEVENSON.COM

Also by Keith Stevenson

H O R I Z O N

Thirty-four light years from Earth, the explorer ship *Magellan* is nearing its objective – the Iota Persei system. But when ship commander Cait Dyson wakes from deepsleep, she finds her co-pilot dead and the ship's AI unresponsive. Cait works with the rest of her crew to regain control of the ship, until they learn that Earth is facing total environmental collapse and their mission must change if humanity is to survive.

As tensions rise and personal and political agendas play out in the ship's cramped confines, the crew finally reach the planet Horizon, where everything they know will be challenged.

"Refreshingly plausible, politically savvy, and full of surprises, *Horizon* takes you on a harrowing thrill-ride through the depths of space and the darkness of the human heart." – **Sean Williams**, New York Times bestselling author of the Astropolis and Twinmaker series

"Crackling science fiction with gorgeous trans-human and cybernetic trimmings. Keith Stevenson's debut novel soars." – **Marianne De Pierres**, award-winning author of the Parrish Plessis, Sentients of Orion and Peacemaker series

Available as a print book and ebook

www.ingramcontent.com/pod-product-compliance
Lightning Source LLC
Chambersburg PA
CBHW020258120726
47904CB00001B/258